OVERWORLD APOCALYPSE

OVERWORLD CHRONICLES BOOK SIXTEEN

JOHN CORWIN

ACKNOWLEDGMENTS

To my wonderful support group:
Alana Rock
Karen Stansbury

My amazing editors:
Annetta Ribken
Jennifer Wingard

My awesome cover artist:
Regina Wamba

Thanks so much for all your help and input!

BOOKS BY JOHN CORWIN

THE OVERWORLD CHRONICLES

Sweet Blood of Mine

Dark Light of Mine

Fallen Angel of Mine

Dread Nemesis of Mine

Twisted Sister of Mine

Dearest Mother of Mine

Infernal Father of Mine

Sinister Seraphim of Mine

Wicked War of Mine

Dire Destiny of Ours

Aetherial Annihilation

Baleful Betrayal

Ominous Odyssey

Insidious Insurrection

Utopia Undone

Overworld Apocalypse

Assignment Zero (An Elyssa Short Story)

OVERWORLD UNDERGROUND

Possessed By You

Demonicus

Coming Soon: Infernal Blade

OVERWORLD ARCANUM

Conrad Edison and the Living Curse

Conrad Edison and the Anchored World

Conrad Edison and the Broken Relic

Conrad Edison and the Infernal Design

Conrad Edison and the First Power

STAND ALONE NOVELS

Mars Rising

No Darker Fate

The Next Thing I Knew

Outsourced

For the latest on new releases, free ebooks, and more, join John Corwin's Newsletter at www.johncorwin.net!

OVERWORLD IN ASHES

Thanks to new friends, Justin and gang are able to return to Eden.

But the Overworld lies in ruins. A top secret nom organization is slowly dismantling the supernatural world, hunting down supers and taking over Obsidian Arch waystations. A new dictator rules what's left and won't relinquish power, even if it means dooming the Overworld.

Together with Conrad Edison and gang, Justin will have to find a way to fight off the noms and restore order. Because another doomsday clock is ticking—one in which either Baal rules the realms, or a rogue Apocryphan draws them back together and kills billions.

CHAPTER 1

Twenty obsidian ships skimmed above boiling seas. Titanic aether vortexes loomed on all sides. Jagged bolts of lightning arced between the gray funnels or sizzled into the ocean. Frosty air crashed against superheated fumes and the turbulence rocked the deck beneath my feet. If not for the weather shields, we'd be frozen or flash-fried in seconds.

Pjurna faded into view, a splash of green behind swirling gray vapors. Baal's dragon army would be here any day now to claim this land and the last city of angels, Tarissa. We weren't on our way to stop him. We couldn't if we tried. Evacuating the last of the citizens was the best we could hope for at this point.

Elyssa and I stood at the prow of the *Listrum*, the newest Mzodi warship to come out of the dry docks in Atlantis. Conrad Edison and his friends, Ambria Rax and Max Tiberius, stared with wonder at the raging sapphire sea, bodies flinching with every quake of thunder.

Conrad turned to me, eyes flaring. "Can you feel it?"

I'd met him a month ago, but we'd been so busy evacuating cities from the path of Baal's dragon army that I hadn't had a chance to talk with him much. I put a finger in the air. "Feel what?"

"The primal fount." He closed his eyes and drew in a deep breath. "It's incredibly strong in this realm."

"Not this hocus pocus again." Shelton leaned against the rail and grunted. "Aether is aether, kiddo."

"He's not a kid." Ambria focused the glare of a thousand suns on Shelton. "He could blow your bloody arse—"

Conrad put a hand on her arm. "Ambria, please."

She took a deep breath and backed off, but her glare turned to me. "Your friend Shelton is rather unpleasant."

"And you act like you know everything." Shelton stuck out his chin. "If this primal fount exists, why haven't I ever heard of it?"

"We don't have time to discuss this." Elyssa stepped between the two. "Stay focused and alert or go below decks and get out of the way."

Ambria shrank back. "I'm sorry, madam commander."

I repressed a snort of mirth, but Adam Nosti couldn't hold in his laughter.

"Please stop calling me that, Ambria." Elyssa sighed. "You're not even a Templar."

"You're the highest-ranking officer in the fleet," Ambria said. "I think you deserve the respect of a proper title."

"Will you just hush?" Max said. "We're on a bloody flying boat with Justin Slade and all you can do is argue!"

Ambria stiffened. "And all you can do is make things awkward with your hero worship."

Conrad didn't seem the least bit fazed by the bickering. If anything, he seemed comforted by it. He regarded Shelton with a serious expression belying his youth. "I'd like to see if you can touch the fount. You're one of the most powerful Arcanes ever. I can't imagine what you could do with that kind of power."

A curious gleam in Shelton's eyes contradicted his gruff exterior. "Yeah, maybe."

"That would be amazing!" Max looked up at Shelton with adoration. "You destroyed an entire mansion with fire meteors. I can't imagine what you could do with the fount."

"What about me?" Adam sidled up to Shelton. "I'm a much better student than this jackass."

Ambria huffed. "A jackass, indeed."

Shelton looked uncomfortably at Max. "Look, kid, I'm just an Arcane. I ain't got nothing compared to the juice Justin's packing."

That didn't seem to dampen Max's enthusiasm. "Would you at least try to use the fount?"

"Maybe." Shelton cleared his throat and looked away.

The *Listrum* cleared the last aether vortex a few miles off the coast of Pjurna and entered the Ooskai Valley. This was our twentieth—or was it our thirtieth?—sortie. We'd evacuated droves of Seraphim already, and this would be the last load. Scouts reported Baal's forces had reached the northern city of Kohvalla and would soon descend upon Tarissa. We were cutting it close enough already.

The valley welcomed us into its wide maw and embraced us in narrower confines a few miles in. The sparkling green waters of the Ooskai River snaked through a lush canopy of aquamarine trees. A flock of golden doves settled into a tree only to explode from it a moment later.

A riot of colors burst from the trees at the sides of the valley. Elyssa tensed, and I instinctively mimicked her. It didn't take long to figure out what put her on guard. Birds fled the vicinity, spooked by something or a lot of somethings. I peered down at the forest floor, but that was the wrong direction.

Scores of blue-white frost wyverns launched from the cliffs above, misting the air before us with frigid gusts. Green and red wyverns swooped from hidden perches to block the valley ahead.

Elyssa tapped on her com badge. "All stop! Battle stations!"

The Mzodi fleet flowed into a semicircle, presenting broadsides to the enemy. Crew manned the cannon turrets and charged the magical gems that amplified their destructive power.

Shelton knocked his wide-brimmed hat off his head and let it dangle by the stampede rope. "Holy farting fairies! I thought Baal's dragon army was all the way north."

"They must have sent a contingent to block the valley." Elyssa stared at the scaly foes. "They're not attacking for some reason."

Adam grunted. "It's a blockade."

"But why?" Elyssa tapped her badge again. "Rise to four hundred. Get us above the canyon walls."

The formation rose until the cliff tops were below us.

"We can't outrun them at this altitude," Adam said.

"That's not the point." Elyssa pointed east. "I need vision."

Armored scales glinted from the long necks of a two-headed wyvern. Crimson covered half its body and neck, and blue tinted the rest. The blue mouth roared and a hailstorm of ice shards exploded from the maw. The red mouth opened an instant later and bellowed a gout of white fire.

It was an amazing spectacle, but all my attention focused on the rider. "It's Baal."

"Or just an infernus," Conrad said.

Demon golems had become an all-too familiar facet of life. Dozens of them crafted in the image of Nightliss still haunted the lands. Baal crafted special versions to contain a sliver of his powerful presence. He could switch to any of them at a moment's notice, or possibly even control them simultaneously, micro-managing them like a seasoned videogame veteran.

I knew this infernus was just a vessel, but it was easier to simply refer to this particular kind as Baal, my dear, sweet grandpappy.

Baal waved a branch. Something white fluttered from it, but it wasn't a flag.

"What the hell?" Shelton shuddered. "He skewered a dove with a damned olive branch."

Adam grimaced. "Savage."

"Good lord, and I thought Victus was bad." Ambria shuddered. "I feel like we've just ventured from Purgatory and into the ninth level of Hell."

"You ain't wrong," Shelton said. "Baal likes to ruin everything."

Conrad clenched his fists. Azure energy crackled across his knuckles. "Does that mean he comes in peace or wants a fight?"

I held up a hand to stop anyone from attacking. "It's his own twisted version of coming in peace." *I hope.*

The two-headed dragon glided closer and hovered a short distance off starboard. Baal's infernus sported a thick beard and bushy eyebrows. He stared at us without concern. "My master comes." He blinked and a blue glow flickered in his eyes.

"Damn, that's creepy," Shelton murmured.

"Hello, son." Baal, the Grand Overlord of Haedaemos, was in the house and he didn't even look surprised to see me.

Does he already know we escaped from Utopia?

It was impossible to say, so I played along. "Don't you mean grandson?" I put on a hurt expression. "You missed my birthday again. I was hoping for a Hallmark card with five bucks inside."

Baal smirked. "It's in the mail."

"You're the best pop-pop ever."

He ignored the jibe and dropped the smirk. "I would parley with you."

"Parley?" I looked at the dozens of wyverns. "You've already taken over most of Seraphina. Why the hell bother discussing a truce at this point?"

"We all wish to preserve the realms." Baal raked his fiery gaze over the others. "We should be allies, not enemies."

Shelton grunted. "World domination ain't exactly our style."

"If I don't seize power, Xanos will." Baal held out his hands helplessly. "Should she gather enough Relics of Juranthemon, she will draw the realms back together into one Earth and unleash a cataclysm killing billions."

"Xanos?" I frowned. "Don't you mean Xanomiel?"

"Yeah, and isn't Xanomiel male?" Shelton said.

"She calls herself Xanos now." Baal shrugged. "The gender of the Apocryphan has always been nebulous at best. I simply go with whatever information I have."

"I'm surprised you'd give us that information for free." He usually wanted something in return.

"We both aim to stop Xanos." Baal offered a smile that was anything but reassuring. "We are on the same side."

"We're not here to join team Baal." Elyssa folded her arms. "Thousands have died in your war on Seraphina. Trading one dictator for another is no choice."

"The Seraphim spent millennia fighting each other. The humans in

Eden have wrecked their world and constantly hover on the brink of self-destruction." Baal shook his head. "Why allow such incompetence any measure of authority?"

"The Utopians seemed pretty competent." I watched for the slightest hint of emotion, but Baal barely reacted. "They had a nearly perfect society until you used Vokan like a wrecking ball."

"Vokan took an unexpected path." Baal shrugged. "I offered the Utopians a peaceful transition of power. They could have maintained their councils and laws so long as they acknowledged my rule."

"When did you offer them that?" I asked.

"Oh, decades ago." Baal shrugged again. "When they refused, I put several plans into motion. Vokan was the first to come to fruition."

Baal didn't play around when it came to long-term scheming. Then again, decades were just the blink of an eye compared to how long he'd been around. "How in the hell did you steer us into Utopia? How did you know we'd go there and not somewhere else?"

"What makes you think I schemed to send you there in the first place?" Baal's expression betrayed nothing.

"Don't play coy." Elyssa stared him down. "Were you surprised to see we escaped your trap?"

"My trap? I only know you went to Utopia because you just now mentioned it." Baal's face remained impassive. "Why would I set a trap for you there?"

"Vokan told us!" I resisted the urge to blast him in the face with magic. "He said, 'Baal sends his regards,' just before locking us in an underground bunker."

"Well, I might have mentioned you in passing." A smirk flashed on his face. "I hope Vokan was a gracious host."

"He's playing mind games." Ambria scowled. "Why bother asking him anything?"

She was right, but I didn't give up. "Did you know about the time dilation in that realm? Did you know our two months there would be nearly six years here?"

"Ah, time dilation." Baal leaned back in his dragon saddle. "Not all realms experience time the same."

"Six years, man!" Shelton threw up his hands. "Bella wouldn't let me leave the bedroom for two days after I got back."

Adam gagged. "Damn it, Shelton. No one wants to imagine your hairy white ass—"

"Ahem!" Ambria cleared her throat. "Let's keep this decent, shall we?"

Conrad interjected a question before I could resume my probing. "Did you influence Victus? Did you help him turn Delectra into a monster?"

Baal turned his gaze on the boy. "I had very few dealings with your father, young Conrad. He chose to go his own path, so I let him. In the end, he proved just as useful."

Anger burned in Conrad's eyes. "By corrupting my mother. By murdering her!"

"Yes, a rather interesting path your father took." Baal shrugged. "I've seen worse, but few with the power to do what he did. Victus was quite accomplished for a mortal and extremely cunning."

Conrad's jaw tightened. "Do you admire him?"

"It's remarkable he banished to Seraphina any who could stand in his way." Baal met Conrad's glare. "Admire or despise him, he was a formidable opponent to all who faced him."

"Not formidable enough," Conrad growled.

Baal nodded. "Sadly, all too mortal."

We all had reason to be angry with Baal. I suspected he had a lot more to do with Victus than he admitted, but it was hard to take anything he said at face value. Even so, I risked more questions. "Who or what is the giant black wyvern, the one we call Enigma?" Before being trapped in Utopia, we'd witnessed the massive dragon giving aid to Baal.

"Perhaps Altash could answer that question for you." Baal shrugged. "It is not for me to trade in such information without equal return."

"We don't even know where Altash is!" Conrad clamped his mouth shut as if realizing he'd just given away free information.

"For good reason." Baal focused on Elyssa. "Ask your father to consider an alliance. My power on Seraphina is nearly consolidated and once that's done I will turn my attention to Atlantis."

Elyssa maintained a stony exterior, but her fair skin paled. "An attack on Atlantis wouldn't be wise."

"Is a week long enough?" Baal nodded. "Yes, I think a week is plenty of time to reach a decision."

"A week?" I scoffed. "There's no way—"

"Where there's a will, there's a way." The demon overlord kept his eyes on Elyssa. "Here are my terms. Alysea will be the grand empress of all Seraphina. This includes any and all sentient beings in this realm. Alysea will represent my interests here, and the armies of Seraphina shall rise to my aid on request." Baal guided his dragon closer and handed Elyssa a scroll. "This is the full text. Read, review, and deliver an answer in one week to me at the coordinates designated in the document."

Elyssa looked at the scroll as if it were a poisonous snake, but reluctantly took it. "We give you an answer, or else?"

Baal nodded. "I'm afraid so. I will not leave a threat at my flank."

I wanted to snatch him off his mount and punch him in the face. "We won't be easy pickings, I promise."

Baal offered a condescending smile. "You've proven to be quite a difficult target. Now kindly turn your fleet around and retreat, lest matters devolve into battle." He nudged his dragon with a knee and it veered away from us and back toward his army.

"I count fifty wyverns," Adam said. "We could probably win a fight."

"Or outrun them," Shelton said.

Elyssa turned to me. "Ideas?"

"Ram through them and finish the mission or turn tail and deliver the message." I shrugged. "Those are really the only options. Provided there aren't a hundred more wyverns waiting in ambush, we could win a battle, but it would cost us some ships."

"Damn." Elyssa gazed at the wyverns. "The citizens of Tarissa are waiting on us. They need us to help them escape. We can't just abandon them." She turned to Adam. "How much speed do we lose if we fly over the valley walls?"

"The altitude is thinner, but we might edge out the dragons in speed." He tapped on his arcphone and showed her a map with some hastily sketched lines. "If we take this route, we can duck back down to lower altitudes and outdistance them."

Elyssa took his phone and went to the bridge. She returned a moment later and gave Adam back his phone. "Brace yourselves." She tapped her com badge. "By now you should have received a flight plan from the *Listrum.* All ships are to proceed along this route at top speed in formation. Do not engage the wyverns unless you have no choice."

Ambria gripped the railing. "Oh, dear. My stomach is in knots."

Conrad put an arm on her shoulder. "Mine too."

Max looked white as a sheet. "You sure those dragons can't catch us?"

"Not unless Baal is hiding their true capabilities." Adam tucked the arcphone in his pocket. "The only wyvern I've seen move faster is Enigma, and she's not here."

The turret gunners strapped into their seats and the rest of us grabbed the railing.

Elyssa thrust an arm forward. "Engage!"

The *Listrum* surged toward the canyon wall. The rest of the fleet flowed from the defensive position and into line behind us. Wyverns shrieked. Reptilian wings beat the air and the enemy army angled to cut us off.

The first few ships would make it easily, but I wasn't sure about the last ones. Elyssa probably reached the same conclusion because she looked back and frowned. She tapped her badge. "*Listrum* and *Halcyon* will provide suppressing fire. All other ships continue onward."

The ship reached the canyon wall and turned broadside toward the oncoming wyverns. The *Halcyon* hovered in place behind us. Elyssa gave the command and the gunners opened fire. Volleys of blazing white spheres crisscrossed before the enemy, but we were still too far away to do much damage.

The dragon army veered away from the onslaught. Cheers rose from the crew.

We did it!

And that was when Baal showed us his surprise.

CHAPTER 2

T he trees below us came alive. Swarms of drakes exploded from the canopy and intercepted the lead vessels.

Elyssa's eyes flared. "All ships, engage!"

The air sizzled with energy. Smoking drakes plummeted into the trees, but there were too many to stop. Dozens more made it onto the ships, spewing fire, ice, and poison at the crew.

I formed a sphere of Brilliance and focused a thick beam at a flock of the small dragons. Only ash and smoking meat remained in the aftermath. I focused my efforts into one finger, raking a concentrated beam through another group, rendering the reptiles into drake chop suey. Shouts drew my attention to the north. While we fought the drakes, the wyverns had made up lost ground.

Shelton whirled his staff overhead and slammed it on the deck. A fiery star storm rained on the wyverns, burning holes through wings and scorching scaled hides.

"Wow!" Max watched as if he had the best seat in a movie theater until Ambria cuffed his shoulder.

"Stop admiring and fight!"

Max blinked from his stupor. "Oh, right."

Conrad rolled to avoid the grasping claws of a diving frost wyvern. He thrust out his hands. Two azure blades of energy blurred through the air and lopped off the wings of the attacker. The wyvern shrieked in agony and spiraled out of sight.

"Jesus Christ on a pogo stick." Shelton's jaw dropped. "How'd you cut through their scales like butter? They're magic resistant!"

"The first power." Conrad's eyes widened. "Look out!" He dove forward and knocked Shelton to the side as a spray of green poison doused the deck where he'd been.

I reflexively channeled a barrier of Murk and the poison goop deflected away from the ship. Another wyvern thudded onto the deck behind me. Massive jaws clamped the air an instant after I ducked.

Elyssa unslung her light bow and snapped it to full length. She drew back her fingers and a beam of light formed the bowstring, an energy arrow nocked in place. She released, and the arrow pierced the dragon's eye. The creature roared and floundered. Ambria and Max scampered away from the thrashing tail.

I unleashed my demon side. Thick muscles snaked around my arms, legs, and chest. Thankfully, my clothes were designed to stretch so I didn't flash demon dong in front of the kids. I charged the giant wyvern and rammed it with my shoulder. A ton of dragon flesh toppled over the side of the ship and vanished below.

We weren't even close to being out of the woods yet.

While drakes swarmed the rest of the fleet, the wyverns seemed intent on ripping our ship apart. Three more landed, barely squeezing into the space on the front deck.

Conrad unleashed a blast of his first power just as I slammed a Murk barrier between the enemy and us. The impact of his strike against my barrier sent currents of electricity up my arms. Conrad cried out and stumbled backwards, stunned from the backlash. The shield shattered, leaving us open to attack from two fire wyverns and their frosty companion.

"Holy dog nuts!" Shelton fended off a flock of drakes. "Take cover!"

"No, Max!" Ambria grasped at the blond-headed boy, but it was too late.

Max ran toward the dragons and threw a handful of rocks at them. They exploded into mist on impact.

"Well that was super effective!" Adam tapped his phone screen and a shield flickered on. "Everyone back off. This won't hold for long."

Apparently, it didn't need to. The wyverns stumbled around, heads bobbing up and down on long necks. I wasn't a great reader of reptilian emotions, but they seemed dazed and confused. They bellowed and grunted at each other, seemed to arrive at a conclusion, and flew away from the battle at top speed.

Shelton turned to Max. "Uh, what in the hell was that?"

"Back in school I was supposed to make a memory fortifying potion, but—"

"It's a memory loss potion," Ambria said. "But it only takes away memories from the last ten minutes."

Max huffed. "If you'd let me finish—"

Another group of wyverns apparently didn't want to let him finish, because they chose that moment to attack.

Elyssa jabbed a finger forward. "Full speed ahead!"

The *Listrum* and *Halcyon* surged after the rest of the fleet. Blue flames licked from the sides of the *Otora,* and the remains of the *Pika* burned on the plateau below us. But the battle had reduced the swarm of drakes to a few scattered flocks.

"This is Captain Shan of the *Ostra*. Our levitation foils are damaged and we're losing power. You have to leave us behind."

"No!" Elyssa looked back at the thirty or so wyverns coming our way. "We have to defend—"

"No, please." Shan's voice was steely. "We will give you space to escape." She sounded almost excited. "We will take many foul beasts with us."

Elyssa's brow furrowed with sadness. Her jaw tightened, and iron masked her emotion. "Permission granted." She took a deep breath. "All ships, full speed ahead."

The *Ostra* rotated toward the mass of wyverns. Flames erupted from its levitation foils. Energy beams sprayed from its turrets. It jetted full ahead. Even crippled, it moved faster than the wyverns and rammed into the peak of their V formation. The aetherite core detonated. A fiery blue sphere expanded, consuming a score of wyverns with it. Glittering like diamonds, the remains of the ship rained from the sky.

The surviving wyverns roared their fury. Baal, a distant figure atop his two-headed dragon, waved, a fond farewell spat in my face. The remains of his ambush force turned and left. We hadn't lost, but we hadn't won. We'd just survived.

Elyssa belted out another command. "Drop to minimum altitude and full speed ahead." The fleet skimmed the dusty plateau and set course for Tarissa.

"Oh god." Ambria leaned against the railing. "This war feels rather hopeless, doesn't it?"

Shelton swallowed hard. "Yeah. And that was just a few wyverns and drakes. We ain't seen nothing yet."

"We need bigger guns." Adam slapped a turret and watched it spin. "How are we supposed to use our ground troops when we can barely win the aerial battles?"

"That's Baal's weakness and his greatest strength." Elyssa wiped sweat from her brow and compacted her light bow. "He's used aerial forces in all his campaigns. The problem is, the wyverns are pretty adept at land battles too."

"It's time to bring back the goliaths and stone golems." Shelton punched a fist into his other palm. "If we combine those with the magic-resistant enchantments the Utopians have, the dragons won't stand a chance."

"Won't be any battle-bots this time around." Adam frowned. "Victus made those the last time."

Conrad's fists tightened. "Science Academy was in bad shape when we left. Arcane University isn't much better."

"Damn, I'm ready to go back to Eden." Shelton ran a hand through his short hair then slapped his wide-brimmed hat back on. "I'm so sick of dragons and flying ships. Ain't nothing but blood and guts in this damned world. And I want a taco."

"What about pizza and burgers?" Adam said.

"I just want to feel like I'm at home again." Shelton sighed.

"That star storm spell was amazing." Max flicked his wand around as if practicing. "I've only read about advanced battle mage spells like that, but I haven't seen many in action."

"Takes a lot of practice." Shelton dropped into a seat next to a turret. "That little trick with your memory loss potion was pretty damned slick. What else you got in that bag of yours?"

Max's eyes lit. "All sorts of things." He produced a shiny yellow marble. "This is Banana Peel. Whatever it covers is so slippery, nothing can stand on it. The potion I used on the wyverns is called Memory Fog."

Shelton leaned over and looked in the satchel. "Anything else?"

"Well, I got this one I'm working on." He dug around and pulled out a vial of red fluid. "Our friend, Shushiel, helped me with this one, but it's not working right."

A shudder ran down Shelton's spine. "The giant spider you told me about?"

Ambria laughed. "Does she frighten you?"

"Anything the size of a horse with eight hairy legs and eight beady eyes would scare me." Shelton grunted. "It doesn't help that she can turn invisible." He looked around suspiciously. "You definitely didn't bring her with you from Eden, right?"

"Maybe." Ambria smirked. "Shushiel might be right behind you, tickling your neck with her fangs."

Adam tickled Shelton's neck with a finger.

Shelton screamed and dove out of the chair, rolling across the deck in his leather duster like a frantic burrito.

Adam and Ambria howled with laughter and it wasn't long before the rest of us joined the chorus.

"You just wait 'til I fill your beds with spiders." Shelton pushed himself up. "Then we'll see who's laughing."

Adam clapped him on the back. "You ever thought about a career in the opera? I think you hit the highest note with that scream."

Shelton mumbled something and sat back down. "Wait until you smell what came out of my other end."

Max laughed. "You've got the best comebacks, Mr. Shelton."

Shelton cleared his throat. "Yeah, I'm a real natural." He pointed at the red fluid. "What's that stuff do, anyway?"

"It's supposed to encase anyone it hits in a web." Max sighed. "Unfortunately, it just covers them in sticky red liquid now."

"Interesting." Shelton took the vial. "Why don't you tell me what's in it? Maybe we can figure out what's missing."

I turned away from the conversation. A few feet away, Conrad massaged

17

his left hand, grimacing with every squeeze.

"Are you okay?" I noticed a burn mark on his index finger. "Is that from hitting my shield?"

He nodded. "I've never seen a shield that could take a hit from the first power. It was like striking a hammer against a metal shield. The vibrations ran right back up my arm."

"Yeah, well that hit felt like I'd jammed my hands in a power socket." I showed him the red skin from the backlash. "I guess we should've coordinated better."

He managed a smile. "Yeah. I'm not used to fighting alongside someone like you. Ambria usually watches our backs while Max flings potions around."

"Maybe you could tell me more about the first power." I glanced to the side as the bridge window misted away and an Mzodi healer walked outside to tend to the wounded crew on deck. She didn't seem to be headed our way, so I ignored the pain as I'd done hundreds of times before.

"The primal fount is the wellspring of all magic." Conrad paused as if trying to put into words an elusive concept. "Every realm has a part of the fount and it's everywhere all at once."

"Can a person go to the source?" I asked.

He shrugged. "I've seen it before, but I have no idea where it is. I think once you touch it, you're linked to it."

"How'd you see it in the first place?"

"The ghost of Moses."

I blinked a few times. "Did you just say the ghost of Moses?"

A smile touched his lips. "Yes. I saw him in the afterlife."

I blinked several more times to convey my confusion. "There's an after-life? It's not just a void?"

The Mzodi healer appeared at our sides without a word and began working on Conrad's hands.

Some of the tension left the boy's shoulders. "Moses called it the birthing chamber, but he didn't really explain anything. You see, the rift guardians outside the Glimmer attacked me. I thought I was dead, but Moses made them with the first power a long time ago, so they just linked me to him."

"Makes perfect sense," I lied. *It's not the strangest thing I've ever heard.* I felt oddly comforted knowing Moses wasn't obliterated; his entire being gone from the universe. Dealing with Vokan taught me a lot about souls, but the mystery of where they went after the body died hadn't been answered—at least not until now.

"It didn't make any sense at all." Conrad inspected the pink but healing flesh when the Mzodi healer turned to me. "The primal fount is the source of life and everything, or at least that's what Moses told me. It looks like pure blue water. He made me wash my hands in it."

"Interesting." I sighed in relief from the Mzodi healing treatment and thanked the healer for her help. "Maybe we need to go on a quest to find the primal fount so we can all touch it and get supercharged."

"Perhaps." Conrad shrugged. "It would be more useful if I could speak with Moses again. The fount is what gave him his longevity and powers. I don't know if you have to be descended from him to use the fount or if just anyone can."

"Yeah, we wouldn't want to risk frying someone who couldn't handle it." I tapped a finger on my chin. "On the other hand, we need all the fire-power we can get to defeat Baal."

Conrad nodded. "I think you're right. Perhaps we should return to Eden after this. I know a few people who might have answers."

"Like Underborn?"

It was his turn to blink. "Yes, though he's not a very reliable source unless you have something to offer."

I snorted. "Believe me, I've dealt with him enough times to know. He only looks out for his best interests."

"There's also a relic hunter named Gwyneth who's done work for Underborn. She might know something."

"What about Cora?"

Conrad's face brightened for the first time. "She's been around since the world was young, but she didn't seem to know much about the primal fount when I asked her."

"I remember the first time you met her." I flashed a grin. "Cora took you onboard her ship, the *Evadora*. She must have ended up back in Eden after ramming the ship into Cephus's crimson arch."

Conrad nodded. "I believe she sought me out, and that's how she became my foster mother."

"It's so odd how that worked out." Then again it might be pretty normal, considering the bizarre happenings in my life.

"I often considered Cora my real mother, but then I got to know Delectra." The light faded from his eyes. "Victus poisoned her soul, but she still died for me. She still loved me."

I swallowed a lump in my throat. "You had a really rough family life. I'm surprised you didn't go to the dark side."

"I think it's what kept me from becoming like my father." Conrad shrugged. "He represented everything I hate."

Elyssa walked over to us and leaned against me. "Getting to know each other better?"

"Yeah. Talking about the first power."

"Mhm." Elyssa glanced to stern. "Well, you've got another hour before we reach Tarissa."

The crash and rumble of rock drew our attention ahead. Something huge burst from the ground and blocked our path.

It was a giant purple dragon.

CHAPTER 3

"It can't be." Elyssa ran to the bow and looked at the massive creature coiling in our path. "All stop!"

It took a few beats, but I recognized the massive reptile. The purple scales were a dead giveaway. Its long, lean muzzle hovered above the coiled form, like a king cobra readying a strike. A terrible premonition gripped my insides.

"Please don't tell me you joined Team Baal, Lulu!"

Your fears are unfounded. A gentle female voice filled my head. The others looked around, confused.

"Anyone else hear that?" Shelton said. "Did Lulu really just send out a public address?"

"I think so." I went to the prow. "Get us closer, please."

Elyssa motioned ahead and the *Listrum* eased forward until we were only a few yards from the massive earth dragon.

"Oh, it's so good to see you again." Ambria raced to my side. "You disappeared from El Dorado."

Events required our swift departure. Lulu turned her great eyes toward someone behind me. *Conrad, you have touched the fount.*

"Y-yes." He stumbled forward. "Moses showed me. Do you know where it is?"

We earth dragons are linked to the fount. We spread it and all sources of magic across the realms. Even we know not where it lies. It is physical, but ethereal. It exists in all realms but none. It births all life and claims the dead.

Shelton groaned. "For Christ's sake, can you just tell us how to touch it?"

I cannot. The fount is not your quest.

"Yeah, but it'd sure be nice if we could juice up on magical steroids." Adam flexed a scrawny arm and completely failed to produce even a tiny bicep bulge.

I posed the obvious question. "What's our quest, Lulu?"

Baal and Xanos seek dominion over all. The nemesis has ended the truce, freeing Altash and I from inaction. Even so, there is little we can do.

"So we're screwed." Shelton knocked off his hat again. "Who in the hell is this nemesis, anyway?"

The mightiest of us. Her wings span the skies, and all of Draxadis bows to her.

Ice formed in the pit of my stomach. "Enigma is the great nemesis?"

I see her in your thoughts, Lulu replied. *Yes, that is Drakara, usurper of the throne, ruler of all dragons.*

Adam gulped. "Except for you and Altash?"

Altash rules those in exile. While our numbers have withered, Drakara's have grown.

I frowned. "If Drakara is the usurper, does that mean Altash is the rightful ruler?"

Drakara deposed the dragon mother eons ago. Altash took up her flame and fought to a stalemate. The truce held for millennia, but open war once again threatens dragon kind.

"You guys can't even fly," Shelton said. "How in the hell do you stand a chance against a giant freaking wyvern with all the flying dragons at her command?"

All dragons fly. Lulu sounded a bit indignant. *Baal's bargain with Drakara is the only reason she fights. Baal must be defeated to end the threat to the realms.*

"You might as well tell us to put out the sun to stop a heat wave," I said. "Baal doesn't physically exist in this realm. There's no way for us to kill him, and Drakara's army is too large for us to defeat."

To defeat a thing, one must understand it. One must discover its source and origin.

"How is knowing Baal's origin supposed to help us?" I said.

Baal's true goals are shrouded in lies.

"Of course they are." I threw up my hands in exasperation. "So what is Baal's origin?"

Even we do not know.

"Now I know why you and Altash never said a thing," Shelton said. "It's because you don't know any more than we do."

Words have power. We could not risk breaking the truce with Drakara lest she ally herself with Daelissa in the last war. If she had, you would have surely lost. Altash lost many powerful allies in the first war against Daelissa. We had hoped to birth new generations of dragons, but even now our numbers are not enough.

"Where is Altash?" I asked.

He gathers allies from the other realms. He asks you to discover Baal's origin so we might defeat him and end Drakara's involvement. It is possible finding Baal's true name will give you power over him.

24

"Where do we even start?" I pinched the bridge of my nose. "You're just throwing us in the deep end with lead weights on our feet."

The first of the Sirens may know, provided she still lives. You will find her in Eden in the land of ice and snow.

"Antarctica? Norway? The Arctic Circle?" Shelton held out his hand expectantly. "We need better directions than that."

The mortals call it the land of ice. I am sorry I have no more for you, but I must go. Drakara's forces converge on the realm of Snix. We cannot allow her to control the snake people. They would be too strong an ally.

Lulu dove back into the ground and it closed behind her as if she'd never been there.

"Hot damn." Shelton face-palmed. "Maybe it's time to move to a new universe, because this one sucks."

"I think I know where the Siren is," Adam said.

The rest of us turned to him.

"Well, where?" I said.

"The land of ice—Iceland." He shrugged. "Seems logical."

"I believe you're right," Ambria said. "I don't know what they'd do without someone as bright as you, Mr. Nosti."

"Adam." He grinned. "I don't want to feel like an old man."

Shelton scoffed. "You're so old you smell like baby powder."

Max burst into laughter.

Ambria rolled her eyes. "It wasn't that funny, Max."

Elyssa stared at the place where Lulu had been for a moment then thrust her hand forward. "Full speed to Tarissa."

Conrad gave me a pensive look. "Guess we'll need to go to Eden as soon as possible."

"It seems so." I wasn't too sure about embarking on an adventure with him and his young friends in tow. They looked and acted like kids, but they had some serious dark streaks lurking behind those innocent faces. Conrad had literally pounded Victus's face to a pulp, they'd fed a were-wolf to a demon, and that was just barely scratching the surface of the stories they'd told.

Then again, I had no room to talk. I didn't like killing but that hadn't stopped me. During my first trip to Tarissa, I'd slaughtered and over-thrown their government. Granted, I was tricked into it by Cephus, but that didn't absolve me.

Elyssa blew out a breath. "I'm concerned about our current timeline."

I blinked from my thoughts. "What do you mean?"

"Hunting through Iceland for a missing Siren could take months. We only have a week before Baal moves on Atlantis."

"I don't need that kind of pressure in my life." I sighed. "What do you suggest?"

"Let's say we find the Siren. What guarantee do we have that she'll know Baal's true name or have info pointing us to the next clue?" Elyssa answered her own question. "None at all. On the other hand, I have concrete ideas for stopping Baal."

I knew where she was going with this. "Recruiting allies from other realms? But that might take just as long to do."

"It might." She shrugged. "But we need more soldiers."

"Hmm." Another thought occurred to me. "Just so happens that we know three Sirens who were around when the Sundering happened."

"Do you think they might know about Baal?"

"Maybe. Even if they don't, they might know the Siren Lulu mentioned." Dolpha, Narine, and Balaena didn't believe in war. Dolpha had helped us fight Kaelissa, but only because the crazy former empress had kidnapped Dolpha's Siren sisters with a blood-stone. I hoped they'd change their minds when it came to defending Atlantis.

Elyssa tapped a finger on her chin. "Well, it's a start. But I still think our time would be better spent finding allies."

"You've brought that up several times at your dad's war council meetings, but you haven't actually mentioned any specific allies." I leaned back against the railing. "I don't think we can count on much help from Eden since Victus demolished the Overworld government."

"No, but we'll have access to weapons, armor, and everything else we left behind." Elyssa waved a hand to dismiss that line of discussions. "Utopia is at the top of my list. We can train their gryphon army to help us and enlist the magi. They also have hundreds of gepheron just sitting around."

"Utopia would be a good place to start," I said, "but we literally just saved the humans there from an apocalypse. Most of the people had their souls ripped from their bodies and stored in a demonic vessel for decades while their bodies were used to steal more souls for Vokan." I grimaced. "Talk about PTSD. I don't know if those are the kinds of people we want to throw into a major war right away."

"It's not like we have a choice." Elyssa's shoulders slumped. "If we could reach the other realms, we could ask the Sirens for help, or maybe even the Nazdal."

I shuddered at the thought of fighting alongside those life-stealing monsters. "Hell to the no on the Nazdal." I sighed. "The problem is, we can only go to Eden, Utopia, or Atlantis. We don't have coordinates for the other realms."

"The ship the Fallen gave us probably has that info." Conrad stepped into our space. "We just don't know how to access it."

"I'll bet I could," Adam said.

"You're overlooking another big source of allies," Shelton said. "The fairies on Pangaea."

Pangaea was the other major continent on Utopia, but it had a big *No Humans Allowed* sign hanging on the doorstep. We'd rescued a fairy from Vokan's home in exile. Pyra hadn't been grateful, but that hadn't stopped her from demanding a ride home. She'd made us stop nearly a mile offshore and flown the rest of the way.

That didn't bode well for an alliance.

"Do I have to remind you that Pyra and her fairy friends don't much care for humans?" I said.

Shelton shrugged. "Maybe they don't like us, but what if we could get the Sirens or someone else to bridge that gap? Maybe we could even get Max's huge spider friend to help out."

Elyssa's mouth dropped open. "Shelton, that's the most diplomatic plan I've ever heard from you."

"Brilliant!" Max said. "Shushiel would love to help, but she's back in Eden working on problems of her own."

I had to admit, it was a pretty smart plan. "Let's back burner that for now. I just want to get back to Eden."

"Oh, hell yeah." Shelton patted his belly. "I could use a taco."

It had been two weeks since we'd returned from Utopia and met Conrad. Though his boat had the ability to take us back to Eden, evacuating Seraphim from Baal's warpath had taken precedence.

The thought of going home tickled me pink. "I guess we'll also have to help boot Xander out of office unless Galfandor has already finished the job."

"Hopefully that's taken care of," Conrad said.

Max grimaced. "I don't know. My father's always dreamed of being a dictator. He might not give up power very easily."

"It also might not be wise to overthrow a democratically elected official." Elyssa shrugged. "We need the people to trust us."

Shelton scoffed. "Hell, I'll be surprised if they even remember us."

I growled in frustration. "Considering the crimes Victus committed, maybe overthrowing the government would be okay, just this once. I don't think anyone would be sad to see Xander tossed out of office."

Elyssa shook her head. "I don't know. Seems hypocritical to depose an elected official just to replace it with our own dictator."

I pshawed. "Baal's not playing by the rules, and Xander Tiberius sure as hell didn't earn that election. It was rigged by Victus."

"Absolutely," Max said. "Can we please overthrow my father? It would be amazing."

Adam burst into laughter.

"For once I agree with Max," Ambria said. "I'd dearly love to overthrow that pompous ass."

Elyssa groaned. "I still think it's a mistake."

"Ah, let the kids have some fun," Shelton said. "I'd have given up my eyeteeth to overthrow a government when I was a kid."

Adams' laughter trailed off. "Wait, you guys are serious about this?"

Conrad cross his arms over his chest. "As a heart attack."

"Let me put that on my list." I mimicked writing on a notepad. "One: eat a taco. Two: overthrow government."

"Can number three be ice cream?" Ambria said.

"Absolutely." I pretended to write that down as well.

"Better put in a facial and pedicure for Shelton," Adam said. "You know how cranky he gets when his toenails aren't hot pink."

Shelton grinned. "Damned tootin'!"

Mountains and valleys gave way to great savannahs where herds of silver antelope fled before sleek gray felines. Seraphina had its share of strange animals but didn't have nearly the biodiversity of Eden. What it lacked there, it more than made up in geographical features. A massive floating landmass appeared across the plains. The skylet hovered above a nebulous aether vortex, rotating slowly on its axis like a small flat world.

Ultraviolet towers stretched heavenward but ended abruptly in jagged points, scars of war. The rebuilt parts of the city center rose proud and true in the middle of the rubble, but the phoenix had barely risen from the ash before more conflict struck. After Cephus, Aerianas had invaded. The rebuilding started again only now to be interrupted by Baal.

It didn't look like Tarissa would be inhabited again anytime soon.

The remnants of the population huddled on the southwestern edge of the city. With the skyways inoperable, there was no other way down or out but by Mzodi ships. Some had tried to glide below on their wings, but turbulence from the aether vortex claimed too many lives.

The Mzodi fleet landed in precise rows. Ultraviolet mist solidified into gangways. Coordinators ran down the ramps and ushered allotted numbers of refugees to each ship. The sky on the north side of the city burned orange. Streaks of light raced back and forth as the city guard fought to hold off the dragons as long as they could.

Elyssa stared at the battle. "We can't just leave those soldiers to die."

"Do the other ships have enough space for the refugees?" I asked.

She nodded. "More than enough."

"Then let's see if we can help."

Elyssa tapped her com badge. "All ships depart immediately after all the refugees are onboard. We're going to give the soldiers a ride." She turned to the bridge. "Head due north."

The *Listrum* rose and rotated north. Crew members manned the turrets and the levitation foils hummed to full power. We raced into the city center. Dozens of Daskar in their crystalline armor streaked in formation above the towers. Dragons swooped after them, flame, poison, and frost claiming victims and destroying buildings. There would be no battle of Tarissa.

Baal had already won.

CHAPTER 4

Twin towers rose in a twisting ladder helix. Three fire wyverns roosted on the conjoined peak, parietal eyes taking in the battlefield. They saw us and roared defiance. The building groaned and wobbled as the huge beasts thrust themselves in the air. Flames speared from their great throats. The Daskar split apart. Ultraviolet beams pummeled the red hide of one dragon. It tumbled out of control and smashed into another tower. Crystal shards rained on the streets below.

Another squadron of Daskar intercepted frost wyverns. Hail and freezing fire filled the air. Any Daskar caught in the way froze and plummeted to earth, shattering on impact. The Daskar picked a target and pounded it, then moved to the next, but there were too many dragons.

Elyssa pointed out a group of wyverns flanking the Daskar. "Intercept and destroy those targets."

The ship veered after them. Crew swiveled the turrets and volleys of destructive energy filled the air. Dragon wings smoked and burned.

Reptilian bodies smashed into buildings and crashed to the ground. A wing of wyverns bellowed in rage and moved on an intercept course.

I unleashed Brilliance at the head wyvern. Conrad summoned his azure powers and tackled another target. Shelton and the others blasted away with everything they had.

The battle might have been five minutes or five hours. All meaning of time seemed to slip away. Blackened blood and ash coated my sweaty arms. Screams and roars rang in my ears. I manifested into demon form and wrestled a beast off the deck. Knocked Adam out of the way of poison spray only to have Elyssa jerk me from the path of fire.

At long last a voice crackled on Elyssa's com badge. *Commander, all refugees are accounted for. Departing now.*

Elyssa hit her com badge. "All Daskar retreat to the *Listrum!*"

Affirmative, came the reply.

Elyssa turned to the bridge. "Slow to one-third speed to let them catch up. Gunners, suppressing fire."

The special armor the Daskar wore gave them the extra speed they needed to outrun the enemy, but the dragons weren't ready to let us go just yet. Forty Daskar made it to the deck and filed below decks to make space for us. The wyvern circled around us, vultures inspecting a dying animal.

"So that's how they want to play it?" Elyssa bared her teeth. "Let's play."

I didn't know where all her confidence came from. "Um, should I be worried here?"

"Gunners, concentrate your fire on the base of that tower!" Elyssa pointed to the twisted helix building. The crew aimed the starboard turrets as low as they could. Solid beams of white sliced into the base. The magic resistant material held up beneath the onslaught but finally gave way. The structure toppled with the sound of a million bulls running through the biggest china shop in the world.

"Drop altitude to fifty. Head due west beneath the falling tower!"

The pilot of the *Listrum* must have been used to crazy orders because she didn't hesitate. The ship plummeted at a gut-wrenching pace. I screamed. Ambria screamed. Emergency restraints sprang from the railings and wrapped around our waists, but I held on for dear life anyway. The ship slowed its descent so fast it knocked most of us on our asses. The restraints snapped tight as the ship thrust toward the toppling building at full speed.

"Son of a three-legged monkey goat!" Shelton's hat flapped in the wind at the end of its string. The weather shields had either failed or been turned off.

The helix tower thundered to earth, throwing up dust and annihilating the road behind us. We rode just ahead of the annihilating wave. The dragons were too busy dodging shrapnel to intercept us. We shot free just ahead of the tip of the tower. The shields sprang back on in time to intercept a blast of shattered crystal.

I would have whooped, but my legs were too wobbly to support me. Elyssa was the only one still standing, fierce violet eyes glaring at the scattered wyverns with the anger of a thousand suns. "Yeah, that's what I thought." She helped Ambria up.

"You're magnificent!" Ambria held onto Elyssa's hand. "How did you know what to do?"

"I didn't." Elyssa wiped sweat from her brow. "Sometimes you just have to pull a Justin and hope for the best."

"A Justin?" Ambria gave me a confused look.

"Yeah, it's called flying by the seat of your pants," Shelton said. "Leap without looking."

"YOLO!" Adam pulled himself up.

"Hellz yeah." Shelton clapped his hands. "You only live once!"

"I'm not that bad," I protested.

Adam snorted. "Dude, you're a regular Leeroy Jenkins."

"Huh?" Ambria looked even more confused.

"I nearly pissed myself." Shelton inspected his jeans for wet spots. "Hot damn that was scary."

Conrad climbed to his feet. "Well, it seems your reputations as legends were well earned."

"Absolutely." Max wiped his forehead. "I never would have thought of blowing up a building and flying beneath it."

"Legends?" I laughed. "More like legendary luck."

"On that we can agree," Elyssa said.

We took the long way home, bypassing the Ooskai Valley for the more treacherous Galdin Pass. It was barely wide enough for our ships to pass through and terminated at the Traskin Maw. There, a giant aether vortex leaned so far sideways that it faced the end of the pass like a gaping mouth.

The Mzodi pilots expertly threaded the needle between the maw and the pass and guided us to open seas.

We reached Voltis in the wee hours of the following morning. Lookouts spotted several wyvern patrols gliding around the perimeter and even a few sea serpents. But the dragons were no match for the fury of Voltis and remained miles away from the heart of the storm. Mzodi ships could handle the violent weather near the storm wall thanks to their shields and hardy design.

Distant wyverns gave brief chase when Shelton thumbed his nose at them but turned back once we crossed the outer threshold. Volcanic ash spewed into the air. Ice crystals rained down on the shields, reduced to steam by superheated air an instant later.

Voltis wasn't a typical vortex as we'd once thought. At its center lay the last fragment of the original Earth before it split apart into realms. The incredible friction of this juxtaposition threw off massive amounts of energy. Inside the storm walls were mountains of dense aetherite, or gems, as the Seraphim called them. Mzodi had fished less concentrated aether gems from normal vortexes, but this stuff was something special.

Shelton and Adam realized it could be a source of incredible power for the Mzodi ships and adapted a whole new power management system. Instead of dozens of crewmembers independently controlling each levitation gem, each ship needed only one pilot with a control stick. Even the flagship, *Uorion*, had adapted it. Unfortunately, dragons bred like rabbits, and the construction of new ships couldn't keep pace.

A ship hidden in the mists of Voltis emerged, its prow bearing a gem shaped like a magnifying glass. It rotated slowly to face the gray storm wall. A Mzodi channeled into the gem. Though it had only a thirty-foot radius, the projected light expanded sixty feet. A portal formed in the storm, a window to calm blue skies.

We went through first and the rest of the ships filed in behind us. Giant silver turrets atop Roman columns rotated to greet us as we came through. Elyssa gave them the clearance codes and the barrels sagged. There were only three entry points into Atlantis from Seraphina, and we had them all covered with dozens of such turrets. If Baal really meant to invade, his dragons would face a gauntlet.

Some turrets utilized nom technology, flak cannons that could take down swarms of drakes and dozens of wyverns at the same time. Though dragon scales were extremely tough, the membranes on their wings were a glaring weak point. Atlantis was small enough to defend quite easily, which made me wonder if Baal truly meant to invade in a week, or if it was just another lie.

A sortie of chariots lifted off from a nearby platform and performed a visual flyby inspection. The aptly named ships resembled their ancient Roman counterparts, complete with wheels. Cannons jutted from

beneath the golden wings, and each one wielded a magical shield generator, but they would be a poor defense against a dragon swarm.

The pilots waved at us when they were satisfied with our identities and
went back to their normal patrols. Though Baal employed mostly dragons, we suspected he might try to infiltrate with infernus if given a
chance. If he did, he might be able to sabotage our defenses. We weren't
taking any chances against the king of deceit.

The ships continued through the gauntlet of turrets and flew across a
seemingly endless ocean. We passed through an invisible veil a few
miles in and an island seemingly appeared out of nowhere. Another
perimeter of turrets trained their sights on us and another sortie of
chariots met us.

Shelton waved to a pilot. "Glad to see they're on top of their game. We're
gonna need all hands on deck if Baal follows through with his threat to
invade."

"He's got to get through Voltis first," Adam said. "Unless he has a way to
make a portal larger than sixty feet wide, he'll have to send the dragons
through in single file."

"Yeah, and we'd mop them up." Shelton frowned. "Still, we're talking
about Baal here. I wouldn't put anything past him. His rift generator
ripped open a gateway big enough for Enigma to fit through."

"That's the trick," I said. "Don't underestimate the Great Deceiver."

Atlantis rose before us, a mountain city of ancient Roman architecture.
Atop the peak, a massive statue of Poseidon held a triton above his head
as if aiming to spear any who came too close. The city held less than a
thousand inhabitants when we first found it, but the streets now teemed
with more Seraphim than humans.

Brightlings and Darklings, once mortal enemies, now occupied the
same city and even shared housing. My mother had tried for years to
unite the two factions and ultimately failed. Baal, it seemed, had
succeeded in forcing them to cast aside their differences and fight as

one. Unfortunately, the unification had come too late and the Seraphim were refugees from their own realm.

The Port of Atlantis teemed with activity. A massive gem on a rotating apparatus focused an ultraviolet beam of Murk on a skeletal mold, slowly forming the next sleek, black war cruiser. Finished cruisers lined the first two piers. Crew swarmed over them, putting the final touches on the massive sky ships.

The *Listrum* set down on Pier Three. The rest of the ships landed nearby and disgorged refugees. Coordinators met them to show them to their new homes and lives.

I'd seen a lot of despair and anguish in my years fighting the bad guys, but the Seraphim took exile extremely hard. Most Darklings ate a vegan diet geared toward food found only on Seraphina. We'd brought seeds and as many stores of their foods as we could, but the farmlands of Atlantis were nearly at peak capacity already.

Mount Olympus, former home of the Fallen, rose a few miles from Atlantis. The citizens of Heval, a city at lower elevations of the mountain, relied entirely on Atlantis for their food supply. Adonis, the governor of Atlantis, had warned us that we would have to import food or risk over-farming the limited arable land. Archon Hippias of Heval had already sent several envoys to demand solutions.

"This place is bursting at the seams." Elyssa sighed. "It feels like the end times."

I couldn't disagree. "Won't be long before soylent green is the only thing to eat around here."

A silver chariot twinkled in the light of the rising sun as it lifted off from the great dome of the central administration building. I stayed on deck to avoid the crowded pier and waited for the chariot. A teenaged girl with long blonde hair guided the vessel alongside us and leaped across the gap.

"Justin!" Ivy wrapped her arms around mine, pinning them to my sides.

Even though we'd been separated for years, she'd hardly aged a day, thanks to Victus. He'd captured her and stored her in a preservation chamber after the rest of us had been trapped in Seraphina. Conrad and friends had found and rescued her and my dear friend, Nightliss, who I'd thought died.

I freed an arm and hugged my sister. "We've only been gone a couple of days."

She let me go and backed up a step. "Yeah, but I was worried that Baal might have blasted you to bits." Ivy turned to Conrad. "Why do you kids get to go and I have to stay here? It's super lame."

"We don't have parents who tell us what to do," Ambria said. "So count yourself lucky."

Ivy stuck out her tongue at the other girl. "I'm totally an adult! I'm literally nineteen—or maybe twenty." She groaned. "God, I don't even know how old I am anymore!"

"Twenty," I said. "Your birthday was nearly a month ago."

"What?" Her mouth dropped open. "I didn't even get a birthday party." Her shoulders slumped. "I guess I'm too old for fluffy unicorns now."

I squeezed her shoulder and laughed. "No female is ever too old for that."

"Damned straight." Elyssa patted Ivy's shoulder. "Stuffed animals for life."

Ivy turned her serious blue eyes on her. "For life."

I felt as if some girl bonding moment passed between them. Ambria looked a little confused, probably because she'd never known such a cushy life. She and Conrad were raised in a god-awful orphanage that sold kids as slaves. It was no wonder they were royally effed in the heads.

"I hardly know how old I am anymore." I sighed. "Thanks to the time differential in Utopia I'm either twenty-three or twenty-nine."

"Whoa, we're almost the same age now!" Ivy grinned. "That's so cool!"

"We need to speak with my father about Baal's ultimatum." Elyssa hopped over to the chariot. "Coming?"

"Yeah." Ivy and I boarded.

"I'll see you later." Shelton nodded toward the city. "Time to go do my husbandly duties with Bella."

Adam gagged. "Man, what an awful visual."

"Yeah?" Shelton winked. "Well you'd better go take care of Meghan before she finds another man."

Adam put on a fake grin. "Yeah, sure."

Elyssa steered the chariot away and their jibes faded into the distance. Before we'd gone very far, a gout of water exploded from the ocean in front of us. Salty spray and mist resolved into the webbed wings and the emerald scales of a sea dragon.

CHAPTER 5

A round-faced woman with blue-gray hair regarded us solemnly from the dragon. Technically, she wasn't a woman, but a Siren.

My heart pounded to the beat of a drug-fueled timpani player thanks to her surprise appearance. When I recovered my wits, I croaked out a greeting. "Hello, Dolpha."

"I would speak with you." The brusque female didn't wait for my consent. Like other Sirens, she seemed to sing rather than speak. "A song is sung. It reaches across the realms and summons us to Aquilis."

I blinked a few times. "Say what? You can hear a song across the realms?"

"Yes. I do not know how or why." She unconsciously stroked her dragon's neck. "We three have known naught but Atlantis since the Sundering. The song summons us home, but Aquilis is no home to us."

Elyssa bit her lower lip. "Does it say why the Sirens need to return?"

Dolpha shook her head. "No doubt it relates to our guest."

I shared a confused look with Elyssa. Ivy blurted the question before I could. "You have a guest?"

"Yes."

I tried to keep the frustration from my tone. "Well, who is it?"

"She knows you and would speak with you before approaching the others."

"That's not an answer," I said. "Who is it?"

Dolpha tilted her head slightly. "Melea."

I hadn't heard that name in years. Melea was not only a Siren, but the person who'd ripped the Chalon from the Grand Nexus during the first war with Daelissa. The backlash had turned her and all Seraphim within range of an Alabaster Arch into infantile husks, and reduced humans to shadow creatures. For millennia they'd been trapped, hungering for the light of the living, until we'd found a way to return the Seraphim back to normal. Unfortunately, we couldn't do the same for humans.

Melea had been one of those we'd restored, but she hadn't stuck around long. "What in the world does Melea want with me? How did she get here?"

"I know not." Dolpha pursed her lips. "Will you meet with her?"

"Like right now?" I shrugged. "Sure."

The ocean surface rippled. A thick tendril of water rose, bearing a woman atop the pedestal. Blue hair drifted about a serene face. Inhumanly large sea-green eyes regarded me as seriously as the first time I'd met her. "It has been some time, Justin Slade." Her mellifluous voice was more pleasant than the abrasive Dolpha's.

"Yeah, it's been a few years." I paused a beat. "What can I help you with?"

"Baal and Drakara wage war against the realms. I invite you to join the only one who can defeat them."

Icy fingers danced across my heart. "Oh god. You're on Team Xanomiel, aren't you?"

"Indeed. Xanos is grateful for release from the Abyss, Justin Slade." Melea offered me a curt nod. "Though it was an impetuous deed unwittingly done, you were the only one able to pierce the barrier."

I didn't know if she was praising or insulting me, but I already felt stupid enough about letting an Apocryphan out of eternal prison. I sighed. "Xanomiel—"

"Xanos," she said.

"Sorry, I forgot he adopted a hip new nickname for the modern age." I didn't tell her Baal was the one who'd told me.

"She."

I rolled my eyes. "Xanomiel was a dude; now he's a female. Xanos isn't even a female-sounding name, by the way."

"It is as Xanos wishes." Melea observed me as if I was an idiot.

"Fine, whatever." I threw up my hands. "Xanos and Baal are two sides of the same coin. One wants to smash all the realms together and the other wants to rule them apart."

"The realms must have structure," Melea said. "Without a ruler, they are prone to self-destruction."

"I'm sorry, but I've heard this argument before and I don't buy it." I crossed my arms to express my unwillingness to entertain her theory. "I'm a big believer in self-determination and free will."

"We don't need a dictator," Elyssa said. "And killing billions to combine the realms is completely unacceptable."

"Why are the Sirens being called to Aquilis?" I said.

"I do not know." Melea looked at Dolpha. "Is there truly a call?"

Dolpha nodded. "You do not hear it?"

Concern pinched the corners of Melea's eyes. "No."

"Maybe good old Xanos doesn't want you hearing it," I said. I didn't plan on joining her team any more than I planned on joining Baal's but wasn't about to let Melea go without wringing some information from her. "Do either of you know a Siren who lives in the land of ice in Eden?"

Melea didn't hesitate. "You speak of Vitania, singer of the black sands. Why do you ask?"

"I just wanted to chat with her." I tried to judge Melea's age, but she looked like a twenty-something who'd undergone extreme plastic surgery to mimic a character from an anime show. "Were you around at the Sundering?"

"I was not born until after the world split. I wish I had known those days and seen the Earth in its golden age." A single tear glistened in her eye. "Torn asunder, the world has withered."

Elyssa frowned. "It hasn't withered; it's just become something different. The Apocryphan warred with each other and split the Earth, in case you've forgotten. One Earth or multiple realms hasn't made any difference in the levels of conflict. If Xanos tells you differently, she's lying."

I piled on. "There were no good old days. That's just a myth coined by people who don't like change or peace."

Melea simply stared at me. "You refuse Xanos's offer?"

"Let me flip that around on you," I said. "How about if Xanos joins us? Together we can kick Baal's ass. We can come up with a new office called Honorary Dictator of the Universe and give it to Xanos. She won't actually have any powers, but she'll have a spiffy title."

Melea's lips tightened. "You are still the impetuous boy so easily tricked into releasing Xanos. You will not see reason."

"Oh, I see plenty of reason not to let billions die just so a jackass can claim dominion over all." I narrowed my eyes. "I think you're the one who won't see reason. You're the same moron who ripped out the Chalon and husked everyone."

"I ended the war!"

I shook my head. "No, you just delayed the war for another few thousand years."

Elyssa scowled. "We cleaned up your mess then, and it looks like we'll have to clean up another one now."

"Yeah, you're a real idiot," Ivy said.

Melea slashed a hand through the air. "I will hear no more of this!"

"That's fine." I reeled back my anger and tried another tactic. "Can I meet with Xanos in a neutral place?"

"I am her emissary. Speak with me and you speak with her."

"I want to talk to her in person." I set my hands on my hips to show I meant business. "If she's so eager to recruit me, we can have a chat about it."

Her lips pressed into a thin line. "She has no time for such things."

"I guess she doesn't want me on her side very much." I shook my head. "Is she scared of me?"

"She fears nothing." Melea scowled. "Xanos will not spare you if you dare go against her. She has already dealt with the three who opposed him." She touched an obsidian necklace around her throat. A pocket of air behind her grew dark. A roiling gray fog enveloped Melea. When it faded away, she was gone. The pedestal of water splashed back into the ocean.

"Uh, where did she go?" I turned to Dolpha. "What kind of Siren magic was that?"

"I know not." she replied. "Melea told me the necklace was a gift from Xanos, but it looks Siren made."

Elyssa flinched. "A necklace that can let her travel between realms?"

Dolpha nodded. "So it would seem."

My stomach sank. "Oh, joy. So Xanos can travel anywhere, anytime."

"Can you help us?" Ivy asked. "We could really use a necklace like that."

"Not to mention Siren songs against the dragons," Elyssa said.

"I do not know how such a necklace is made." Dolpha turned to Elyssa. "Neither I nor my sisters will fight for anyone."

"My god, the fate of the realms lies in the balance!" I hated to sound overly dramatic, but it was true. "Are you saying you won't even help us prevent Xanos from merging the realms together and killing billions?"

"We will do what we can to preserve life but killing is unacceptable."

My inner demon decided to toss in his two cents. *Destroy.*

Put a lid on it, Fred. I didn't like how mouthy he'd become lately. Even shutting him in his cage didn't quiet him like it used to. Also, he hated his new name.

Convincing Dolpha and the resident Sirens of Atlantis to fight with us was out of the question, but they weren't the only ones in the universe. "Is there a way to reach Aquilis from here?"

Dolpha twitched, as if surprised by the change in subject. "We have no arch, no way of traveling there. Only the Fallen possessed that ability."

"Yeah, but they're dead," Ivy said. "Someone really powerful killed them."

Elyssa's eyes flared. "My god, I wonder if those were the three Melea said Xanos killed."

Conrad, Ivy, and the others had traveled to Bermuda to rendezvous with the Fallen so they could catch a ride to Seraphina. But the Fallen weren't there. All that remained was a hole in the ground where their house had been. No other house in the neighborhood had been touched.

The Fallen had programmed their neighbor to give Conrad and gang instructions for reaching Seraphina.

"If Xanos was strong enough to find and kill three of the most ancient Seraphim in existence even while she's not at full strength, I don't know how we stand a chance."

Elyssa dropped a rotten cherry on my poop sundae. "We already don't stand a chance against Baal."

"Man, you guys are making me sad." Ivy slumped. "I mean, Conrad overcame impossible odds to beat his dad. He saved me, Nightliss, and the Fallen, and managed to get us to Seraphina where we finally found you again." A faint smile lifted the corners of her lips. "I know everything looks hopeless, but I think we can beat anyone or anything if we just work together."

Elyssa's mouth dropped open. "That's the most profound thing you've ever said, Ivy."

"Yeah." I grinned. "Usually you just want to blast people."

"Well, I do want to blast bad guys, but I've learned a lot since Conrad saved me." Ivy brushed blonde locks from her eyes. "We just need to handle one bad guy at a time."

I looked at Elyssa. "Sounds like it's time for a quest to the land of ice."

She nodded. "Yeah. Maybe Vitania can help us unravel Lulu's riddle."

"Lulu?" Ivy's eyes went wide. "You saw her?"

I'd forgotten Ivy hadn't been with us. "Yeah, she popped out of the ground and talked to us in Seraphina." I gave her the details. "It's a long shot, but maybe if we dig into Baal's origins we can find his weakness."

"Yeah, like who is that guy really?" Ivy shrugged. "He's like the devil or something, but where did he come from?"

"It would seem you have many journeys ahead of you." Dolpha stared out at the ocean. "I am content to remain here."

"I hate to say it, but you Sirens aren't much help." I didn't bother softening my words. "Literally the only time you helped us was when your Siren sisters were kidnapped by Kaelissa."

Dolpha scowled. "We may not fight your wars, but we have done much to help."

"How about diplomacy?" I said. "Maybe you could use the song to communicate with the Sirens in Aquilis and see if they might help us."

"My song cannot pierce the barrier." Dolpha's forehead pinched. "If help is something you need, I will give you a gift greater than any spear or sword." She and her dragon dove into the ocean and vanished.

"So ditching people is the gift?" I stared at the ocean waves. "Hey, I already know how to ditch people I don't want to hang with!"

"Maybe her absence is the gift." Elyssa smirked. "Dolpha never was that pleasant to talk to."

Ivy nodded. "I never met her 'til now, but she is kinda rude."

"But seriously, are we supposed to wait here?" I looked up from the water.

Elyssa shrugged.

"We could give her five minutes," Ivy said. "I really want to know what she's going to give us."

"I'd rather not wait." Elyssa engaged the levitation foils and the chariot resumed course toward the great domed administration building. "It's imperative we tell the council about Baal's threats."

"I don't think five minutes will kill us." But Elyssa nearly had us at our destination before I finished my sentence. I looked out at the ocean for any sign of the Siren, but Dolpha was nowhere in sight.

I hurried to catch up to Elyssa and Ivy as they entered the arched entrance to the administration building. Voices echoed down the marble halls, words too muffled to make out what they were saying. The tones were heated enough to indicate the council session wasn't all giggles and hugs.

We stepped into the public chamber, a round auditorium with stadium seating. A homely man with a pot belly and thinning gray hair paced in the circle at the center. He held up an open hand. "Those are the facts, my friends. We cannot avoid reality."

The woman most people knew as Alysea, Grand Empress of Seraphina, stood from her seat. I knew her simply as Mom. Her hand rose. "I would speak, Archon Adonis."

He nodded. "Granted."

Mom clasped her hands at her waist. "Adonis is correct. Atlantis cannot sustain such a population for long, but neither can we send the Seraphim refugees en-masse to Eden. The Overworld strives to keep the noms there from discovering its secrets for good reason."

"If not Eden, then where?" Adonis said. "There is plenty of room there. I'm certain we could explain the rules to the Seraphim."

"We have thousands of displaced Seraphim," Mom said. "The Overworld government is recovering from war. It would be a recipe for disaster."

"Ugh, this is boring." Ivy hugged me. "I'll see you later, bro." She pranced away.

Commander Thomas Borathen stood and raised his hand. "I would speak."

Adonis sighed. "I know what you're going to say, commander." He threw up his hands. "Say it anyway."

"Eden is not the place. But we may have access to another realm that would be perfect." He waved a hand to a man in a gray business suit.

Cinder nodded gravely. "May I speak, Archon?"

"Yes, honorable golem." Adonis waved him in.

"Thank you." Cinder stepped into the circle. "As you know, we recently ventured to the realm of Utopia. Due to the apocalyptic conditions of the realm, the citizens have desperate need of help."

Adonis frowned. "Pardon me if I'm wrong, but isn't Utopia subject to extreme time dilation?"

"During our stay there, yes." Cinder tapped a gem on the table in the center of the circle and projected a spatial map of the known realms. Utopia was further from the Abyss than it had been the last time I'd seen it. "Utopia reached the apogee of its closest pass to the Abyss during our time there. It has now passed out of that phase and will not reach it again for one year of Atlantean time."

"So there's no time dilation there now?" Mom asked.

"Every hour there is two here for the next month," Cinder said. "After that, the effect lessens to almost nothing."

"The Utopians are agreed on sending the refugees there?" Adonis asked.

"I have not broached the subject with them," Cinder said. "It seemed unwise to do so before securing the approval of the council."

"You have my absolute approval," Adonis said. "Shall we call a vote?"

"Seconded," Mom said.

"All yeas show your hands." Adonis raised his.

Mom and Thomas raised their hands. Captain Takei, de-facto leader of the Arcanes, joined them. But they were still several hands short of consensus.

Kassallandra, ruler of the Daemos, walked down the aisle, fiery red hair flowing down icy white shoulders. Her scarlet dress glittered beneath the lights, long splits on the side allowing tantalizing views of long, fair legs. She stepped into the circle, not bothering to request permission. "You speak of finding displaced Seraphim new homes. Of aiding a destroyed civilization. Yet you have refused to grant us and the other

Overworld factions immediate passage back to Eden." Her ice-blue eyes shaded crimson. "We are not your conscripts. We are not your slaves. We joined you to stop another invasion from Seraphina. The threat is over. It is time for us to go home and rebuild the Overworld."

"Aye, the war is over." Colin McCloud, pack leader of the lycans, raised a fist. "It's time to go home."

Komad Rashad, vampire faction leader stood and lent his voice. "Agreed."

Baal and Xanos were about to drop the hammer on the realms, and our allies were ready to take their armies and go home. The Eden coalition was falling apart, and with it, any hope of winning this war.

CHAPTER 6

I couldn't stop myself from responding to Kassallandra's preposterous statement. "The threat is over?" I topped my words with a sarcastic laugh. "Are you kidding me? The threat is even worse than before. Baal and Xanos are about to tear the realms new assholes. Without our coalition, Eden can't last."

McCloud turned to me. "Aye, lad, it might fall. Hell, all the realms might fall. But what good can the likes of us do against gods? Lycans can't fly, last I checked, so how are we supposed to fight dragons?"

"It's true, I'm afraid." Komad wore a teal Atlantean tunic with gold stitches. Even worlds away, the vampire leader managed to appropriate the pinnacle of fashionwear. "The mighty archangels and Daskar could not defeat the dragons. What are we to do, flail our arms uselessly while they roast us from above? It is better to let us go home. We have been away for nearly a decade. We must set the Overworld right and protect what is ours."

Much as I wanted to counter his argument, I couldn't. The battles in Seraphina had been almost exclusively aerial. The Arcane military wing, the Blue Cloaks, had lost most of their flying carpets and brooms over the years and didn't have the facilities to replace them fast enough. Daemos, vampires, lycans, and felycans were foot soldiers. Even the Templars had limited air support without supply lines back home.

Thomas didn't want to return everyone to Eden for fear they'd scatter to the winds, never to return when we needed them. He hoped to set up shop in Atlantis and build new facilities to manufacture everything necessary for an aerial war, but resources were too limited in this pocket remnant.

We had the means to return to Eden, but it would be painstakingly slow with only the portal device on the boat the Fallen had given Conrad. It was a logistics boondoggle.

Thomas spoke before I thought of a response. "Perhaps you're right." He stepped into the circle next to Kassallandra. "Some Daemos have wings in demon form, but they can't fly." He nodded at Komad and McCloud. "None of you have aerial fleets, and even if you did, what chance would you have against wyverns?"

"Earth-bound dragons would have no chance against lycans," McCloud said. "Get us in the air and we'd show them a grand beating."

"He's goading us," Komad said. "Commander Borathen is well aware we could defeat the dragons, provided a level battlefield."

"Agreed." Kassallandra raised a fiery eyebrow. "We are simply being realistic."

"I wasn't goading you," Thomas said. "I, too, was being realistic."

Fire flashed in her eyes. "We've never had a chance to fight dragons on the ground."

That sparked an idea. "What if we could force the dragons to fight on our own terms?"

All eyes turned my way.

McCloud chuckled. "How in the world would you manage that, lad?"

"The elemental magi on Utopia can control the weather to some extent. If they allied with us, they could conjure storms to force the dragons to retreat or fight us on land."

He grinned. "That might actually work. Force those bastards into the mud and see how they do when they can't rain fire from above."

"An interesting proposal," Komad said. "But we will not agree to anything until our passage home is granted."

Kassallandra nodded. "Agreed."

And there it is. None of their excuses meant anything. They just wanted to take their kickball and go home.

Thomas's jaw tightened, but he didn't argue or get angry. He just nodded. "We will have to work out a schedule. As you know, the *Angel Wings* is the only vessel with a portal device that can access Eden." He turned to Cinder. "When is the next Voltis alignment?"

"Two days, three hours, and fourteen minutes." Cinder tilted his head slightly. "I will need precise numbers of those returning to calculate how long it will take."

Kassallandra held out her hand to Thomas. "So we have an agreement, commander?"

He shook her hand. "Yes."

"Then I vote in favor of relocating Seraphim to Utopia, and the motion to secure them as a new ally in return for swift passage back to Eden."

"Aye on all counts," McCloud said.

Komad nodded. "Agreed."

A hulking figure in the back of the auditorium stood. "Felycans vote yes." Saber, as usual, didn't have a lot to say and sat back down.

"It's agreed," Thomas said. "Please provide Cinder the information he needs, and he will create a schedule to get everyone home."

I intercepted Kassallandra on her way out.

She regarded me coldly, but it wasn't anything personal. Kassallandra just wasn't the friendliest person in the world. "What would you have of me, Kohvaniss?"

"Wow, I haven't heard that title in a while." On the day Kassallandra was supposed to marry my father so she could be the queen bitch of all the Daemos, Aerianas had ambushed the ceremony and tried to banish Kassallandra to the Abyss. I'd saved the day and won the endorsement of the Daemos houses. Kohvaniss, loosely translated, meant supreme devourer of souls. It was a lot to live up to, especially since I was on a soul-free diet.

The fire in Kassallandra's eyes faded to hazel. "You devoured many souls during your time in Utopia, did you not?"

"They were demon spirits, not souls," I said.

"Few Daemos dare devour demon spirits," Kassallandra said. "They have a tendency to influence their human halves."

"Shouldn't be a worry for you," I said. "You don't share your body with a human soul."

"Perhaps." She shrugged. "How did it feel?"

"You've never tried it?"

"No. The few Daemos who did such things went mad." Kassallandra raised a red eyebrow. "So, how may I be of service, Kohvaniss?"

Is she playing mind games with me? A knot of worry formed in my stomach. My demon half had definitely become stronger since devouring all those demon spirits, but I hadn't sensed any overt signs of madness. I noticed her waiting on my answer, but it took a moment for me to remember what I'd wanted to talk to her about in the first place.

"Will the Daemos come to our aid if we need you again?"

"Of course." Kassallandra looked mildly offended. "I swore an oath to you all those years ago, and nothing has changed. I am the leader of the Daemos, but I am also duty bound to the Kohvaniss."

"What happens if I die?"

Her full lips pursed into a rosebud. "Never fear. I will still do what I must to protect my people." Her other eyebrow arched. "If you wish an even more formal arrangement, we could bear a child who would serve as a symbol of an eternal alliance."

I frowned. "Yeah, my girlfriend might not approve."

Kassallandra shrugged. "Then my word will have to suffice. Good day." She gave a curt nod and left.

Damn, she's cold.

I knew McCloud and Saber would round up their troops if we needed them, but Komad was an unknown. Unfortunately, he'd already left. Elyssa stood in the circle with Thomas and my parents, so I walked down and joined the conversation.

"Certainly need to," Mom said.

"Certainly need to what?" I asked.

"Begin evacuations," she said. "Utopia is in alignment for three more days. We have thousands of Seraphim to send through."

"We can adapt the portal device on the *Raptor* to open a larger gateway," Cinder said. "That will allow us to send through several ships at a time and transport the refugees in time."

"I told them about Baal's ultimatum," Elyssa said. "I still don't know if he will actually invade Atlantis or if it was just an empty threat."

"That's the trick," Dad said. "Misdirection is the name of the game, and Baal's the master."

Thomas turned to me. "Justin, I'd like you and Elyssa to be our emissaries to Utopia. Hopefully they agree to take in the Seraphim quickly so we can get them resettled."

"I think they will." At least I hoped so. We had just rescued them from their own apocalypse. Maybe they'd save us from ours. "It's the part about getting their elemental magi to help us fight dragons that I'm not sure about."

"One step at a time," Mom said. "I know you just got back, but we really need you to leave for Utopia right away."

I turned to Elyssa. "I'm ready if you are."

She nodded. "Let's go."

I looked around. "Where's Nightliss?"

Cinder's eyes tightened. "She has resumed her duties as Clarion."

I blinked in surprise. "I thought she was going to wait."

"She insisted," Thomas said. "Hundreds of Atlanteans want to join the Templars, so she's bestowing as many blessings a day as she can."

"Atlantean Templars?" I scratched my head. "Are they coming to Eden with us?"

Thomas shook his head. "No, they'll form a new Templar legion here. We've also had Seraphim ask to join."

"Seraphim?" I almost scratched my head again but didn't want to make myself prematurely bald. "Why wouldn't they join the archangels or Daskar?"

"I asked them the same thing," Thomas said. "Many see the Templars as a neutral organization, whereas Daskar and archangels are exclusively Darkling or Brightling. The Mzodi are neutral but they don't take recruits."

"We need all the manpower we can get," Elyssa said. "We've buried so many of our own, I lost count."

I sensed the heavy weight of loss in the pit of my stomach. It was always there these days. We'd lost people and now an entire realm to Baal. The best I could hope for was to just not think about it. "It seems we'll have to bury even more in the days to come."

Thomas nodded grimly. "I'm afraid so."

"Let's get the *Raptor* ready for launch." Elyssa headed toward the exit.

I touched her hand to stop her. "I'll catch up in a minute."

"Okay." She kissed my cheek. "Meet me in thirty."

I saluted. "As you wish."

"That's right, farm boy." Elyssa winked and walked away.

Mom frowned. "Farm boy?"

I chuckled. "Inside joke." I put a hand on Dad's shoulder. "I have some questions for you." Kassallandra's warning about demon spirits wasn't sitting well with me and I needed some better answers.

"Oh, one of those talks." Dad tutted. "I guess it's time we explained the birds and the bees."

Mom rolled her eyes. "If he doesn't know by now, he never will."

I groaned. "Your dad jokes are the worst."

Dad chuckled. "What's the special talk you want to have, son?"

"It's about the demon spirits I ate in Utopia."

"Mhm." His grin faded. "I meant to talk with you about that, but you didn't seem overly concerned about it."

"Kassallandra freaked me out. She said Daemos aren't supposed to devour demon spirits."

Mom's forehead pinched. "How many did you eat, Justin?"

I gulped. "Um, a lot. Over a hundred. I kind of lost count because it took weeks."

"Wow." Dad's eyes widened. "I didn't realize it was that many."

"They were tiny." I held my thumb and forefinger a fraction apart as if that illustrated the size of a spirit. "Just baby demons."

"Oh, dear." Mom grimaced. "Baby demons?"

"That's unlikely, son." Dad's grin returned. "A powerful demon can separate slivers of its own spirit to create new entities. I'd bet that's what you devoured, not actual demon babies."

"Do demons mate?" I frowned. "I really don't understand how things work in Haedaemos."

"So it *is* time for this conversation." He winked. "Like the physical realm, there are males and females." Dad looked up and squinted as if recalling ancient memories. "They mingle their spirits and form an essence, a tiny seed that either can bear." Dad cupped a hand as if holding a ball. "This seed can mature into an imp. If the parents can prevent lesser spawn from devouring the imp, it will eventually become a new demon."

Mom shuddered. "Lesser spawn devour demon children?"

Dad nodded. "Haedaemos is a dangerous place. Powerful demons devour the weak, adding to their strength. That's not always in their best interest, because they also want other demons to do their bidding."

Mom grimaced. "Sounds a lot like everywhere else, minus the devouring part."

"True." Dad made a cutting motion with his hand. "Powerful demons can also take a fragment of their own spirit and implant it into other demons to exert greater influence."

I squinted. "They can make their own mini-me?"

"In a sense, yes." Dad clasped his hands behind his back. "The fragment has no life or consciousness of its own, but it can assimilate into another spirit and alter it."

I didn't like the sound of that. "So, do I have to worry about the spirits I devoured in Utopia? Did I corrupt myself?"

"You fed your demon side the equivalent of steroids," Dad said. "For most Daemos, that would spell big trouble. But you have a Seraphim element to your soul that seems to have offset the worst effects."

"I dunno. My inner demon's been a lot more active lately."

"Yeah, you probably fattened him up." Dad clapped me on the back. "But if you haven't lost control yet, that probably means you're okay."

"So I'm safe?"

Dad waggled a hand. "Give yourself time to assimilate the caustic spirits you absorbed. Think of your demon spirit as a glass of clean water. The more pollution you dump into it, the dirtier it gets. If your spirit is powerful enough, it will clean itself. If you overload your spirit, it will turn caustic."

Do not fear power. My demon seemed amused by my apprehension.

Why don't you hush and go back to your cage? "My demon side seems happy."

"It's grown stronger." Dad didn't look terribly worried. "The good news is your Seraphim side seems to have countered the usual side effects."

"Have you ever devoured demon spirits?" I asked.

"Once or twice." Dad patted his belly. "Made me sick as a dog. Thankfully, since I'm originally from Haedaemos, I'm a little tougher than the average Daemos."

"Believe me, they made me physically ill. But it was the only way to free those sprites and humans." My gorge rose just thinking about the experience. Devouring caustics was like sucking down wriggling, rotten zombie worms but instead of giving me a sour stomach, they soured my soul. I took a deep breath to ward off nausea.

"Shake it off, champ." Dad squeezed my shoulder. "You'll be right as rain in no time."

"Thanks. At least I know I'm not going to go insane." I sighed. "Well, off to another adventure."

"I'd sure like to visit Pangaea," Dad said. "In my thousands of years of life, I never knew fairies actually existed."

"I guess only those who lived before the Sundering would know," Mom said. "Even we're just babies compared to those folks."

I nodded. "I'll be sure to ask Vitania about the fairies if I find her in Iceland."

"If only I knew where to find an ancient Seraphim." Mom shook her head. "Unfortunately, most ancients have long since vanished."

The word ancient tickled a memory from a long time ago in a realm not so far away. It wasn't the most pleasant memory because it involved my introduction to Kaelissa, the mother of Daelissa, and the former empress of the Brightling nation. "Kaelissa said that Fjoeruss was an ancient."

Mom laughed. "Fjoeruss? How could he possibly be that old? I knew him when I was growing up. He was one of Daelissa's friends."

"Did you know him as a child?" I asked.

Mom pursed her lips. "I don't remember. I lost so many memories in the Desecration, and plenty more to old age."

I pressed her a little harder, hoping she'd remember something. "You don't remember seeing him as a child at all?"

Mom shook her head. "I only remember him being part of our little gang. Most ancients were aloof and strict. He never acted that way when we were younger."

"Did you know any ancients back in the day?" Dad asked.

Mom nodded. "Only a couple. Most had moved away, unhappy with society."

"Kaelissa claimed Fjoeruss's real name is Ussor." I'd never actually told Mom about this conversation. Not because I was afraid of her reaction or anything important, but mainly because I'd just forgotten to bring it up again. "She said his greatest love and adversary was Seaa, the golden ruler."

Mom's face went white as a sheet and she gripped Dad for support. "Seaa was the originator of my bloodline. Did she say—"

I nodded. "Kaelissa said you're the great-great granddaughter of Ussor."

"Whoa." Dad clapped his hands together. "Who's your granddaddy?"

Mom's mouth hung open. "I can't believe it. I don't want to believe it."

"Well, now that we can get back to Eden, I can go to the source." I put a hand on Mom's shoulder. "I'll ask Fjoeruss."

"It just can't be." Mom's nose wrinkled. "I can't imagine Fjoeruss as anything but the troublemaking trickster I knew all those centuries ago."

"People change. I've never known Fjoeruss as anything other than Mr. Gray, the mysterious jackass who doesn't care about anyone but himself." I shrugged. "Maybe he's just exceptionally good at acting."

"Probably," Dad said. "He didn't get the name Trickster for nothing."

"I'll find him and ask him when we get to Eden."

"Fjoeruss can wait," Mom said. "Go to Utopia and secure a place for my people to live."

"And ask the fairies for help," Dad said. "They can fly, right? Maybe they can sprinkle fairy dust in dragon noses and win the war."

I snorted. "I wish. Unfortunately, I don't think they'll help us. I did my best to convince Pyra, but she blew me off."

"Maybe you could try again," Mom said. "You've got a few days before Eden aligns with Voltis."

I sighed. "Yes, Empress."

Mom kissed my cheek. "Good luck son. I love you."

Dad gave me firm hug. "Try not to vanish for six years again, okay?"

I hugged him and Mom. "Love you. I'll see you soon."

I hope.

CHAPTER 7

O n my way to the *Raptor*, I used my com badge to contact Shelton and let him know about my mission.

"Are you crazy?" Shelton groaned. "We just got back."

"It can't wait. We've got to make the window to Utopia and be back in time to make it to Eden." I updated him on the council meeting.

"Son of a biscuit eater! Didn't you tell them that Baal promised to attack in a week?"

"Yeah, but what can they do against dragons?" I headed down a short pier and disturbed a flock of gray seabirds. "On the other hand, Baal might have just said that to scare us."

"Well, it worked." Shelton sighed. "Baal's guessing games really stress me out."

"Yeah, well, Atlantis is a tough nut to crack, even for Baal. We've got layers upon layers of defenses." A group of Atlanteans waved enthusiastically at me as they passed by, so I waved back. "He'd pay a heavy price."

"What if he moves on to Eden next?"

Amber wings glinted in the sunlight. The hull of the *Raptor* resembled a giant hawk, talons extended for the kill. Those same talons angled forward to provide perfect balance for the ship when it landed, a masterpiece of form and function. "If Baal sends a dragon army there, the noms will crap their britches, panic, and respond with fighter jets. I don't care how many dragons Baal throws at them, that's a fight he won't win."

"Yeah, well what about Drakara? She could probably take on the entire United States Air Force."

"Maybe." I stopped walking. "So, do you want to come or not?"

"I can't." He sighed again. "Bella will castrate me if I leave so soon."

"With my bare hands," Bella said in the background. "Justin can survive without you for two days."

"But, baby—"

"No." Bella's Spanish accent underscored the severity of punishment Shelton would face if he crossed her. "You are mine."

I hadn't realized she was listening in on the conversation. "Harry can't come out to play?"

"No, Justin, Harry is under house arrest." Bella laughed. "Oh, why the sad face, Harry? Is it really so bad?"

I could only imagine his puppy-dog eyes. "Look, I'll be back in a couple of days. Then we're off to Eden. We can all go."

Shelton's voice brightened a bit. "Really? God, I can't wait to go home."

"Me either. Later, man."

"Hey. You be careful. No getting trapped by Vokan again, okay?"

I nodded even though he couldn't see me. "I'll do my best." I ended the call. I heard the patter of bare feet and something slammed into my back. I stumbled forward and nearly plunged over the side of the pier. I caught a glimpse of silver skin before hands clamped over my face.

"Guess who?" said a sprightly voice.

It wasn't hard to guess. "Evadora."

"Yes!" She jumped off my back and burst into giggles. "He's so smart, Ivy."

"Well, duh, he's my bro." Ivy took Evadora's hand and they skipped ahead of me toward the *Raptor*.

I hurried to keep up. "Where are you going?"

"It's our turn to go on an adventure," Ivy said. "I'm tired of being cooped up in Atlantis."

I really didn't want the kids on this trip. Without Shelton coming, I could have at least had some alone time with Elyssa. "I don't think Mom will let you go."

"I'm an adult, Justin." Ivy stuck out her chin. "Maybe I don't look like one thanks to Victus, but I'm twenty like you said."

"Maybe in years, but not in maturity." I sighed. "Look, I'll check with Mom."

"Too late." Ivy tapped her own com badge. "Mom, I'm going to Utopia with Justin, okay?"

Mom replied after a brief pause. "Ivy, maybe you should—"

"No, I'm going and that's final. I love you, bye." She tapped it off.

My com badge pinged. I answered. "Hey, Mom."

"Ivy wants to go with you to Utopia."

"I know. She's standing right in front of me."

Mom sighed. "Try not to destroy anything, okay?"

"Whatever happened to be careful?" I said.

"Well, that too, but you and Ivy are a dangerous combination."

"Yes, Mom." I tapped off my badge. She wasn't wrong. Ivy and I had blown up a lot of things over the years.

"Yay, we're going!" Evadora leapt about ten feet straight up and spun like a ballerina. The silken material of her dress glittered in the sun and puffed out like a cloud.

"Well, so much for a quiet trip." I trudged up the gangway and boarded the ship.

Conrad sat cross-legged on the deck with Max and Ambria. "Hey, Justin." He put down a hand of cards and stood up.

I stared at him in confusion. "You're coming with us too?"

Ivy and Evadora ran up behind me. "Conrad!" The pair of girls smothered him in hugs then launched themselves at Ambria. Ambria struggled to escape but didn't stand a chance. "Max!" Ivy and Evadora turned to him. He glowed with happiness.

Considering the puppy-dog eyes Max gave Ivy, I suspected the poor boy had it bad for my slightly crazy sister.

When Conrad recovered from the assault, he brushed off his pants. "Is it okay that we're coming?"

"Um." My desired alone time with Elyssa evaporated like a fart in a breeze with five kids onboard. Considering what they'd been through to find us, at least I knew I wouldn't have to babysit. "Sure. It's totally fine."

One of the bridge windows misted away and Elyssa stepped outside, a sheepish grin on her face. "I saw Conrad on the way here and kind of let slip where we're going."

"Elyssa!" Evadora launched herself across the deck.

Elyssa deftly sidestepped the girl and caught her in one arm. She swung Evadora in a circle and set her down.

Evadora wobbled on her feet. "Whoa, you're fast."

"I would dearly love to see fairies," Ambria said to me. "Thank you for letting us come, Justin."

Max gave me a hopeful look. "Is Shelton coming?"

"No, he's under house arrest." I grinned. "The wife won't let him go."

"Oh." Max's shoulders slumped a bit. "Do you think she'd let him talk to me?"

I shrugged. "I don't see why not. Didn't you want him to train you?"

His face brightened a little. "Yeah. It's kind of like a dream come true to be trained by Harry Shelton."

I tapped my com badge. "Shelton, one more thing."

"Yeah?" He sounded miserable.

"Max wants to know if you can train him."

"Yeah, sure!" A pause. "Is that okay, honey?"

"As long as you don't go far, Harry," Bella replied.

"Alright," Shelton said. "Send him over."

A grin split Max' face from ear to ear. "Hey, you guys go see the fairies. I'm gonna train with Harry Shelton, okay?"

Conrad patted Max on the back. "I think that's a grand idea."

"Please do, Max." Ambria hid a smile. "You might actually learn something."

"Aw, you're not coming, Max?" Ivy puffed out her lips.

Max swallowed hard. "It's a big opportunity, Ivy."

"It's just Shelton." Ivy fluttered her hands like wings. "We're going to see fairies!"

"Maybe another time." Max hugged Conrad and Ambria goodbye. "Please don't die, okay?"

Conrad nodded somberly. "We'll do our best."

Max bolted down the gangway and headed back into town, leaving the rest of us on the ship.

Ambria laced her fingers through Conrad's and leaned on his shoulder. "This should be a nice trip."

Conrad gave us an embarrassed look. "Are you certain it's okay if we come?"

I nodded. "Sure. Maybe we can talk more about the first power and all that."

"I'd love to."

Chattering excitedly, Ivy and Evadora vanished below deck.

Ambria trailed behind Elyssa to the bridge. "Could you teach me how to operate your ship?"

"If you'd like." Elyssa powered on the ship and gave her a live-action tutorial as she guided us out of dock.

Conrad went to the prow and stared out at the horizon. "Do you really think Baal will attack Atlantis?"

"There's no telling." I leaned against the railing. "Baal likes to manipulate people. That's how we ended up trapped in Utopia. He might have threatened Atlantis just to make us concentrate our forces here and leave Eden unprotected."

"And also to keep us from finding more allies." Conrad nodded. "It sounds like an effective ploy."

"On the other hand, he might have a secret way into Atlantis we don't know about. Maybe Drakara can portal the entire dragon army right over the city and blast us to ashes."

"I certainly hope that's not the case." Conrad looked up at blue skies. "If Drakara has that kind of power, there's not much we can do to stop her."

"Ain't that the truth."

A plume of water rose into the air, propelled by Dolpha's sea dragon. She glided next to the *Raptor*. "You almost left without your gifts."

"Well, you left us and went for a swim," I said. "We couldn't just sit around for an hour."

Dolpha leapt lithely from her dragon and landed on the deck. She opened her hand and displayed dozens of tiny seashells. "Here are your gifts."

"Um." I took one in my hand and held it between thumb and forefinger. "Gee, just what I always wanted. Miniature shells."

"It truly is better than a sword or spear." Elyssa examined a pink shell. "Do I flick it in someone's eyes?"

Dolpha scoffed. "These shells hold the song of understanding. She took one and pressed it to my neck just under the jawbone near the carotid artery. My skin burned for a brief instant. I tried to slap her hand away, but she'd already withdrawn it. "May the song of understanding light a new path to friendship."

I touched my neck. The skin was rough to the touch, but not like a seashell. Elyssa examined it. "Weird. It looks like a tattoo now."

"Great, just what I always wanted." I glared at Dolpha. "What's the song of understanding? Does this mean I can sing now?"

Dolpha scowled. "Impertinent boy. For your insolence, I will let you discover it for yourself." She huffed and leapt back over to her dragon.

"Wait, I'm sorry!" I held out a hand. "Please, what do these do?"

But the siren was just done with me. Dolpha gave me a final glare before vanishing into the ocean depths.

Elyssa sighed. "Maybe we should've been nicer."

"Yeah, maybe so." I touched my neck. "Well, I hope we figure out what this thing does."

Elyssa pressed a shell to her neck. It glowed, and her skin seemed to absorb it, leaving a faded tattoo of the pink shell. "Kind of burns, but I don't feel any different."

"Try singing," Ambria said.

"Hey baby. Oh, baby, baby." I hummed a little ditty. "You know you want it, baby."

Ambria clamped her hands over her ears. "Just stop, please!"

Elyssa snickered. "Yeah, I don't think it improved your singing voice, Justin." She tucked the rest of the shells into the side satchel she always wore. "At least we have matching tattoos now."

Ambria looked longingly at Elyssa's shell tattoo. "May I have one?"

Conrad held out his hand. "I'll take one too, just in case."

Elyssa obliged, and smirked when Ambria gently applied one to Conrad's neck. "They're so cute," she whispered to me, and went back onto the bridge.

"I'll take some to Ivy and Evadora, too." Ambria ran below to make sure everyone had their cool new tats.

The *Raptor* resumed course for the towering gray wall of Voltis. Once there, I went below deck and pulled Argus out of the storage room. Shaped like a huge magnifying glass, the glass was actually an aetherite gem. Metal rods attached to the side of the gem angled down and out to form a socket. Inside the socket sat a small sphere, the Chalon, which was the key to opening portals.

I pushed the base of the portal device into a clamp on the prow just behind the weapon turret and locked it in place. After straightening it out, I channeled Stasis through the Chalon. Energy flowed through the portal gem and magnified it into a broad circle against the storm wall. A breach formed, a gateway to Seraphina.

The coordinates for Utopia could only be reached from the outer storm wall of Voltis, as far as we knew. Cinder had examined the enchantment code in the portal gem but hadn't found a matching location we could use on the Atlantis side.

We emerged from the portal just outside the violent storm wall. A wave of heat turned a curtain of mist into steam. The moment of visibility revealed a score of dragons only a few hundred yards from our position. One of them roared, alerting the others, and the wing of four wyverns veered toward us.

"Great." I ran onto the bridge. "Distance from coordinates?"

"I need five minutes to get us precisely into position," Elyssa said.

"Five minutes? We've probably got sixty seconds."

"Nothing I can do about it." Elyssa looked out the window. "Should we go back to Atlantis?"

I cracked my knuckles. "No. Maybe Conrad and I can fend them off long enough."

Elyssa swung the ship around and jammed the throttle to full. "Let's do it."

I went back outside and manned a turret. "Lay down suppressing fire."

"Okay." Conrad swiveled the port turret toward the enemy.

"What can I do?" Ambria said.

"Nothing until they get closer," I said. "Even the turrets can barely reach them now." I fired a volley of flak spheres. They exploded into brightly burning shrapnel in front of the dragons but were too far away to hit them. The wyverns closed to within a hundred yards.

Ivy and Evadora ran up to the deck.

Ivy leaned over the railing. "What's the commotion?"

"Ooh, dragons!" Evadora clapped her hands.

Conrad turned to her. "Can you mind control dragons, Evadora?"

Evadora shook her head. "I don't control creatures, Conrad. I talk to them and ask for their help."

"Well, if you could do that it'd be grand."

Evadora shouted, but the thundering fury of Voltis drowned out her words. "They'll have to get closer."

Conrad shook his head. "I'd rather not take the chance." Azure energy crackled in his palms. He pressed his hands to the power gems on the turret handles. Energy hummed. A brilliant blue beam sliced through the air and hit the lead dragon. It roared in pain and lost speed. The other wyverns came straight for us.

CHAPTER 8

"**W**ell, now the dragons definitely won't help us," Evadora said.

"Blast 'em!" Ivy shouted.

Elyssa rotated the ship to face Voltis and began fine-tuning our position. Conrad moved to the aft turret. I abandoned mine since it couldn't aim directly behind us and channeled a sphere of destruction around my right hand. We couldn't let the dragons hit the ship. That would knock us out of alignment. Opening a portal at the wrong spot was a very bad thing. It might open a breach to the void and unleash the Beast on Seraphina.

Conrad charged the turret and waited until the next dragon was less than thirty yards away. The power gems amplified his energy two-fold, unleashing a crackling lance of light. The frost wyvern tried to dodge, but it had nowhere to go. The magic-resistant scales blackened and burned. It fired back a stream of frost, but the onslaught was too great.

The wyvern went limp and spiraled toward the ocean.

I fired a bolt of Brilliance at the left wing of the next dragon. The scales on the thick webbing weren't as tough as those on the hide, but it still took a concentrated blast to burn a hole through it. The fire wyvern retaliated with a gout of flame. Before I could channel a shield, Ivy splayed her fingers and formed a protective barrier.

"Nice!" I blasted the wyvern's other wing. It couldn't maintain altitude with two holey wings and dropped beneath us. Unable to turn in time, it entered the outer edges of Voltis. Jagged bolts of lightning caught the wyvern and roasted it like a giant pig.

The last two wyverns roared in defiance but veered away from us. One of them glared at me. *I will burn you for this.*

Conrad and I flinched at the same time.

"Ooh, it talked to us," Evadora said. "And he isn't happy."

"That's for sure." Conrad backed up a step. "I didn't realize wyverns could speak."

"Neither did I." I waved after the retreating form. "Are you intelligent? Can we talk about this?"

The wyvern didn't reply. It and its companion flew back out to sea to assist the first wyvern Conrad injured.

"Next time you want me to talk a dragon into helping us, don't hurt it, okay?" Evadora tutted. "If I punched you in the nose, you wouldn't want to help me very much, would you?"

I didn't like being lectured by a child, even if she was right. "Do you really think you could have talked those wyverns out of attacking us?"

She pursed her lips. "Probably not. Cora thinks they're just following orders from their queen just like the Glimmer creatures do what she says."

Something passed behind Conrad's eyes. "We should have brought Cora with us. I'll bet she could talk to them."

"If I can't talk them into being friends, Mommy can't either." Evadora shook her head. "She taught me everything."

"Got it!" Elyssa's shout jerked us from our conversation. "Do your thing, Justin."

I channeled Stasis into the Chalon. A large beam speared from the portal gem and into the storm. The clouds ripped open into a gateway, creating a transition bubble between the two realms. Elyssa took us through.

I braced myself. The last time we'd been here, the time differential seemed to freeze us in place when the transition bubble receded. This time I felt nothing except a slight tweak in my stomach.

Elyssa checked the chronometer on the ship. "Cinder was right. Looks like time is almost the same here as it is in the other realms."

I looked out over the railing at a vintage nineteen-seventies split-level house. Curious faces stared out behind windows. In Utopia, Voltis aligned in someone's front yard. During the dystopic era, i.e. a few weeks ago, the population of this entire city had consisted of mindless eidolons, their souls used as a power source for Vokan. Now those citizens were returning home after decades of unlife.

The front door opened. A man and woman stepped outside and waved.

"Are you the saviors?" the man shouted.

I hoped we hadn't accrued another nickname. I had too many to keep up with these days—Kohvaniss, Destroyer, commander, punk-ass kid— enough to make my head spin. "We helped bring down Vokan, if that's what you mean. I'd love to stay and chat, but we're on another mission."

"Thank you so much!" the couple shouted.

"The saviors!" Another voice echoed from next door. "They're back!"

Neighbors stood outside waving and jumping up and down. More doors opened, and people rushed outside, waving and shouting thanks.

Elyssa turned the ship around and took us above the trees. "That was unexpected."

"Yeah." I grinned. "Feels kind of good, though."

Ambria wiped tears from her eyes. "So much gratitude. It's beautiful."

Ivy clapped her hands. "That was neato!"

Twin silver towers rose from the city center a few miles away. The current Grand Council had taken up residence in Solan since this city suffered the most under Vokan's rule. The roads had been clogged with rusting, abandoned cars when we left, but most had been cleared or moved to the sides. Magic carriages now ferried citizens through the streets. People stopped whatever they were doing and looked up at the amber bird of prey swooping across the city.

Many of them recognized the ship on sight, waving and clapping as we passed by.

Sunlight shone on the golden hides of gryphons lifting off from the roof of the left tower. The magnificent creatures glided our way bearing familiar faces.

"Elyssa, you are back!" Ki guided her gryphon alongside us. "We had not expected your return so soon."

"Oh my!" Evadora danced in place. "They're so beautiful!"

Ivy clapped her hands. "And fluffy!"

Ki's mouth dropped open. "Are these your children, Elyssa?"

Ivy burst into laughter. "No, silly. Justin's my brother."

"They're friends." I introduced the lot of them to Ki and got to the point. "We need Utopia's help."

"I will take you to the council. They are in session now and would gladly hear your requests."

"That would be great." I motioned ahead. "Lead the way."

A Viking-sized blonde steered her gryphon closer. "So, the child has returned with more children." Gemma stared at Evadora curiously. "It has been some time since I saw humans so tiny. Is silver skin common in your lands?"

Evadora looked at her skin and shaded it pink. "My skin is whatever color I want!"

"They could use a firm hand and warrior training." I gave Gemma a serious look. "Do you want to be their mommy?"

Ambria's mouth dropped open in shock. "What in the bloody hell are you talking about?"

Gemma scowled at me. "You are as annoying as I remember, Justin Slade." She drew her sword and it blazed to life. "Perhaps a bout of sword fighting will shut your mouth."

"Man, I'd love to, but we just don't have the time." I blew her a kiss. "Maybe next time."

Ki laughed. "Oh, Gemma, you're an easy target."

Gemma spat. "Perhaps one day we will see." She flew ahead of us.

Conrad watched her fly away. "I take it she lacks a sense of humor."

I chuckled. "Completely."

Elyssa landed the *Raptor* in the courtyard outside the council tower. We debarked the ship and Ki escorted our group inside. The council chamber was a large, circular room with stadium seating on the sides. Four triangular tables sat in the middle, but only one was occupied. Apparently, they hadn't gotten around to electing officials from all four cities.

An old man with bright eyes sat at the tip of the triangle. A petite blond woman sat to his right, and a medium-sized brunette to his left. A citizen droned on about farmlands and production schedules.

People nearby oohed when they saw the children. Due to population controls, long lives, and the apocalypse, Utopians had very few children. I imagined seeing Conrad and the others was quite a novelty.

Magus Agula saw us and blinked. He held up a hand. "Excuse me citizen, but we have guests."

There was a commotion of rustling clothes and shifting bodies as all eyes locked onto us.

"The saviors!" someone shouted.

"Children!"

The auditorium burst into applause.

Ambria and Conrad shrank behind us while Ivy and Evadora pranced around each other, ballet dancers before an adoring audience.

I waved at everyone. "Howdy, y'all!"

Agula stood and held open his arms. "Justin and Elyssa, it is good to see you again."

"It's good to be back." I motioned the others to stay. "Just wait back here, okay?"

"But I want more cheers," Ivy said.

"You'll probably get them." I walked down the aisle between the seats and into the circle. I nodded at the other councilors. "Daana and Elaine, it's good to see you."

"Delighted," Elaine said. "What brings you back?"

I looked back at the citizen who'd been speaking before. "I don't want to interrupt this man."

The man bowed. "Without the saviors I would not be here. You may take my place."

I gave him a short bow back. "We're always happy to defeat tyranny and evil."

Applause filled the room for a second time. I turned to Agula. "Is it okay if I address everyone?"

"Of course." He held up his hands. "Justin Slade would like to speak."

The room went from jubilant to quiet as a graveyard in a split second.

"Thank you, citizens of Utopia." I bowed slightly. "The last time we met, we helped liberate your souls and cities from the clutches of the evil Vokan. I wish we could let you live in peace to rebuild this great society. Unfortunately, Vokan was assisted by an even greater evil, the Grand Overlord of Haedaemos himself, Baal."

A chorus of oohs and ahs rose from the crowd.

"Baal wishes to conquer each realm and rule them separately. He says this is for our own good, to protect us from one of the former rulers of the world, an Apocryphan named Xanos." I rotated in place to face the other parts of the crowd around us. Thankfully, the room's acoustics amplified my voice. "Xanos wants to recombine the realms into one Earth. This would kill billions of people and compress us all back into one realm."

Gasps echoed. Fear twisted faces.

"What would you have us do?" Agula said.

"Baal has already conquered Seraphina with an army of dragons." That elicited a fresh round of gasps. "Since he is allied with the ancient dragon queen, Drakara, we have been unable to stop him because most of our army is incapable of flight."

"Whereas we have hundreds of gryphons and gepheron," Elaine said. "You desire military help."

"We also believe the elemental magi of Utopia can conjure storms and ground the dragons." Elyssa strode down the aisle and stood next to me. "Our backs are to the wall in Atlantis. We need help to defend it, so we can seek out more allies and turn the tide on Baal."

Agula pinched his chin between thumb and forefinger. "We abhor war and destruction. Before Vokan, we knew peace and tranquility. We maintained equilibrium with the world and prospered." He sighed. "Vokan showed us how easily such balance can be destroyed. He plunged us into a seemingly endless dystopia. Though gone, deep scars remain."

"Scars which may never heal," Elaine said. "But these scars have also taught us that sometimes violence must be met with violence." Elaine rose from her seat. "The Science Council stands with you."

"Evil must not be left unchecked." Daana stood. "The Citizen Council stands with you."

Agula pushed up. "As does the Magus Council."

A woman in the front row held up a fist. "Utopia stands united behind the saviors. May tyranny and evil perish!"

The crowd jumped to its feet and deafened us with applause.

Well, that was a lot easier than I thought. It had been a rough few weeks, but this totally made my day.

Ambria wiped tears from her cheeks. Conrad smiled in satisfaction. Ivy and Evadora looked ecstatic.

The roar quieted to a murmur and Agula spoke. "We will send as many troops as you need, but we do not have enough trained riders for all the gepheron."

Gepheron were bat-like creatures bred and trained by Vokan's loyalists. Though they looked spooky, they enjoyed pets and nom-noms like any other domesticated animal.

"Actually, that's perfect," Elyssa said. "We have troops who can ride the gepheron, if that's okay."

"Absolutely," Agula said. "Our gryphon forces are at your disposal."

"One other thing," I said. "Knowing how you guys value population control, this is kind of a biggie."

"Tell us, please," Agula said.

"We have a few thousand Seraphim refugees who need homes. Can they stay here temporarily until we reclaim Seraphina?"

"We have hundreds of empty homes here in Solan, and many more in the other cities," Agula said. "We will welcome the Seraphim as our own."

"You guys are the best." *If only the rest of the universe was like this.*

"Is that everything?" Agula said.

"Yes. We'll work out the logistics and get back to you." I nodded at Daana and Elaine. "The citizens of the realms are grateful for your assistance."

"Will you stay for a meal?" Agula said. "We will not be in session much longer."

I smiled regretfully. "Unfortunately, we're on a very tight schedule. We have to go to Pangaea and ask for their help."

The councilors grimaced.

"A very dangerous task," Agula said. "Please go with caution."

"We do not know much about them," Daana said, "but the beings in Pangaea despise humans."

"Exercise extreme logic and prudence before approaching them," Elaine said.

"We will." I waved to the audience. "Thank you, citizens. You have our gratitude."

The cheers followed us through the room on our way out. I noticed cameras training their glass eyes on us as well. It seemed this visit was being televised.

The world will know our might. Fred apparently enjoyed the spotlight.

Ki waited on us outside. "It went well."

"Yes, it did." I gripped her shoulder. "Thank you and wish us luck. We're off to Pangaea now."

"Pangaea? You will need more than luck." Ki's face blushed when she turned to Elyssa. "Farewell, warrior. I hope to see you again soon."

Elyssa returned a smile. "Thank you, Ki."

"We took the liberty of supplying you with armor and other supplies." Ki pointed to several satchels near the ship. "I hope you find them useful."

"Wow, thanks." I opened a satchel and found strips of metallic cloth inside. When worn, they could expand to cover the body, much like Nightingale armor. The Eden army was woefully short on com badges, armor, and other necessities. I turned back to Ki. "Do you have enough supplies to outfit a thousand troops?"

She shook her head. "The magi who produce the armor have only just begun producing a supply for our own troops. It will take months before production meets demand."

"Well, thanks so much for this." Everyone grabbed a satchel and we boarded the *Raptor*.

"I think Ki likes you, Elyssa," Ambria whispered in a conspiratorial tone.

"Duh." Ivy rolled her eyes. "They fought Vokan together."

Ambria laughed. "I meant she likes-likes her."

I groaned. "This is so middle school."

Elyssa snorted. "Yes, Ki likes me, but we already discussed it. I'm not in the market for a girlfriend right now."

"Right now?" I said incredulously. "I hope you're not planning to dump me anytime soon."

Elyssa grinned. "No, you're kind of handy for saving the world and all that."

I rolled my eyes. "Glad I'm useful for something."

"Why are you stuck with just one person, Elyssa?" Evadora tilted her head. "My mother says a woman should not limit herself to one experience."

Amusement shone in Elyssa's eyes. "Oh, I'll try not to limit myself too much."

Ambria's arm tightened around Conrad's. "I'm happy with one boyfriend, thank you very much."

Ivy sighed. "Yeah, I really like Conrad, but he likes you a lot more than me."

Conrad's face burned bright red.

I changed the subject before the conversation matured from middle school to high school. "Maybe we should get underway."

"Yes, great idea." Elyssa fled onto the bridge. The *Raptor* rose into the air just above the trees, gathering speed and heading southeast. When we cleared Solan, Elyssa put the levitation foils to maximum and the earth blurred beneath us. Even at this velocity it would take a day and a half to reach the coast of Pangaea.

Thick forest stretched on for miles. Rolling hills and plains eventually took prominence before opening to grassy savannahs. Giraffes with unicorn horns grazed on a grove of trees. Hulking orange felines stalked a herd of antelope. I tried to take in all the strange wonders of the land, but the speed of our passing didn't allow much sightseeing.

Though Utopia was a massive continent, nearly eighty percent was unsettled thanks to the strict population controls. We wouldn't pass anywhere close to the city on the eastern coast. In fact, we wouldn't see another city out this way unless the Pangeans lets us in.

Judging from the last time we'd been there, I calculated our odds of success at zero. I just hoped they wouldn't kill us for trying.

CHAPTER 9

I t was late in the afternoon when I decided to alter our course. The idea came to me out of nowhere, but it felt pretty damned smart.

"You want to go to Vokan's hideout?" Elyssa's brow furrowed when I proposed the idea. "What makes you think he'd even be there?"

"I just know he'll be there."

"Because?"

"Remember the fairies he kept imprisoned there? I'd be willing to bet they were his backup plan in case he ever lost power." I tapped my temple. "He doesn't know we freed them."

"Unless he's already been back and gone." Elyssa pursed her lips. "On the other hand, if he is there, he'd be an invaluable bargaining chip with the fairies."

I hadn't considered that angle. I just wanted to catch the snooty bastard and punch him in the face a few times. "Why do you think that?"

Elyssa crossed her arms and leaned back against the railing. "Think about it. He sacrificed dozens of Pyra's crewmembers."

The light blinked on in my head. "Pyra would love to punish Vokan for his crimes."

"Yep." Elyssa grinned. "And maybe she'll let us talk to the queen fairy."

"Wow, that's a good plan." I grunted. "Let's hope the old bastard is there."

I let Conrad and Ambria know what we were doing.

"What a brilliant idea," Ambria said. "It's obvious Elyssa is the thinker."

"Hey, I do some thinking too."

Ambria pursed her lips. "Well, maybe you think a little bit, but certainly not much."

"Damn, you're savage."

She flushed with pleasure. "Yep."

Conrad seemed to filter out the entire exchange, leading me to believe Ambria was like this most of the time, not unlike someone else I knew. Someone who wore a cowboy hat and a leather duster ninety-nine percent of the time. Yeah, that guy.

Dusk darkened the sky by the time we neared the destination. Elyssa dropped the ship lower until it skimmed just above the trees. I activated the camouflage, and the hull shimmered into chameleon mode. The levitation foils whined, and the ship lurched as if we'd just hit the brakes.

Emergency restraints extended from the railings and kept us from sliding across the deck.

"What happened?" Ambria gripped the emergency strap.

Elyssa grimaced. "I forgot how much energy the camo takes from the levitation foils." She looked at the holographic control panel and tapped a finger on a jagged red line. "We're limited to one-third speed while under camo."

I looked at the destination, a crag of volcanic rock jutting above the tree line. The flat top of the inactive volcano that birthed it rose in the distance, an ominous silhouette against the night sky. An old lava tube housed Vokan's hideout beneath the crag, a spiraling tunnel carved from intense heat.

"Everyone, suit up." I slipped a strip of armor cloth around my neck and showed Conrad and Ambria how to do it.

We reached the rocky beach and Elyssa set the ship down near the forest.

Ivy and Evadora emerged from below deck. "Are we there yet?" Ivy asked.

I shook my head and put a finger to my mouth. "Quiet. We're hunting bunny wabbits."

Evadora frowned. "Why would you hunt innocent rabbits?"

"It's a joke." I told them about our plans to capture Vokan.

"Ooh, can we blast him?" Ivy whispered conspiratorially.

I shook my head. "No. We need him to help us get into fairyland."

Ivy's eyes widened. "Well then, he's super important, because I really want to meet some fairies."

"Yep." I touched the band of dark material at my throat and the black Utopian armor spread across my body. "Go suit up. We need to be as quiet as possible."

Ivy went to change, but Evadora remained on deck. Ambria and Conrad activated their armor and grinned at each other.

"I feel like a spy," Ambria said.

"The name's Edison." Conrad held out a hand to her. "Conrad Edison."

Evadora's eyes locked onto something in a tree. She squawked. A crow squawked back at her and she laughed. "Oh, he's funny."

"You going to put on your armor?" I asked.

Evadora's skin shaded green. "I don't need it."

"What if he shoots you with a spell?" Ambria said.

"I'm too fast." She zipped back and forth, a green blur. "He'll never hit me."

"You might be surprised," I said. "Vokan's no joke."

"He'll never see me anyway," she said. "I can hide in plain sight in the forest."

"That's true," Ambria said. "Evadora's a master of hiding."

"You can be our lookout, Evadora" Elyssa said. "Can you scout ahead for us?"

"Already am." Evadora grinned and pointed up at the crow. "He's looking for me."

The crow circled above for a while then drifted down to land on Evadora's shoulder. He cawed softly in her ear.

"He says he saw someone go into the rock earlier," Evadora said. "He only caught a glimpse through the trees."

Elyssa grinned. "He's here." She rubbed her hands together. "Let's go get him."

"I'll find him." Evadora streaked into the forest and vanished like a ghost.

"Vokan might have traps." Elyssa gathered Ivy, Conrad and Ambria. "I need you to hang back a dozen yards in case you have to rescue us."

Ambria saluted. "Yes, madam commander."

Elyssa groaned.

Ivy frowned. "Why did you call her commander?"

"Because she's our leader," Ambria said.

I rolled my eyes. "Shall we move out?"

Elyssa nodded, and we jogged into the forest. Weeds and bushes jutted from cracks in the streaked rock left behind by molten lava, making footing treacherous. We reached a clearing a few minutes later.

I skirted wide of dead, black soil. The old demon patterns etched into the earth had killed it long ago. Going too close to them filled my head with frightening visions.

Closer. Intense longing filled my inner demon. *Touch them.*

It had been a long while since my demon half tried to control my body, but now I felt him tugging at the strings. With great effort, I slammed him back inside. *Why do you want me to touch them?*

The demons they belong to are powerful. We should consume them and gain their strength.

Devouring demon babies had nauseated me. Consuming a full-grown caustic demon had knocked me on my ass. I couldn't handle anything more powerful. *We're here for something more important.*

No. My demon half seemed to swell inside the psychic cage.

I pushed back, gritting my teeth so hard I got a headache. *Stop it, Fred!*

"Justin?" Elyssa got in my face. "Why did you stop walking?"

"What?" I blinked and looked around. The others watched me curiously. "Sorry, I guess it was the demon patterns." Now wasn't the time to bring up Fred's troubling behavior. I started walking again. "I'm good now."

The entrance to the lava cave was empty so we sneaked over. A pair of eyes formed in the black rock. I nearly shouted in alarm, but Elyssa clamped a hand over my mouth. Evadora faded into view, a mischievous grin on her face.

I took a deep breath to calm my racing heart. "Neat trick. Can you take a look inside the cave?"

She nodded and went down the volcanic tube, skin tone blurring to match the rock as she went. The rest of us followed into darkness. Water dripped somewhere in the distance. Cool air whispered past my ears. It was like entering a tomb without a light. We treaded as quietly as possible.

Yellow light shone softly ahead, growing brighter as we wound our way down. Faint voices reached my ears, but I couldn't make out the words. I should have been apprehensive, but excitement infected me. *Vokan is going to be our bitch!* I couldn't wait to punch him in the face.

I slid along the wall and bumped into something warm. Evadora nearly gave me another heart attack, but this time I controlled myself and only slightly wet my pants. Her wide eyes met mine. *Not a good sign.* We were too close to the chamber to speak so I put a finger to my lips. The voices had quieted. Silence hung heavy in the air. Vokan might be weak without his cantrap of souls, but he would still be a challenge.

I went around Evadora and crept down the ramp to the opening at the bottom. I saw Vokan at once. His appearance shocked me into a brief stupor. He hung in the air naked as a jaybird, arms and legs restrained by gossamer threads. Blood trickled from cuts on his limbs, his chest, and his tender bits, dripping onto the floor in a steady pitter-patter.

Vokan's head lolled over his chest. His long blond hair, filthy and blood-stained, hung to his belly button. The former grand magus didn't look so grand.

His captor crouched in front of him, drawing long fingers through puddled blood and sketching alien designs on the smooth stone floor. Translucent amber wings fluttered on her back. Crimson hair hung over her face, matching the bloodstains on her pale skin.

Vokan had returned to his hidey-hole, but his former prisoner had made him her bitch.

I was ready to fight an elemental magus, not a fairy. Even Elyssa stared in stunned silence at the scene. *We should back off and reassess.* Pyra hadn't shown us what she was capable of and I didn't want to go in blind against a refugee fairy who might be able to turn us all into frogs.

Ivy cured my indecision by leaping inside the cave, a ball of Brilliance in her palm. "Hands up lady, or I'll blast you!"

The fairy leapt into the air, wings fluttering, and spun to face my sister. Black flames blazed around her hands. An alien language flowed from her lips—another reminder that Pyra had used magic to translate for us.

I walked into view, hands held up. "Wait. Can we talk about this?"

The fairy spoke again. "...evil...die...defend..." It was like listening to someone with a severe speech impediment. Some words made sense, but others were gobbledygook.

"My name is Justin." I spoke slowly, as if that would help. "We came here to capture Vokan. We mean you no harm."

Her eyes widened. "Justin. No harm." She spoke with a thick accent that could have passed for Italian. The flames around her hands died. She touched her chest with a bloodstained hand. "Thal."

I pointed to my sister. "Ivy." I waved out the others. "Elyssa. Conrad. Ambria."

When Evadora faded into view, Thal's eyes widened. She said another word I didn't understand.

"I'm Evadora." Her skin brightened from basalt to muted silver. "Are you a fairy?"

Thal tilted her head. "Fae."

Pyra had used that term instead of fairy, so I made a mental note to adopt it whenever possible. It felt like imminent danger had passed, but there was the matter of the bleeding magus in the room.

"Are you torturing Vokan?" I said.

Thal cocked her head slightly. "What?"

"Torturing, hurting Vokan?"

Comprehension lit her eyes. "Yes. And make magic."

"Magic?" I grimaced. "What sort of magic?"

"He imprison me. I take his magic." Gibberish still mangled most of what she said, but I got the essentials. Every time we spoke, the words became clearer.

"How did you meet Vokan?" I asked. She started off with a stream of nonsense, so I held up a hand to stop her. "Please repeat." I said it twice and she seemed to get it the next time.

"The ancient gods went away long ago, many say to create new worlds and leave us on our own. I sensed the stirring darkness, the threads of existence pulled to benefit a great power. The Fae had no interest, so I broke covenant and went to the humans." After that remarkably clear opening, the language barrier slammed down between us again.

"How is it we can understand her the second time?" Ambria said. "Is it a spell?"

I shrugged. "Maybe Pyra's translation spell is still working."

Elyssa shook her head. "No, it's not that at all. Ambria wasn't here with us last time."

I frowned. "Oh." Turned to Ivy. "Can you understand Thal?"

"Yeah, mostly." She shrugged. "What kind of language is she using?"

"Fae," Thal said. "How are you able to speak it?"

"We're not." I had no idea what she meant.

"I know what it is." Elyssa tapped the seashell tattoo on her neck. "It's the gift Dolpha gave us."

"Oh." I dragged out the word for emphasis. "The song of understanding is a universal translator."

Thal drifted lightly to the ground. She stood maybe four feet tall but with all the features of a fully-grown woman. "Translator?"

I turned my neck so she could see. "A Siren gave it to us."

Her eyes flared. "Siren! They are all gone."

"They have their own realm, yes." I looked at Vokan again. "You can steal his magic?"

"I make blood magic to see inside his head and understand his magic." Thal tucked her hair behind an ear, unconcerned by the blood drying on her fingers. "I will know how he trapped me, so I can trap him."

I was really curious about this blood magic. "Once you learn, can you use his magic all you want?"

"The effects do not last." She tapped a finger to her temple. "The memory fades over time."

Well, there goes my shortcut to elemental magic. "These dark stirrings you sensed, we're trying to stop them too, and we could use another ally."

Thal's eyes brightened. "Yes, an ally. The humans must fight because the Fae do nothing."

"We're actually on our way to request help from the Fae," Elyssa said. "It would help greatly if we could take Vokan, because he imprisoned you and another Fae named Pyra."

Thal bared her teeth. "Pyra would see me dead. She hates humans. She would rather all die than to ally with them."

"Maybe we can change that." Elyssa stepped a little closer to the fairy. "Thal, may we take Vokan with us to use as a bargaining chip with the Fae?"

"No, he must suffer my wrath. I will trap him as he did me."

"That would actually be a favor to Vokan," I said. "The spell he used preserves the prisoner."

Thal walked toward her prisoner. "Then I will kill him slowly."

"Imagine what Pyra would do to him," I said. "She hates humans and he kidnapped her too."

The Fae tilted her head slightly. "Pyra would torture him more. Make him scream for years."

"If you want to form an alliance with humans, you don't have enough time to really focus on a proper torturing." I held out my hands pleadingly. "If you let us take him, you'll kill two birds with one stone."

Thal's eyes narrowed. "Kill birds?"

"It's a saying. It means to accomplish two things with one effort."

"I would still like to torture him." Thal shook her head. "No, he is mine to kill."

It looked like we'd have to fight a fairy if we wanted Vokan for ourselves.

CHAPTER 10

I opted for an alternative to fighting and pulled out what I hoped was my ace in the hole. "Do you remember how you escaped from Vokan's prison?"

Thal stared at me without speaking for several uncomfortable seconds. "I awoke and saw Pyra talking to people."

"Yes." I pointed to myself. "We're the ones who saved you."

"I remember you now." She walked in a circle, agitated, then stopped and stared at me. "We are forbidden to bargain with humans, but I broke covenant. You saved my life, so I must offer something of equal value."

"Like Vokan's life?" I asked.

Thal shook her head. "No, his life is forfeit, worthless."

"Can I have him anyway?" I asked.

She went silent for a moment. "Yes, but by covenant I am still in your debt."

All this talk of covenant was confusing, but I sensed a large can of worms I didn't want to get into with the pitter patter of Vokan's dripping blood in the background. "I would like to take Vokan to our ship and stop his bleeding, so we can transport him to Pangaea without getting blood everywhere."

Thal's shoulders slumped. "Very well. Take the evil one."

"I would also request that you come with us to Pangaea to help us negotiate with them."

"No!" She held up her bloody hands defensively. "Pyra will see me undone and remade. I will be erased for breaking covenant."

"Oh, we don't want that," Ivy said. "I like you just the way you are."

Evadora held up a fist. "I will not let Pyra ruin you."

"An elf would truly rise to the aid of a Fae?" Thal looked uncertain.

"Elf?" Evadora scratched her head. "What's that?"

I clapped my hands. "I knew it!"

"It makes sense," Conrad said. "They call themselves the folk of the wood."

Elyssa waved off our nerdish enthusiasm. "Will you at least come to our ship and tell us more about yourself and the Fae?"

Thal stared down at the crimson patterns on the floor. "Yes. I will do that." She wiggled her fingers and Vokan dropped to the floor with a meaty thud.

His eyes shot open and he cried out. "Who dares attack me?"

I stood over him and grinned. "We dare, you son of a bitch."

"You!" Vokan shouted.

I punched him in the face and he went back to dreamland.

"Oh, I like that," Thal mimicked throwing a punch. "Humans are so brutal."

"Because cutting him a hundred times isn't?" I stared at the naked magus, unwilling to heft him because I didn't want to get blood and private parts all over my clothes. I channeled a web of Murk and slid it beneath him like a sled, levitating him in front of me. "We're good to go."

Thal followed us back outside and toward the ship.

Fred squirmed inside, pressing against his psychic cage as we walked. I shoved back, using as much willpower as I could while still channeling the Murk sled. It must have been in the midst of that when I went off course. I didn't even realize it until blackened bones crunched beneath my feet.

Fred laughed.

Nausea wormed through my guts. The world flickered, and the color drained from my surroundings.

I looked around, confused. Vokan was gone. Elyssa was gone. I stood alone in a field of ash, surrounded by a translucent haze that hid the world in silhouette. Crimson liquid flowed through an intricate pattern beneath my feet.

Voices emanated from the mist, the tonality all wrong as if the language were spoken backward. A huge shadow skittered past on dozens of legs. Its body seemed to distend, stretching like a snake, growing longer as it encircled me. Brilliance hummed to life in my palms, crackling and sparking like grease in a hot pan.

"Stay away from me!"

The creature began to tighten the noose. "Stay away!" It screamed back. "From me! Stay away!"

Shivers ran down my spine and my ass clenched tight. "What the hell are you?"

"Are you?" It echoed back. It burst through the fog and reared up, hundreds of tiny human arms and hands flailing from the body of a millipede. The head was a single glowing red eye with screaming human faces pressing against the translucent barrier.

I let loose with everything I had. White fire burned through the eye. Decapitated heads rolled from the inside, screaming in a discordant chorus of agony. The millipede body kept coming even as more human heads spilled from its guts. My throat burned raw, but I couldn't stop screaming, couldn't stop the torrent of destruction blazing from my hands.

Sliced to pieces, the millipede's hands still grasped, and the heads still screamed. Nothing I did could make it shut up. I tried to run. An invisible barrier at the edge of the crimson pattern knocked me backwards. Whatever it was hadn't kept out the monster, but it held me in.

I looked up. A rip in the air throbbed red, like a hole in a beating heart.

Black vapor drifted outside the pattern. It swept inside, swirling around the millipede. The screaming heads and flailing arms went still. The creature froze and disintegrated. Neither dust nor ash remained of the thing.

I channeled a barrier to keep out this deadly new threat. Rather than come at me, it swirled into a mass. The mass took shape and form, a head, torso, and an appropriate number of arms and legs. The darkness turned to flesh, light red in tone.

A smile spread across a familiar face. It didn't look identical to the infernus, but it was close enough. "Well, a personal visit from my grandson. Well done, Kalesh."

My inner demon swelled with pride.

The red man grinned. "Devouring all those caustic demons had the effect I hoped it would on your spirit."

It took a moment to find my voice, and even then, it came out a harsh whisper. "Baal?"

He rapped knuckles against the shield I channeled. "You don't need this. The reverse summon pattern protects you."

"It didn't protect me from that monster!"

"It didn't make it through did it?" Baal smiled.

"Why should I believe you?" I cast my gaze wildly around, expecting an ambush at any moment. "Who's Kalesh? Did he bring me here?"

Baal shrugged. "He facilitated it."

"Is this Haedaemos?"

Baal shook his head. "This plane exists between the physical and spiritual realms, a place with no name. Some call it Nowhere."

"Nowhere?" I tried to look through the surrounding haze, but everything past a few feet blurred to an indistinct nothing. *I must have stepped on one of the patterns in the field.* "Is this how Vokan communicated with you?"

"It is one of the ways, yes." Baal traced a black claw along the Murk shield. "You cannot physically enter Haedaemos, at least not for long. Eventually your body would lose its grip on the soul, and they would part ways, sending the physical shell elsewhere."

"Am I here physically?"

"Indeed. Nowhere allows both spiritual and physical beings, though it is a much nastier place than Haedaemos."

I spun in a circle. "How do I get back?"

"With the magic word." He flashed a wicked grin. "If you trust me enough to lower the barrier, perhaps I will tell you."

"Is it please?"

"No."

"What if I don't trust you enough to lower the barrier?"

"Then we'll have plenty of time to talk."

I didn't like the sound of that. I couldn't imagine what Vokan might use for a magic word, though it probably had something to do with his immense ego. Another wave of sickness passed through me. My skin seemed to squirm and shift. Pain wracked every fiber of my being, driving me to my knees.

An entire body ripped free of my skin. Pain scorched every nerve fiber. I half expected to see my flesh hanging in tatters. Instead, a figure that looked hauntingly like me stared back with flaming blue eyes and sapphire skin. Sickly yellow lines coursed through its form. A thin tube extended from my body to the other like an umbilical cord.

My jaw dropped open. "Fred?"

Flaming eyes glared back. "I am Kalesh." The flames in his eyes flickered yellow.

My demon spirit should have been a strong healthy blue, but I'd polluted it with the essence of too many caustic demons.

"I do love it when a plan comes together." Baal peered through the barrier. "Well, at least one of my thousands of plans. You see, I felt confident you would defeat Vokan, and if you didn't, I would be rid of someone who vexes me greatly." He smiled. "As usual, you struggled to victory, driven by your compassion for the downtrodden."

"Something you'd never understand."

"Oh, I understand it." Baal shrugged. "It is how I knew you would throw your own body into the void if it meant saving the Utopians. How I knew you would consume as many caustic demon shards as needed to free the sprites and eidolons. It is why your demon spirit is so strong and out of balance." He looked at Kalesh. "It is why your spirit influenced you to come to this place. It is why you blindly stepped onto this pattern and came to me."

I thought of all the gentle psychological nudges that gave me the idea to come here. My corrupted demon half had pulled an inception on me and led me here.

Baal nodded. "Yes, you see it now. Kalesh was supposed to have delivered you to me the last time you came here but missed the opportunity."

I regarded my traitorous demon side. "How does my spirit even know what you want?"

"Daemos spirits are difficult to reach." Baal chopped a hand on his palm. "They are walled off to an extent, protected. But when you summon spawn, there is a brief window of vulnerability, an instant where I can send a message."

I glared at the traitor. "How could you do this to us?" I spun back to Baal. "And what in the hell do you want with me?" My knees buckled. The strain of holding up the shield grew heavier by the second. I wondered if Kalesh stepping outside had anything to do with it.

"Lower the barrier, grandson, and I'll show you." Baal raked claws across it. "You can trust me."

"No, I can't, you lying bastard!" I summoned all my strength and poured it into the shield.

The sapphire color of my demon spirit rippled sickly green. His hand thrust out, gripping my neck and squeezing. I gasped and tried to pry his fingers away. My concentration faltered, and the shield cracked.

Kalesh released me. "Baal is strong. Listen to him."

"You traitorous bastard!" I rubbed my throat. "You're an idiot!"

"No, I am strong and wise."

It was like talking to a child.

Baal tapped a claw on the barrier. Another crack ran down the surface. "Let me in so we can talk."

I tried to bolster the shield, but Kalesh moved to hit me. It was all I could do to quell the terror rising in me. *What will Baal do if the shield is gone?* I was trapped in a cage with an animal while an even larger predator waited outside.

Baal scraped his claws down the barrier, fingernails on a chalkboard. "Open up, Justin."

I cringed. "So you can devour me like you did that giant millipede?"

"It was a spirit." He shrugged. "I have power over them. I cannot do the same to you here."

"I don't believe you!" I held out a hand to keep Kalesh at bay and tried to summon more power to the shield. My spirit grabbed my arms. His spirit skin felt cool one instant and burned feverishly the next. In my quest to save the Utopians, I'd completely jacked up my aura.

There was no way out of this—not until Baal got his pound of flesh. I just hoped the reverse summoning pattern protected me from the worst of it. I stiffened my spine and laid on the bravado thick and heavy.

"Fine, Baal." I dropped the shield. "It's down. Now what?"

Baal regarded me coolly. "Will you join me, grandson?"

"No, no, and no again. How many times do you have to ask?"

"That was the final time." Baal stepped closer to Kalesh. My demon side tried to act brave, but it shrank back from the Grand Overlord of Haedaemos. Baal held out the palm of his hand and gently pulled a scarlet thread from his flesh. It snapped free, squirming like a worm. "Would you like more power, Kalesh?"

"Don't take anything from him." I grabbed my demon half, but he shoved me aside like a rag doll. The umbilical cord stretched tight and jerked me back. I stumbled against Kalesh and fell to the ground.

Baal tossed the wriggling worm. It crossed into the pattern without harm.

"I would always have more." Kalesh caught it and dropped it into his mouth. His skin glowed bright red for an instant and dimmed back to sapphire. "Power."

"Yes, power. It will flush out the caustic pollution the boy filled you with." Baal looked down at me and smiled. "I hope you don't regret not joining me, but I suspect you will."

"The only regret I'll have is if you win." I struggled to my feet. "And I'll do anything to stop you."

"Yes, I believe you will." He paced around the pattern. "Eventually, you will see that my way is right. Once I am ruler, there will be no more wars. Peace and prosperity will reign. Once all our peoples are strong again, we can look to other horizons."

I had no clue what he meant. "What other horizons?"

Baal smiled. "Oh, there is so much more than your limited mind can comprehend. So much more than the realms." He sighed. "If you'd only joined me. You could have seen through my eyes. You could have felt the pulse of the universe beneath your fingertips. You could have ruled by my side."

"Why would someone like you want anyone to rule by their side?" I wanted to spit in his face but reigned in the urge. "Let's face it, Baal. No matter how much power you have you'll always be empty inside."

For once, his grin faltered. "The word you need is absolution."

I stared in confusion. "Absolution?"

The umbilical cord snapped tight and jerked me and my demon half toward each other. Kalesh roared in outrage. My feet skidded across the pattern. The impact jarred me to my bones, the agony so great I nearly blacked out. Strength rushed back into my veins. I felt as if I could punch the world and crack it in half.

The red hole above me thrummed with power. The last thing I saw was Baal waving goodbye as I shot into the sky.

I opened my eyes. Blackened bones and charred grass stretched around me. Crimson runes burned beneath my feet. I yanked my feet to uproot them and leapt back to the safety of the path.

"Justin!" Elyssa jumped up from a nearby rock and grabbed my shoulders.

The others watched me like someone who'd just woken from a coma.

Conrad walked closer and sniffed the air. "Where did you go?"

"Nowhere." I shuddered. "Literally. I was in a place between here and Haedaemos."

"You just walked right into the middle of the pattern when we were passing it," Ivy said. "I tried to grab you, but you vanished too fast."

Ambria grimaced. "The ground swallowed you."

Evadora clapped her hands and giggled. "It was a neat trick."

"It wasn't a trick." I felt Kalesh's smugness seeping into my own emotions. *You did this.*

Yes. He seemed quite happy.

"I thought you were dead." Thal inspected me. "You smell of the dark world."

"I don't doubt it." I looked at my hands, touched my face. Even my own body felt like it belonged to a stranger. "I had a talk with Baal."

Elyssa's eyes flared. "What happened?"

I clenched my fists to keep from shaking. "My demon side—Kalesh—lured us back here. He got me to step into that pattern. It was all part of Baal's plan."

"I remember you walking toward that pattern when we first came here looking for Vokan," Elyssa said. "I grabbed your arm."

I didn't even remember it. "Yeah. That was Baal's original plan. All those caustic spirits I absorbed corrupted my demon spirit and made him stronger. I can't even trust myself anymore."

Ambria winced. "Surely there's a cure."

"Maybe there was, but not anymore." I took a deep breath. "Baal gave Kalesh a piece of himself. I think he'll use it to completely take over my body."

Elyssa's eyes flared. "We won't let that happen. Your father can probably help."

I swallowed the panic rising in me. "Yeah, I hope so." I wasn't so sure.

Elyssa hugged me. Ivy and Evadora crowded around and joined in.

"You'll get better bro." Ivy's eyes glowed white. "I promise!"

I swallowed the lump in my throat. "Thanks, sis."

Vokan slumbered peacefully on the trail. "How long was I gone?"

"Twenty minutes or so." Elyssa peered into my eyes as if trying to see my soul. She looked away. "Let's get back to the ship."

I took a breath and nodded. "Yeah, that's a good idea."

As we walked, I couldn't stop thinking about what Baal had given Kalesh. What did it mean for me? I had a terrible feeling I'd soon find out.

CHAPTER 11

W e made it back to the ship without further incident. I dumped Vokan in the Mzodi equivalent of a shower in one of the restrooms. Ultraviolet mist filled the square stall, concealing the unconscious magus. When it cleared, it left behind a sparkly clean Vokan. Unfortunately, his multiple cuts soon began to ooze blood again. I levitated him out of the cleaning room and into our medical bay.

Once there, I let the healing gems do their magic, closing the dozens of razor cuts all over his body. Then I put a sleeping gem on his forehead and left him in La-La Land so we could converse with our new fairy acquaintance on the front deck.

"Maybe it would help to start with some history," I said. "Why do the Fae hate humans so much?"

"That ancient enmity predates the realms." Thal's wings flattened against her back and vanished. She sat on the deck next to Evadora and leaned back. "In those days there were few humans, their tribes threatened by the unman hordes who sought dominion over the lands. The humans begged us for refuge, and the Fae granted it."

"I never heard of this," Evadora said. "My mother was alive before the Sundering, but she forgot a lot."

"The unman hordes threatened us with war, but they had already provoked the Lyrolai, the elven folk. Caught between our peoples, the hordes fled for distant lands. The Lyrolai warned us also to banish the humans, for their kind did not live in harmony with nature but bent it to their will." Thal wrapped her arms around her bent legs. "Lumia made a bargain with the humans, that they would have their own lands forever separate from the Fae. The humans agreed to this bargain and Lumia helped them settle on the opposite end of the Earth from the unman that they might be safe and prosper."

"Was Lumia a Fae queen?" Ivy asked.

Thal tilted her head. "Lumia is more than a queen. She is the mother of our kind."

"She's still alive?" I asked.

"Of course." Thal seemed surprised I would even ask the question and continued her narrative. "Centuries passed and humans appeared in the Fae lands. They destroyed ancient forests and plowed land to make way for crops. Lumia sent emissaries to remind the humans of their bargain. These humans knew nothing of the past agreement and refused to leave. Lumia sent guardians to drive them out, but the humans returned with armies. Thus began a short, brutal war."

Evadora grimaced. "I hope the evil humans didn't win."

Ambria cleared her throat. "Excuse me, but we're human."

"Yeah, but you're not bad ones."

Thal didn't seem to register the side banter and kept right on going. "These humans were no match for our magic. They forced us to kill many of them, putting a darkness in the hearts of Fae that had never existed before. Lumia sent spies to the human lands only to find they had spread across the world like a disease, destroying everything in their path." Thal spread her hands as if to encompass the globe. "But the humans were not the only threat. In isolation, the Fae had not realized another threat already seized much of the world. The Apocryphan controlled the great empires of the Sirens and Seraphim. Even the great city of Juranthemon was no longer independent. Lumia realized that there was no room on Earth for the Fae."

If I'd been in a seat, I would've been on the edge. I'd heard about the Apocryphan and knew the basics of the Sundering, but I hadn't heard much about the world before that.

"Lumia long desired to create a Fae realm separate from the rest of the world, but even she did not have the power to do it. The Apocryphan, she realized, could make it so. She studied these beings for many years to understand them and chose Xanatas to aid her, for she was the outcast, the lowest of the Apocryphan." Thal held a hand near the deck as if to illustrate just how low.

I waved my hand. "Hang on, who's Xanatas?"

She put a finger to her chin. "That is one of the many names of the outcast. We recorded her as Xanatas in the ancient days. She became Xanomiel during the earlier epoch and chose a male form. I do not remember her other names."

"Whoa, she could turn into a man?" Ivy's jaw hung open. "Like with all the stuff between the legs and everything?"

"The Apocryphan were godlike, though not actually gods." Thal shrugged. "They could change appearance and gender if desired."

Xanatas, Xanomiel, Xanos. All the same dudette or dude, depending on her mood. "Sorry to interrupt. Please continue."

Thal tilted her head as if she didn't understand everything I said but seemed to get the gist and returned to the story. "At first Xanatas saw an opportunity to rule the Fae, a kingdom unknown to the other Apocryphan, but Lumia convinced her otherwise. She showed her how to manipulate the others of her kind into war and how to fracture the world into realms. And so it came to be."

I blew out a breath. "Wow, so Lumia's the one responsible for the realms?"

"Her magic combined with the power of the Apocryphan." Thal waved a hand around. "This created our realm, but unbeknownst to us, many humans were also cast into Pangaea with us. They built a city on the far coast and prospered for many years before we discovered them. Once again, there was war between the Fae and humans. Those Fae who killed suffered the great darkness."

"So the Fae didn't kill anything before they fought humans?" I said.

"We do not kill animals for food. Nature provides sustenance and we take only what is necessary. Those Fae infected by the darkness began to act more like humans. They killed animals and ate their flesh. They saw violence as a means to an end." Thal smiled. "Lumia's daughter, Glacia, was among the first guardians who slew humans. It was she who realized they could no longer remain among the Fae lest they infect the others. She took her people to the shadow of the great mountain and called her people the Unfae."

"Are their kids also Unfae?" Ambria asked.

"They are born of the darkness, yes."

I lifted an eyebrow. "So Glacia is evil?"

Thal frowned. "No. I am also of the Unfae, and I am not evil."

Why am I not surprised? "I take it Pyra is not Unfae."

"Correct." The fairy sighed. "She does not like our kind."

"What does Lumia think about the coming darkness?"

"Lumia no longer abides among us," Thal said. "She simply vanished, leaving behind only the mark of power on her daughter, granting her authority over the Fae."

Ambria shook her head. "Wait, she put Glacia in charge?"

"No, Glacia's twin sister, Pyra."

I knew from experience that twin sisters in charge of supernatural kingdoms were big trouble. "Why in the world would Pyra herself come after you? If she's the ruler, she could have just sent guardians instead."

Thal looked down as if ashamed. "Because I willingly killed that I might become Unfae. Because I forsook my heritage." She looked up at me. "Because I am her daughter."

Shelton wasn't here to say it, so I did. "Holy farting fairies."

"Amen to that." Elyssa blew out a breath. "Justin, I don't think we stand a chance in Haedaemos of convincing Pyra to help us."

"Glacia might," Thal said. "But you would have to enter the Fae kingdom first, and no one enters without Pyra's knowledge."

"What if we brought her Vokan?" I asked.

"I cannot speak for my mother," Thal said. "She may grant you an audience or she may command the Unfae to end you."

"Just because she has someone else do her killing doesn't absolve her of it." Elyssa shook her head. "We rescued Pyra. We took her all the way home, and even then, she didn't budge an inch on letting us into Pangaea. If saving her life didn't help, I don't think gifting Vokan will make a difference."

"Are all the Fae tiny like you?" Ambria said.

Thal tilted her head. "Just because we are not lumbering giants does not make us tiny. It means you are large." She stood and looked down at us. "And ungainly."

It took me a moment to realize she'd grown a few inches and put on some girth. I jolted to my feet and stared at her in shock. "You're our size now." She'd grown as tall as Elyssa, but her face remained disconcertingly childlike.

"Yes." She looked down at her legs. "I feel heavy like this."

"That's really neat!" Ivy jumped up and inspected her. "You can shrink and grow anytime you want?"

"Within certain limits, yes." Thal turned to Evadora. "What are your people doing about the coming darkness?"

"Oh, our people are all asleep." The silver-skinned girl made a sad face. "Our realm was destroyed by the Sirens so they could keep the other realms from drifting apart."

"Destroyed?" Thal's eyes widened. "And the elven folk slumber?"

"Yes, but Mother wants to wake them." Evadora shrugged. "Her evil twin from the reflected world put them to sleep."

Daelissa and Nightliss, Cora and Naeve, and now Glacia and Pyra. "Twins are just bad news in general. One of them always turns evil and wants to rule the world."

"Oh, yes. Every single one." Elyssa rolled her eyes at me.

Conrad spoke up. "Thal, what was your objective once you asked the humans for help?"

"I wished to alert them to the danger, so they could prepare," she replied. "If my mother refused to do anything, at least others might fight the darkness."

"Do you have any idea where Lumia went?" Ambria said. "I'll bet she could exert some influence."

"It is a mystery that none have solved." Thal shrank back down to four feet tall. "There was great intrigue in the court when she vanished. Many suspected foul play. The guardians investigated Pyra but absolved her. They said only Lumia could have given Pyra the mark of power. The only question was if it had been made under duress. They concluded Lumia was too powerful for Pyra to control."

Conrad asked another good question. "What sort of powers do the Fae have?"

Thal vanished.

"Whoa!" Ivy waved a hand in the air where she'd been. "She's not invisible."

"I'm here."

We turned to see Thal atop the bridge. The fairy blipped away and appeared back where she'd been a moment ago.

"So you can blink from one place to another," I said.

"Blink?" Thal tilted her head. "As in the shutting and opening of an eyelid?"

"What's the maximum distance?" Ambria said.

"Not far. Perhaps a hundred feet." Thal's hand blurred and the air shimmered in front of her. "I open a rift and travel through the between place." She gripped Ivy's hand and the pair vanished inside. The disruption in the air vanished. Seconds ticked past and they leapt from another rift in the middle of the deck.

Ivy looked pale as a ghost. "So cold!" She shivered violently. "I don't like the between at all!"

Thal seemed amused. "It takes some time to grow accustomed to it."

I raised my hand and waved it like a little kid. "Can I have I a turn?"

"Of course." Thal grabbed my wrist and blackness swallowed us whole. We stood in a void, blue as the ice of a glacier. Intense cold penetrated my skin and seeped into my core.

I shivered violently. "H-h-holy smokes, it's freezing!" My words faded almost instantly, absorbed by the void. Before I could say another word, warmth melted the frost and I stood in front of my friends, a few feet from where I'd been before.

Evadora jumped in place. "Me next, me next!"

Thal graciously gave everyone a turn, even Conrad who didn't seem very keen on going and seemed even less enthused when he returned.

"I'll stick to a blink stone and nausea." Conrad rubbed his arms and shivered. "How many can you take at once?"

"As many as can touch me," Thal said. "The rift is only visible when I will it so and will not permit any who are not in contact."

"Can you rift up into the sky?" Elyssa said.

Thal looked up. "Yes, of course, but not very far."

"That could be a powerful ability." Elyssa tapped a finger on her chin. "What else can you do?"

"You use magic, yes?" Thal nodded at me.

"Most of us can," Ambria said sourly, as if Thal ignored her on purpose.

The fairy turned to her. "Do magic."

Ambria flicked her wand and formed a ball of light. "Like that?"

Dark flames ignited on Thal's fingertips. She waved an arm, leaving behind a trail of sparkling dust. The light on Ambria's wand flickered and died.

"What?" Ambria tried to revive the light but nothing happened. She tried several more spells, but none worked.

"You are silenced," Thal said. "The effect lasts only a moment."

Conrad's mouth dropped open. "You can silence anyone?"

"Yes. I block them from the aether." She looked at him. "You try."

Conrad summoned azure fire in his hands. Thal spread the sparkling dust over him. Instead of dampening his fire, the dust popped and crackled like gunpowder.

It was Thal's turn to look shocked. She gripped Conrad's wrists and stared at the flames. "A human who touches the Allmother!"

Conrad flinched. "You mean the primal fount?"

I peered at the azure energy. "You can't interrupt his magic?"

"Obviously not." Ambria looked quite proud.

"What about mine?" I ignited orbs of Brilliance and Murk in my hands.

Thal snapped out of her confusion and sprinkled her fairy dust on me. It felt like someone turned out the lights. My connection to the aether around me disintegrated. I felt disoriented, an integral part of my being suddenly nullified.

My magic was gone.

CHAPTER 12

My demon half growled happily. *Your Seraphim side is cut off.*

Well aren't you just observant, Fred?

I am Kalesh!

I mentally rolled my eyes at him and switched to demon vision for a better look at my situation. Clouds of aether drifted around me, but I couldn't feel or touch them. The fairy dust had completely deadened my connection to aether.

"I don't like this at all." The magic and traits from my demon half still worked, but not external magic.

"It's quite unsettling." Ambria massaged her hands. "Oh, it tingles when it comes back."

I felt the sensation a moment later, pins and needles up and down my body.

"Yeah." Conrad looked at his hands. "I feel it too. I guess because it silenced my normal Arcane magic even if it couldn't stop me from touching the primal fount."

Thal stared at Conrad. "I would know how a male human touches the Allmother."

Conrad shrugged. "The earth dragons gave the ability to my grandfather and allowed me to use it as well."

"It's a long story," Ambria said.

Elyssa held up a hand. "Before we move on to that, do you have other powers?"

"I can steal some powers with a blood ritual." Thal formed the black flames in her hands and juggled fireballs in the air. "I can use darkfire as a weapon." She walked to the railing. Her hand blurred and a ring of black fire spread on the ground below, twisting into a pattern. Hands of flame lunged upward, grasping at anything within reach. "There are many things darkfire can do."

"Neato!" Ivy peered at Thal's hands. "Can you teach me?"

"It is not in your blood to grasp Fae magic just as I cannot grasp human magic without a blood ritual."

"I use Seraphim magic," Ivy said. "It's real simple. You just channel the forces of the universe and weave them into stuff, or just blast things."

Thal's brow arched. "You are Seraphim?"

Ivy puffed out her chest. "Mostly, but I might have some demon in me like my big bro."

"Part demon?" Thal turned to me. "We know very little of demons. Pyra said they did not exist before the Sundering."

"Well the grand overlord of demons is one of the entities behind the coming darkness." Baal's smug face played back in my mind. "We're also looking for an ancient Siren named Vitania who might know about his origins."

Thal's gaze riveted on me. "You know of Vitania?"

"Barely." I shrugged. "We were told to look her up."

"Vitania once took refuge in our kingdom." Thal looked up as if remembering something. "It was after the Sundering, but the Apocryphan still ruled the realms."

"Goodness, how old are you?" Ambria said.

Thal raised an eyebrow. "I am only a few hundred years old, but our history is kept in great detail. The Sirens were forced to build bridges between the realms so the Apocryphan could restore their power."

I really wanted to get my hands on their history books. "How did the Sirens trap the Apocryphan in the Abyss?" That information could come in handy against Xanos.

Thal's forehead pinched. "The volumes about that have been missing for some time."

Elyssa's eyes narrowed. "Did those books go missing before or after Lumia vanished?"

Thal seemed to ponder it for a moment. "I do not know."

"Hmm." Elyssa tapped a finger on her chin. "What else did you read about Vitania and Lumia?"

I could practically see the gears turning in her head. She was onto something.

Thal shrugged. "The two were close. Vitania gifted Lumia with a necklace of obsidian and alabaster."

I snapped my fingers. "Hey, that sounds just like the necklace Melea had. I think Vitania gave Lumia a portal necklace"

"Lumia and Vitania were friends." Elyssa's eyes gazed into the distance. "I'm willing to bet Lumia used the necklace to travel to wherever Vitania was at the time."

I blew out a breath. "Man, if we could get a portal necklace, that would be dope."

Ambria's eyebrows popped up. "So Lumia and Vitania might be in Iceland together?"

"Yep." Our next moves were clear. "Let's go to Eden and find Vitania. If Lumia's with her, maybe she'll agree to an alliance with us nasty humans."

"It is possible," Thal said. "Lumia is still the Fae queen and could order Pyra to help you."

"I wouldn't be surprised if Lumia helped the Sirens trap the Apocryphan." Elyssa bit the inside of her lip. "It's possible she and Vitania could help us against Baal and Xanos."

"Two birds, one stone." Conrad clapped his hands together. "I feel very good about where this is going."

"Me too." Ambria leaned her head on his shoulder. "But I guess that means we don't get to see fairyland."

"Man, I really wanted to see it too." Ivy scuffed her shoe on the deck. "You sure we can't just go for a quick look?"

"I doubt we'd get close enough," Elyssa said. "We need Lumia or other nonhumans to convince Pyra to let us in."

"Agreed." I looked at the volcanic wasteland Vokan once called home. "I'm ready to get out of here."

Elyssa nodded. "Let's get underway back to Atlantis. We can drop Vokan in Solan and ask the Utopians to keep him locked up until we decide what to do with him."

"Is it really a good idea to give him to the Utopians?" Ambria said. "They might not give him back later."

"I think they will," Elyssa said. "The Utopians kind of owe us."

"Because Justin totally saved them." Ivy grinned. "I bet they'd do anything for him."

"Plus, we're giving them the chance to administer justice to the one man who ruined everything." Elyssa crossed her arms. "They won't sentence him to death, but they'll lock him up. Then we can have the pleasure of telling Vokan the Fae want a word with him too."

"Ooh, I like the way you think." I almost felt sorry for Vokan. *Nah, not even close.* After all the people he'd killed and souls he'd consumed, he deserved everything he got.

"You trust these humans?" Thal asked.

"They're good people," I said. "Way better than the humans back in Eden."

Elyssa pursed her lips. "You originally looked for humans because you sensed the darkness. It just so happens that we're already fighting the darkness."

Thal's lips pursed. "You said a being named Baal is behind it?"

"Yeah, that's why we wanted to talk to Pyra." I sighed. "We've got two bad dudes who both want to rule the universe. Baal, the Grand Overlord of Haedaemos, wants to control the realms but keep them separate. Xanatas, now known as Xanos, escaped the Abyss and wants to recombine the realms and rule Earth."

"Xanatas?" Thal shivered. "She alone is a powerful threat. I hope you are right and Lumia is with Vitania, for even the violent humans cannot defeat her without help."

"Then let's not waste another second." Elyssa set her hands on hips. "Thal, do you want to come with us?"

The fairy looked at the others as if measuring her reply. "It seems fate led me to this moment that I could join your quest. Lumia might enjoin the Fae to your cause."

"Wow, now we've got a fairy on the team." Ivy pumped a fist. "This is so cool!"

"And I'm an elf!" Evadora danced in a circle, chirping like a bird on crack cocaine.

Ambria clamped her hands over her ears. "Do you have to be so loud, Evadora?"

Conrad watched, a glint of amusement in his eyes, but barely cracked a smile. *That kid has been through hell and back.* It was a wonder he hadn't turned out like his father.

Elyssa guided the ship up and turned us back toward Solan. It was late when we reached the council towers, but the streets were alive with lights, music and dancing. Agula watched from the top of the first tower, unaware of our approach. He jumped with surprise when he saw us docking.

"My friends, you've returned!" Agula gripped my hands enthusiastically. "How was your mission?"

"We didn't make it to Pangaea, but we made a new friend." I motioned to Thal. She stepped hesitantly off the gangway as if the ground was lava. "This is Thal of Pangaea."

Agula froze. "My goodness. Are you Fae?"

Thal remained a safe distance from him. "I am Unfae."

"Technically still Fae," Ambria noted dryly.

"Might I greet you?" Agula held out a hand.

The diminutive fairy regarded his hand like a poisonous snake. She reached tentatively toward it and placed her small hand in his palm.

Agula patted it gently. "It is an honor to greet you, Thal."

She stared at him for a moment then looked at me. "He does seem gentle."

"You were one of the Fae imprisoned by Vokan." Pain filled Agula's eyes. "I am so sorry that monster was the first human you met."

"Just so happens we also brought you a gift." I couldn't help but grin. "We've got Vokan."

Agula went still with shock. "You captured him?"

"Technically, Thal caught him. We were going to take him to Pangaea as a peace offering, but plans changed." I put on my serious face. "We think the people of Utopia deserve to put him on trial but with the understanding that we may need to take him to Pangaea at a later date."

"Absolutely." Agula tapped his pendant. "Daana and Elaine, I require you for a very important vote."

"Oh?" Music blared in the background, but Daana spoke loudly enough to overcome it. "I will be there soon."

"What is so important?" Elaine asked in a tired voice.

"Justin has brought us a gift." Agula giggled like a kid. "We have Vokan."

"Yes!" Elaine whooped. "I'm on the way!"

Within an hour, the council had voted to put Vokan on trial and to return him to us as a peace offering to Pangaea, should we request it.

Elyssa replaced the sleeping gem on Vokan's forehead with a pair of Templar sleeper cuffs on his wrists to keep the rogue magus unconscious during the transfer. "How do you plan to imprison him?"

"We created a special cell just in case we ever caught him," Daana said. "It is where the cantrap used to be."

"Ooh, symbolism," I said. "I like it."

"Yes, it was a nice touch," she said. "I'm rather pleased we get to use it."

"It is made of transparent quartz and enchanted with the same magic resistance as the bunker where he trapped you," Elaine said. "That way we can watch him."

"Vokan is still powerful even without a cantrap of souls," Elyssa said. "I'd recommend you keep several guards around his prison and a magus on standby."

"And Baal might try to pull a jail break, too." I didn't know how likely that was, but better safe than sorry.

"We shall take all necessary precautions," Agula said. "Thank you for allowing us this chance at justice."

We said our goodbyes again and headed back to the house on Dilling Street where the nebulous cloud of Voltis hovered in the front yard. I channeled through Argus and opened a portal in the hazy fog. Thunder rumbled my bones as we emerged near the storm wall of Voltis back in Seraphina. Sheets of rain and ice rapped against the weather shields. Lightning and volcanic bursts lit the night sky.

Thal's eyes flew wide with wonder. She went up to the shield and peered out at the storm. "Such magnificent power."

I half expected to meet a dozen dragons waiting for us, but none emerged from the darkness to challenge our entry into Atlantis. I used Argus to channel a portal and we slipped inside quickly just in case. I couldn't stop thinking about Baal's gift to Kalesh. *What if he can track us now? Can he read my mind?* There were just too many insidious possibilities to consider so I tried not to think about it.

That just made me think about it even more.

"You're pale as a sheet, Justin." Elyssa hooked her arm in mine while piloting the ship with her other hand.

"Yeah." My mouth felt dry. "What if Baal is connected to me now? What if my dumbass demon soul just screwed us royally?"

"I think you should speak to your dad. He might know."

I dared feel a little relieved at the thought. "I hope so."

It was the middle of the night when we landed, but this couldn't wait. I gave Elyssa a kiss. "I'll meet you at our house later, okay?"

"Of course." Elyssa kissed my cheek. "We'll make it through this, I promise."

I swallowed the knot in my throat. "I hope so."

I jogged to the end of the pier where they parked the public chariots and flew one to a domed marble house near the administration building. It was small and quaint compared to the royal palace in Cabala, but still the size of a small mansion. I traced a secret pattern on the door and it clicked open.

The grand staircase took me to a short hallway with the master bedroom at the end. The door clicked open before I could knock, and Dad stepped outside with only a pair of linen pants on. He put a finger to his lips and led me to a balcony on the opposite side of the house.

"How did you know I was here?" I said.

"What did Baal do to you?" Dad gripped my head and peered into my eyes.

Uncertainty and fear swelled in my throat. "Is it that obvious?"

"The smell woke me up." He backed away. "Did he give you something?"

I gave him the short version of our journey to Vokan's hideout, Baal's trickery, and everything else in between and after.

Dad blew out a breath. "Baal gave your demon a fragment of his spirit."

"Am I marked? Can he read my mind now?"

"No, nothing like that." He patted my back as if that might console me. "Think of it as a highly concentrated dose of spirit. Your demon side will absorb it slowly, gaining more power as it does."

"Just like what you told me about earlier?" I gulped. "What does that mean for me?"

"It means you might lose control." Dad pursed his lips. "It takes decades to bring both human and demon soul into harmony, Justin. By giving your demon side more power, it's possible the balance of power will tip to Kalesh."

CHAPTER 13

"**M**y demon could rule the roost?" I gasped. "That's insane!"

"Baal couldn't get you on his side, so he's trying to exert influence another way." Dad's hands clenched. "A spirit seed would work on a demon, but I have no idea how it affects Daemos."

"So he can't read my mind or possess me, or track my whereabouts?"

"Anything is possible, but I highly doubt it." Dad's nose wrinkled. "Man, that is a strong odor."

I sniffed my armpits, but my deodorant was holding up. "Why don't I smell it?"

"Probably because your senses filter out your own odor."

I sniffed again to be sure. "So I reek like sulfur to everyone else?"

He shook his head. "No, only Daemos can sense it."

It was stupid, but I felt relieved. "Good. I don't want Elyssa to think I stink."

Dad gripped my shoulder. "My advice would be to stick around here for a while. It's possible I can siphon off some of the spirit and keep your demon side from growing too strong."

"I can't. We're going to Eden first thing tomorrow. We have to find Vitania and hope Lumia is with her. By then, you guys should already be on your way after us."

"Surely Elyssa and the others can handle that without you." Dad leaned his elbows on the balcony railing and looked out at the empty streets. "I don't know how hard or fast the spirit seed will affect you."

I didn't like the uncertainty, but I couldn't just sit on my hands. "My human and Seraphim genetics might slow it down."

"I hope." Dad sighed. "I'd come with you, but we have an army to transport back to Eden. I also have to go visit Heval in a couple of days. Their leader wants assurances about food supply and defense." He shrugged. "Your mother and I will probably be on the last ship out."

"When is Kassallandra going back?"

He chuckled. "Oh, you know her. She'll be on the first ship." He tapped a finger on his chin. "If worse comes to worst, maybe she can help you."

Asking Kassallandra for help wasn't ideal, but it was better than letting Kalesh overcome me. "Can you ask her for me tomorrow?"

Dad nodded. "Be careful, son. Baal makes Daelissa look like a playground bully."

"Yeah, I figured that out." And if Baal was that powerful, what did that make Xanos? I didn't even want to think about it. I felt like an ant versus an elephant.

"Well, let me take a look before you go." Dad stepped back, eyes flickering with blue flames. "Yep, it's there all right. Your demon spirit should be sapphire, but now it looks like someone bleeding out in a swimming pool."

"That's a lovely visual." I switched to demon vision and looked down at myself, but it was hard to see anything without a mirror.

"The sliver Baal put in you is slowly staining your spirit." Dad extended a tendril of his own soul essence.

I felt a slight tug as he latched in and a steady pull as he drew on my soul essence. "Is it helping?"

"No, it's not. I can't separate the sliver from your spirit." He untethered and shook his head. "I've got good news and bad news."

My stomach twisted in knots. "Give it to me, doc."

"The good news is, the seed Baal planted isn't staining your spirit as fast as I thought it would. The bad news is, once it hits critical mass, Kalesh is only going to get stronger and influence your decisions more."

"Could he control me like a puppet?"

Dad shook his head. "No, but your emotions and feelings will be heavily affected by your demon side. Just like the time you lost control during your first visit to Tarissa and slaughtered all those people."

My knees wobbled, and I choked down a wave of nausea. "I don't want to turn into a monster. Is there anyone who can remove the spirit sliver?"

"I know of one person, but I haven't seen her since before we left for Seraphina."

"Well, what's her name?"

"Emily Glass."

"Emily Glass?" I'd met her once during the Crystoid Incident. She and her boyfriend, Tyler Rock had been with the Custodians. "Did she come to Seraphina with us?"

"No, I don't think so." He shrugged. "I joined up with her and Vallaena to stop Domathus from physically manifesting and taking over Eden around the same time you were fighting Maximus and his vampire army."

"The Demonicus Incident."

"Yep." His lips pressed into a flat line. "I'd look her up first thing when you get to Eden. She's got some very special talents that might be able to remove the sliver."

I raised an eyebrow. "Talents?"

"She could literally remove the vampirism from a vampire." Dad whistled as if to underscore how impressive that was. "She single-handedly banished a demon lord back to hell and sent Overlord Domathus packing along with him." He met my eyes. "She might be able to extract Baal's thorn as well."

Warm hope crept across the ice in my chest. "Any idea where to look first?"

"Maybe what's left of the Overworld government can help." He shrugged. "Tyler Rock is also a pretty powerful businessman in Atlanta, so he might be easier to find."

"Thanks." I gave him a one-armed man hug. "Guess I'll see you in a few days."

Dad embraced me with both arms. "Be careful, son. I promise we'll figure this out."

"Thanks, Dad." He walked me outside and waved goodbye as I flew off in the chariot. Despite the seed of hope, anxiety circled, a shark in bloody waters. I had to stop and hover in place as the walls closed in.

Deep breaths. Emily can help me. I will not let Baal win.

It wasn't the first time I'd felt crushing depression and anxiety, and it wouldn't be the last. As much as I wanted to curl up into a ball and scream in terror, I couldn't give in. I gripped the chariot reins and steeled myself the best that I could. Even so, it felt as if the air held no oxygen. My vision wavered, and a ringing grew louder in my ears.

Mine soon. Kalesh sounded so smug I wanted to punch him.

There was only one person who made me feel better when everything felt hopeless, and I had to reach her fast. I urged the chariot to full speed and landed outside a small bungalow halfway up the mountain. Poseidon's spear seemed poised to strike the house, should the statue on the mountain ever unleash it.

It was an accurate representation of my emotional turmoil.

I dashed inside. Elyssa was already curled up in bed, but her glowing violet eyes opened when I stepped into the room. I got in bed and curled up next to her. She snuggled against me.

"Justin, your heart's racing."

"Yeah." I shivered, and my throat locked up.

She kissed my forehead. "Baby, it'll be okay."

"Maybe." I swallowed a lump in my throat and gave her Dad's prognosis. "We've got to find Emily Glass before I lose my mind."

Elyssa hugged me tighter. "We've faced worse. Remember the vampling curse? Remember when I almost died, but you traveled to Seraphina and brought back a healer? We've beaten impossible odds before."

"I know." The anxiety lost its grip and began to slide away. I put my head to Elyssa's chest and listened to the steady rhythm of her heart. The constricting dread loosened its hold on my chest. "Baal's poisoned my demon side in the hopes I'll join him. I hope Emily can help."

"Me too." She pressed her head to my chest. "Me too."

I took a calming breath. "Where's Thal?"

"Staying with Evadora." She traced a fingernail down my shoulder. "Evadora, Cora, and Ivy will go with us to Eden, so we can drop them off at Arcane University. From there, they'll go to the Glimmer and try to break the spell holding the Lyrolai prisoners. Conrad and his crew might go with them, but they haven't decided yet."

"Let's hit Atlanta right after we drop them off," I said. "We need to find Tyler Rock."

She chuckled. "Sounds like the main character's name in a romance novel."

"Nah, more like an action hero name."

Elyssa kissed my nose. "Well, let's hope Emily Glass can be your hero."

WE HAD a full crew on the *Raptor* the next morning. We couldn't take *Angel Wings*, the ship the Fallen left for Conrad, since its portal device was needed to make gateways for the ships carrying everyone returning to Eden. Adam Nosti added camouflage spells to the *Raptor* so it wouldn't stand out like a sore thumb in Eden.

Conrad and his friends claimed a room below deck. Cora sat on the back deck, gazing out at the sea while Ivy and Evadora played a seashell game the Sirens had taught them. Everyone bore the tiny seashell tattoo, taking advantage of Dolpha's translator gift. I'd hoped to speak with her before leaving to see what she knew about Melea's portal necklace, but the Siren didn't make an appearance.

Shelton, unfortunately, was still under house arrest by Bella.

Cinder parked the *Angel Wings*, a sleek double-decker yacht, next to the *Raptor* and walked across the gangway to our ship. "Hello, Justin."

"Hey, Cinder." I shook his hand.

Nightliss came across the gangway behind him, a sad look on her face. "Justin, you're leaving already?"

I gave her a hug and kissed her forehead. "We don't have any time to waste." I gave her a quick account of my encounter with Baal.

Her eyes widened. "This cannot be!" Nightliss pressed her hands to my chest and closed her eyes. "I sense the change in your demon spirit, but there's nothing I can do to remove the splinter from your soul."

"Apparently, my only hope is finding Emily Glass."

Nightliss's eyes filled with concern. "The last I knew of her, she fought off a demonic invasion."

Elyssa's ears perked. "The Demonicus Incident?"

"No, it was after that." Nightliss touched a finger to her own chest. "I only know because I gave blessings to several Custodians recruited to assist Emily's team. I once tried to bestow a blessing on her, but her body rejected it."

"Rejected it?" I blinked. "So she fought two demon invasions with ordinary human strength?"

"She is very brave." Nightliss sighed. "I don't know much about the second incident. We were in the middle of the Crystoid Incident at the time, so we couldn't devote more resources to her."

Just thinking about that period of time reminded me how lucky I was to have Nightliss back in my life. I couldn't resist giving her another hug. "Is Emily still alive?"

"I believe so." Nightliss gripped my hands. "Justin, I must remain here to assist with the evacuation of Atlantis. Please be careful."

"I'm really sad you can't come." I kissed the tops of her hands. "I hope they're not piling on too many duties."

She smiled. "It's actually quite nice. We're creating a new Templar League with members from all supernatural types. It's our hope they can be the guardians across all realms."

"Wow, that's ambitious."

Shelton huffed and puffed up the gangway and onto the ship. "Thank god I got here in time." He took off his hat and fanned his face with it. "I thought you'd leave without me."

Adam emerged from the bridge. "How in the blazes did you escape from Bella?"

"He didn't." The petite Colombian appeared at the top of the gangway, amusement dancing in her violet eyes. "I told him we would go together. Why hello, Nightliss!" She hugged the equally petite angel.

"Hello, Bella!" Nightliss released her and stepped back. "I didn't know you were going with them."

Shelton ignored them in true Shelton fashion and talked over their conversation. "Bella coming along is a win-win. I get to go with you guys, and we can hit the bedroom anytime I want." He winked.

Adam gagged. "Always TMI, dude."

"Where's Meghan?" Shelton looked around as if she might be hiding behind a bulkhead.

Adam scratched the back of his neck. "Um, she's busy and all that."

"Busy?" Shelton frowned. "She wasn't at our reunion dinner after our grand return from Utopia either."

"Dude, it's cool. She's got a lot on her plate, especially with the evacuation to Eden." Adam jabbed a thumb over his shoulder toward the bridge and changed the subject. "With help from our Mzodi friends, I attached an arctablet to the wall. It's got a full complement of camouflage spells and other fun stuff built into it, so the *Raptor* doesn't trigger UFO sightings when we get back."

I looked around. "Let's get a headcount to make sure everyone's onboard, and then I think we're good to go."

Shelton rubbed his hands together. "Man, I can hardly wait to get home."

"Me either," Adam said. "Being in an alien environment really wears you down after a while."

I walked to the railing and gazed at the large crystal cube affixed to the prow of the *Angel Wings*. A small black orb etched with lines was encased inside the large gem. "So that's the new and improved portal gem you're using for the evacuation?"

Cinder nodded. "We had to deconstruct the smaller one the Fallen left to us so the Mzodi gem enchanters could fabricate a larger one. The volon at the center is the key."

"Volon?" I used my super sight to zoom in. "I thought that was a Chalon."

"The Fallen named it a volon since it only works with Voltis and not the Grand Nexus." He turned back to me. "It will take several Seraphim channeling into it to maintain the large portals necessary for the transport ships."

"The nifty thing about the volon is that you don't need specific coordinates in Voltis to make a portal," Adam said. "You just have to be able to envision the spot where Voltis aligns in the realm you want to visit. We don't even have to leave Atlantis to use it."

"That's a relief." I didn't want to worry about a dragon ambush in Seraphina.

"Voltis aligns near Kratos in Eden." Cinder displayed a tiny island on his arcphone. "It is not far from Bermuda."

Shelton grunted. "Figures Voltis would be in the Bermuda Triangle."

"That does explain a lot," Adam said.

I took Cinder aside. "I guess you're staying to assist with the evacuation?"

"Yes. Issana and Nightliss are helping me improve the portal technology." Cinder paused as if processing a thought. "It is rather strange, but they have become friends."

Issana was one of Nightliss's infernus doppelgangers. "Maybe because they share the same soul."

"Perhaps."

I sensed a slight strain in his voice. Emotion was new to Cinder. I hated that the first thing he felt was the loss of Bliss, another of Nightliss's infernus. "How are you doing?"

He stared blankly into the distance for a moment. "I think about Bliss more than anything else." Cinder turned to me. "Every time I see her face, I feel empty and hollow."

"That's how I felt when I thought Nightliss died." I squeezed his shoulder. "In a way, Bliss is still alive. She's part of Nightliss again."

"Yes, her memories are there, but she is not alive." Cinder seemed lost in his thoughts again. "It is quite strange, but Nightliss has a magic that helps abate the pain sometimes."

My eyebrows shot up. "Really? I don't know of any magic that helps with that."

"Perhaps it is not exactly magic, but it feels like it."

"What does she do?"

Cinder's lips curled into the tiniest of smiles. "She hugs me."

I couldn't help but grin. "You know, that is a special kind of magic." I gave my golem friend a hug. "You'll get through this, Cinder. I promise."

He hugged me back, albeit a bit awkwardly. "Thank you, Justin. You are a true friend."

I said my goodbyes to Nightliss, then she and Cinder went back to the *Angel Wings* and led the way to the storm wall of Voltis. Once there, Nightliss channeled into the crystalline cube. The volon blazed to life. A narrow ultraviolet beam speared into the raging storm.

Like the sun dissipating fog, a window to another world spread across the clouds, creating a gateway large enough for the *Raptor* to navigate. Kratos, a hump of sand with a few palm trees, waited on the other side.

We waved goodbye to Cinder and Nightliss as Elyssa guided the *Raptor* through. Once on the other side, the portal faded away behind us. Voltis in Eden resembled a dark, billowing fogbank no more than a hundred feet tall and wide. It spat lightning bolts into the water and rumbled ominously like an angry thunder child.

"My god, it's beautiful!" Shelton raised his arms to the sky. "Is this Eden? Are we really home?"

Adam held up his arcphone. "Dude, I've got four bars! We're really home!"

They whooped and jumped around like maniacs. I hooked my arm in Elyssa's and danced a little pirate jig. "We're home, baby!" I almost leapt off the boat so I could touch Kratos, but didn't want to chance getting struck by lightning from Voltis Jr.

After so many years of fighting in an alien realm, we had finally made it back to Eden.

CHAPTER 14

Once the celebrations died down, Elyssa got back to business. "We'll go to England first to drop off Cora and anyone else who's going to Queens Gate. The rest of us will head to Atlanta and look for Emily Glass."

"Emily Glass?" Shelton looked puzzled and I realized I hadn't told him or Adam about Baal's unholy gift.

"Yeah. Baal sort of poisoned my demon spirit." I shrugged as if it were no big deal even though it ate me up inside. "He planted a sliver of his own essence in my demon side and we need Emily to get it out before it takes over."

Shelton snarled. "Damn it. Why does Baal have to piss in our cereal all the time?"

"Uh, how long do you have?" Adam asked.

"A couple weeks, maybe longer." I shook my head. "Even my dad couldn't do anything to help. He thinks my human and Seraphim genes might slow down the process but didn't know for sure."

Shelton clapped his hands together. "Then let's do it. Can't wait to see the old stomping grounds again, anyway."

Adam frowned and turned to Elyssa. "If Justin's a ticking time bomb, why go to Queens Gate first?"

"So I may return to the Glimmer." Cora stepped up beside us. "We have some promising new ideas to restore my people from their long slumber, and it's imperative we start immediately."

"It won't take long to get there, anyway." I shrugged. "The *Raptor* can get us back across the Atlantic from England to Atlanta in a few hours."

"On that note, let's get going." Elyssa went back to the bridge and steered the ship northeast. The weather shields flickered on and we got underway.

"How did your people get put to sleep in the first place?" I asked Cora.

She gazed out at the seemingly endless horizon. "I do not have all my old memories, so whatever Naeve did to them is a magic I have long forgotten. But after speaking with Thal last night, she told me of a sleep magic the elves knew before the Sundering."

"I read about it in the great histories." Thal seemed to materialize next to me, probably using her rift magic. "It might be the same magic Naeve used on the elves."

"Naeve summoned the Glimmer folk to the village one day and used the sting of nightshade thorns to paralyze and sedate them." Cora's hand tightened to a fist. "Then she cast the old magic on them."

"If it's the same magic I read about, Cora might be able to reverse it." Thal rubbed her fingers together. Black dust crackled in the air. "My silencing magic might also dispel it."

"I do not know what good my people can do against Xanos or Baal, but we must do everything in our power to stop them." Cora put her hand over mine. "I remember the great battle we fought in Seraphina against Cephus. It is good to see you persevered."

"Yeah, you rammed your giant sky ship into the crimson arch." Shelton punched a fist into his palm. "It was freaking epic."

"Yeah, we won that battle thanks to you." I sighed. "Unfortunately, Victus also got us out of the way for nearly a decade."

"But now we're back, baby!" Shelton drew in a long breath, savoring the air. "And Victus is dead."

"Amen, brother." Adam looked out at the water. "Amen."

The *Raptor* skimmed a few feet above the water to keep us below radar and out of sight of any nom sea-going vessels so we didn't have to employ the camouflage spells. Though we had extra aetherite power gems, we didn't want to chance burning through our power too quickly, nor slow to a snail's pace to accommodate the power drain.

When we neared England a few hours later, Adam selected an appropriate illusion and activated it. The air around the *Raptor* shimmered and the vessel lurched with the sudden decrease in speed. From the inside, everything looked the same, but if I poked my head out over the railing, the wicked bird of prey now looked like a small corporate jet.

"Nice!" I flicked through the selection of illusion spells. Unlike camouflage, they didn't have to constantly change to match the environment and didn't burn nearly the same amount of energy. The *Raptor* was tiny compared to most Mzodi vessels, but still large by most nom standards. It stood as tall as two city buses even without the retractable bird claws, stretched nearly fifty feet wide, and spanned a hundred feet in length.

I giggled like a schoolgirl when we passed over the English countryside. "Look at all the normal houses down there!" I wanted to feel the earth beneath my feet and frolic in a field like a bunny rabbit.

Shelton wiped a tear from his eye. "Damn, it's good to be home."

Bella wrapped her arms around his waist. "Yes it is, dear."

Adam stared blankly out at the passing countryside as if it wasn't even there.

I'd seen this expression enough to know something was eating him up inside. "Adam, what's wrong?"

He blinked and looked at me. "Nothing, just overwhelmed."

"Dude, you've been moping around for the past week." Shelton nudged him in the shoulder. "What's the deal?"

Adam let out a long sigh. "I guess I saw it coming even before we got trapped in Utopia."

Bella nodded as if she knew exactly what he was about to say.

Shelton blurted it out in his usual caring manner. "Meghan dumped you."

Adam winced. "Yeah, you could say that." His eyelids fluttered like someone trying to stop tears. "She thought we'd died or gotten lost when we vanished. Six years without me around made it easy for her to move on."

"But we were only gone a couple months in Utopian time." Shelton huffed. "Impatient woman."

Bella cleared her throat. "It may have been no time to you, but do you know how long I mourned you, Harry? Do you know the kind of pain everyone went through?" She wiped her eyes. "No one wanted to admit that you'd died. Justin's parents thought he'd made it to Eden but couldn't return. The Borathens refused to admit Elyssa might have died. I was the first one to break down and hold a service for you, Harry."

Shelton's gaze softened. "I know it was hard on everyone, babe, but there wasn't much we could do about it."

"Meghan waited a year," Adam said. "Then she moved on."

"Who's she dating now?" Shelton asked.

"No one." Adam shrugged. "She said our paths were too divergent and that unless we finally settled down, we'd see each other so rarely that we might as well not be together."

I grimaced. "Why doesn't she just come with us on our adventures?"

Adam shook his head. "Not everyone wants to jaunt around the world risking their life as often as we do."

"I, for one, would dearly love to settle back down in Eden," Bella said. "At least enjoy it before Xanos and Baal destroy everything."

I scoffed. "That's an optimistic way of looking at it."

"Yeah, well things ain't looking good." Shelton shrugged. "Might as well enjoy life while we can."

"Are we there yet?" Ivy bounded up the stairs to the deck. "I'm so tired of traveling."

The outskirts of London already passed below us. "Almost there."

"Where should I drop off Cora?" Elyssa said. "There's nowhere to land in the city."

"Try Hyde Park near the Serpentine," Conrad said. "That's near the secret entrance to Queens Gate."

"Maybe we should get some food while we're here," Shelton said. "There's gotta be tacos in London, right?"

"Of course." Conrad took out his arcphone and pointed to a spot on the maps near Hyde Park. "There's a place where all the food trucks line up and you can get anything you want."

Shelton licked his lips. "Sounds perfect."

Elyssa guided the ship to the coordinates. Wide fields and few trees offered plenty of space to land, so she guided the ship down.

"Why are all those people pointing up and yelling?" Ivy said.

Car tires screeched and horns honked. I peered over the side and saw wide-eyed people staring at us in horror and fleeing for their lives. It was then I remembered the *Raptor* was disguised as a corporate jet. Unless technology had progressed rapidly over the past few years, most jets couldn't hover in place and none of them would dare land in the middle of Hyde Park.

I turned to Elyssa. "We're not invisible! Everyone sees a plane trying to land in the middle of the park."

She face-palmed. "Gah! I forgot to switch modes!"

Thankfully, this was London, and storm clouds blanketed the sky. "Take us straight up."

Elyssa yanked on the controls and the *Raptor* shot upward, concealing us in the foggy haze moments later. She put the ship in hover mode and groaned. "I'm so used to flying everywhere in Seraphina that I forgot to turn on the environmental camouflage."

"That was funny." Evadora giggled. "I like it when people scream and run."

Thal trembled with apprehension. "So many humans."

Max grimaced. "The authorities will be on full alert now. How are we supposed to land?"

Shelton grunted. "I say we just put on full camouflage and try again."

"Too risky." Elyssa sighed. "What was I thinking?" She fiddled with the tablet and turned on full camouflage. The air rippled, but the effects weren't visible from the inside. I stuck my head over the railing and nearly freaked out when the ship seemed to vanish.

But it hadn't—not completely, at least. The camouflage mimicked the gray clouds, making only a slight shimmer in the air. I gripped the railing a little tighter and pulled myself back in. "Looks good."

Elyssa consulted the map for a moment and seemed to settle on a plan without bothering to tell the rest of us. I was perfectly fine with that since she usually had more sense than the rest of us combined.

Ambria hovered behind her. "That's brilliant, madam commander."

Elyssa's shoulders stiffened. "Please just call me Elyssa, okay?"

Ambria drooped a little. "Well, if you insist...Elyssa."

"Better."

Max chuckled. "You've got something brown on your nose, Ambria."

She scowled at him.

Elyssa guided the ship down toward the River Thames. We glided over signs advertising river tours and along a narrow canal diverging from the river. The canal ran between apartment buildings and ended at a stone wall. Small boats bobbed next to equally small docks. It was a perfect place to hide a sky ship in the middle of the city.

The *Raptor* floated on water just fine, so Elyssa set us down in the water and extended the gangway to one of the docks.

I looked around to make sure the coast was clear and went down to the dock. From the outside, only a slight shimmer in the air indicated anything was there at all, but ripples in the water would give it away to anyone observant enough. I gave a thumbs-up even though I couldn't see anyone on the ship. "Good enough."

One by one, our crew appeared out of thin air as they descended the gangway and left the cover of camouflage. The air wrinkled and the illusion of a large yacht blinked into existence. The illusion didn't line up perfectly to the dimensions of the *Raptor*, so Adam and Elyssa seemed to walk right out of the hull.

"I don't want to chance burning through too much energy with full camouflage," Adam explained when he joined us. "But we probably shouldn't leave the ship here for long or someone's bound to start asking questions."

Bella nodded. "They might wonder how a boat that size fit into the canal."

"Well, let's not worry too much." Shelton patted his stomach. "Where are the food trucks?"

Conrad looked at his arcphone. "Nearly three miles from here. We'll need to take a taxi or a bus."

Shelton huffed. "Considering I haven't stepped foot in Eden in years, how in the hell am I supposed to pay for a taxi?"

Conrad removed a wad of currency from his wallet. "Perhaps with this."

Ambria glared at Shelton. "You really should think before you speak."

Max entered the fray. "Pot, meet kettle."

"Oh, hush, Max." Ambria put a finger to her lips. "Just because he's your idol doesn't mean he isn't an ass."

"Well, Harry can be quite a *culo*," Bella said. "But I love that about him."

Shelton snorted. "Yeah, I'm a lovable jackass, kid."

Ambria rolled her eyes. "I wouldn't go that far."

Conrad, as usual, seemed to ignore the entire exchange and walked down the sidewalk toward the road. "We might have to take two taxis."

"There are a lot of us." Cora hooked her arm in his. "Perhaps we could get ice cream like we did so long ago."

He looked at her, eyes wide. "You remember that?"

A little gasp escaped her lips. "Yes, I do." A tear trickled down her cheek. "Oh, Conrad, I wish I could remember it all."

Shelton lowered his usual speaking volume and leaned toward Max. "What's that about?"

Max ran a hand through his blond hair. "When Conrad revived Cora from the dead, she'd forgotten a lot of her former life, including Conrad."

"Ouch." He sighed. "I didn't have much of a family life when I was a kid."

"Me either." Max looked down. "My parents are pretty evil."

I didn't want to agree, but Xander had joined forces with Victus. "We can't control what our family is like, Max."

"Yeah, but it still sucks." He looked at Cora. "Conrad had it worse, but I'm glad he found someone like Cora."

Shelton patted him on the back. "For better or worse, you've got us now, kid."

Max beamed. "I like you all a lot better than anyone in my family."

The giggles of children echoed from a balcony above. I looked up and saw Thal fluttering near the fourth story of an apartment building.

Shelton stared up at her. "What in the holy hell is she doing?"

"Thal, get down here!" I said. "You need to disguise yourself."

Her forehead wrinkled. "Why?" She drifted down and hovered eye level with me. "Are the tiny humans here dangerous?"

A little girl on the balcony shouted, "Come back, tooth fairy!" Her little hands grasped the railing, but she was apparently too short to look over.

"I do not harvest teeth!" Thal shouted back. Her brow furrowed. "What monstrous, tooth-stealing Fae haunts the children of this land?"

"They think you're the tooth fairy?" Shelton guffawed. "Oh man, that's rich!"

"It's just a myth," Ivy said. "I used to put my teeth under a pillow so the tooth fairy would give me money for them, but Daelissa told me the truth. She said it was just Bigdaddy and Bigmomma who left me the money."

"Money for teeth?" Thal shuddered. "Barbaric."

Shelton huffed. "Look, can we just go get tacos?"

"Thal, it's important that you disguise yourself to look like us." I waved a hand toward the street. "Humans here don't know about magic, fairies, lycans, vampires, or any magical creatures. If they did, they'd freak out."

"Magical creatures?" Thal frowned. "I don't understand."

Light dawned in Elyssa's eyes. "Because you come from a land where most of the creatures are magical, at least according to our standards."

"Holy fart knuckles." Shelton scoffed. "Can't you just disguise yourself? I'm in dire need of a damned taco!"

Thal drifted to the ground, scowling at Shelton the entire time. Her body stretched and grew until she stood nearly eight feet tall, towering over us. "Fine. Let us go get this taco, whatever it is." Despite her giant stature, her voice remained diminutive."

Ivy giggled and jumped up. "You're so huge! Can you grow to fifty feet tall?"

Cora walked in a circle around Thal. "Impressive." She touched the fairy's arm. "This is not an illusion?"

"It is my limit." Thal shrugged. "Not all Fae can grow to such a size."

"Um, can you tone it back a little?" I said. "You'll draw more attention like this than if you walked around with fairy wings."

Thal patted my head like a dog's. "Do you feel tiny?"

I looked way up at her. "A little, but that's not the point."

She sighed. "Very well. Maintaining this size is strenuous anyway." Thal shrank back down to five feet and some change. "I can hold this form indefinitely."

"How does that work?" Adam looked her up and down. "Do your insides and everything grow with the rest of you?"

"Everything maintains proportion." Thal shrugged. "Some of the Fae can shift to animal forms. Some cannot shift at all but are powerful in other ways."

Shelton clapped his hands. "Dude, tacos! We can talk about this stuff on the way."

"For once, I agree with Shelton." Ambria pointed where the path met the road. "Shall we get him his taco fix?"

Conrad took her hand and started walking. "It's a grand idea."

We'd hardly taken a few steps when two police stepped around the corner. The taller of the two brandished a baton. "You, there. Halt!"

CHAPTER 15

C onrad stopped. "Who, us?"

The police held their batons at the ready but didn't seem to have any other weapons. Both wore tall domed helmets with a band of black-and-white checkers near the brim. Navy vests covered white shirts.

The tall one held up a hand. "All of you, halt."

The other officer did a double-take when he saw the ship. "How in the bloody hell did that get in here?"

I stepped to the front. "What's the problem, officer?"

He grunted. "What sort of accent is that? Where are you from?"

That was a good question considering how long I'd been away from Atlanta. I probably had one hell of a mashed-up accent going. "I'm American."

"Don't sound like it." His eyes wandered around our group. "We received calls of a disturbance."

"I can assure you it wasn't us," Elyssa said. "We're just out to get some food."

The second officer tugged the sleeve of his partner. "Where did that yacht come from, Albert?"

"I don't know, George." Albert jabbed a finger toward the canal. "We'll just have to ask the river authority, won't we?" He turned back to us. "I'd like to see identification, please."

Oh, crap. "I don't have any with me," I said. "We're just out for some food."

Ambria put her hands on her hips. "I'm sorry, but do you have proof we've done anything wrong?"

"Miss, I received reports that a girl was climbing up the balconies and that a large group was disturbing the peace." Albert raked a stern gaze around. "Your group fits the bill."

Thal walked up to them and flicked her fingers. Black dust sparkled and the officers burst into bouts of sneezing.

"Chemical attack!" George gripped his throat and dropped limply to the ground. Albert followed him an instant later.

Shelton jumped back. "Holy farting fairies, did you kill them?"

"Of course not." Thal knelt next to Albert and put an ear to his mouth. "He is asleep, as I had hoped."

Elyssa groaned. "Well, now we've got to leave. They'll be sure to set off an alert when they wake up."

"But, tacos." Shelton sounded like he wanted to cry.

"They will sleep for hours," Thal said. "We still have time for this taco thing."

Elyssa looked down at the slumbering police and back at the camouflaged ship. "Ugh. I don't like it, but I could use a taco myself." She lifted

George off the ground and slung him over a shoulder like a sack of potatoes. She looked around. "Find somewhere to put them that won't look obvious."

"Up there." Ivy pointed to the second-floor balcony fifteen feet above us. "No one will see them."

I tapped Ivy's shoulder. "Give me a boost."

She cupped her hand and counted to three before thrusting upward. I jumped at the apex and flew up and over the railing. The apartment was dark, so I leaned over and motioned to Elyssa. "I'll take George first."

She held him out. I channeled webs of Murk and wrapped them around him, then pulled him up and laid him down on the tiled floor. I repeated the process for Albert and snuggled him up against his partner. I leapt over the railing and nearly face-planted when I tried to execute a three-point landing.

Elyssa laughed. "You really need to practice those, babe."

I threw up my hands. "It's harder than it looks."

"We good?" Shelton said. "Tacos now?"

"Yes, Shelton, tacos now!" everyone shouted back at him.

He looked mollified. "Good."

Bella rolled her eyes. "That's my man."

Conrad and Ambria took the lead and headed down the path. The rest of us trailed behind them. Max walked next to Shelton, asking him questions about spell casting. Shelton's hangry scowl vanished as he started discussing techniques.

Elyssa raised an eyebrow. "I can't believe I'm saying this, but Shelton might actually make a good teacher."

Adam came up beside us and spoke in low tones. "I think Max reminds Shelton of himself when he was a kid."

"Rough childhood?" Elyssa said.

Adam snorted. "That's putting it mildly."

I nodded toward the head of the pack where Conrad and Ambria walked. "Can't imagine it's rougher than what Conrad had."

"Or Ambria for that matter." Elyssa shook her head. "I still can't wrap my head around half the stories they told us. An orphanage selling Arcane kids as slaves? How did they not go insane?"

"Or turn evil." Adam shuddered. "They've seen nearly as much blood and gore as the rest of us, and we've fought wars."

Thal looked around in wonder when we emerged from the alley. "So few trees." She scuffed her shoe against the sidewalk. "Everything is stone."

"Concrete and buildings," Ivy said. "Humans bulldoze everything else."

Evadora growled. "They have no respect for nature."

"It is a wonder a single forest still stands," Cora said.

A man bumped my elbow in a hurry to get past. My fists clenched and heat rushed to my face. I growled and lunged for him.

Elyssa gripped my arm and spun me around. "Justin, what's wrong?"

The anger evaporated, leaving me confused. "Nothing. My temper flared."

She grimaced. "I wonder if Baal's spirit is already influencing you."

Fear seeped into my stomach. "My god, I'm losing it." I grabbed her hand. "You'll have to help me keep my chill."

"I'll do what I can." Elyssa gripped my hand tighter. "I hope Emily is easy to find."

Adam fiddled with his phone. "I looked up Tyler Rock on the nom internet. He apparently vanished a long time ago and is presumed dead. There's nothing about Emily Glass that I could find."

"Dead?" I shook my head. "How?"

"The nom sources have no further information." Adam shrugged. "Emily and Tyler worked with the Custodians, so maybe they have a record."

"My phone's updating about a decade worth of apps." Shelton held out his phone to show a screen full of progress bars. "There's one hell of a system update coming from Orange. I hope it works with all those modifications we made to the software."

"Same with my phone." Adam tapped on his screen. "The Templar website isn't coming up, so I can't look up any info on the Custodians."

"Emily and Tyler worked with someone named George Walker," I said. "Maybe we can find him."

"Let me try the Atlanta office." Elyssa took out her arcphone and dialed some symbols. The phone beeped and a recording came on. "The symbols you dialed are disconnected and no longer in use. Please check the symbols and try again." She disconnected. "That's not a good sign."

"Whoa, the Atlanta branch is disconnected?" Adam fiddled around on his phone. "Hey, most of the Overnet sites are gone."

"Because the Overworld was practically dismantled by Victus." I tried a few sites on my phone, but none worked. "Looks like we've got to do this the old-fashioned way."

"You mean travel to Atlanta and dig around?" Adam said.

"Yep, exactly."

"My phone's lagging with all these updates," Elyssa said. "I'm going to wait until it's done then we can look some more."

"Yes!" Shelton's jubilant cry drew the attention of everyone on the street. He didn't care. He didn't even look back as he raced toward food trucks two blocks away.

The rest of us hurried to keep up. Ivy and Evadora held hands and skipped down the sidewalk, singing gaily about taco time. Thal's face screwed up in comical confusion, but she ran to keep up.

"Bloody tourists," a man said. "You'd think they never had tacos before."

"Can't blame them, really," a woman replied. "I could use a few tacos myself."

By the time we caught up with Shelton, he'd already located the taco truck, a beat-up old box on wheels with the longest line. Shelton stood impatiently at the end of a long queue, lines of pain etched in his face. "Man, this is going to take forever!"

Thal tilted her head. She flicked her fingers and yellow sparkles drifted onto some of the people in front of Shelton. They burst into shouts and screams of alarm and ran off in all directions. Those untouched by the dust saw the others scattering and took off after them, a flock of sheep following the leaders. Only a stout few remained in place, determined to get their prize no matter the danger.

A confused woman at the neighboring vegan food truck held out her hands defensively and looked around. "What's wrong? Why is everyone running?"

"A big rat," Ivy said. "Run before it eats your foot!"

The woman blinked a few times then shook her head in disapproval before carrying on with her business.

Shelton grinned at Thal. "You're a real gem."

"There are so many people that you must wait behind them for sustenance?" Thal turned in a circle. "It is no wonder my people cannot abide humans. They are everywhere!"

The woman in front of her gave her a concerned look as she paid for her meal.

The food truck chef leaned out of the window and looked around.

"Where the bloody hell did they all go?"

"Doesn't matter." Shelton stepped up to the window. "I haven't had a taco in years. This is an extreme emergency."

"Extreme emergency?" The man frowned but took Shelton's order for three fish tacos, two fried chicken tacos, and one of all the others. When asked to pay, Shelton nudged Conrad. "Thanks for lunch, Daddy Warbucks."

Conrad sighed and produced the cash.

"If you buy mine, I'll pay you back later." I turned my pockets inside out to demonstrate my lack of funds.

Conrad shrugged. "Fine. Everyone, get what you want."

Everyone ordered, even Thal, and we sat down at benches in a nearby plaza.

"I thought Fae didn't eat meat," Elyssa said.

"I am Unfae. Even so, I prefer seafood." Thal regarded her shrimp taco suspiciously. "What is the chunky liquid on the green leaves?"

"It's salsa." I took a bite of my barbeque taco and moaned in pleasure. "Oh man, it's so good."

She took a tiny bite, tested it, took a larger piece in her mouth. "It is delicious!" Thal devoured the rest and turned to Conrad. "May I have another taco?"

Conrad counted his dwindling funds and sighed. "Yes, go ahead."

Thal returned with four more tacos.

"That was an interesting trick you pulled earlier, Thal." I wiped my mouth with a napkin. "What did you do to those people in the line?"

"I filled them with fear." Thal bit into another taco and moaned in pleasure. "Some Fae can incite emotions with their dust, but fear is the easiest. Hate is also easy."

"You can make them feel fear indefinitely?" Elyssa asked.

"Well, if you continue to sprinkle them." Thal picked up a fish taco. "There are other ways to increase the duration, but you risk damaging the psyche."

"Fascinating." Adam sipped on a beer. "So your magic centers on the fairy dust that comes out of your hands?"

"The aether flows through us." Thal formed black flames on her hands. "Enchanting it only makes it look like dust." She rubbed thumb and forefinger together and green dust fell on the wooden table. A flower stem sprouted from a crack and grew several inches. A yellow flower blossomed at the end.

"Whoa." Adam leaned forward and sniffed the flower. "You can grow plants from nothing?"

"There was a seed trapped in the crack." Thal took another bite of taco. "I gave it the energy it needed to grow."

"We can make plants grow too." Evadora hopped up from the neighboring table and waved a hand at the flower. It bent toward her, as if yearning to touch her. "Not all of them can outgrow their original size, like this one." She touched the flower. Its roots came free and she transferred it to the soil where grass and trees grew in the plaza. "Now it can be happy and thrive."

"Beautiful." Thal smiled. "I hope you can free your people from slumber. This world needs help."

When we finished with lunch, it was time for goodbyes. I hugged Ivy. "Be careful in the Glimmer. It's crazy dangerous there."

"I know." She kissed my cheek. "But it'll be so cool."

"I would love to see the Glimmer," Bella said. "Harry, why don't we go with them?"

"I've had enough of other realms." Shelton wiped a stain off his leather duster. "I want to enjoy Eden all I can before Baal shows his ugly face."

Bella smiled. "Would you mind if I went with them?"

"I told the guardians to let people pass," Conrad said. "Any of you who want to go won't need to worry about them."

Shelton winced. "Well, yeah, if you want, hon. I was kinda hoping for some snu-snu on the ride back to the States."

Adam's face screwed up into a grimace.

"I'm still sore from yesterday." Bella pulled him down for a long kiss. "I'll make it up when I see you in a few days."

"We might be all the way across the world by then," Shelton said.

"That's what Obsidian Arches are for," Bella replied.

"Oh, yeah." Shelton scratched the back of his neck. "We've been in Seraphina for so long I forgot we have those here."

"Your old underground mansion is still intact at Arcane University," Max said. "You can even use the omniarch."

"I'm afraid it's a bit untidy from fighting my father," Conrad said.

"Dude, the Mansion." I sighed with longing. "If we weren't in such a hurry, I'd love to go see it."

"I wonder whatever happened to Cutsauce," Elyssa said. "We left him there when we went to Seraphina."

"Galfandor might know," Conrad said. "We need to go to Arcane University once we get Justin's situation sorted anyway, because the Overworld needs to be put back in order."

"There's a lot that needs to be fixed." Elyssa sighed. "Well, we should get going."

Cora, Ivy, Evadora, and Bella climbed into a taxi and left. The rest of us walked back to the ship.

"I don't see why we need to go with Justin," Ambria said to Conrad. "Why don't we go to Arcane University and get started putting it back together?"

"I'm certain Galfandor can manage things for now," Conrad said. "Hopefully, he's already deposed Xander and restored order to Queens Gate."

Max's jaw tightened. "I hope Xander is rotting in jail."

I slowed down to walk beside Conrad and Ambria. "You guys don't have to come. If you want to help Galfandor fix things on this side of the pond, that's fine."

"No, I definitely want to come." Max glanced at Shelton. "I've got a lot to learn."

Ambria reasserted her opinion. "I most definitely think we should stay, Conrad. They can find Emily without us."

Conrad looked uncertain. "Well, I suppose there is a lot to do here."

"I'll hail a cab." Ambria waved her arm.

"I'm staying with Shelton," Max said.

"I would prefer to stay with you all." Conrad looked back and forth between Ambria and me. "But I guess you don't really need us along."

"We'll be fine," I assured him. "We've also got all the Templars, vampires, and more that'll soon be pouring back into Eden. I still have no idea what we plan to do with them."

"Okay." Conrad seemed to deflate a little. "Let me know if you need me, okay?"

"Definitely." I shook his hand and waved goodbye to Ambria who'd already procured a taxi.

After they left, it was down to Me, Elyssa, Shelton, Adam, Max, and Thal.

"This is exciting." Max grinned. "I get to go on an adventure without Ambria."

"You guys are always at each other's throats." Shelton chuckled. "I don't know how you deal with it."

"Well, we love each other like sister and brother, but we fight like it too." Max shrugged. "I wouldn't give it up for the world, but even siblings need a break from each other."

"I feel, ya." Shelton clapped him on the back. "I'll give you some tips for dealing with women."

Elyssa groaned. "I'd be wary of any advice Shelton gives you on females."

Shelton looked hurt. "Hey, I got Bella, didn't I?"

"I'm still trying to figure that one out." Elyssa couldn't hide her grin.

"All charm, baby."

Adam snorted. "You can even hide the stink from an asshole if you put on enough body spray."

Shelton rubbed his fingers together like a cook adding ingredients to a recipe. "Little bit of bleach on the anus, some deodorizer, and presto!"

Elyssa's nose wrinkled. "Ick!"

Thal's forehead pinched with confusion. "What is bleach and why would one apply it to an anus?"

Adam burst into laughter. "I'm not sure you want to know."

"Do Fae poop?" I couldn't resist asking.

Thal blinked. "What?"

"Do you poop?"

It seemed Dolpha's translator hadn't converted that word before— surprising considering all the scatological humor we enjoyed.

"Yes. The Fae must poop, as you call it, the same as most creatures." Thal frowned at my burst of laughter. "You find this humorous?"

Shelton, Adam, and I doubled over with laughter

"Pooping and farting are the funniest things in the worlds to boys." Elyssa let out a sigh of the long-suffering. "Don't ask me why."

Thal pursed her lips. "Farting?"

"Passing gas." Shelton blew a raspberry.

"Ah. Fae farts are quite odiferous, but I will make sure to indulge you so you can enjoy it."

Shelton and I burst into more laughter.

Adam made a face. "I can't imagine they're any more stinky than Shelton's."

I chuckled. "Yeah, talk about supernatural."

Elyssa groaned and quickened her pace.

When we reached the alley with the ship, I peeked around the corner to make sure George and Albert hadn't woken and summoned an army of police. They must have still been snoozing on the balcony because there wasn't a single person in sight.

Elyssa released a breath. "I expected to find more police waiting for us."

"Great minds think alike." I took her hand and headed in.

The alley stretched for thirty feet before opening up into the area with the canal. When I stepped onto the path, it was as if I'd crossed behind a curtain. The empty canal vanished, replaced by one teeming with people in tactical gear.

"What the hell?" Shelton shouted.

I didn't even have time to identify the uniforms before someone aimed a big silver rifle at me and fired.

CHAPTER 16

Time seemed to slow as my demonic reflexes kicked in. I dodged left. A black sphere the size of a marble flew toward Elyssa. Her reflexes were even better than mine. She ducked and rolled. The marble struck Shelton in the chest. Electricity crisscrossed his body. He convulsed and went down in a heap.

I didn't have time to check on him because more pistols and rifles oriented on us. Elyssa swept the feet from beneath the nearest attacker and drew her light bow from the holster on her side. She drew back her hand and a glowing white bowstring appeared with a crackling blue arrow already nocked. She fired. The arrow exploded on impact with a uniformed figure and knocked them back twenty feet.

Every attacker wore a black uniform and a full-faced helmet concealing their identity. The grunts from the first two people Elyssa took out sounded feminine.

I swung up a foot and kicked an attacker in the full-faced helmet, eliciting another feminine cry. She spun around and face-planted on the ground. Two more operatives fell to my fists. Spells crackled past me. I looked back and saw Max guarding Shelton's unmoving form. These people seemed to be noms, but I couldn't afford to play nice. I channeled a shield and deflected another volley of black projectiles.

A figure appeared on the second story balcony behind the other attackers and shouted in a foreign language. I couldn't understand her at first, but then she repeated herself. "Seraphim! Seraphim!" The accent sounded Italian.

"Who the hell are you people?" I channeled a sphere of Brilliance. "Don't make me blast you to ash!"

More operatives appeared on the balconies. One of them aimed a rifle with a wide muzzle at me. I channeled more power into my shield. Gray energy rings rippled through the air with a high-pitched whine. Even though I felt no impact, cracks formed in the shield and it began to crumble.

The same voice shouted again. "Fire electro rounds!"

A volley of black spheres came at me. I slashed at them with a wide beam of Brilliance. Electricity crackled in the air. My shield crumbled so I rolled away from the gray beam and fired a burst of Murk at the closest attacker. I heard a familiar cry and looked back. Elyssa lay on the ground. Max sprawled unconscious across Shelton. Thal was nowhere to be seen.

"No!" Demonic rage surged. Before I could stop myself, I leapt into the air. Agony tore through my back. Webbed wings unfurled to either side and caught air. A part of me was stunned by this development. I'd never sprouted demon wings before. My demon side roared in fury.

"None shall attack Kalesh and survive!" My voice was deep and guttural even though I hadn't manifested into full demon form. "You will burn in the fires of my wrath!"

About a dozen electro rounds hit me at once. Electricity burned through every nerve fiber in my body. My arm stretched toward the leader on the balcony, black claws displacing my fingernails. A roar of rage and pain filled the air. Then I fell to the ground and the lights went out.

CONRAD

"Something's wrong." Conrad banged the partition window in the back of the cab.

The cab driver glanced back. "What is it?"

"Stop here, please." Conrad read the meter and handed him payment.

"Conrad, what in the world?" Ambria resisted the pull of his hand but finally got out. "What's wrong?"

He pulled her to the sidewalk and stared across the road. The entrance to the Queensway subway station was there. Not far from it was the narrow entrance to the parking deck where they needed to go. A hidden lift inside would take them deep beneath the London to the Queens Gate waystation.

The dark entrance always looked menacing, probably due to protective enchantments meant to keep noms away. But something else triggered Conrad's unease. Something about the two groups of watchful women hovering near the entrance. They wore dark clothes, mostly jeans and long coats. Though it was London, today was far too warm for coats. The furtive glances they cast at everyone who walked past the entrance only increased Conrad's suspicions.

"I think those people work for Xander." Conrad took Ambria's hand and pretended to look at pastries in the display window of a bakery. "They're watching everyone who goes in."

Ambria's eyes widened. "Do you think they got Cora's group?"

"I don't know." Conrad watched them from the corner of his eye. "They were only a few minutes ahead of us."

"Maybe they work for Galfandor," Ambria suggested. "They might simply be rounding up anyone loyal to Victus."

"Maybe." Conrad felt a little foolish for not thinking of that. "What do you suggest we do to make sure?"

"We bait them." Ambria squeezed his hand. "I'll go toward the entrance. You protect me if they do anything."

Conrad's eyes widened. "There must be eight of them. I don't know if I can handle that many Arcanes."

"I can protect myself too." Ambria grinned. "I'm no weakling."

"It's too risky." Conrad stared at an eclair in the display and caught a curious look from the baker behind the counter.

"We might not have a choice." Ambria tugged his sleeve. "They're coming this way."

Four of them crossed the road, eyes locked on Conrad and Ambria. Conrad resisted the urge to draw on the primal fount. The magical glow would be a dead giveaway. "Don't stare at them, Ambria. Pretend you're interested in the bakery."

"Conrad, we've been standing here for five minutes."

A woman with shoulder-length blonde hair held a shiny black cube in her palm. Glowing lines on the surface grew brighter as they approached. She looked up from the object. "Confirmed."

All four women drew small silver pistols from beneath their coats. Ambria's wand flew from her holster and into her hand as if drawn by an invisible string. Conrad reached through the darkness in his mind and found the glowing blue waters of the primal fount. His spirit-self plunged both hands into the well.

Azure fire crackled across his skin. Even before the pistols fired, he spun a shield. Black spheres exploded from muzzles. Electricity arced across the shield where they struck.

Conrad held blue fire in his hands. "Who are you?"

"Submit," the woman with the black cube said. "Or face the consequences."

"I'll show you consequences." Ambria held up her wand threateningly. "Did you attack a group of women who came through here before us?"

The woman tilted her head slightly, black eyes showing no emotion. "You are the first to come here today. You will submit."

The other group of women near the parking garage entrance sprinted across the street. A tall woman with a shaved head unslung a rifle with a conical muzzle, almost like an old-fashioned musket. She stepped in front of the others and leveled her weapon. Three broke off from the group and flanked toward the street, unable to fit between the shield and the bakery. Conrad wove a curve into the shield and stretched it out into the street.

A car struck the shield. Tires screeched and horns blared. Nearby noms blinked from their everyday stupor and stared at the spectacle unfolding before them. Phones appeared in hands, cameras recording.

The woman with the rifle opened fire. Gray rings of energy pulsed forth, rippling against the shield. Conrad felt the shield weave unbinding. He reinforced it, adding another layer. But even if he could hold this barrier, the other women would soon make it around the end.

A car on the other side of the road lost control and skidded across the median. One of the women leapt onto the hood of the car and aimed her silver pistol over the shield.

Ambria slung a spell. The green energy bolt struck the pistol from the woman's hand. "Who are you? What do you want?"

"Submit," the blonde woman said. "You cannot escape."

Three women made it around the shield. A double-decker bus jerked to a halt, temporarily blocking their path. Noms scattered, screaming. Others remained in place, phones recording.

Conrad tied off the weakening shield and grabbed Ambria's arm. "Run." They dashed the opposite way from their attackers. "We've got to get back to the ship."

Something whirred overhead. A black quadcopter drone paced them from above. Ambria flicked her wand and blasted it from the sky. The wreckage crashed onto the sidewalk behind them. People screamed and jumped away.

"Bloody hell!" A man in a business suit jumped back. "She's got a gun!"

Panic erupted. The crowds of pedestrians scattered, antelope racing from a cheetah. A man in police uniform brandished a baton and waved at them. "You there, halt!"

"I don't have a gun!" Ambria brandished her wand. "It's just a stick."

The officer ducked behind a rubbish bin as if he'd just shot at her. "Drop your weapons!" Like most of the police in London, he was unarmed. But it wouldn't take long for others to respond.

Conrad dodged down an alley and blocked the entrance with another shield weave. Ambria sprinted past him and stopped at the intersection of another alley to consider their path.

"Straight ahead." She ran to the end and slowed once she reached the sidewalk. "Act normal."

Pedestrians crowded the sidewalk and cars waited their turn at a busy roundabout. No one here had heard the disturbances a block over. Four of the attackers emerged from an alley on the other side of the round-about. The woman with the black cube held it up. It seemed to tug her in Conrad's direction.

"Is that some sort of Arcane detector?" Ambria clenched her wand. "We can beat four of them, Conrad."

"Right out in the open?" He looked around for a sign of the other pursuers. "We can't stir up the noms any more than they already are, or it'll be Paris all over again."

Ambria shuddered. "You're right. We don't want an army of police descending on us."

"On the other hand, we can't keep running if they can track us."

"It must have a limited range." Ambria looked back down the alley, but it remained empty. "Otherwise it would drag them back and forth every time it caught a signal from another Arcane."

"It took them a moment to lock onto us earlier." Conrad watched as the women slowly made their way toward the hidden prey.

"We can't use our illusion spell to trick the detector, so we have to either outdistance it or forcibly take it from them."

"We can't sneak up on them either." Conrad put a shrubbery between himself and line of sight with the women. "It'll take them a while to get across the road. Let's use the time wisely."

"I think we should circle around and go to Queens Gate. That woman said we were the first, so that means Ivy and the others haven't crossed paths when them yet." Ambria peeked around the shrubbery. "We can't just let them walk into a trap."

"If they haven't been through there, where could they be?" Conrad led her down the sidewalk away from their stalkers and around the corner at the next intersection. A siren wailed in the distance. It might be random coincidence, but it was probably backup for the policeman.

Ambria took out her arcphone and looked at the map while they walked. "Got it."

"Got what?" Conrad leaned over her shoulder. "Are you looking for a getaway route?"

"No, I think I know where Ivy and the others are." She grabbed his hand and tugged him down the street. They went a block over and cut left, making a wide circle that would eventually take them back toward the parking deck.

Ambria scanned the sky for another drone while Conrad looked behind and all around for the attackers. They spotted the second group three blocks ahead, coming their way. This group also had a black box.

"Yes!" a jubilant shout drew the attention of passersby. Ivy danced on the sidewalk, a double-scoop of ice cream bouncing precariously atop a cone.

The others were right where Ambria suspected—at an ice cream shop.

"I love ice cream." Evadora bounded along beside her, skin flushed peach to blend in with the noms. Cora and Bella sat at a nearby table, oblivious to the threat lurking behind them.

The woman with the cube rotated her head toward Ivy and their group stalked toward them.

"Oh no." Ambria cupped hands to her mouth, but Conrad gripped her arm.

"Wait. We don't want to draw attention again." He shouldered through the throng of pedestrians and walked quickly, trying not to stand out from the crowd.

The woman with the cube locked eyes with Conrad. She said something, and her companions ran toward their quarry. At this pace, they'd reach Ivy and the others at the same time as Conrad. A drone drifted over the buildings and flew toward Ivy and the others. A turret with a muzzle aimed their way. It would open fire long before Conrad reached Ivy.

Before he could shout a warning, Bella perked up, as if a sixth sense warned her of danger. She dropped her ice cream and spun, a wand appearing in her hand. A narrow beam sliced the drone in half. It crashed to the ground sending great arcs of electricity surging across the sidewalk. Pedestrians convulsed in silent agony and went down. Panicked noms shouted and screamed in alarm, scattering like sheep.

With the sidewalk clear, the attackers drew pistols and came at Bella.

The dhampyr blurred to the side and leapt twenty feet. A quick chop to the neck took down the first assailant. Bella swept the legs from beneath a second attacker and slammed a fist into her chest. Cora waved her hand at a tree growing from a planter in the sidewalk. It whacked a third attacker with flailing branches. Bella incapacitated the final one.

Conrad and Ambria reached the scene, breathless.

"That was amazing!" Ambria looked down at the fallen women. "Where did you learn to fight?"

Bella rifled through the clothes of the first woman. She took the silver pistol and tossed it to Cora. "I took magitsu a century ago, but I'm a bit rusty."

Conrad grabbed the black cube. It hummed and sparked. "Ah!" He threw it into the street just as it crackled and burned into a molten husk. Another crackle and pop drew his attention to the silver pistol Bella had tossed to Cora. It melted into slag where she dropped it.

Ambria touched another pistol. After several seconds, it too began to melt down. "If we can't have them, neither can they!" She grabbed the other two and let them self-destruct.

Evadora watched with great interest as she licked her ice cream cone.

Ivy paused eating for a heartbeat. "Who are these crazy people?"

"No identification." Bella perked up and looked around. "I hear sirens."

Clusters of frightened and enthralled noms hovered nearby, phones out and recording video.

"We should go." Cora stepped over unconscious pedestrians and motioned the rest of them to follow.

Conrad caught up and slowed her down. "We saw these people outside the entrance to the Queens Gate parking deck. For all we know, it's not safe to go inside."

"If we're to reach the Glimmer, we have little choice." Cora shook her head. "We must take the chance."

Ivy skipped over to Ambria. "Why are you and Conrad here? I thought you were going with my bro."

"We decided to contact Galfandor and let him know everything that's happened," Ambria said. "But those women in black were waiting outside the parking deck. They have black cubes that can track Arcanes."

"Or magic users in general," Conrad added.

"Cora is right. We should go to Queens Gate." Bella stared at one of the assailants. "These women are noms."

"Are they infernus?" Ambria said.

Bella shook her head. "Infernus are very good copies of people, but their blood doesn't taste the same." She flashed her fangs. "I took a sample to make sure."

Ambria flinched. "I didn't realize you were a dhampyr like Elyssa."

"Come, let's go." Cora stepped around unconscious bodies.

The others hurried to catch up.

"This is troubling." Bella looked back over her shoulder. "If the noms have technology to hunt supers, the entire Overworld is in grave danger."

CHAPTER 17

J ustin

A sharp pain in my ribs tore me from slumber. I jerked awake and lashed out. A gloved fist hit my ribs again and there wasn't squat I could do about it. Thick metal shackles held my wrists together. An even thicker bar connected the cuffs to leg restraints. Clamps held the contraption to a metal chair.

I blinked, tried to take in on my surroundings, but my bleary eyes had trouble focusing. Water splashed in my face. It was probably meant to shock me even further awake, but all it did was clear the gunk out of my eyes. An imperious woman in black tactical gear stood next to another woman with a shaved head.

They spoke to each other in English, but it took a moment for me to make sense of it.

"Definitely one of the class three bogies, Commander," the woman in tactical gear said to the woman with the shaved head. "It's a good thing we took him by surprise."

The commander traced a finger along puckered scars on her neck. "You said he demonstrated demon class abilities as well."

"Yes, commander. Wings and a tail."

The commander walked in a circle around me. "A hybrid?"

"We don't know."

I blinked water from my eyes. "Who the hell are you people?"

The commander motioned with her hand.

A man stepped from the darkness. He shoved a metal device into my ribs. Electricity burned through my nerves. It wasn't the worst pain I'd ever felt, but I screamed anyway. If that wasn't enough, the muscle spasms released everything from my bladder.

"No!" A neck clamp limited movement, but I managed to look down enough to see I was naked as a jaybird. "You just made me piss myself, jackass!"

That earned another jolt. I gritted my teeth to stop from screaming and nearly bit off my tongue.

"You will speak only when given permission." The commander's ice-blue eyes reminded me of Thomas's and the edge in her voice made it clear she was used to absolute authority. She ran a hand over her smooth-shaved scalp. "When I give you permission."

I flashed a grin but held my tongue this time. There was no sense in getting shocked to hell and back when I could bide my time and cut my way out of these shackles. I channeled a trickle of Brilliance to my right index finger just to test. Crystals on the handcuffs glowed and the energy dissipated.

The commander noted it. "Definitely class three."

I tried again with more power, but the crystals drained the energy almost immediately. *Some sort of magic-dampening gems?* I'd seen my share of devices meant to interdict magical abilities, but nothing like these. Testing them out in front of my captors didn't seem like the brightest option, so I fought back my panic and stared at the commander.

She asked a question. "Are you a hybrid?"

There's no harm in answering. Plan B for escape was to use my demonic strength. If I let them shock the hell out of me, I'd be too dazed to do anything. "I'm part Daemos and part Seraphim."

The commander raised an eyebrow and turned to her subordinate. "I did not realize the two species could mate."

"The creatures will mate with anything," the other woman replied. "But it is interesting their genes are compatible."

"Where is Dr. Sidana?" The commander looked back towards the door.

"I assume she is on her way." The other woman tapped her watch. "Locate Dr. Sidana."

"Prison level, quadrant one," a robotic female voice replied. "Enroute to class three holding."

"Very good." The commander walked around me. "Are there others like you?"

"No," I lied. As she stood behind me, I realized something even more disturbing than the anti-magic crystals. *I can't sense her at all.* I closed my eyes and hoped my demon abilities worked. My demon vision flicked on. In most cases, I could easily seduce women by latching onto their auras. But where I would normally see golden or white soul essence hovering around humans, I saw only a flickering blackness around these. Either these women didn't have auras, or something masked them.

For the first time, real fear speared its icy cold claws into my guts. If I couldn't sense their auras, I couldn't feed my demon side. Any brute strength I burned would be unrecoverable. The crystals ensured I couldn't use magic. In other words, I was helpless as a human.

"Where are you from originally?" the commander asked.

I answered in a meek voice. "Atlanta."

"Very good." She stepped in front of me. "Since you've been a good boy, I will let you ask one question."

I stared blankly, unsure what to ask.

The commander broke the silence. "Very well. I will answer your earlier question—who are we?" She clasped her hands behind her back. "We are Razor Echelon. The secret weapon that keeps humans safe from the monsters, and I am Commander Edge."

The other woman slashed a hand sideways like sword and saluted. "Razor, Aye!"

"Wow." I scoffed. "Razor Edge. So original."

The electric prongs stabbed into my ribs and I screamed in surprise and pain. *These assholes better pray I never get loose!* I glared at the man with the cattle prod. "What the hell is your problem, Proddy McMasterson? Were you unloved as a child?"

His forehead pinched, and he looked like he wanted to jab me again. A flick of Edge's fingers sent him back to his corner.

Edge regarded me with a dispassionate smile. "We have moved from one tumor to another, cutting each blight from this world, purifying it. We know the approximate location of another hidden city somewhere below London."

Queens Gate. How many other pocket dimensions have they purified? Had they destroyed them? Imprisoned the people there? I didn't dare ask a question, so I waited for hers even though I knew what it would be.

The commander leaned toward me. "How do you reach Queens Gate? Where is the secret entrance?"

I didn't want her to have the answer, so I lied. "I don't know. I'm not from here." *Do they know about other realms?* I had to be careful about spilling the beans on anything else. Then again, if they wanted to go to Seraphina and fight Baal, they were totally welcome to try.

She stared unblinkingly into my eyes. A finger twitched and the jackass with the cattle prod did his job again.

I gritted my teeth and glared at the witch with all the hatred I could muster. Simmering anger flared. My inner demon snarled and slammed against his cage. Between the shocks and the inner turmoil, I lost control. My inner monster broke free.

The man with the cattle prod yelped in alarm and leapt back. Even Edge took a few steps back. My skin shaded blue and my head felt heavier. It took a moment to realize I'd grown horns and partially manifested into demon form. The effects faded as quickly as they'd come. My horns clattered to the floor, thin ebony spirals not much larger than a goat's.

I will devour her. Kalesh licked his chops and strained against my control. *I grow stronger and soon you cannot stop me.*

In case you hadn't noticed, I'm covered from head to toe in magic-proof shackles. We can't feed on her essence. How do you propose we devour the commander if we can't even move?

Kalesh mentally snarled at me but didn't supply an answer.

You're a moron!

He didn't rise to the bait. Or maybe since he was part of me, I didn't rise to the bait against myself. *Damn this is confusing.*

The commander picked up one of my horns. "Fascinating. We have encountered only a handful of spawn."

A young woman with a thin computer tablet entered the room. Her dark eyes flared when she saw me. "Whoa. This is the hybrid spawn?"

"Indeed, Dr. Sidana." Edge turned to her. "A very rare breed. Run the usual battery of tests."

"Yes, Commander." Dr. Sidana secured a loose strand of black hair behind her ear and began tapping on the tablet. She looked up every so often and softly spoke into the tablet.

The commander turned back to me. "Back to my earlier question. Where is the secret entrance to Queens Gate?"

My mind still felt scrambled from all the shocking, but I'd had a moment to contemplate what I needed to do. I couldn't give up information about Queens Gate. I had to do everything I could to keep them in the dark. "I told you I don't know." My ribs felt the agony of the prod again.

The commander grabbed a handful of my hair and yanked me closer. "Tell me the truth, beast."

"That is the truth, bitch!"

Proddy McMasterson must have cranked up the voltage because I saw stars when the prods stabbed into my ribs the next time. The room faded in and out of vision.

"Please don't damage him too much," Dr. Sidana said. "I need him to be conscious for the physical."

"Very well." Edge slapped me repeatedly on the cheek until my bleary eyes focused on her. She was practically nose-to-nose with me. "We will see you soon." Edge backed away and touched the puckered scars on her neck. What I hadn't noticed before were the dozens of tiny white scars dotting her skin—the kind of scars left by sharp fangs.

I bared my teeth. "Not if I see you first."

Miraculously, Johnny McProdmeister didn't jolt me again.

Once the room cleared of everyone except my favorite cattle prod handler and the doctor, Dr. Sidana attached her tablet to a rolling cart and cleared her throat. "My name is Dr. Pari Sidana, but you may call me Pari. I have three certifications in supernatural taxonomy, including vampires, werewolves, and general shifter studies. Though I am not certified in either the Seraphim or the Daemos physiology and super-natural composition, I do have a working knowledge."

"Where do you get certified for that? DeVry University Online?"

"No, our organization has its own teachers and certification programs." The jab at her credentials seemed to have sailed right over her head. She strapped a white device with a digital display around my lower bicep. It swelled with air and took my blood pressure. "Interesting." She entered the info on her tablet.

"My name is Dr. Evil, but you can call me Justin."

Pari didn't even look up from her tablet. She took blood. Brandished a Q-Tip and took some samples from my privates then used a control stick that tilted the chair forward so she could violate me with a gloved finger.

An inhuman bleating noise escaped my throat. "Get your finger out of my ass!"

She snapped off the rubber glove and discarded it in a red trash can. "Subject's prostate is normal. Stool sample taken and will be sent for analysis with other fluids."

I couldn't remember feeling so completely humiliated in my life. "Why are you doing this to me?"

"We've never captured a spawn before," Pari said matter-of-factly. "It's important we form a baseline even if you are a half-breed."

She didn't seem as closed-mouthed as Edge, so I risked another question. "How does your organization know about us?"

Pari frowned and tapped a finger on her chin. "I suppose various governments have known for a long time. I was in Nimbus, the paranormal agency in the United States. We took down covens of vampires and packs of were-wolves but nothing like what we've done the past year with Razor." She took a metal file and scraped beneath my fingernails. "We always knew there was more to it than just vampires and werewolves. We'd had some scrapes with demons, but they'd just leave the bodies when we captured them." Pari deposited the filings in a glass vial and put it on the tray with the rest of my specimens. She picked up a stethoscope and put it against my chest.

I waited a moment in the hopes she'd keep talking, but she didn't. "How is Razor related to Nimbus?"

Pari blinked as if coming out of a trance. "Razor is the new international group. The best of the best from participating countries were put under the jurisdiction of the UWO. Our counterparts from Colombia had some very close calls with a vampire invasion years ago, but it was shut down before they could investigate."

I grimaced. Maximus, a rogue vampire, had built an army of blood-suckers so he could overthrow the Red Syndicate, the legitimate vampire ruling body. The Custodians had done their best to cover up the incident, but even they weren't perfect.

She took one of those ear-checking devices and stuck it in each ear while continuing to speak. "Everything was status quo until we discovered supernatural agents embedded in nearly all of our organizations. That was the catalyst which drove the formation of Razor." She put the device against my lips. "Say ah."

I opened wide. "Ah."

"You're the healthiest specimen I've ever seen." Pari spoke into her tablet, listing observations as if I wasn't even here. "After I'm done with you, I have to go look at the magician we captured with you." She sighed. "They're not nearly as interesting."

Magician as in singular? I wondered if any of my friends had escaped.

"We don't harm noms—normal humans. In fact, we're here to keep bad things from happening." I tried to offer a reassuring smile despite the anger boiling beneath the surface. "Eden is in great danger."

Pari flinched. "That's the second time I've heard that term. Do you mean the garden of Eden?"

"I meant Earth." It wasn't accurate, but I wasn't ready to let these crazies know more than they needed to. "There are bad supernatural organizations and good ones, kind of like the Justice League versus the Legion of Doom. We're the good guys."

"I find that rather hard to believe." She pursed her lips and regarded me for a moment. "It won't matter long anyway."

I waited for further explanation, but she took a rubber mallet and started testing my reflexes instead.

"Why won't it matter long?"

"Hmm?" She looked up. "Why won't what matter?"

"You said it won't matter long when I said we're the good guys."

"Oh." Pari took a white device that emitted a high-pitched whine and ran it over my leg. "The Colombians confiscated a super serum from the vampires. We're modifying it to enhance our soldiers."

My stomach dropped. "Super serum?"

"Yep." She looked at me and frowned. "Why are you wincing?"

"The sound that device puts out is killing my ears."

Pari nodded. "Ah, you have super hearing. This body scanner emits ultrasonic frequencies humans can't hear."

I couldn't stop thinking about the super serum she mentioned. There was only one kind that the vampires in Colombia had and it was made with my blood. If Razor was truly modifying it to enhance their soldiers, we were in big trouble.

CHAPTER 18

The noms already had a massive numbers advantage. If this shadow organization jacked up their soldiers on supernatural steroids, the Overworld would have a real war on its hands— one we couldn't win.

I've got to escape.

"Where is this place?" I asked.

"One of our secure facilities." Pari didn't elaborate.

Two technicians wheeled in a machine. A helmet that looked like something from an old-timey deep-sea diving outfit hung from a bundle of wires. A tech put it over my head. Inflatable pads inside swelled until they pressed securely against my head.

"We're doing a brain scan, so please remain as still as possible." Pari's voice echoed in the confines of the helmet. "Try not to think of anything unless I tell you to."

Aside from a splinter of light, the helmet was pitch black and stuffy. It took everything I had not to freak out. "I can hardly breathe in here."

A fan whirred to life and fresh air circulated. "It might be best if you took a short nap. I'll let you know when I need your brain to be active."

I didn't like all these tests, but there wasn't squat I could do about it. I closed my eyes and took deep breaths to fight off the claustrophobia threatening to smother me. An image flashed into my mind.

Black liquid pools form on a white floor. Hundreds of black spiders congeal from the primordial goo. They skitter up the legs of the man with the cattle prod. His screams fade and his body melts beneath the onslaught of feeding monsters.

The spiders weren't spiders, but scorps. The miniature demon spawn devoured flesh more efficiently than a swarm of piranhas.

Yes. Summon the spawn and destroy them. Kalesh sounded eager to unleash hell.

Can I even summon spawn with these magi-cuffs on?

We manifested earlier.

I didn't like him using a plural pronoun to refer to me. *So my demon abilities aren't cut off.*

He didn't answer.

Provided I summon a swarm of scorps and kill these people, how am I supposed to get out of these shackles?

Again, he had no answer. Or maybe I didn't have the answer. *Damn this is confusing!* He was me, right? Or was I slowly becoming him?

I didn't think scorps could eat metal. Hellhounds could morph into human form, but what good would that do if they didn't have the key to my locks? It seemed unlikely a hellhound could easily carry my shackled body out of this place, wherever we were. I also needed line of sight to visualize the spawning pool. If there was a way to do it without vision, I hadn't learned it yet.

"Your brain is too active," Pari said. "Please stop thinking so I can form a baseline."

"I'm naked, shackled to a metal chair, have been violated, probed, and cattle prodded. How in the hell am I supposed to not think?" The helmet pads made it difficult to talk.

"Go to your quiet place so the probe can complete."

I am going to probe her quiet place with my fist when I get out of here!

"Your serotonin levels are spiking again," she said. "I don't want to sedate you because it will skew the results."

I didn't want to play along, but I knew I had to. The sooner she finished the brain scan, the sooner I'd be able to see the room again and at least test summoning spawn. I closed my eyes. Using the meditation techniques that allowed me to switch to demon vision, I withdrew inside my mind. I'd spoken to my demon spirit this way before, but I didn't want to see that jackass right now.

Light bled through my eyelids. *Did I fall asleep?* I blinked awake. Instead of the cold LED lab lights, warm daylight welcomed me. Since I knew for a fact I hadn't escaped, I realized I must have gone into such a deep trance that I was in a lucid dream state.

I stood on a gray boulder, an island in the center of a crystalline stream. I spun around. A dense fog slowly receded, revealing mossy riverbanks and fields of flowers. Water burbled past my feet. The reflection of an unfamiliar face stared up at me. I reached down and touched the water.

My consciousness seemed to shed my body and I stared at myself, a stranger peering through the window of another soul. A gentle voice echoed all around me, a judge listing every little thing about me. An undercurrent of emotions, vast and deep, threatened to drag me into a void. I felt empty and hollow one moment and swelled with hope and joy the next.

I tuned in to the judging voice and realized it was my own.

Hope. Unfounded optimism. Rage. Murderous intent. Two spirits war for domi-nance of one vessel. Neither is right. Both are wrong. Intense love for friends. Hatred for those perceived as bullies.

It went on and on and on, the negatives piling up against the positives. A deep crimson stain spread slowly across the white canvas of my soul. I felt as if I were about to explode into a million pieces or be crushed beneath the weight of emotion.

"Ah!" I jerked my hand out of the water. My body trembled, and my throat felt raw. "Oh, god, I'm so woke right now." The water wasn't water at all. I looked behind me and confirmed what it was. Three tribu-taries cascaded down waterfalls—one of Murk, one of Brilliance, and the third of Stasis, swirling together for form a stream of Clarity, the ultimate truth.

Clarity had bared my soul down to its rotten core. I couldn't resist the demon seed. When it grew strong enough, it would overpower me. Emily Glass was my last hope. Every moment I remained locked up here was another moment closer to becoming the demon Baal wanted me to be.

"Why am I here?" I cried out. My voice echoed across the fields of flowers beyond the stream. I'd been here before, a long time ago. The universe had wanted me to make a choice between the primal forces. Most Seraphim chose their affinity to Murk or Brilliance, becoming stronger in the force of their choice. Fjoeruss had taught me that there was a lot more to choose from than just those two, so I'd taken all four— Murk, Brilliance, Stasis, and Clarity.

With the choice far behind me, I didn't understand why I was back to this place, wherever it was.

That was when I saw something else—something far upstream. The waterfalls were only shoulder height to me, the streams no wider than four feet. They all sprang from a common source perhaps a hundred yards away.

Time to investigate.

I leapt to the riverbank. The ground swallowed me. Screaming, I fell from the sky and landed hard on my feet. "What the hell?" I spun around and got my bearings. I was back on the boulder. "Playing games?" I jumped to the opposite bank.

Another terrorizing fall took me right back to the boulder. I tried vaulting to the waterfalls but rebounded on an invisible shield. Growling, I paced back and forth. "What are you hiding from me?"

There was no answer, but a light bulb flickered on in the dark recesses of my mind. I faced the source and leapt sideways to the riverbank. When I fell through the ground and looped around to the sky, I saw what I'd missed before. A pool of azure energy fed the other forces. It flowed in all directions, each branch a different color, each stream a completely different form of magical energy.

It's the primal fount.

Seraphim magic was only a fraction of all the different kinds of power. What I'd thought were the primal forces of the universe were only one tiny offshoot of the source of magic. I dropped into a sitting position on the boulder and laughed. "I'm not special at all. Not even a little bit!"

I was on the brunt end of a huge joke. The universe had played me like a fool. I might be strong with Seraphim magic, but Conrad had touched the freaking primal fount. He drew straight from the source itself!

You are not strong. You are insignificant. There is only one who sees your worth and will make you even more powerful.

I flinched. Kalesh hadn't said that and I knew I hadn't. As much as I knew the words were twisted and wrong, a part of me agreed. A part of me hungered for power and recognition. All I had to do was join Baal.

"No!" I stood up and slapped my cheeks. "Wake up!"

An invisible force shoved me into the stream of Clarity.

I desperately clung to the boulder, but my legs splashed in. Layers of lies and misconceptions peeled away like an onion, opening my core to the light. I saw everything I'd seen before, but there was more, so much more I couldn't even verbalize. Clarity reduced everything to a stream of emotion, boiled down, skinned, and raw. My soul flickered, a tiny speck of sand in a vast ocean of bright stars.

You are nothing.

"No!" I clawed my way up the boulder and lay panting. Daelissa had died when confronted with her absolute truth. Elyssa had merely thought it was a strange out-of-body experience. Clarity hadn't killed me, but it absolutely terrified me.

I wiped tears from my eyes and looked downstream. I'd been so preoccupied with the source that I hadn't seen where the river of Clarity led— up a steep mountain and into the clouds. What did that mean in this impossible world? Was that the way to heaven or hell?

The waters shimmered and morphed into a ghostly figure. A reflection of myself stared back at me. I'd met myself here before, so it wasn't terribly surprising to see me again.

"How do I get out of here?"

"You ask yourself a lot of questions," the reflection said. "And you know the answers."

"Why can't I reach the primal fount?"

"Why do *you* think I can't reach it?" he said back.

A growl rumbled in my throat. "If I wanted a shrink, I'd hire one!"

"You and I both know why you can't reach it." My reflection shrugged. "You just can't admit it."

"Tell me the truth!"

"You want the truth?" He laughed maniacally. "You can't handle the truth!"

Anger rose like a wave of bile. I wanted to lash out at this ghost, this misrepresentation of me. "What is this place? Why am I here if I don't even matter?"

More than anything, I wanted out. I wanted to get back to reality even if it meant I was shackled naked in a top-secret black-ops lab. I closed my eyes and concentrated on the real world. *Take me back!*

"...astonishing amount of data. I have never seen such bizarre activity before!" Pari's jabbering brought a sense of relief.

"I'm back." My voice sounded hollow and broken.

"Back?" The pads in the helmet deflated. The pressure on my head relented and light flooded into my eyes. Pari came into focus. "Did you meditate?"

I blinked bleary eyes. Nodded. "You told me to quiet my mind, so I did."

"That explains the brief pause in synaptic activity." She turned her tablet to me. Dozens of colored lines rose in a series of spikes. "But then you went absolutely crazy."

"I *am* crazy." *I am nothing.*

The power is ours to take, Kalesh reminded me.

His words sounded right. I shook my head. "No, he's not right!"

Paris' eyebrows rose. "Who's not right?"

"No one."

I saw movement out of the corner of my eye an instant before the cattle prod struck my ribs again. Prodmeister Pro pressed it harder and harder against me. "Answer the question, prisoner!"

Pari waved him off. "Stop it, Private Brills!"

"I will when he answers." Brills smiled sadistically. "Commander Edge's orders."

I was raw, both physically and mentally. An animalistic scream tore from my throat. Pain pierced my forehead. Muscles swelled and pressed against unyielding metal. My throat constricted against the collar. I couldn't breathe, couldn't see through the haze of red in my vision. All my hate and rage focused on the man with cattle prod.

But it was all for nothing. The world disintegrated into black sand and scattered to the wind. I must have briefly lost consciousness, because when I opened my eyes again, the man with the cattle prod stood back against the wall. Pari paused speaking to her tablet and nodded when our eyes met.

"You are the most fascinating and frightening creature I have ever encountered." She stepped closer. "There is so much to learn from you. So much to study." Pari's eyes widened. "I could become the first specialist on spawn."

In other words, I would be a rat in a cage for a very long time.

CHAPTER 19

C onrad

THESE NOMS after Conrad and the others were highly organized and well equipped to hunt supers. The drones, weapons, and tracking cubes couldn't have just been cobbled together by a small group. These people probably belonged to a larger organization—one that might be sweeping the city for supers even now.

"What if these people found Justin and the others?" Conrad couldn't stop looking over his shoulder every few seconds as their group walked away from the ice cream shop. "Maybe we should go check on them."

"Justin and the others are long gone by now," Ivy said. She took out her arcphone. "I can call him to be sure."

"Yeah, good idea." Conrad took out his phone too. Dozens of notifications appeared on the screen. The phone manufacturer, Orange, had pushed out several updates since his return to Eden.

"I can't get service." Ivy glared at the phone. "It keeps saying I need authorization to use the network."

Conrad tried his and received the same message from a robotic voice. "Network authorization required. Please contact your local Overworld authority."

"I'm sure the others already left." Cora glanced down an alleyway as they walked past it. "We need to get into Queens Gate before more of these people block the entrance."

They were probably right. Justin and the others had been right near the ship when Conrad and Ambria parted ways with them. For now, it was best for them to reach the safety of Queens Gate.

Ambria grabbed Conrad's arm. "We're being followed."

Conrad looked back at the ice cream shop, now two blocks behind them. A small crowd of people trailed behind them, phones out and recording. They couldn't just go into the secret elevator to Queens Gate with noms trailing them.

Conrad wove an invisible blanket of static electricity in the air, leaving a trail of charged ions behind them as they walked. The first nom reached the charged area and shouted in alarm when his phone crackled and popped.

"My new phone!" he wailed.

A woman screamed and threw her smoking phone to the ground. The other noms stopped and milled about, confused and uncertain.

That'll do. The rest of the way should be easier without a crowd.

Tall black vans roared up to the ice cream shop. Dozens of uniformed women piled out. The uniforms weren't standard police issue. A cube in the hands of one woman confirmed they were with the hunters.

She held up the cube. Her hand jerked toward Conrad. Drones rose from the tops of the vans and zipped toward them.

"Clear the way, people!" One of the women shouted. "Government business."

Cora stopped in place, eyes staring blankly. She blinked and looked at Bella. "I peered through the eyes of a bird. The other streets are blocked off by similar vans."

"I've encountered hunters and slayers of the supernatural, but these people are something else." Bella motioned the others onward. "We've got no choice but to get to Queens Gate, no matter what. There's nowhere to hide so long as they have those cubes."

"Agreed," Cora said.

Conrad removed a yellow marble from his satchel and tossed it on the sidewalk behind them. Max's Banana Peel potion splatted on the sidewalk and spread in all directions for dozens of feet. Pedestrians slipped and fell on the frictionless substance. The uniformed people in their military-style boots had no better luck. Feet flew in the air and bodies slid in all directions.

Ivy and Evadora giggled.

"Don't just stand there," Conrad said. "Run!"

Ivy blurred away, Evadora close behind her. The rest of them jogged down the sidewalk, shoving through the enthralled crowd of onlookers.

"These bloody people and their phones." Ambria pushed between a pair of hefty men who stared at their phone screens. "They're like zombies!"

Conrad looked up and over his shoulder. A pair of black drones followed their every move. He thought of striking them down but didn't want to draw the unwanted attention of the noms and their camera phones.

Unfortunately, Ivy didn't have the same restraint. Explosions rocked the intersection ahead. Conrad hurried down the sidewalk and saw Ivy hurling spheres of destruction at two more of the black vans. An empty car burned in the middle of the road. Noms ran screaming in all directions. Others took cover and aimed their cameras at the fight.

"Stay away from us, you jerks!" Brilliance speared from Ivy's fingertips, slicing off the top half of a van.

"It's a freaking blonde Hermione!" a boy shouted.

"Kick their asses!" his friend shouted through cupped hands.

"Ivy, stop it!" Conrad grabbed her arm. "You've just let all these noms record you doing magic!"

Rage shaded Ivy's face deep red. "I don't care. The people chasing us are noms so they must already know about magic."

"We don't know that." Conrad pulled her toward the parking deck entrance. "We don't know anything about them."

"We know that they're mean!" Ivy jerked her arm away. "I should blast them all to atoms."

Evadora shimmered out of camouflage. "That was exciting."

Cora thrust her finger forward. "Into the parking deck now, girls!"

Cowed, Ivy and Evadora ran inside.

The group raced down the winding ramp of the garage, through an illusionary wall, and stopped at a thick concrete column. Conrad reached through the illusion hiding the levitator call button and touched it. Seconds ticked past like hours. Sirens wailed in the distance. Shouts echoed through the parking deck, hunters on the prowl.

"Did any noms follow us?" Ambria said.

Bella shook her head. "There's an illusion spell over the entrance to this section. Unless they touch the fake wall and realize it isn't solid, no one will find us."

The lift doors opened, and everyone piled inside. Conrad braced himself for the abrupt descent, but even then was hardly prepared when the bottom seemed to drop out beneath them. After a few seconds of near freefall, the levitator slowed so abruptly only those with supernatural strength were able to stand without holding onto the handrails.

Ivy giggled. "That was fun!"

"About as fun as a cricket bat to the knees," Ambria muttered.

They stepped off the levitator and into the Queens Gate waystation. The ancient creators had carved and smoothed the cave walls, though centuries of erosion had etched lines and grooves in the stone. A soft yellow glow suffused the air, a light source from everywhere and nowhere that lit nearly every square inch of the great cavern.

Even on a slow day, the Queens Gate waystation was a busy place, but today it resembled a madhouse.

A purple Rolls Royce with a massive set of demon horns affixed to the hood sat just outside the levitator. Cars lined the walls of the cavern, as if moved there to make space for the hundreds of white tents in the middle.

"Halt!" A man in white robes stood before them, hand upraised. "By order of Overlord Tiberius, none are to enter the city of Queens Gate without proper documentation. All refugees from other Overworld cities must apply for entrance and take residence in a tent until their application is considered."

"Overlord Tiberius?" Conrad could hardly believe his ears.

"Refugees?" Ambria looked aghast. "What in the bloody world is happening here?"

The man looked at something behind them. His eyes widened, and he tapped a comm badge on his robes. "Security detail report to the levitator! We have—"

Evadora ripped the badge from his robe and threw it into the tent city. Ivy grabbed his robes and yanked him to the side of the levitator. It soon became evident why the man had called for help. Giant posters with Conrad's, Ambria's, and Max's faces plastered the wall.

"Xander rules the Overworld." Ambria groaned. "Galfandor failed."

"How could things go so terribly since we left?" Conrad turned to the man in white. "How did Xander become the Overlord?"

"Traitorous scum." The man spat at Conrad, but only a few flecks reached his face.

Ivy gripped his wrist and squeezed. "Tell us what's going on or I will rip off your arms."

"Dear heavens!" The man swooned. Ivy slapped his cheeks until he recovered his wits. He trembled but answered the question. "The Overworld is under attack. La Casona, Four Ways, and three other cities were attacked. Some citizens escaped, but hundreds of others were captured by a group called Razor Echelon. Overlord Tiberius is working on a retaliation plan and has declared martial law."

"Overlord?" Ambria spat the word. "How did he stay in power after we killed Victus?"

The man puffed out his chest. "The Overlord is too powerful for scum like Galfandor to defeat. He has too many allies."

Just hearing the title Overlord triggered seething fury in Conrad's stomach. His fists clenched so tight, they hurt. He forced back the anger and posed another question. "Is Galfandor still alive?"

The man turned away, but Ivy gripped his chin and forced him to face her. "Well, is he?"

"Yes. He's imprisoned with the other traitors." His face burned bright red. "You'll join him soon enough, scum!"

It took everything to not slap the man. Conrad took a deep breath to remain calm. "Where, exactly, is he?"

"In the cells beneath the old courthouse." The man bared his teeth. "Try to save him, and you'll suffer his fate."

"The old courthouse?" Ambria looked confused. "You mean the Overworld Grand Court in the government sector?"

"There are hundreds more guardians in the waystation." The man struggled uselessly in Ivy's grasp. "You stand no chance against us."

Ivy rapped him on the head and he slumped unconscious. She looked at Conrad. "Can I blast him, please? He'll just tell the others when he wakes up."

"Much as I'd like to, we should let him live," Ambria said. "Elyssa doesn't kill unless she's forced to. I think we should follow her example."

"You really have your head up her butt," Ivy said. "Elyssa's not perfect."

"Oh, and Justin is?" Ambria crossed her arms and glared at the other girl.

"My bro is awesome." Ivy's eyes flared. "I dare you to say something bad about him."

"Hey!" Conrad waved a hand between them. "We're in the middle of enemy territory with nowhere to go. Now is not the time to fight among ourselves."

Ivy scowled and looked away. "Whatever. Let's just get out of here."

Ambria cleared her throat and looked at distant double doors in the rock face. Queens Gate was on the other side of that wall, but dozens of white cloaks patrolled the area. "How are we supposed to get past border control?"

Conrad tapped a finger on his chin. "Kanaan took us out of the Grotto through a hidden exit in the control room. I wonder if Queens Gate has something similar."

"There are no roots this deep in the earth," Cora said. "Otherwise I might be able to sense hidden passages."

"It might be as difficult to break into the control room as it would be to get past border control." Ambria pointed out a contingent of white-cloaked guardians standing near the stables. The hidden entrance to the control room was just behind them.

Ivy pounded a fist in her other hand. "We blast our way through."

Conrad frowned. "Evadora, can you camouflage and scout out all the guards between us and the doors to Queens Gate?"

"Yep!" Evadora scooted into the tent city and blurred into near-invisibility.

"We'll wait for her to come back." Conrad dragged the unconscious white cloak behind the purple Rolls Royce and went back to the levitator.

"Something with a really loud motor is coming down the parking ramp." Ivy cocked her ear. "I wonder how they got past the bad people."

The levitator was one of two entrances into the Queens Gate waysta-tion. The other was a winding ramp hidden behind an illusory wall. It corkscrewed into the earth for a mile before reaching the parking lot.

"More refugees, no doubt." Ambria sighed. "The Overworld is on the verge of collapse!"

"Certainly seems that way." Conrad walked down the line of cars parked against the cavern wall. The faint squeals of rubber on stone emanated from the tunnel. He climbed onto the hood of an SUV and looked over the tents toward the main entrance to Queens Gate. There were too many tents and bodies in the way to get a clear view.

Squealing tires and roar of an engine grew louder with every passing second. Moments later, a bright orange sports car skidded inside and spun out of control. It plowed into the parked cars with a screech of metal and shattering glass. A man in nom attire staggered out, wand in hand. "They followed me! They're coming!"

The ambient noise in the cavern was too loud for most to hear him, but a few nearby witnesses stared in horror.

It didn't take a genius to know who he was talking about.

"Oh no." Ambria drew her wand. "It must be Razor! We've got to go!"

"We have to wait for Evadora." Conrad hopped down off the truck and ran where he'd stashed the unconscious man. He tried to wake him, but he slumbered on. "We need to warn the authorities."

"But they're the bad guys," Ivy sad.

"They might be, but they're at least with the Overworld." Warmth trickled into Conrad's palms as the primal fount responded to his summons for power. "We've got to warn someone."

"I'll do it." Bella straightened to her full five feet. "They're not looking for me."

Cora followed her. "I'll come with you." The two women ran to the white cloaks near the control room.

Conrad and the others watched nervously. The first person they spoke with tapped a comm badge. A moment later, a man with a gray patch on his robes appeared with a grumpy frown. The frown vanished, replaced by wide eyes and fear. A klaxon whined. Shouts and cries of alarm filled the cavern.

The klaxon turned off and a voice echoed. At first, Conrad couldn't understand what the man said due to the ambient noise, but the magical amplification cut through the noise.

"Quiet, you fools!"

It took a while, but the cacophony of frightened voices faded enough so the man could speak.

"We are in a state of emergency. All citizens are expected to fight in the defense of Queens Gate. All Arcanes report to the stables. All others report to the Obsidian Arch. You will be given your orders."

The rumblings of discontent drowned out the rest of what he had to say. Despite the anger, most people began filtering toward their assigned locations. A handful of vampires grouped together and brandished a sign that said *Vampires are citizens too!* They began shouting, "We won't go! We won't go!"

White cloaks scrambled to herd the willing into appropriate groups but ignored those who didn't cooperate. Conrad was impressed with how quickly they arranged people into squads and set up barriers.

Bella and Cora returned a moment later.

"Well, I hope they can assemble a defense," Bella said. "I think we should use the distraction to get inside Queens Gate."

"Why don't they just blow the parking lot entrance and block it?" Ambria said.

Bella shook her head. "I don't know. In any case, we can't reach it now."

"There are still a lot of guards at the city entrance," Cora said. "I suggest we discreetly walk that way so we can slip through at a moment's notice."

"There are twenty guards at the doors." Evadora shimmered into sight. "But there were fifty before all this started."

Ambria nodded somberly. "We can get past them, forcibly if need be."

"You mean blast 'em," Ivy said.

Ambria sighed. "Yes, we can blast our way past them."

Groups of Arcanes tore down tents while others levitated barriers into place. Vampires and lycans grappled cars and dragged them to block the tunnel exit. It only took two or three to lift a car and move it as easily as someone might relocate a piece of furniture.

"It would've been so easy to build a blast door there," Ambria said. "But instead, they just left it wide open!"

"Well, we can mention that to Overlord Tiberius," Bella said. "I'm certain he'll take your advice to heart."

Conrad and the others edged their way around the organized chaos, trying to avoid white cloaks who might draft them into duty. But a white cloak leading a group of Arcanes grabbed Bella's arm as they walked past. "You there, what's your assignment?"

"We're going to help with barriers," she lied.

"Well, you're in the wrong place." He pointed to the stables. "The magic barriers are stored over there." His brow furrowed. "Which means you're lying."

"No, I'm not—"

He waved away her excuse. "I won't let cowards like you waste my time. If you don't want to fight, go hide in the stables and stay out of the way. It'll be on your heads if we lose." He opened his mouth to say something else, but diesel engines roared and a giant metal beast crashed through the blockade of cars.

Ambria shrieked. "It's a bloody tank!"

CHAPTER 20

onrad

C Dozens of troops in black flooded in behind the war machine. They wore tactical armor and full-faced helmets equipped with breathing apparatus and tinted visors. The butts of silver rifles pressed against their shoulders, the muzzles pointing at the defenders.

A massive barrel slowly extended from the tank turret. Arcanes dove behind barriers and a multi-colored array of spells flashed through the air. The Razor troops responded with their rifles. Black electro bullets filled the air.

Despite the onslaught of magic, the enemy barely faltered. Their uniforms absorbed the brunt of the magical attacks. They were slowed, but not stopped.

"They're wearing different uniforms than the people up top," Ambria said. "They must be reinforced against magic."

"But how?" Conrad ducked behind a barrier with the others. "How would noms know how to block magic?"

"Does it really matter right now?" Ambria gripped her wand tight. "We can't fight them."

Howls and war cries rose above the bedlam. Lycans shifted to wolf form and vampires blurred forward. The enemy front line faltered beneath the physical onslaught. The tank turned its barrel toward the front row of Arcanes and fired. A great boom thundered through the cavern. A huge black sphere flew overhead and exploded, unleashing a wave of electrical impulses. Convulsions seized swaths of Arcanes and drove them to the floor.

More troops emerged, these in metallic exoskeletons. They grappled with the vampires and werewolves, machines matching supernatural strength. What had been a triumphant blitz turned into a full-on retreat.

A squad of enemies broke through the first barrier. Conrad summoned the first power and leapt to his feet. Azure power arced from his hands and lanced into the first two soldiers. Magic-resistant armor smoke and burned. They cried out and ran into each other in their haste to escape. Ivy channeled Murk into a giant sledgehammer and batted three soldiers like cricket balls. They flew back into their comrades, bowling them over and foiling the blitz.

The tank turret rotated their way. In a moment, the entire area would be blanketed with electricity. Conrad speared more soldiers with the first power, but there were too many for him to stop them all.

The tank fired. Ivy wove a sphere of Murk and intercepted the electro shell. It exploded inside, disintegrating the shield, but not before all its energy dissipated into the air. "I can do this all day!" Ivy shouted.

"I have an idea." Conrad spun a rotating shield to deflect electro bullets. "Ivy can you plug the barrel?"

Her eyes lit. "Oh, that would be neat!"

"Can you do it from this distance?" The tank was fifty yards from their position.

Ivy frowned. "I need to be a little closer."

"Then let's do it." Conrad pushed his hands forward and the shield flew back at the soldiers, bulldozing them out of the way. Lycans and vampires surged from the enemy's right flank, forcing the mechanized units to engage. The backline Arcanes moved forward while healers dragged the unconscious out of the fight.

"Surrender!" A voice boomed from a loudspeaker on the tank. "This waystation is hereby placed under the authority of Razor Echelon. All resistance will be met with force. Cooperation will be rewarded."

An Arcane in singed gray robes raised his staff above his head. "Go to hell, you bastards!"

"Go to hell!" Others took up the battle cry, and in a terribly unorganized stampede, the Arcanes fired spells and ran blindly at the enemy.

The tank turret lowered and aimed at the oncoming mob.

Ivy blurred forward. She ducked beneath a volley of electro bullets. Leapt over a line of soldiers. Landed on her feet and channeled a beam of Murk at the tank. An ultraviolet shell encased the barrel. A boom thundered. The barrel exploded. Great waves of blue electricity arced across the enemy. Mechanized suits whined to a halt and soldiers convulsed in agony.

Enemy operatives grabbed fallen comrades and scrambled backward. A hatch on the tank flew open and the crew abandoned the dead machine.

The cavern erupted with cries of triumph and the citizens of the Overworld ran toward the retreating enemy.

Ivy stared in disbelief. "Holy smokes, we did it!"

"I didn't think we had it in us." Ambria looked at Ivy with a hint of respect. "Bloody well done."

"We should use the opportunity to our advantage." Cora took Conrad's hand. "The door guards have all but abandoned their posts."

Conrad blinked. "Oh, yes." He looked around and located the others. Only Evadora was missing, but she was probably in camouflage. A small woman fluttering above the bedlam caught his gaze. "Is that Thal?"

"I thought she was with Justin!" Ivy waved at the fairy. "We're over here!"

Thal spoke to someone below her and flew toward them. A few Arcanes looked at her in confusion, but most were too busy celebrating and chasing the enemy soldiers to notice.

"Why aren't you with Justin?" Ivy asked when she came into range.

"Because people like them"—she jabbed a finger at the Razor soldiers —"caught him."

"What!" Destructive energy blazed in Ivy's hands. "Where are they? We have to save him!"

"You'll not be getting out that way." Thal shook her head. "The entire construct up there is surrounded by thunderous metal beasts and hostile humans."

Max squeezed out of the crowd, Shelton close behind.

"Harry!" Bella nearly plowed him over with a hug. "You're safe!"

Shelton tried to talk, but the impact seemed to have knocked the air from his lungs.

"Max!" Conrad hugged his friend. "How did you escape?"

Max slumped. "Thal did it somehow. But we couldn't save Justin, Elyssa, or Adam."

"They nailed us with shocker bullets," Shelton said. "By the time we woke up and went back to find Justin, the women in black were long gone. We got to the parking deck right when that army was rolling in, but Thal used her rift magic to get us past."

"Yeah, there's no way to get back out," Max said. "We're stuck in Queens Gate."

"I'm just glad you're safe, Harry." Bella stood on tiptoes and kissed his cheek. "I promise we'll rescue Justin."

Shelton sighed. "Man, we've got to do something. God only knows what those soulless assholes are doing to him."

"We really should enter the city and talk about this later," Cora said. "In a few moments, the door guards will return."

Shelton scowled and looked around. "Jesus. Looks like we missed one hell of a battle."

"Razor is only a small part of our problems," Ambria said. "Xander's minions run Queens Gate and they won't let us into the city if we dawdle about."

Shelton recoiled like someone hit him. "Xander's in charge? I thought your buddies here were supposed to take over."

Ambria scoffed. "Things didn't work out."

Conrad felt as if someone had blindsided him. Justin was a prisoner. Xander ruled the Overworld. The noms had a secret army to fight supernaturals. It was like being caught in a nightmare with no way of waking up.

"Conrad, are you okay?" Ivy shook his shoulder. "We need to get going."

Conrad blinked. "Yes, yes. Let's go."

"Are you sure we can't rescue my brother?" Ivy said.

"Not right now." Shelton growled. "Believe you me we will, though."

The group made their way through the throng of victorious Overworld citizens while white cloaks desperately tried to restore some semblance of order. Only ten of them barred entrance through the double doors to the city.

Shelton walked right up to them. "Open up. We're going in."

"Let me see your papers," one of the men said.

"I don't need no stinking papers. I'm Harry Shelton, bitch." Shelton leveled his staff at the men. "Open the damned doors."

Max held up his wand. "Yeah, he's the great Harry Shelton!"

Ivy summoned Brilliance into her hands. "I'm a Seraphim, bitch. Don't mess with me or I'll blast you."

Thal rose on gossamer wings. "I'll curse you with my Fae magic if you don't do as they say."

The white cloaks' mouths dropped open in astonishment.

"You're a real fairy?" One of them asked.

"I'm Fae!" Thal flung her dark dust at the man and he slumped unconscious. "Open the doors!"

The white cloaks held up their hands and backed away.

"So you'll open up for a fairy, but not me?" Shelton scoffed. "Man, I've been gone so long, they forgot me."

Conrad tugged on the handles and the doors swung open. A giant green valley spread out, sparkling in glorious sunlight. Cliffs towered on either side. The spires of Arcane University touched the sky on the western cliffs. The organic silver curves of Science Academy sparkled on the cliffs to the east. The city of Queens Gate sat in the middle, its grand old buildings reminiscent of ancient Rome and London.

"Impossible!" Thal flew through. "An entire underground world?"

Shelton snorted. "A Fae thinks something is impossible?"

"It's a pocket dimension." Ivy shut the double doors behind them and patted the rock face. "Places like this exist where the Glimmer touches Eden, for some weird reason."

"They are fragments of old Lyrolai and Eden combined." Cora looked wistful. "Now my realm is but a shattered world."

Ivy jogged over to the pirate ship gondola that carried people up to

Arcane University. "We need to get to the Mansion. I'll bet we could use the omniarch there to rescue Justin."

"What about overthrowing Xander?" Ambria said. "We can't just let him stay in power."

Max pounded a fist in his palm. "Absolutely. There's no way he could stand against all of us."

"If he had a hundred white cloaks in the waystation, how many does he have guarding him?" Conrad felt torn about not confronting Xander, but if all the people who followed Victus now followed the new over-lord, victory would be difficult.

"Conrad is right," Cora said. "We don't know Xander's capabilities. I think it would be wiser to go to the Glimmer. Perhaps Thal can wake my people."

"No, I'll remain at the university." Conrad boarded the pirate gondola behind the others and took a seat. "I need to scout the Mansion and see if Xander has it and the omniarch locked down. Maybe I can find out where they're keeping Galfandor."

"I'm staying with you." Ambria plopped down beside him and took his hand.

"Me too." Max sat on his left. "Last time, we beat your dad. Now, it's time to beat mine."

Images of the bloody last fight with Victus flashed through Conrad's mind. He'd pounded his father's head to a pulp. Killed him. It was the least Victus deserved, but victory had left scars that would never heal.

"I kind of want to stay with Conrad, but I kind of want to go with Evadora to the Glimmer." Ivy quirked her lips. "Maybe we should blast Xander first and then go to the Glimmer."

"No, it's better this way." Conrad looked out the window as the gondola rose toward the cliff and Arcane University. "Besides, I have a feeling even getting onto the grounds of the university won't be easy. Xander will probably have the entire place locked down."

"Don't worry, kid." Shelton wrapped an arm around Bella's shoulder. "The others can go to the Glimmer, but we've got your back."

"Absolutely." Bella smiled. "We'll stay with you."

Shelton grunted. "The sooner we get control of the omniarch, the sooner we can save Justin and the others."

The gondola came to a stop at the top of the cliff and the group debarked. There were no guards waiting there, so they cautiously made their way down the path through the woods to the security station at the main gate.

"We should camouflage," Max said. "Maybe we can sneak past the guards."

"We can't sneak past the wards." Ambria clucked her tongue. "The entire place is mined with wards against disguises and camouflage."

"I will have trees lift us over the walls," Cora said.

Ambria shook her head. "The barrier wards will still zap us."

"Just so happens I'm an ace at de-warding." Shelton flourished his staff. "But if all else fails, we'll just overpower the guard and waltz right on through."

"I like that plan," Max said. "I could use that stun spell you taught me."

"Not right away." Shelton patted Max's shoulder. "If charm and guile fail, then you stun them."

Ambria groaned.

Prepared for the worst, they paused at the end of the path and looked out at the wall. Conrad wasn't prepared for what he saw. Warped, broken gates hung open. Piles of rubble lay beneath holes in the wall. Two of the towering spires seemed to have been sheared off, and blackened pockmarks marred the white walls of the main castle. The crystal dome of the library had survived, but it was apparent a great battle had been fought not long ago.

"Good lord, they wrecked the university!" Ambria stepped out of the woods and looked around. "There's nobody here."

"That don't mean nothing." Shelton strode forward, arcphone in hand, and began scanning the perimeter.

Ambria rolled her eyes. "Your use of double-negatives is nothing if not consistent."

"Thanks, darling." Shelton winked at Conrad. "She's got a tongue sharper than the claws on a cross-eyed cat in a mule barn."

"A what?" Ambria stared at him blankly, apparently unable to decide if she should be upset or simply confused.

Shelton continued his scan while Max observed and asked questions. Shelton mumbled and nodded and seemed genuinely pleased that Max took such a keen interest in the spell.

After a short while, Shelton tucked his phone back in his leather duster. "Something rolled through here and blew all the wards to hell. Destroyed the gate and left a hell of a mess. The few wards left are fizzling out because they haven't been recharged."

"What in the world could do that?" Bella said.

"That's a damned good question." Shelton knelt and looked around. "I don't know what could survive going through all those wards, but I don't see any bodies."

"Could've been cleaned up," Bella said.

"Maybe." He stood and projected a holographic image from his arcphone. "This is the visual representation of the wards scan."

A maze of glowing lines and symbols appeared in the holographic display. In several places, the lines were broken and crackling, as if a giant bull had smashed through an electric fence.

"There must have been a battle between Xander's and Galfandor's forces," Ambria said. "That's the only explanation I can think of."

Shelton ran a finger along the brim of his hat. "Dollars to donuts you're right."

A surprised smile crossed Ambria's face at his agreement.

Bella walked to the smashed gate. Before anyone could stop her, she stepped past the wall and inside. "Without wards, it is safe to enter."

"Yep." Shelton headed through, Max at his heels.

Blackened and scarred, the giant oak doors of the university hung open to darkness and ominous silence. Bella cast a light spell and sent the glow ball ahead. The temperature dropped several degrees inside. Dust and soot dirtied the stone floors. A tarp in the center of the hall covered a great heap.

Shelton hissed between his teeth and stopped. It didn't take Conrad long to see what gave him pause. Pale, bloodied hands stuck out from beneath the covering. Bella flicked her wand and the tarp lifted away to reveal the horror. Dead eyes met their gazes. Ambria gasped. Max recoiled. Conrad felt sick to his stomach, but it was no different than the mass grave he'd discovered at Victus's foundry.

The university was a tomb.

"Some of these are infernus." Bella directed a glowball to a body that looked as if it were covered in jelly. "The demon flesh is decomposing."

"Holy house of horrors." Shelton shuddered as he walked around the pile. "Looks to be about as many real bodies as there are infernus." He stiffened and dropped to a knee. "Oh, man."

"What is it Harry?" Bella hurried around to the other side. Conrad and the others followed.

An old man with curly hair and broken round spectacles stared blankly out from beneath a dead infernus. A tear trickled down Shelton's cheek. "Damn it, Miles. What in the hell were you still doing here?"

"Oh, Harry, I'm so sorry." Bella kissed his cheek and rested her head on his back. "I know how much he meant to you."

"He was just an old man." Shelton gritted his teeth and wiped away tears. "Why in the hell would he fight a damned battle when he should be retired and on the beach?"

Ambria's lower lip trembled. "This is awful. How many professors died here?"

"Too many." Cora closed her eyes and let out a long breath.

Ivy wiped tears from her eyes. "Some of these people were my teachers when I was here." Her fists balled up. "Max, I'm going to scorch your daddy to dust."

Max gulped. "Be my guest."

Evadora shivered and looked around. "It feels like ghosts are here."

Shelton reached over and gently closed Miles's eyes. "Rest in peace, professor. If it wasn't for you, I wouldn't have done a damned thing with my life."

Ambria tentatively reached over and touched Shelton's sleeve. "I'm very sorry for your loss."

Shelton wiped away another tear. "Not as sorry as Xander's gonna be when I ram my staff up his ass and light him up like a Christmas tree."

Max nodded somberly. "He deserves it."

Conrad felt strangely numb. Death had become an all-too familiar face. It had taken so much from him. He'd taken Cora from its grasp, only to have her barely remember their time together. It was almost as if the woman who'd been his only real mother had never returned from the grave.

"Humans are a violent lot." Thal fluttered around the room. "Sometimes I wonder if I made the right decision to come to you for help."

"As flawed as we are, I'm afraid you have no choice." Ambria looked at her sadly. "We are our own worst enemies."

Conrad walked past the pile and through the main hallway toward the back exit of the building. His footsteps echoed in the lonely void. The others hurried after him.

"Where are you going?" Ambria said.

Conrad didn't pause to look back. "There's nothing for us here. Only the Mansion matters now."

Arcane University was dead.

CHAPTER 21

J*ustin*

Pari, the mad little scientist, drugged me to sleep when she was done with me, and drugged me to screaming wakefulness when she wanted to run more experiments. The bright fluorescent lights were always on. With no clear day or night cycle, my body and mind were completely off kilter.

How long have I been here? What day is it?

Between Johnny Cattleprod's tender jolts and Pari's constant experiments, I barely knew which way was up. Only one thing remained constant: every time I woke up, Kalesh loomed larger in my consciousness. My demon side steadily grew stronger and angrier. It didn't matter how strong he was, the physical shell encasing our consciousness was helpless in this prison.

"Meal time." Private Brills held a stainless steel cup with a straw to my mouth after Pari finished with me for the time being.

I greedily slurped down the pasty shake that passed for meals in this hellhole. Brills wore a crooked smile and leaned close enough so his bad breath washed over my face. "You be a good boy today and I'll get you strawberry flavoring for supper."

I desperately clung to the time reference. "Is this lunch? Is it noontime?"

He smiled smugly and left the room. It was one of the few moments they'd left me alone and conscious. I turned my head the best I could with the constrictive head brace. Aside from Pari's work bench and the cattle prod hanging from the wall, there was little else of interest. I tested my shackles, but the thick metal didn't even creak no matter how hard I pressed against it.

More power.

My demon took control. Muscles bulged and my skin shaded blue. Strength surged into me. I twisted and jerked. The edges of the shackles cut into my skin. Blood oozed down my arms. Frustration mounted into full-blown fury. I strained with everything I had. The wrist shackles creaked and cracked. But no matter how hard I tried, they wouldn't break.

The adrenalin rush faded and Kalesh retreated, pacing in the back of my mind like a caged beast. My arms went limp as noodles. Sweat burned the chafed skin on my wrists and neck.

Pari entered a moment later. Her eyes narrowed when she saw the blood. "You'll only injure yourself if you try to escape arrestor shackles." She frowned. "I should have sedated you before I left."

"What day is it?" My dry throat croaked.

"An important day." She opened the door and a man in a white orderly uniform wheeled in a cart with an array of sharp objects. "Vampires have shown an incredible ability to heal, but their regeneration seems somewhat more limited than myth would have us believe."

"Regeneration? How is that different from healing?"

"If you cut off a finger or an arm, the wound heals quickly, but there is no sign they will grow a new limb to replace the old."

My chest constricted. "You're going to cut off my finger?"

"No, your arm."

My heart froze.

"Don't worry. I'll use local anesthesia to numb the pain."

"Are you insane?" I struggled uselessly. "You're talking about cutting off my arm as if it's nothing!"

Pari ignored me and tapped on her tablet. "I discovered something quite interesting." She turned the tablet to face me. Twin DNA helixes rotated side-by-side. "The mutant vampire serum from Colombia contains DNA that matches precisely with yours."

The secret is out. "Because it is mine. A rogue vampire captured me and took my blood without permission."

"We have been unable to replicate the serum because it was apparently crafted using magic." Pari turned the tablet back toward her. "Then again, we don't wish to create mutant vampires."

"You want to use the very thing you're fighting against to help you." I bared my teeth. "That's called irony."

"It's called making good use of resources."

"Why are you fighting us? Why not simply engage supers in good old-fashioned diplomacy?" I slumped against my bonds. "We're pretty reasonable when you're not using us as lab rats."

"I personally have nothing against some supers." Pari put down her tablet. "I believe magic is somehow rooted in science. Perhaps your magicians are telepathic or telekinetic. I will do everything in my power to understand how this works and perhaps open a doorway so humans can utilize so-called magic in their everyday lives."

"Why not let us help you?"

"I draw the line at magicians. They are merely normal humans with extraordinary abilities." She pursed her lips and shook her head. "But I cannot abide the inhuman mutants."

"Vampires are people too," I croaked. "Just like the Arcanes."

"No, they are fundamentally changed by an outside process." Pari went to the table and began sorting through her tools. "Much like yourself, they are something else, something alien and very dangerous. If I were religious, I might even say soulless."

"Woman, I've got more soul than I can handle." I shifted to demon view, but the same darkness that protected Edge and Brills protected Pari. Even though I couldn't latch on to this shadow aura, I probed it with tendrils of my own essence. Gray static crackled across the shadow aura and across my essence. It felt as if I'd dunked my brain in ice water.

My body locked up, frozen in shock. For a seeming eternity, I was a child with his fingers in an electrical socket, unable to even yank back the probe from Pari's protective field. Through no action of my own, the probe unlatched and I was able to breathe again.

What in the hell is protecting her?

I switched back to normal vision and examined her up and down. A fading glow in the comm badge drew my attention. The badge was about the size of a silver dollar but square and a quarter of an inch thick. It looked metallic except for a transparent oval in the shape of an eye.

The sedation and experiments hadn't made me the most observant person in the world, but I would have noticed if the comm badge glowed all the time. I took a chance and tested my theory. I extended my essence and endured another icy electrocution from the shadow aura. My teeth clenched tight and my muscles locked up. For a moment, I didn't think I'd be able to withdraw, but Kalesh stepped in and cut off the probe.

You have no understanding of our true power.

I ignored him and looked at the comm badge. It glowed a little brighter than last time, fading to dark after a few seconds. It didn't take a genius to connect the dots. The badge had anti-magic technology and shielded the wearer from my demonic abilities. It probably protected them from vampiric compulsion as well.

If I could yank off her badge, I could seduce her with my demonic powers. Accomplishing that would be an incredible feat, considering Pari would have to put her chest right up against my shackled hands or near my mouth. She invaded my personal space all the time, but usually stood to the side.

Specialist Brills came back into the room and eyed the instruments. "Slice and dice day, doc?"

Pari rolled her eyes. "You have no appreciation for the scientific process." She took a wax marker and drew a dotted line across my forearm.

Cold sweat broke out on my forehead at the thought of losing an arm. I might have supernatural healing, but I doubted my limbs would grow back. Plus, I'd look really stupid channeling magic through a stump.

"I ain't got no appreciation for these freaks." He picked up his cattle prod and stood nearby. "God didn't make these things."

"Oh, how quaint. A religious man." Pari went to the table and chose a large serrated bone knife for the task. "If your god is omnipotent, he's responsible for everything on this earth. If he's not, he's not a god."

I needed to extend this conversation any way possible or I was about to get mutilated by this crazy scientist. So I took a shot in the dark and offered them some information they might not have. "Even the Apocryphan aren't omnipotent."

Brills brandished his prod, but Pari put up a hand. "Apocryphan?"

"Godlike beings who used to rule the world."

Brills sneered. "The world was never ruled by freaks."

"Private Brills, you will remain quiet and at your post." For once, steel shone in Pari's eyes. "Commander Edge is keen on gaining all the information we can."

Brills's fingers clenched around the handle of the prod, but he backed off and stood by the wall.

Pari put aside the knife and came closer. "Tell me more."

"Four or five Apocryphan—I don't remember exactly—once ruled the Earth. A rogue named Xanomiel—she goes by Xanos now—tricked them into fighting each other. This allowed the Sirens to banish them into a prison called the Abyss."

"Sirens?" Pari tapped on her tablet and aimed the camera at me. "Yes, keep going. This is fascinating."

"There was another war not long ago. A rogue Seraphim tried to invade Eden—Earth—and we had to fight her off. I accidentally freed Xanos from the Abyss and now she's loose and set on world domination."

Brills growled. "Can't you see he's making this up to buy time?"

"Perhaps." Pari pursed her lips and regarded me for a moment. "I'll let the commander decide the merits of the information."

"There's tons more." I planned to give a blow-by-blow replay of the war against Daelissa—whatever it took to keep my arm intact for another minute more.

"I'll let you tell me more after the procedure." Pari rubbed her hands together. "I'm excited to see your regenerative abilities. If they're as grand as I imagine, you'll be a very important part of our Weapon X program."

I struggled uselessly. "Why cut off my arm? How about starting small—like yanking out a fingernail or something?"

She filled a syringe with clear fluid, squeezed out the air, and jabbed it into my arm. "I promise this won't hurt."

My stomach constricted. I wanted to vomit and scream. "But what if my arm doesn't grow back?"

"Then I'll be disappointed." Pari withdrew the needle and patted my arm. "It should be numb in a moment." It seemed only scant seconds passed when she grabbed the knife and brought it back. She pinched my skin. "Do you feel that?"

"Yes!" I writhed in my bonds, but the shackles held my arms firmly in place. "Please don't do this. I like having two arms."

"Shut up!" Brills rammed the prod into my ribs.

A scream tore from my throat.

"Private Brills, there's no need to traumatize him further." Pari shooed him away with the knife. "I don't want anything to affect his regeneration." She put the knife to my arm and sawed it back and forth once. Blood seeped out. She wiped away the blood and watched as my skin knitted itself back together. "Fascinating."

Despair and fear coiled around my insides. "Don't do this!" All my negative emotions boiled in a cauldron. "You have no right!"

"Please remain calm. This will only take a moment." Pari put the bone knife against my forearm and began to saw. My skin was numb, but I felt the vibrations. Nausea snaked up my throat as the metal hit the bone.

You are weak. Kalesh surged against his cage. *I am strong!*

My cauldron boiled over. Hatred and rage filled my body. "I have had enough!" I focused on the floor, even as the knife sawed into my bone. I didn't even stop to think if it would work. I just did it. My mind reached through the window of my soul and found a nest of lesser spawn spirits. A pool of pitch black formed on the floor.

Brills leapt forward. "We've got a class four breach!"

Pari ignored him and continued to saw.

The pool bubbled. Tiny black scorpions struggled free from the primordial goo.

Brills rammed the prod into my chest. "Submit! Submit!"

I bared my teeth and endured the pain, focused on the creatures crawling forth from the depths of Haedaemos. "You will submit," I snarled.

Pari stumbled back, confused. Then she saw the seething mass. "What sort of breach is that?"

"Demonic!" Brills reared back with the prod and slammed it into my chest with everything he had.

I roared in pain and my concentration snapped. But it was too late.

A swarm of shiny black scorps covered the floor behind Brills. They rolled into a mass, like ants clustering to survive a flood, and surged toward him. Brills screamed as they swarmed up his legs, devouring everything in their path.

Hold. It took everything I had in my weakened state to keep the scorps from finishing him. "Release me or die."

Pari backed away slowly, edged toward the door. Part of the swarm covered the door at my command. She held up her hands. "I don't have a key for your restraints!"

I glared at Brills. "Release me!"

"I don't have them, you bastard!" His pants were shredded. Blood trickled from raw flesh. Muscle and bone showed through his wounds.

"Then you will be devoured." My voice rumbled in demon mode. "There will be nothing left."

"No!" Brills held up his hands. "I'll go get the keys, I promise."

"You lie." My rage began to subside, replaced by frustration. I had all the power in the room, but no chance of escape.

217

Brills yanked something from his ankle. It was covered in blood, but recognizable. He'd had a pistol in an ankle holster! A pop rang out. A bullet pinged off my shackles. I reacted without thinking. The scorps swarmed Brills. He screamed in agony and dropped the pistol.

Pari's screams of horror joined his.

I made the scorps stop, but it was too late. Brills dragged himself across the floor, a mess of torn flesh and blood. An eye dangled from a socket. His lips were gone, teeth and sinew exposed. His hand reached for Pari's shoe, trembled and went limp. A death moan rattled from his throat and he went still.

Pari hadn't stopped screaming. It was a wonder no one else had come to check on the ruckus. I didn't know much about scorps, so I directed them to eat the shackles. They were like a hive mind, a hundred impulses bound into one directive. The pressure of controlling them grew slightly easier as I became accustomed to the sensation.

The swarm rolled closer to the shackles but refused to eat them. Apparently, metal wasn't on their list of approved foods.

What now? If I killed Pari, I'd still be imprisoned. I might be able to summon a hellhound and have him carry me out of here, but that would be extremely awkward. I could also have a hellhound mimic Brills's appearance and send him out to search for the keys, but that would take forever. I would have to find a very specialized demon spirit for that role, and it would take time.

I had all the power in the room, but I was still a prisoner.

CHAPTER 22

"Please don't kill me." Pari held out her hands defensively even though the scorps didn't advance on her.

That was when a much simpler solution presented itself. "Remove your comm badge."

Her eyes flared. "Why?"

"Do it or die." I was done playing games with this woman.

Pari gingerly plucked it from her lab coat and put it on the table. The shadow aura faded, leaving behind an ordinary dim white halo. I extended a tendril and latched onto Pari's essence. Her eyes flared, and a gentle gasp escaped her throat.

I amped up the sexual aura just enough to attract her to my filthy, naked self.

She moaned. "Oh, wow. I'm super aroused. These must be the powers we were warned about."

My incubus powers were great at emotional manipulation, but it was a far cry short of mind control. I turned it up a little more. Pari moaned and pressed herself against me despite the shackles between us. *Feed!* Kalesh drew on her essence without so much as a by-your-leave from me. I was too hungry to resist and siphoned her emotional energy into me.

"I can't help myself!" Her eyelids fluttered. "Take me now!"

"I need to get out of these restraints first. Get the keys and release me."

"There are no keys." She leaned down and pressed her lips to my cheek. "There's a magnetic release in the observation room through that door."

I was instantly suspicious. On a conscious level she knew what I was doing to her and might have some modicum of control. If she got far enough away from me, I'd lose my connection to her. On the other hand, I did have a swarm of scorps to babysit her.

"Go release me." I moved the scorps away from the door. "But they'll be watching you."

She was too consumed with pleasing me to even give the little monsters a glance. Pari yanked open the door and dashed through. The shackles snapped open in a chorus of clicks. I groaned at the sweet, sweet release. I rubbed my chafed wrists, massaged my sore neck.

Pari burst back inside. "You're free!" She straddled me and nuzzled my neck. "This is fascinating. I'm so aroused I can't control my primal urges even though your body odor is abysmal." She abruptly shoved me so hard she fell from my lap and onto the floor. "Release me, you monster!"

I stood on wobbly legs and glowered down at her. "After everything you've done to me, we both know who the real monster is." I fed on her aura, gaining strength and recharging my demon batteries.

Pari crawled toward me, body trembling as she tried to regain control of her hormones. I'd never seen a non-supernatural female with so much control. "Your kind have no right to this world. I worked so hard to be the best." Tears trickled down her cheeks. "It's unfair that you are born with these gifts."

I genuinely felt bad for her, but she was my ticket out of this joint. One thing was certain. "I need clothes." I amped up the demonic persuasion even more. It was nowhere near as good as vampiric compulsion, but Pari's eyes glazed over as her baser functions went into hyper-drive.

"Anything for you." She whimpered and went back to the other room, returning with a short lab coat.

"Where are my clothes and my things?"

"I don't know. Most prisoners' items are kept in the control rooms. Yours are not."

I put on the lab coat even though it barely covered my privates. "I was captured with five other people. Where are they being held?"

Pari moaned and pressed her face to my chest. "Please take me. I can't stand it anymore." She bit my neck. "Do it now!"

This was the downside to my incubus abilities. Sexual persuasion worked to a point, but too much made the subject unable to do much but think about sex. I held her at bay and turned down the sexual volume. "Where are my friends?"

She trembled and glared at me. "There were only three of you. The others escaped."

I felt intense relief that some of my friends had escaped this torture. "Where are they being held?"

Pari was done with questions. She grasped at my tender bits. I dodged back and gripped her shoulders. Her hormones had completely over-whelmed her higher brain functions. Considering what she'd done to me in the name of science, I shouldn't have felt bad, but I did. I felt like a class A mind rapist.

Consume her soul. Kalesh had his own plans, but I wasn't about to drain her dry.

I released her aura. Pari cried out and fell to the floor, just missing a puddle of Brills's blood. She sobbed softly for a moment then abruptly jumped up and tried to make a run for it. My legs were wobbly, but I was still too fast for her. I snagged her arm and dragged her into the control room.

Two rows of seats offered observers a view through the two-way mirror. A touchscreen control panel displayed a variety of options, including the magnetic lock release for the chair shackles. I tapped the screen "Can I find my friends with this?"

Pari struggled in my grasp. "I refuse to help you."

I directed the scorp swarm closer. "Then they will eat you."

She shivered. "It is better I die protecting us from your kind. You can't escape without my help."

"Then I'll send my little monsters to kill everyone in this facility."

Pari's eyes flared, but just as quickly narrowed. "No, if you could do that, you would have done it to escape days ago."

I clung to her time reference. "How long have I been here?"

"Three days."

For some strange reason I felt relieved. Without a sense of time, it seemed as if I'd been a prisoner for weeks. Unfortunately, Pari was right. I could summon more scorps, but I didn't have the skills to simultaneously control several swarms and send them everywhere at once. Then again, I might have another option.

"How large is this building?"

She scoffed. "I won't tell you anything else."

I grabbed her by the neck. "Then suffer the consequences."

Fear filled her eyes. She wormed in my grasp, but there was nothing she could do. I dragged her into the other room and pushed her into the shackles. I had a scorp tap on the control tablet and the magnetic locks clacked shut, shackling the scientist from head to ankle. I picked up a piece of Brills's bloodied, shredded uniform and shoved a wad in her mouth.

Kalesh didn't like where this was going. *You are weak. Use our powers to control her!*

For a moment, I was tempted. This woman tried to cut off my arm. She'd repeatedly violated me for three days and even stuck a finger up my ass. I felt the urge to crush her windpipe and watch her die. My hand clamped around her neck and squeezed. Her eyes bulged, but she was helpless to resist, just as I'd been.

"No!" I yanked my hand back. "Stay in your cage, demon." I forced Kalesh into a prison of willpower. He seemed amused. It was getting easier for him to influence me and that didn't bode well at all.

I picked up the bone saw from the floor. Pari squirmed and shook her head. I touched the bloodied metal to her arm. I leaned close and whispered in her ear. "I'm excited to see if it grows back."

The gag muffled her screams. I burst into laughter.

What am I doing?

I dropped the saw and backed away. Kalesh laughed in my mind. I pressed a hand to my forehead. *This is worse than I thought.* My demon side was already gaining the upper hand.

You are weak, but soon we will be strong.

I backed away from Pari and went into the control room. I eased open the outer door and peeked out. I blinked a few times to adjust my eyes to brilliant lights. Polished white concrete stretched in all directions. My prison was a large concrete cube, as white as everything else in sight. I counted over a dozen more cubes, each one spaced about fifty yards from the next. There were dozens more beyond those.

The room seemed to stretch on forever in all directions, an illusion only enhanced by the white walls, white ceiling, and white prison cubes. It was like being snow blind on a sunny day. I squinted, trying to gain perspective, and made out a wall a few football fields away.

The facility was enormous. "Who in the hell are these people?" They had to be well-funded to afford a place like this.

Footsteps echoed in the distance. I put my back to the wall of my former prison and looked around. A woman in black marched past several rows down from me. I took my time and observed the other directions. Three more guards walked past, but none patrolled down the row toward me.

I took a moment in between patrols to walk around my cube, looking for identifying marks. A small bar code outside the door was the only thing I found. My legs felt a bit stronger since feeding on Pari, so I crouched and leapt. My fingers caught the top of the cube, some fifteen feet high. I pulled myself up and looked around. The roof was also nearly blank aside from a small barcode in the center.

The elevated position wasn't much use since my cube sat in the middle of a sea of identical buildings. If there were any exits on the walls, they were hidden from here. I dropped back down to the floor. Exits or not, getting out of the building wasn't my top priority right now. I had to find my friends first. Pari said they'd captured three of us, but I didn't know which three. I just had to hope they were all in this facility.

I dashed across the fifty yards to the neighboring cube, my bare feet barely making a sound, my unsecured junk bouncing around uncomfortably beneath the hem of the lab coat. I located the door and pulled on the handle. It was locked. *Why was my door unlocked?* Maybe Brills and Pari didn't lock it when they were inside but locked it when they left. There was no keyhole, number pad, or biometric scanner mounted near the door, just the bar code.

A gentle yank with my demon strength didn't work. I braced myself to rip it off its hinges but paused. The sound of shrieking metal would probably alert the guards. If one of them stumbled across a jacked-up doorframe, they'd definitely raise the alarm. There had to be a better way to unlock this door.

I went back to my prison cube and searched the control room. There were door controls, but they only worked on this cube. I examined the outer door. Thick metal bolts extended from all sides and slid a foot into the concrete. I'd have to fully manifest into demon form to smash through one.

No biometrics, no keycards, no keys—how in the world did they control access? I went back into the room where Pari slumped in her shackles. She glared at me accusingly. I knew she wouldn't give up answers unless I got really mean. But a square object on the floor caught my attention.

Pari's comm badge.

I face-palmed. "Duh." I grabbed it and went back outside the cube. After careful examination, I found a small square imprint in the middle of the door. I touched the badge to it and the bolts in the door clanged into place. Another tap released them.

I'm in business!

I peered carefully around before making a move to the next cube. I heard boots on concrete, but the sounds were distant. I sprinted across the space to the same cube I'd tried moments ago. Pari's badge unlocked it, and I went inside. Instead of a control room, I stood in a white room with a drain in the floor. A body lay on a metal table, blood streaming through channels and into the drain. The skin was held open with clamps, the few organs inside exposed.

"Oh my god." Bile rose in my throat. Though the head was shaved bald, the face was feminine. A stainless steel tray held teeth, among them vampire fangs. A video screen on the wall displayed a diagram of the body and notes. The initials *Dr P.* were at the bottom.

She's the monster.

I wanted to squeeze Pari's head between my hands. Hear the crack of her skull. She deserved it for this atrocity. Fear swelled, a tide of icy water freezing my heart. *Is Elyssa here somewhere? Is she still alive?* In the days I'd been here, what if Pari had dissected all my friends?

I didn't have a moment to lose. I rushed back outside and went to the next room down. It held a deceased man. The notes on the board indicated he was a lycan. Much to my relief, the next few cubes were empty. I kept count so I'd know how many cubes back returned me to my former prison. Since every row of cubes looked the same, it was difficult to orient myself without tracking every step.

When I reached the wall at the far end, I peeked cautiously up and down the outer aisle. The wall was concrete like everything else and seemed to have no doors. I mentally labeled it as the northern wall just to give me some sense of direction.

The next row of cells was empty, but uncleaned bloodstains hinted at unpleasant activities. Anxiety gripped my heart. What if this room previously held Shelton or Elyssa? What if one of my friends had died in here? My heart pounded faster; my throat constricted. What if I'd escaped too late to save them?

Get a grip!

I closed my eyes and took deep breaths to drive away the panic attack. Elyssa and the others were still alive. They just had to be. No matter the situation, I had to search every last cell. If they weren't here, that meant they had to be somewhere else.

I found another living being in the next cube.

Like my cell, it had a control room. Instead of a chair, a clear cylindrical container held a naked androgynous creature with smooth, gray skin. It stared at me with a look of human confusion on its alien face.

"Who the bloody 'ell are you?" it said in a British accent.

For a moment, I couldn't think of an answer. "*What* the bloody hell are you?"

Its skin shaded pink, gained pores and texture. Nether regions morphed into all the glorious detail of a male. "Like I told the others, I'm a Flark."

CHAPTER 23

C onrad Shelton took off his cowboy hat and put it over his chest. "Hot damn, it's good to see this place again." He put the hat back on and ran a finger around the brim. "It ain't the original, but it still feels like home."

The Mansion loomed like a great shadow in the dim cavern. Only a few of the magical lights used by Victus and his cronies still flickered, and the stone building was an empty, haunted shell. Shelton rapped his staff on the ground and launched several glowballs into the air. "Once we get the aether generators up and running again, this place will be just like new."

The glowballs drifted higher, revealing black patches of old blood and piles of ash and bones littered around the cavern.

"Oh my." Bella grimaced. "There must have been another fight here."

"Your home was Victus's headquarters." Ambria shuddered. "His murderous minions lived like rats down here."

"Murderous minions, eh?" Shelton chuckled. "I like that."

Ambria opened her mouth as if to respond, but his amused tone disarmed her.

"I can't believe the entire campus is empty." Ivy scuffed a shoe against a bloodstain on the stone floor. "It's like everyone killed one another."

"Humans." Thal scoffed. "You'll destroy each other long before the gods do."

"Probably." Shelton grunted. "We need to get this place up and running so we have a base of operations. Then we can figure out what happened."

"In the meantime, we will go to the Glimmer." Cora took Evadora's hand. "There is little we can do without an army."

"Yeah, fine. You go do that." Shelton walked toward the Mansion. "I'm gonna figure out how to rescue Justin."

"Yeah!" Ivy pumped a fist in the air.

"We'll probably need an army to do that as well." Bella studied a pile of bones from afar. "Perhaps it would be safer if we all went to the Glimmer for now."

"Maybe." Shelton turned around and took her hands. "Look, I know you're dying to see the Glimmer, so why don't you go with the others like you planned and the rest of us will get the Mansion cleaned up?"

"A trip to the Glimmer certainly sounds better than scrubbing blood off the ground and dusting furniture." Bella stood on tiptoe and kissed Shelton. "Just don't run off and do something foolish, my love."

"I promise I won't do anything stupid without letting you know first." He kissed her nose. "Have fun."

Conrad stared at the Mansion. It had been his home too, for a while. He wondered if it would feel the same knowing his father had lived here. Knowing his father had died here by Conrad's own hands. Victus's blood probably still stained the stone ground where Conrad had killed him.

Ambria's fingers laced through his. "Maybe we shouldn't stay here. This place feels haunted."

"It's just a building." Conrad shrugged off his unease. "We'll make it ours again."

"I hope you're right." Her hand tightened on his. "It looks rather foreboding."

"It's got the death cooties," Shelton said.

Ambria blinked. "The what?"

"Death cooties." Shelton shrugged. "Something dies in a place and infects it like a ghost."

Ambria grimaced. "Sounds awful."

"We'll make it ours again." Max bared his teeth. "I'm not gonna let Victus ruin everything we ever loved."

Shelton clapped Max on the back. "That's the spirit. A little soap and elbow grease, and we won't even think about all the dead bodies around here." He took in a deep breath and let it out slowly. "Everything is gonna be all right."

It sounded to Conrad as if Shelton needed to convince himself of that. "Let's check on the omniarch." Conrad turned around and went through the large opening in the cavern wall to the stone tunnel outside. An opening straight across led to a gauntlet room where Kanaan had trained him and his friends. The corridor to the right led into the Burrows, a maze of old prisons where Victus formerly housed his army of battle mages. The tunnel to the left ended at a smaller opening.

Conrad led the others through the latter opening and into a round room. As tall as it was wide, the black omniarch sat in the middle, a band of silver encircling the perimeter. Conrad knelt and sealed the circle then imagined the place he knew so well. The crack in the world appeared in his mind. The arch hummed. A silver line slashed the air and breached into a window to that very place.

"Now that looks interesting." Shelton stepped through and peered inside the crack. "Where does it go?"

"Across a great void and into the Glimmer." Evadora skipped behind him. "You should come see!"

Shelton backed away. "Later. We've got a lot of work to do."

Cora kissed Conrad on the cheek. "Be careful."

Conrad smiled. "You too."

Thal hovered behind Cora, her wings a silver blur. "It will be nice to leave the human realm."

Ivy stared longingly after Evadora. "I want to go, but you'll probably need my help cleaning up, Conrad."

"Go if you want," Shelton said. "If I can get the house golems up and running it won't be that hard."

"But I also want to help find Justin." Ivy bit her lower lip. "Maybe I'll stay here."

"Aww." Evadora frowned. "I wanted to show you everything."

"Okay!" Ivy bounced through the arch. "I'll just come back when they need me."

"Kids." Shelton chuckled. "Really had to twist her arm."

"Yes, kids." Bella wrapped her arms around his neck and pulled him down to her level for a long kiss. "You're the biggest kid I know, Harry." She tapped a finger on his nose. "Stay out of trouble."

"Yeah, yeah." He straightened up and watched his wife go through the crack after Cora and Evadora. Ivy and Thal followed close behind.

Shelton came back through the portal to the omniarch room and Conrad shut it off.

Ambria looked over at Max. "Well, it's just us again."

"Plus Shelton." Max grinned. "This is going to be fun."

"Yeah, loads." Shelton headed back into the corridor and turned right toward the Mansion. He ignored the ash, bones, and bloodstains and went straight inside the house. Conrad followed him through the east wing and into a room with dozens of rectangular aether generators plugged into a central matrix. Only one of the generators glowed. The rest looked undamaged, but they weren't drawing aether from the leylines.

Shelton rubbed his hands together. "Let's get these puppies up and running."

With help from a few spells and a lot of physical labor, all but two of the generators eventually glowed with life. It had been a long day and everyone was exhausted, but the pantry was bare, so Shelton opened a portal behind a Chinese restaurant and ordered everyone takeout.

Since no one wanted to sleep amidst the dust, blood, and ash in the Mansion, they set up camp in the gauntlet room and spent the night there. Aside from a few grunts and groans, even Shelton had little to say and retired to his sleeping bag shortly after their late supper.

CONRAD WOKE before the others the next morning, his neck stiff and sore from the hard ground. His funds were quite low thanks to paying for everyone's meals, so he forced down leftover ramen noodles for breakfast.

Shelton joined him moments later. He munched on baby corn and wolfed down General Tso's chicken before saying anything. "Not my favorite breakfast." He set down the cardboard container. "I can't wait to get this place cleaned up. Then it's pancakes and bacon forever."

"Sounds delicious." Conrad's mouth watered at the thought. "I would dearly love a shower."

Shelton chuckled. "Yeah, I'm a bit ripe myself."

Ambria rose, complaining about stiff muscles and a sore back. She had nothing positive to say about the cold Chinese food. Max, however, finished off his pork fried rice with relish.

"This is really quite good." He crunched into an eggroll. "Not bad at all for being cold."

And then it was back to work.

"Are we supposed to clean the entire Mansion ourselves?" Ambria asked as they walked back toward the house.

"Nah." Shelton shook his head. "Find the house golems. If they're salvageable, they can do the work for us."

That was apparently all the encouragement Ambria needed, because she found them within ten minutes. The previous owners had carelessly tossed them into a maintenance room in the east wing. Many were damaged, but most functioned once Shelton reactivated their sparks. Before long, a crew of wooden servants dispersed throughout the Mansion with instructions to clean it and its environs thoroughly.

Conrad expected a few surprises might lay in wait around the premises, but even he wasn't ready for the corpse a golem carried downstairs moments later. The shaved head and tattoos identified the man as one of Garkin's former followers even though his face was so burned it was unrecognizable.

"Hope they can clean the death cooties out of this place." Shelton studied the dead man for a moment then straightened with a shudder. "Let's check out the war room."

"It's right over here." Max rushed ahead of the others and went inside the first room in the west hall.

A scarred wooden table ran from one end to the other of the long, otherwise empty room. Shelton studied a bloodstained knife someone left buried in the center. "Damned people got no respect." He flicked his wand. The knife pulled free and landed in the hallway with a clang.

Max hovered behind him. "Is this where you planned the war against Daelissa?"

"Yep." Shelton sat on the edge of the table. "Standing room only in those days." He sighed. "Seems like yesterday."

"Maybe we can use it to plan the fight against the new bad guys." Max twirled his wand. A tiny tornado funneled the dust off the table and deposited it in a pile near the door. "We just need to bring the army here somehow."

Shelton jolted upright. "That's the ticket! We've got an omniarch. All we have to do is open a portal to Kratos and bring everyone through."

It was the best idea Conrad had heard in a while. "We could march straight to Xander and take back Queens Gate without a fight."

Ambria looked impressed. "Who would have thought Max and Shelton had a good idea?"

Max was in too big a hurry to retort. "Let's go to the omniarch. We don't want to miss the army if they already started evacuations."

Shelton checked his arcphone. "That shouldn't be a problem. It'll take 'em a few days to get everyone through."

Max dashed out of the room and shouted in alarm almost immediately.

Conrad hurried after him and skidded to a stop in the foyer. The single body had grown into several neat rows of ten. "This place is more like a mausoleum than a house."

"Holy smoking goat turds." Shelton waved over one of the golems. "Don't just leave corpses in the foyer. Take them out back."

"Out back?" Ambria's nose wrinkled. "Take them to the omniarch so we can portal them somewhere else."

Shelton snapped his fingers. "Yeah, what she said." He winked at Ambria. "See, you ain't so dumb after all." He stepped around the bodies and headed to the door.

Ambria's fists clenched. Conrad squeezed her shoulder to ward off an angry response.

She narrowed her eyes at Shelton's retreating form. "That man is insufferable."

Conrad thought the man was funny in a sarcastic way, but he wasn't about to tell Ambria that. "You shouldn't take him too seriously."

Her eyebrow arched. "You like him, don't you?"

He wisely avoided answering. "Let's catch up with him."

A gateway to the tiny island of Kratos already hung open within the omniarch when they entered the room. Max stepped through first and the others followed.

A warm ocean breeze greeted Conrad on the other side. Waves lapped gently at the sandy shores. Instead of a portal to Atlantis, only the dark clouds of Voltis rumbled offshore beneath blue skies.

"What the hell?" Shelton paced the shoreline and peered out at storm. "They should have started bringing people through already."

"We only just arrived in Eden yesterday," Ambria said. "It probably takes time to organize such a large exodus."

Shelton grunted. "Yeah, you're right. Problem is, we need to know when they actually start so we can redirect them through our portal."

"Maybe we could leave a sign." Max scrawled a glowing message in the air with his wand. *Call Shelton when you see this!*

"It could work," Ambria said. "Provided it lasts long enough."

"What would really be useful is an ASE." Shelton's lips pressed into a thin line. "Problem is, I don't know where to get one."

Ambria's forehead scrunched. "ASE?"

"All-seeing eye." Shelton formed a circle with his index finger and thumb. "About the size of a marble. It's a surveillance device the Templars use. I could leave one here and have it ping me when a portal opens."

"Maybe we could find a Templar and ask them," Max said.

Shelton snapped his fingers. "I'll bet Big Creek Ranch would have a supply."

Conrad frowned. "Why would a ranch have ASEs?"

"It's an undercover Templar compound." Shelton waved his hand. "Come on. Let's check it out." He went through the portal and back to the omniarch room. The house golems had already started stacking bodies outside the door. Shelton ignored the corpses, closed the gateway to Kratos, and opened a new portal. Cold air washed out from pitch black. Shelton's face blanched. He waved a hand and the gateway vanished.

Max shivered. "Was that the Void?"

"Yeah, and it ain't a place you ever want to open a gateway to." Shelton shivered and walked in a circle, rubbing his arms like a man who'd brushed shoulders with the grim reaper. "Why in the holy hell did it open there? I'd never forget what the Ranch looks like."

A sick feeling wormed into Conrad's gut. "What if it's not there anymore?"

Shelton turned even whiter. "You think Victus destroyed it?"

"Anything could have happened in all the years you were gone," Ambria said. "I don't think we ever visited the place."

Shelton closed his eyes. "Well, let's hope the gas station across the road is still around." He opened his eyes and activated the arch. A gateway formed behind a brown brick building with a square red logo. Shelton let out a sigh. "Thank sweet little baby Jesus that worked." He peeked through. Looked both ways. "Looks good. Let's go."

Conrad and the others followed him through. The portal was only three feet from the backside of the building. Since the portal was only visible from the front, no one would see it unless they walked to this very spot. A line of trees concealed their entrance from anyone at the car dealership behind them. Shelton cast an illusion to cover the portal just in case, and the group walked around the side of the building.

It was nighttime in this part of the world, but cars and trucks occupied nearly all the many petrol pumps. Conrad hadn't seen such a large petrol station in all his life. Shelton led them across the lot toward a busy highway. Traffic hummed both ways down six lanes. There didn't seem to be a place for pedestrians to cross.

Ambria looked back and forth. "Dare we risk our lives?"

"Nah." Shelton tapped on his arcphone and the green light turned red. Speeding traffic screeched to a halt. One car swerved to avoid rear-ending the truck in front of it. Shelton chuckled and traipsed across the road without a worry in the world. Once they were all across, another tap on his phone turned the light green again.

Max looked at him with wonder. "Did you hack the traffic system?"

"Heh, no." He showed Max the spell. "I just used illusion to make it look red."

"Smart and simple," Conrad said.

Ambria quirked her lips. "Clever."

"Hey, if it works, it works." Shelton shoved the arcphone in the pocket of his leather duster and continued down a residential street. A tall wooden fenced offered a modest obstacle against intruders. Shelton took out his phone again and scanned as they walked. He stopped where a gravel driveway led into pastures. Knelt and peered through the closed metal gate. "No active wards. No grass growing through the gravel. The lawn is short but uneven, so I'd bet horses are the ones trimming it." He stood. "Someone's here, but who?"

"Only one way to find out." Max drew his wand. "Let's take a look."

Conrad tapped into the primal fount just to be ready and followed his friend through the gate. They walked beside the gravel drive, keeping near a wooded area so they could conceal themselves if necessary. The silhouette of a large structure loomed at the end of the driveway. Two bright sconces lit a dark wooden door and a front stoop. A concrete walkway connected it to a stone carriage house on the left.

A horse whickered somewhere in the darkness, but the lack of lights and the sliver of moon made it impossible to see the animal.

Shelton stopped dead in his tracks. "No damned wonder I couldn't open a portal here. There's a four-car garage where the house used to be, and the church looks different."

"We'll take your word for it," Ambria said dryly. "What now?"

"What now?" Shelton huffed and walked straight toward the front door. "We find out what in the hell is going on here!"

Conrad grabbed his arm. "Wait! Are you sure that's a good idea?"

Shelton glared at the door as if he wanted to blow it off its hinges, then took a deep breath and looked around. His eyes lit on a large barn about fifty yards away. Without another word, he marched straight toward it.

"I really wish you'd verbalize your intentions," Ambria said.

Shelton grunted.

Dark green trim accented lavender wood—a far cry from most barns Conrad had seen. The barn looked large enough to house an entire herd of horses.

"It's so cute." Ambria ran a hand along the trim.

Shelton scoffed. "Yeah, exactly how the Templars like things—cute." He tugged on the door, but it wouldn't budge. "Son of a bitch."

Ambria tapped the latch with her wand and it clicked open. "That certainly worked better than your curses."

"I was gonna do that next." Shelton opened the door and peered inside. "Let's just hope the next lock isn't too hard to pick."

Conrad followed him inside. A light switch to the right activated florescent lights overhead. Instead of hay-covered dirt and stalls for livestock, they found a polished concrete floor. Vintage and exotic cars sat in neat rows along the walls, leaving the middle completely clear.

There was a loud double-click behind them. Conrad spun and faced a man with a black shotgun pointed squarely at him. The sides of his head were closely shaved, leaving a long thick patch of hair on top combed to the side. His neatly trimmed beard looked nearly six inches long.

"I think you've broken into the wrong place, people." The man spoke in a calm, unwavering voice. He locked gazes with Shelton. "I don't take kindly to thieves."

"Thieves?" Shelton bared his teeth. "Who are you and why do you live here?"

"You've got some nerve demanding answers when you're the one at the wrong end of a SPAS Twelve." He motioned to the left with the barrel. "Move ten feet to the left."

Keeping the gun trained on them, the man reached around a wooden beam and tapped on something on the other side. The center of the floor shifted, sloping down into a ramp that led into darkness.

Shelton didn't seem surprised, but his eyes burned bright with anger.

The man motioned with the barrel again. "Go down the ramp."

Shelton stopped Max from complying. "Why? Ain't you gonna call the police?"

The man's right eye twitched. "Already did. I'm going to tie you up in the basement until they get here."

"Sure you are." Shelton cocked his head slightly. "Let me ask you this. Are you a nom who stumbled across the complex underneath, or a turn-coat Templar?"

The man's eyes narrowed. "You aren't the first person to ask questions about this place." He motioned with the shotgun again. "I guess you'll just have to keep wondering."

"Until you take us below and kill us, that is." Shelton grinned. "You're a real sack of shit—"

The shotgun exploded in rapid fire.

CHAPTER 24

J*ustin*

I STARED with horror at the shape-shifting monster inside the cylindrical cell.

"You're a Flark?" My face screwed up with disgust. The only Flarks I'd known had fought for Daelissa. Ivy's former bodyguard had been a Flark named Mr. Bigglesworth. I didn't know much about the creatures except they could shapeshift like Silly Putty and touching them caused excruciating pain.

"You've heard of Flarks?" He seemed amused. "Who are you?"

"I'm Justin Slade. I fought against your kind in the Second Seraphim War."

"Yeah?" He scratched his head. "I told me mates no good would come from that crazy angel, but they got stars in their eyes." He made jazz hands. "Cost 'em their lives, it did."

"You didn't fight with them?"

"Me?" He scoffed. "Nah. I opened a bakery. I like Eden a lot better than Seraphina or the other hellholes I've visited. I copied a nice British gent and created an identity of my own. Apparently, the spooks here figured it out and came for me one day." He sighed. "Bloody shame. My cupcakes were selling like mad."

This was not the conversation I'd expected with a Flark. "Did you know a Mr. Bigglesworth?"

"Yeah sure." He scratched his head. "Right arsehole he was. I think he lived in Daelissa's bum hole half the time."

"If I release you, what will you do?"

"Well, I'd like to go back to me bakery, but I suppose it's a bust now." He slumped. "It's almost too sad to ponder."

I didn't know if the Flark was putting me on or not, but I also didn't relish leaving him here. He might be useful to my rescue efforts. "Hang on." I went to the control room and released the magnetic locks. The container clicked open.

The Flark stepped out and managed a wistful smile. "Much appreciated, mate." He held out his hand.

I regarded it like a snake. "I don't want to touch your hand. Bigglesworth tried to eat me!"

He guffawed. "I wouldn't do that. You just sprung me from jail."

"So touching you won't burn like a million fires?"

"Naw." He put out his hand. "It'll feel just like the real thing."

I patted his hand like a kid testing a hot stove. It felt normal. Still suspicious, I gave his hand a wimpy shake and released it. I tried not to look at his junk, but we were both free-balling it about a foot from each other.

"You can call me Tommy." The Flark grinned.

"I need pants."

He looked down and shrugged. "I suppose. Humans don't like prancing around in the nude for some reason."

"I just feel very vulnerable."

"Well, I'll put mine away if it makes you feel better." Tommy's genitals smoothed over into Ken-doll nothingness.

I winced. "Well, maybe a little." I went into the control room and opened the outer door to show him the giant room of cube prisons. "My friends are locked up in here somewhere. I have to find them before I can leave."

"I suppose the least I could do is help you find them." He pointed to the comm badge in my hand. "What's that?"

"It's the key to the cells." A guard patrolled two rows down, so I pulled my head back into the room. "I got it from Dr. Sidana."

Tommy scowled. "I'd like to give that woman a piece of my mind. She wanted to boil me in water to see if I melted!

"Yeah, she's an evil little bitch." I checked outside but the guard was coming this way. "We need to hold here until the guard goes past." I considered confronting the guard but all it took was a tap on his comm badge and more baddies would come running.

Something white slithered past my foot. I barely held back a cry of alarm. The guard turned left, oblivious to the tidal wave of white rising behind him. The Flark lunged and engulfed the man. The guard struggled for a moment then went limp. The doughy Flark morphed back into Tommy. "He'll be unconscious for a while."

"You didn't kill him?"

He shuddered. "I've never killed, and I don't plan to start now."

"Huh? But I thought Flarks had to eat their victims in order to morph into them."

"What?" He chuckled. "That's an old Flark's tale if ever I heard one."

I dragged the guard inside the cell. He was much shorter than me, but I didn't care. I stripped him down to his bright red briefs and tried to squeeze into the uniform, but it the pants were painfully tight. As much as it disgusted me, I took off the man's underwear and put them on. It felt mighty fine to secure my junk even though I looked more ridiculous than ever in a short lab coat and bright red briefs.

"May I?" Tommy took the pants and shrank his body to fit them.

"I guess nothing is ever too tight in the crotch for you."

He chuckled. "I can size to fit whatever I please." He put on the shirt and pointed to the guard's comm badge. "Can't hurt to have a spare."

"Can't you just morph your own clothes?"

He grimaced. "Aye, but nothing feels quite so good as cloth on the skin." He held up the guard socks and wriggled a finger through holes in the toes. "What a bloody shame to wear socks like these."

I dragged the guard into the cylindrical container and locked him inside. "Let's go."

Tommy pocketed the holey socks and we went to the next cube. The guard's badge opened the door. A green-skinned horror was shackled to a chair inside. It looked like a man, but slimy tentacles with suckers on the end wriggled from holes in its ribs and lunged for us. Smaller shackles held each one at bay.

I backed away. "What in god's name is that?"

"It's a blasted leecher." Tommy whistled. "They were predecessors to the vampires. The Seraphim created all kinds of little monsters by accident back in the day. I haven't seen a leecher in ages."

"How old are you?" I asked.

"Oh, about a thousand, give or take." He shrugged. "I didn't get over to Eden until Daelissa opened the Alabaster Arch. Coming to Eden was just the change I needed."

"So you could open a bakery."

"Yep." He grinned.

I waved at the leecher. "I'm Justin. I'm here to save you."

"Feed." It strained at the shackles. "Feed!"

"Oh, poor soul's pretty far gone," Tommy said. "They must've starved it so much that it can't even pretend to be human anymore."

"How do we save it?"

Tommy winced. "Best not to let it loose or it'll come after us. Believe me, it's so hungry it'll kill the next thing it gets its tentacles on."

"I'm tempted to feed Pari to it."

"Nah, mate." Tommy clapped my shoulder. "Killing only turns your soul black."

It was my turn to wince. "Then I'm in trouble."

"Oh, yeah. War with Daelissa and all that." He nodded. "Bet you killed lots."

"More than I wanted to."

"Yeah, most say that." He shrugged. "We moving on?"

I nearly cried with relief when we found Adam in the next cell. The inside of the cube resembled a normal jail cell, complete with stainless steel toilet, sink, and a thin mattress on the floor. Apparently, they didn't think Adam dangerous enough to shackle down. His phone and clothes were on a table in the control room which made me wonder why my clothes and Tommy's hadn't been on location too.

I turned on his arcphone, but it didn't have a signal. Something in the place was blocking it so I couldn't use the GPS to find our location.

Adam slumbered naked but peacefully and didn't wake when we prodded him. I covered his nethers with his shirt, because I'd seen enough man junk for one day.

"Must be drugged." I took in a deep breath. "Thank god he's okay."

"They really like to strip folks naked in here." Tommy shook his head. "Bloody perverts."

I couldn't argue with that. "I have one more friend to find. Let's leave Adam here since he's asleep and we'll come back when we find the other."

"What's your other friend's name?"

"Good question." I pinched the bridge of my nose to fight the headache of maintaining the scorps while we wandered around. I wanted them when we made our escape from the main complex, but the effort of maintaining them was wearing me out. "There were six of us, but three escaped, according to Pari. I don't know who else is here."

"You're bloody lucky the others escaped." He gazed longingly at Adam's socks. "Do you suppose he'd mind if I wore his socks?"

"Um, probably not."

Tommy slid the first sock on slowly, moaning with pleasure. "Oh, these are fresh. They must've cleaned them when they brought him in."

The pressure in my head continued to build as the scorps fought to get free so they could run wild and devour everything. While Tommy enjoyed his sock experience, I stepped outside the cube and summoned the little monsters. The death ball of pincers, claws, and sharp teeth rolled up to me. I concentrated on the floor. A black pool formed, and the creatures melted back into it, hissing and screeching with unsated hunger.

"Now that's a trick." Tommy knelt next to the fading goop and touched it. "Feels like slime."

"I suppose that's what it is." With the scorps gone, the pressure in my head subsided and the headache faded. I took a moment to listen for patrolling guards and heard nothing but the background hum of electricity and air conditioning.

"It's a wonder they don't have more guards in this place." Tommy wiggled his toes in the socks. "Seems awfully large for just two or three."

"Yeah, it does." Either Razor was confident no prisoners ever escaped from their cubes, or this building was inside a larger guarded complex.

The next cube held the bodies of two men and a woman. The transparent spheres on a nearby table told me they weren't real people at all, but infernus. It seemed Razor had a way to hunt them down as well.

Tommy picked up a sphere. "What are these things?"

I prodded one of the bodies. It wasn't too mushy, indicating it hadn't been dead long. "These bodies are made of demon flesh. The soul spheres combine a golem spark and a soul fragment to give them life."

"Like golems?"

"The most realistic golems you've ever seen."

"Too real." Tommy brushed the hair from the female's face. "They could pass for genuine humans."

"That's the point. They were made to replace officials in the Overworld government so Victus Edison could take over." I gave him a brief history of Conrad's experiences. "There are probably hundreds of infernus moles still out there. I'd like to know how Razor is able to track them down."

"Same way they track down everyone—with these little black cubes." Tommy held his hands a couple of inches apart to approximate the size.

"They showed up in my bakery with one of those bloody things and went right for me."

I went back out to the corridor and looked around before heading to the next cube in the row. It felt like I'd been searching for hours, though it had probably only been an hour. Even so, I feared someone would discover my escape and we still had a lot of real estate to cover. We cleared the last three cubes in the row, all empty, and moved to the next. The first one held the remains of something resembling a giant, dead fish. The next one, nothing.

The third had a jail cell like Adam's. A figure huddled beneath a blanket on the mattress. My hopes soared. When I opened the door, the person in the cell leapt to their feet, hands crooked like claws, teeth bared. She didn't seem the least bit concerned about her lack of clothes. Recognition spread across her face.

"Justin?"

I froze in place, grasping for words. "Stacey? Is that you?"

She clapped her hands and jiggled in all the right places. "Bloody right it is!"

Tommy scratched his head. "This your missing friend?"

"No, it's another friend from a long time ago." I hit the release and opened the cell. Stacey sprang through and gripped me in a crushing hug.

"Oh, my dear, sweet little lamb! You came to save me."

"Not exactly."

She backed off and looked down, a mischievous grin spreading across her lips. "Oh my." She tugged on the base of the lab coat, nearly grazing my nuts beneath the red briefs. "You wish to indulge in a prison fetish?"

I gulped. "Dude, you're with Ryland."

"Yes, but, exceptions could be made." Stacey laughed and kissed my cheek. "You're the same innocent boy I remember."

My face flushed with heat. "Not innocent, exactly."

Tommy tossed a heap of clothing to Stacey. "You're a ripe little peach, you are, but I suppose you should cover up."

Stacey was every bit as curvy and sexy as I remembered. She caught me looking and smiled. "Are you certain you want me to cover up?"

"Please," I said in a strained voice. "You're awfully chipper for someone stuck in captivity."

"Well, I only just arrived yesterday." She pulled on skintight yoga pants and a T-shirt with *Kitty Mistress Supreme* scrawled across it. "Ryland took the children to Montana for a wilderness experience. I was supposed to join them, but a group of noms took me completely by surprise." She cocked her head. "My god, are you a prisoner too?"

"I was, but I escaped." I motioned to the Flark. "This is Tommy."

"Pleased, I'm sure." Stacey nodded at him. "Can anyone explain what this is all about?"

"An organization called Razor Echelon is capturing supers and experimenting on them." I tugged on the hem of the lab coat, feeling very exposed even with the underwear. "They seem to be hell bent on capturing or wiping supers off the face of Eden."

Stacey took my hands. "Speaking of which, where in Eden have you been for the past nine years?"

"That's a long story, and we still have someone else to save."

Her eyebrow quirked. "Who?"

"It could be a fairy, a wizard, a kid or my girlfriend, but I won't know until we find them."

She laughed. "Oh, Justin. Always on an adventure."

I squeezed her hands and kissed her cheek. "It's really good to see you again."

Stacey cupped my cheek. "You too, love. I should've known my lamb would rescue me."

Tommy squinted at us. "You two must have an interesting history."

"Oh yes." Stacey smiled. "Oh, the things we've done."

I put up my hands. "But nothing sexual."

"Shame." Tommy shook his head. "She's got a lovely figure."

"Why, thank you, Tommy." Stacey blushed.

I groaned and went to the exit. "Let's get moving. I don't know how much time we have before someone realizes I'm missing."

"How are you able to enter the cells?" Stacey said.

I showed her Pari's badge. "This opens them."

"Interesting," She said. "So we can't split up and search?"

"Maybe with this." Tommy held out the guard's badge. He demonstrated its use in the door to her cube and it opened. "Works fine, as you can see."

Stacey's eyes widened when we stepped outside of her cube. "This place is absolutely monstrous."

"Bloody right," Tommy said. "It'll take us a while to make it through every row."

Stacey took the guard's badge from him. "I'll make quick work of the next row over. You finish this one."

I put an arm on her shoulder. "Be careful. There's at least two more guards wandering around this place."

She purred. "They'll never catch a cat on the prowl." With that, she blurred away.

"Feisty one, she is." Tommy nodded in approval. "I like her."

"Yeah, me too." Something in the ambient sound changed—a high-pitched whirring. I looked up and around and spotted the source. A small black drone rose in the air near the far corner. Our window of escape had just narrowed considerably.

CHAPTER 25

"Take cover!" I pulled Tommy behind the cube and let him peer around the corner at the surveillance drone. "That thing probably has a camera. If it sees us, we're screwed."

"I didn't notice it earlier." He frowned. "You think they know something's up?"

"Maybe. I don't know. Let's not waste any more time." I sprinted to the next cube and went inside. The control room window looked into a white room filled with people. Their naked forms huddled together, faces down. They moaned and whimpered. Their skin looked painfully red and blistered.

"Look at this." Tommy showed me the control panel. "Says the ultraviolet light level is at thirty percent."

"They're vampires!" I turned it down to zero and the light in the other room dimmed. I released the door lock and opened it.

"Please, no more!" one of the men sobbed. "You're killing us!"

One of the women's eyes narrowed. "Uh, he's not wearing any pants."

A girl snickered. "Nice undies."

"My name is Justin Slade and I'm here to save you," I proclaimed, red underpants flashing beneath the lab coat.

"More like Captain Underpants," one of the women said.

"Wait, you're *the* Justin Slade?" One of the men rose. "I thought you and everyone who went to Seraphina were gone forever."

"Almost, but not quite." I waved off the question. "Look, we've got a small window of opportunity to escape, but I'm still trying to find someone."

"Can't we make a run for it?" another vampire asked.

"Not yet." I bit my lip and tried to think of a plan. "Wait here until we come back for you."

"Just sit here?" The crying vampire wiped his eyes. "They've been torturing us for days. They took away Belinda and Reed and we haven't seen them since."

I thought of the vampire fangs in one of the other cells and grimaced. "I'm afraid they killed them."

"No!" A male vampire dropped to his knees. "Who are these damned monsters?"

"Ain't that the question?" Tommy gave him a sad look. "But it's best if you wait until we come back. Otherwise, we might set off an alarm and we'd all be right back to these bastards' tender mercies."

The girl who'd commented on my underwear stood up. "I'd like to know where my clothes are. I didn't just buy that shit off the rack, you know."

Vampires were very fashionable creatures even in the worst of times. Seeing them huddled in this naked mass was definitely off-putting.

"Out here." Tommy opened a black chest filled to the brim with attire. "You lot certainly love your fancy underwear."

The girl shoved past us. "They're more than panties. They're a way of life." She sorted through the chest, tossing articles of clothing everywhere.

I could see this would take a while. "We'll be back. Please don't go outside without us."

"You've got fifteen minutes," the girl said.

"Jesus, Clarissa." The crying man gave her a look of disbelief. "He's Justin Slade. He knows what he's doing."

"I hope he can do it in a hurry."

I grabbed her arm and spun her around. "You'd better listen to me, or I'll throw you to the wolves."

"As if!" She held a lacy bra in her hand—one far too busty for her and shook it in my face. "I won't risk staying here just so you can run around and play hero. Fifteen minutes, and we're leaving."

"You realize he just played hero with us, right?" One of the other women got in her face. "I swear to god, Clarissa, if you screw this up, I'll snap your neck."

"Makes two of us." Another woman bared her fangs. "And give me my damned bra."

Clarissa gulped and handed over the lingerie. "Fine, bitches. Don't come crying to me if he gets us all killed."

"We might as well have been dead before he came along." The crying man took a deep breath. "We'll be here."

I gave Clarissa one last glare. "Thanks. We won't be long."

And we really weren't. Tommy and I left the cube and peered cautiously around for guards and drones before heading to the next cell. A slap on my ass scared me so bad I almost screamed. I spun around and saw the most beautiful sight in the world. Elyssa looked bruised, but gorgeous as ever.

"Babe!" I wrapped my arms around her and drew in her scent. "I didn't know if you were here or not."

"Thank god, Justin." She melted in my arms. "I didn't think I'd ever escape."

"We're about to." I looked at Stacey. "Thank you."

"My pleasure."

"What about your other friend?" Tommy said.

I slapped my forehead. "Yeah, we need to go get Adam. He's asleep a few rows over." It took a moment to orient myself toward the correct cube. "Third one down."

"I'll be back." Stacey blurred away.

I looked around for the drone and spotted it drifting back and forth across the vast space, but slowly making its way here. I took the moment to pepper Elyssa's cheeks with kisses. "I'm so happy these evil asses didn't kill you."

"Aside from a man who brought me food, I didn't see anyone else." Elyssa looked around. "This is the oddest prison I've ever seen. Cubical cells in a warehouse space. Why not use something more conventional?"

"No idea." I rubbed a hand on the glossy white wall. "I think they went for style over substance."

"I'm just so relieved you're okay." Elyssa leaned her head on my chest. "Did you find everyone else?"

I told her what Pari had said. "Using the power of deduction, that means the three who escaped were Shelton, Thal, and Max."

"I hope they made it somewhere safe."

"Yeah, me too." I motioned to my new pal. "This is Tommy the Flark. I found him along the way."

"Pleased to meet you." Tommy doffed an imaginary cap.

"A Flark?" Elyssa flinched. "Since when are they friendly?"

"Most of us aren't the bad sort," Tommy said. "Just like all Seraphim ain't out for world domination."

Stacey appeared around a corner, Adam slung over her shoulder. She set him down just outside the vampires' cube. "I can't wake him up. Suppose I'll have to carry him out."

"Yes, please." I opened the door and poked my head in. Most of the vampires were clothed. "It's time to go."

"I can't find my Roger Wilhelm alligator boots!" one of them complained. "They cost over a thousand dollars."

"Yeah, well, be ready to barefoot it out of here in a moment." I closed the door. "We don't know where the exit to this place is or what's outside. Let's hope they're as lax about guarding the outside as they are the inside."

Elyssa's eyes locked onto the drone. "In another ten minutes, we'll have to take cover or risk that thing spotting us."

"We don't even know where the exit is yet." I paced back and forth anxiously. "Those vampires need to shift into high gear or I'm leaving them."

"Should we search the other cells?" Stacey said. "There might be others we can rescue."

I estimated we'd cleared about a third of the cells. That left far too many to search. "We shouldn't risk it. If they catch us again, we might never get out. At least we can get help from the outside if we escape."

"Oy, you've got it mate." Tommy winked. "Ain't many places can hold me, but this lot did. We gotta run for it. Come back later to save anyone we left behind."

"Provided they don't lock down the facility even tighter." Elyssa frowned. "But you're right. Every moment we're here, we risk being captured. Judging from the size of the force that captured us, they have a small army at their disposal."

"First things first," I said. "Where do we get out?"

"I'll scout the perimeter." Stacey saluted with a wiggle and some nice jiggle. "Lamb."

I grinned. "I missed you."

She blew me a kiss and dashed away.

Elyssa gripped my hand harder than necessary. "Shall I scout too, boo bear?"

"Boo bear?" Tommy chuckled. "I like that name better than Justin."

"Uh, I wasn't flirting with Stacey."

Elyssa quirked an eyebrow. "Mhm."

"For realz!" I kissed her hand. "But it would be totes amazeballs if you looked for an exit too."

"You got it, Commander Boo Bear." She slapped my ass and blurred away.

Tommy grunted. "I certainly know who wears the pants in your relationship."

I threw up my hands. "She's a freaking ninja. Of course she wears the pants."

"Nyug nyug!" Adam struggled to his feet and dashed away in a drunken fervor. He made it two feet before flopping on the ground like a dying fish.

Eyes wide, he opened his mouth as if about to shout, so I clamped a hand over his pie hole. "Hush! You're safe."

Adam struggled uselessly in my grasp. His dilated pupils gradually shrank, and his gaze seemed to focus on me for the first time.

"Adam?"

He nodded. I released his mouth. "Justin, where in the hell am I?"

"We're breaking out of the slammer." I brought him up to date on our progress. "Once the vampires get dressed and we find an exit, we're getting out of here."

He nodded sluggishly, still fighting off the drugs in his system. "Wow, you've done a lot and all I did was sleep."

"Did anyone talk to you since you've been here?" I asked.

Adam frowned. "This one nasty dude who'd shock me with a cattle prod if I didn't take the drugs they gave me."

I bared my teeth. "Private Brills."

Adam turned to Tommy. "I'd really like to know more about Flarks. Do you mind answering some questions?"

I groaned. "Is that seriously at the top of your to-do list right now?"

"Dude, he's a Flark!"

"Dude, we're in a top-secret prison dedicated to holding supers."

Adam slumped. "Yeah, I guess you're right." He looked down at his shoes. "I hate wearing shoes barefoot. I wonder what happened to my socks."

"Oy." Tommy chuckled and pointed to his feet. "I borrowed 'em earlier, mate. I took a set from a guard earlier, so you can have yours back."

Adam waved him off. "Nah that's okay. But I'll take the guard's socks if you don't mind."

"Of course not." Tommy tossed over a black ball. "They've got holes in the toes."

"Anything is better than barefoot," Adam said.

"Sock swapping is just gross." I shuddered and peeked back in the door at the vampires. "Are you ready yet?"

Clarissa primped in the two-way mirror. "I need five minutes."

"You've got until the others get back."

"Back from what?" one of the males asked.

"Scouting." I closed the door and watched the drone. It worked its way from the eastern side about five rows down. "We don't have much time until that thing's here."

Adam fiddled with his phone. "I don't have a signal to make calls, but I do have my spells." He flicked through a list. "I wonder if they protect the drones from hacking."

"You can hack it remotely?" I said.

"Nom devices usually aren't that hard." He activated a spell called *RV Shenanigans*. A wall of code scrolled down the screen and a green laser speared from the holoprojector. Adam pinpointed it on the drone.

"They have a lot of anti-magic devices." Apprehension tightened my stomach. "I hope that thing isn't protected or it might set off an alarm."

The drone wobbled back and forth before stabilizing. The code on the phone flashed green and the laser blinked off. A holographic control panel appeared next to a camera feed.

"Gotcha." He flashed me a grin. The camera has a narrow field of view." Adam tapped on the virtual buttons. "It has an auto-patrol mode so the remote operator was probably just looking at the camera feed. I'm looping the last sixty seconds, so they'll think it's still patrolling."

Tommy looked over his shoulder. "Bloody impressive, mate. I never got into these gadgets. Too much to learn."

"Maybe you can find an exit with that thing," I suggested.

"It's possible." Adam directed the drone higher and zoomed in to the distant wall. He scanned from one corner to the next, but it was just a seamless canvas of white. He continued the rotation, but there wasn't so much as an exit sign in sight. "How in the hell do people get in and out of here?"

"It's because we're looking in the wrong place," Elyssa said behind me.

I yelped and jumped five feet off the ground.

Elyssa giggled. "Too easy."

"Supernatural hearing but no awareness." Stacey tsked. "My lamb, you really must be more careful."

I turned to face the women. "Ha. Ha." I rolled my eyes. "Tell me you found something."

"I found this." Elyssa handed me a clear bag with my clothes and arcphone inside. I was so happy I almost cried. She grinned. "The red underwear is cute, but not quite your style."

I gave her a big hug and kiss, then tore open the bag and swapped the red briefs for my own boxer briefs. I finally felt like me again, and it was good to have my arcphone, Nookli, back. "Did you find anything else besides my dignity?"

Elyssa pointed across the vast space. "Far right corner."

Adam directed the drone's camera that way and peered at the screen. "What am I looking for?"

"I see a white wall."

"Probably because you're so far away." Elyssa looked at Adam. "Good to see you're awake and functioning."

"Barely." He chuckled. "This place doesn't spare the drugs. They wanted to see how I performed magic while under the influence of various narcotics."

I frowned. "They got you high?"

"That's putting it mildly." Adam sighed. "Crack is a hell of a drug."

"More fun than the torture they put me through." I rubbed my now-healed wrists. "That crazy doctor wanted to saw off my arm and see if it grew back."

Adam winced. "Holy shit, that's insane."

"Are the damned vampires ready yet?" Elyssa opened the door. "Gather outside. We're moving out."

"Who are you?" someone said.

"The person telling you to move out!" Elyssa jabbed a thumb over her shoulder. "Come now, or get left behind."

A chorus of groans greeted her, but Clarissa and her blood-sucking troupe filed out, looking remarkably glam for the situation. Hands on hips, Clarissa gave me a regal gaze. "We are ready."

"God, I should hope so." I shook my head. "You realize we're trying to escape a prison, not dressing up for a night on the town."

"If you can't look great escaping, why bother escaping at all?" She made duck lips. "Let's get on with this."

"I'm sorry she's such a bitch," one of the men said. "We deal with her attitude all the time."

"*All* the damned time," the others muttered.

Clarissa shrugged. "As if I care."

Elyssa sighed. "You are such a vampire."

"Yeah, well you do you, honey."

I put an arm around Elyssa's shoulder before she took Clarissa's advice as an excuse to kick her ass. "Lead the way, babe."

Elyssa narrowed her eyes at Clarissa but nodded. "Okay."

We hauled ass toward what I labeled the southwest corner of the building. Adam used a spell to grant him extra speed and managed not to fall too far behind. Tommy's legs stretched like rubber, allowing him to take four strides for my every one.

We crossed the equivalent of four football fields to reach the coordinates. Only when we got closer did I see what the ubiquitous white camouflaged. What I perceived as the corner of the wall was a square protrusion running from the floor to the ceiling.

"I think it's an elevator shaft," Elyssa said. "But I couldn't find a way inside."

"I can get us in." Adam pulled up the drone controls and tapped on one labeled *Auto-Return*.

The drone zipped toward us and stopped overhead. It paused, then dropped to a few feet off the floor. There it remained for a solid minute before someone complained.

Clarissa stalked around it. "What's that stupid thing doing?"

"Waiting." Adam put a finger to his lips. "Hush and be patient."

"Not one of her strong suits," one of the vampires said.

"Patience can suck it," Clarissa said.

With a soft *snick*, the wall slid open and the drone drifted toward it.

"Everyone in, now!" Elyssa dashed inside.

I followed her inside a mid-sized elevator and the others squeezed in until we were packed like sardines. Tommy morphed into a stick figure to give the rest of us a little extra space. The drone sensed the objects in its way and rose higher to hover over our heads. The door shut, and the elevator began to rise.

"Oh, shit." Adam struggled to free his arm so he could point up. "There's a camera in here!"

"Hack it!" Elyssa said.

"I can barely move, much less reach my phone," he said.

"Fish in a bloody barrel." Tommy chuckled. "I hope we don't meet a firing squad when the door opens." He extended a slender limb to cover the lens.

"You've killed us all," Clarissa hissed. "I should have known better."

"Shut up!" Another vampire said. "It's better than frying to death."

"Yeah, at least we can go out in style."

"Whatevs, you morons." Clarissa scowled. "Just be ready to fight."

The elevator slowed to a halt, and we waited in dread to find out what waited on the other side of the door.

CHAPTER 26

C onrad

The barrel of the shotgun exploded into rapid fire.

Conrad barely had time to weave a shield. The buckshot that would have shredded Shelton's face sank into the shimmering barrier and hung a moment before dropping to the floor. The shotgun fired four more times in quick succession. Pellets stopped midair and rained down on the floor.

The man's eyes flared. He began to shove more shells into the breach, but Ambria twisted her wand and the gun flew from his grasp. Max swung his wand in a twirling pattern and a lasso of energy wrapped around the man's arms and legs.

Shelton chuckled. "Damn, you kids are good."

Conrad lowered the shield and they walked over to the man. "You planned to kill us all along."

"Yep." Shelton leaned in until his face hovered an inch from the prisoner's. "Now tell me who you are and how you got this place, or I'll start peeling off your skin with an army of carnivorous roaches."

The man blanched. "Don't hurt me!"

"Says the man who planned to kill three kids." Shelton's eyes narrowed. "Answer me or face the roaches."

"There's no such thing as carnivorous roaches."

Conrad lit a flame in his hand and singed the hairs on the man's arm. "Just like there's no such thing as conjuring fire in my hand?" Conrad had never heard of roaches eating living flesh and he certainly didn't want to see them in action.

Sweat beaded on the man's forehead. "The name's Jay Butler. I stumbled into this place a few years ago while looking for land to develop." He gulped. "The main house was burned to the ground and the church looked like someone tried to blow it up. I tried to find who owned the place, but it wasn't in the county records. It was like it didn't even exist."

"Because the previous owners hid it." Shelton backed away and stared at Jay for a moment. "You don't know how the place was destroyed?"

"No, I swear." Jay stared uneasily at Conrad. "Now let me go."

Shelton looked around at the exotic cars. He pursed his lips and tapped a finger to his chin. "Looks like you're living pretty high off the hog." He walked to a shiny red car and peered inside. "Either you're a very successful land developer, or you've been making a mint off something else." He motioned to Max. "Cut him loose."

Max flicked his wand and the magic ropes vanished. Jay scrambled toward the door. Another rope looped around his foot and yanked him so hard he flopped on his belly. Jay clawed at the concrete, but the aether rope dragged him back to Max's feet.

"Don't try to run." Max released the spell. "We may look like kids, but you won't stand a chance against us."

Shelton snorted. "Never bring a gun to a magic wand fight."

"Get up." Ambria pointed her wand at Jay.

"It can't be!" He rose on shaky knees, unable to tear his eyes off her wand. "That's a real magic wand?"

"Yep." Shelton slapped him on the back of the head. "It's real magic, doofus!"

Jay's legs wobbled. "I thought it was advanced tech."

Shelton got in his face again. "You've been selling everything you found below, haven't you?"

The other man quailed. "Yes."

"Son of a bitch!" Shelton held up a fist. "Are you the only one who knows about this place or are there others?"

"I swear I'm the only one!"

"Yeah, we'll see." Shelton shoved him toward the ramp. "Lead the way, bucko."

The ramp was wide enough for three cars to fit alongside each other and about a hundred feet long. Bright lights blinked on when they reached another concrete floor at the bottom, illuminating a massive underground garage. Several black sedans occupied parking spaces along the walls. Two metal boxes sat in another corner. Yellow paint sectioned off several small squares not far from two sets of elevator doors.

Shelton jabbed a finger at the sedans. "Did you sell any of those cars?"

Jay shook his head. "No, I couldn't figure out how to start them."

"Thank god for miracles. Last thing we need are noms with flying cars."

The other man's eyes flared. "F-flying cars?"

Shelton ignored Jay's outburst and prodded him toward elevator doors. "Let's take the levitator below and see what kind of damage this bozo has done."

The doors slid open and Shelton shoved the prisoner inside.

Jay huddled in the corner of the levitator car. "What is this place?"

"Headquarters for the supernatural cops." Shelton gave him a grin. "And they're all gonna be here within a day or two."

"What?" The other man's face twisted with fear. "Why? Where did they go?"

Shelton didn't answer. "How many people did you kill to keep this secret, Jay?"

Jay hesitated a moment. "I didn't kill anyone! I wasn't going to kill you, I swear to god!" He dropped to his knees just as the levitator stopped and the doors opened. "Please, let me go. I promise I won't tell anyone about anything."

"Yeah, I believe you." Shelton grabbed the man by the collar and hauled him to his feet. "Keep on walking, Jaybird."

It seemed to Conrad that Shelton was enjoying himself. Conrad felt a certain sense of satisfaction watching the would-be murderer fear for his own life.

A smoothbore corridor stretched ahead of them. Shelton let Max keep an eye on the prisoner and navigated to a plain room with a single window in the wall. The doorway next to the window hung open. Beyond it lay a warehouse. Shelton led them down a long aisle. Aside from a few knick-knacks, the shelves were bare.

Shelton stopped in front of a box with a few silver marbles inside. "Do you know what these are, Jay?"

The other man shook his head.

"They're something real special. All-seeing eyes." Shelton put a marble between thumb and forefinger and spun it into the air. The ASE hung in the air just in front of Shelton. "Control menu." A holographic menu appeared. Shelton tapped in a few commands and the ASE zipped away.

Jay's teeth chattered. "What did you just do? What was that thing?"

"It's gonna find out if you lied to us, Jay." Shelton flashed a grin. "It's gonna find all your deepest darkest secrets so I know just how much you need to be punished."

"I didn't do anything!" Jay screamed and scrambled away.

"Ah, shut it!" Shelton flicked out his staff to full length and knocked the other man on the back of his head. Jay slumped to the floor. "I'm gonna look around for more useful stuff."

Conrad looked at the unconscious man. "What about him?"

"Tie him up, I guess." Shelton clapped Max on the back. "Good job, by the way."

Max beamed. "Thanks!"

Ambria groaned. "We helped too, you know."

"I know, I know." Shelton motioned at the shelves. "Let's go exploring."

After Max secured Jay, Conrad and the others spent the next hour scouring the shelves. Conrad found a few swords and Ambria located several strips of black cloth Shelton identified as Nightingale armor. Max found crates with handfuls of elemental grenades labeled soggers, icers, and scorchers.

By the time they were done, they'd accumulated a crate of loot.

"Good work." Shelton dumped the ASEs into the loot box. "It ain't much, but it'll work." He booted Jay until the man jerked awake with a scream. "Time to go, bucko."

Jay staggered to his feet. "Let me go. Please."

"Yeah, we'll see." Shelton led them back to the levitator and took it up to the parking garage. They'd just reached the ramp going up into the barn when the ASE zipped into view. A holographic map flickered on in front of Shelton. Several red markers were scattered in the woods around the estate. Shelton's lips peeled back into a snarl. "Didn't kill anyone, huh?"

"I didn't!" Jay's eyes darted toward the ramp and the open barn door beyond. His muscles tensed, but he didn't try to run again.

"Yeah, well let's take a look." Shelton tapped the holographic menu on the ASE and it drifted back up the ramp slowly enough they could follow it. As they neared the woods, Jay's shaking intensified.

"Don't even think about running." Max poked his wand in Jay's back.

Shelton lit the way into the dark woods with his staff. When they reached a mound of dirt, his jaw went tight. "Do me a favor, Jaybird, and dig up that mound."

Jay kicked Max's leg and rammed into Ambria. He dodged around a tree and ran. Conrad lashed out with an azure beam of light and sliced a sapling off at the base. It fell in Jay's path. The man tried to leap it, but his foot caught a branch. Conrad ran over to him and put a foot on the man's throat. "If you run again, I'll cut off your left foot."

"Whoa, easy there, cowboy." Shelton grinned. "Let's take it a toe at a time."

Jay squirmed frantically. "Let me go, you lunatics!"

Conrad wove a band of energy and clamped it over Jay's mouth, muffling his screams.

Shelton pointed his staff at the other man. "Now get up and dig."

Tears pouring down his cheeks, Jay shoveled dirt with his hands. A few leaves covered the mound, but it was fresh enough that roots hadn't taken hold. A man in a filthy gray business suit rested inside. Blood blackened with age stained the chest. Grimacing in disgust, Shelton dug through the dead man's pockets and found a wallet. The driver's license was missing, but a business card inside told the truth.

Shelton read the name on the front. "Jay Butler." He scowled at the prisoner. "With Butler Land Developers."

"You little liar." Ambria pointed her wand at the fake Jay. "What's your real name, you murderous wretch?"

Conrad released the binding over the man's mouth.

Tears streaked down the killer's filthy face. "What does it matter? You're going to kill me anyway."

Conrad held out his arcphone and scanned the man's face. He ran an image search using the nom internet. It didn't take long before it matched with a face from a social media website. "His name is Alan Combs. It says he worked at Butler Land Developers."

"The plot thickens." Shelton clicked his tongue. "Poor Jay was going to develop the land, but then Alan discovered the armory and all the magical gadgets. He killed Jay to keep this place secret. And he would've gotten away with it, if not for us meddling kids."

Ambria blinked. "Meddling kids?"

"What now?" Max looked with disgust at the weeping murderer. "Do we really have time to make him dig up all the people he killed, or should we get back to more important things?"

"Good question." Shelton tapped a finger on his chin. "We can't turn Alan over to the nom authorities because they'll find out about this place. I guess we could bring him back to the Mansion and lock him up there."

"We need to discover the identities of the poor souls he killed," Ambria said. "Their loved ones need to know."

"You're right, but we ain't exactly got time to do that." Shelton glared down at Alan. "You're one sorry sack of shit." He wove his staff in a pattern, muttering to himself. Glowing amber light surrounded the corpse of Jay Butler and solidified into a shell. "That'll keep the body preserved for now. Let's get back to the Mansion."

"Let me go!" Alan tried to run again.

Conrad knew the world would be better off without such a man, but he couldn't bring himself to kill him. Instead, he wove a needle of energy and pierced the man's calf. Alan screamed and went down. Shelton knocked him on the back of the head with his staff and the screaming stopped.

"Biggest crybaby killer I ever met." Shelton sighed. "Give me a hand, Max."

"You got it." Max helped Shelton haul the unconscious man upright and they dragged him along between them. When they reached the road, Shelton cast a camouflage spell to make Alan look like a rolled-up carpet. They dragged him across the wide highway right in front of dozens of cars.

Ambria giggled nervously. "I feel as if I'm on a stage and all these people are watching me."

Shelton snorted. "All they care about is that light changing to green so they can get on with their boring little lives." He waved his staff and the illusion making the lights red in all directions faded away. Right on cue, the noms gunned their cars and were off to the races.

Conrad led the way around the petrol station and found the portal despite Shelton's camouflage spell. They went through to the omniarch room and into the hallway beyond. Corpses lined the floor, their rotting aroma more than Ambria could handle. She waved her wand and sprinkled them with deodorizing magic.

Conrad stopped in front of a body with a head so covered in blood it was nearly impossible to identify. It was missing a right arm, and the left hand had been cut off at the wrist. A blackened hole gaped in the chest. Conrad didn't need to see the face to know who it was. Conrad's bloody handprints still stained the dead man's shirt.

Ambria gasped. "Is that...him?"

Conrad nodded. "Yeah." His voice cracked.

"Holy shit." Shelton unslung the unconscious Alan off his shoulder and handed it to a nearby golem. "Wait here."

The golem remained in place.

"Galfandor never even had a chance to secure the Mansion," Max said. "All the bodies from our battle must still be here."

"No wonder it stinks to high heaven." Ambria wrinkled her nose.

Shelton did a double-take. "Hang on—that's Victus's body?"

Conrad nodded.

Shelton growled. "I wish he was alive so I could tie him down and tweeze his nose hairs one at a time."

Even dead, Victus made Conrad tremble with hatred and anger. Victus had taken everything from so many people. Death was too good for him.

Shelton squeezed Conrad's shoulder. "I'm sorry you had to deal with that, Conrad. We left a huge mess behind when we went to Seraphina, but you three did a damned good job in our absence."

Ambria blinked and tears pooled in her eyes. "Thank you, Shelton."

Conrad wiped moisture from his own eyes. "We never had a choice."

"Yeah." Max put a hand on Conrad's other shoulder. "But we made the best of it."

Shelton released Conrad and took a deep breath. "Well, let's separate the good from the bad and give the good ones a burial."

"These all look like Victus's people," Ambria said. "They're all the dead from our last fight against him."

"I don't remember so many dead," Conrad said. "Ivy must have killed more than I realized."

"It makes it easier for us." Shelton shrugged. "We'll drop 'em in a volcano somewhere."

"Even Victus?" Max said.

Conrad nodded. "Especially Victus."

"All right, let's go lock up this bastard." Shelton motioned for the golem holding Alan to follow them and they went to the great stone house. The golems had made tremendous progress. The foyer and other ground-level rooms practically sparkled. Shelton had the golem toss Alan on a bed in the first room in the east wing and locked the windows and door with a spell.

With that taken care of, they went back to the omniarch and opened a breach to Kratos again. Shelton took out an ASE and started programming it. "Once we get this thing up and running, we'll dispose of the bodies."

"I don't think you need to bother with that." Ambria pointed out a sleek, black shape drifting outside the storm clouds of Voltis. Its organic hull reflected off the calm blue waters.

It was an Mzodi ship. Two more hung in the air nearby.

The Eden army was home.

CHAPTER 27

J *ustin*

I DIDN'T KNOW what to expect on the other side of the elevator door. A military base teeming with soldiers? A control room? A giant hedge maze or maybe a battalion of tanks? Literally anything could have waited on the other side of that door and I wouldn't have been surprised. The elevator opened to an Obsidian Arch waystation control room.

Boy, was I surprised.

It wasn't just any old control room either, but one featuring an Alabaster Arch. Alabaster was something of a misnomer since it wasn't pure white. Thick black bands spiraled around pale stone. They were the only kind of arches capable of opening portals to other realms, at least before Victus sabotaged them to trap us in Seraphina.

Neat rows of small black arches, each one with a Cyrinthian symbol before them, were capable of opening portals to their corresponding arches in other waystations. A niche to the side contained omniarches capable of opening gateways to any destination you could precisely envision.

I processed all of this in a split instant—much faster than the surprised soldiers standing outside. That was a good thing because getting out of the cramped elevator was no easy matter. Tommy literally sprang into action, a wave of doughy flesh blanketing the first soldier. Vampires poured out after him. Before the soldiers could ready their rifles, their asses hit the ground.

"Get the comm badges!" I shouted.

"Holy shit!" A surprised man in a white lab coat turned tail and ran down the center aisle. Clarissa blurred after him and yanked him back by the collar. He slammed to the ground with a strangled yelp.

I waved a hand around. "Split up and find any other stragglers."

The other vampires vanished into the rows of arches.

Stacey sniffed the air. "I think someone soiled their pants."

Elyssa wrinkled her nose. "God, what a stench."

Three of the five female soldiers lay unconscious from the brief altercations with the vampires. I addressed the conscious ones. "Where are we?"

The two women glared at me in silence.

Clarissa walked behind the captives and traced fingernails on the backs of their necks. She knelt behind the woman on the left and breathed into her ear. "I will drain the lifeblood from the last one to answer."

"Do what you have to do, bloodsucker," the other soldier said.

The first didn't even flinch or look back. "I will gladly die for the cause."

"These people are hardcore," I muttered. My eyes wandered to the man in the lab coat. Sweat trickled down his forehead. His eyes cast furtive glances around the group.

The other vampires returned with another four unconscious female operatives.

"The control room is clear," Stacey said, "but the cavern outside is another matter."

Elyssa raised an eyebrow. "What do you mean?"

"There are dozens of military barracks, machinery, and other buildings." She frowned. "It's rather odd, but I counted only fifteen soldiers out there."

"The main force might be deployed elsewhere." Elyssa waved a hand at the arches. "Even without magic, they're using our own arches against us."

The captive soldiers remained stubbornly quiet, so I went for the easy target. "Keep them here." I took the male scientist from his vampire ward.

"Let me go!" He squirmed uselessly in my grasp. "Don't eat me!"

I ignored his pleas and dragged him well away from the soldiers, Elyssa pacing behind me. Once we were out of earshot of his comrades, I let him go. "Don't try to run." He did. I grabbed him before he took a step and shoved him against a black arch. "You can't get away."

Elyssa hemmed him in from the side and flashed her fangs. "Next time you try to run, I'll take a liter of your blood."

His face blanched. "Don't, please. I have a family."

"I don't care if you have puppies and kittens." I folded my arms across my chest. "Answer my questions or we'll turn you into a vampire."

He recoiled as if I'd just backhanded him. "I'd rather die!"

"I'll bet you would, but we won't let you. You'll be a bloodsucker forever." I gave that a moment to sink in. "Now tell me, where are the other soldiers?"

"I don't know."

"I can tell when you're lying." Elyssa took his arm and forced it toward her fangs. "Tell us the truth."

He screamed and tried to jerk free. "No!"

I ignited the blue flames in my eyes and growled. "Answer the question."

"They're in London!" Tears pooled in his squinty little eyes. "They found Queens Gate."

Alarm flashed in Elyssa's eyes. "They sent an army to conquer Queens Gate?"

"Yes." His voice quavered.

"Where are we now?"

He shrank back from the fury in my voice. "Katoomba, Australia."

Recognition lit in Elyssa's eyes. "The Three Sisters."

I grabbed the scientist's coat lapels and yanked him close. "What's your name?" I figured I might as well make this personal.

He gave me a blank look before stuttering an answer. "Jacob."

"Okay, Jacob. Tell me everything about the Queens Gate operation."

"I'm just a researcher! I don't know all the tactical details."

"Tell me what you do know." I nodded at Elyssa. "Let me know if he's lying."

"Oh, I will." Elyssa was adept at questioning suspects, but she certainly wasn't a lie detector. Thankfully this guy hadn't called our bluff.

Jacob's face turned green. "The Artemis cubes pinpointed a high level of supernatural presence in London."

"Artemis, goddess of the hunt?" Elyssa scoffed. "How cute. Keep going."

Jacob gulped. "They sent an expeditionary force to track and observe. As the vampire specialist, I went with them to find nests so we could mark and eradicate them."

"Nests?" Elyssa scoffed.

"Yes, vampires are social creatures that nest together." He straightened his shoulders, but the tremble in his hands betrayed him. "We tracked several supers to a nondescript parking deck and overheard mentions of Queens Gate. Our people located the entrance. Apparently, the concentration of supernaturals at the location was extraordinarily high, so they sent nearly all local forces to secure it."

Elyssa pursed her lips. "How many soldiers are there?"

"Five hundred."

Her eyebrow quirked. "You're hiding something." She paced to his side. "How many soldiers does Razor Echelon have worldwide?"

Jacob gulped. "I don't know exactly."

Her eyes flashed. "Guess."

"Several thousand?" He shrank back. "I swear I don't know."

That number sent a chill up my spine. Years of fighting and surviving in Seraphina left us with just over a thousand in the Eden army. If all went according to plan, they were just now arriving from Atlantis, half a world away at the island of Kratos. I doubted they were ready to jump back into battle even if I could reach them quickly.

Elyssa kept going. "What's an Artemis cube?"

"It tracks supers."

"Are they magic or science based?"

"Science, of course. All of our equipment comes from ARD—Advanced Research Division."

That triggered another quirk of Elyssa's eyebrow. "Where is ARD?"

"I don't know." He trembled. "It's top secret."

Elyssa pressed her lips together. "Who's your leader?"

"Commander Edge."

"Worldwide?"

"All I know is that she answers to the Overseer." He shook his head. "Please, I don't know much else."

"Bull." I showed him my teeth. "Are your people using the arches for transport?"

"Yes." Jacob clenched his jaw as if to keep from saying more than I asked.

I gave him an expectant look. "Which ones?"

"Ones like these." He patted the small one behind him.

"What about those?" I turned him around and pointed to the omniarches.

"We can't get them to work. They just open up to darkness, and there's a monster inside."

The Void. I gave silent thanks they hadn't unleashed the Beast on this world. It would consume everything if let loose. Razor didn't know the omniarches required a precise visual on the destination or it would create a gateway to the Void. I tapped on the small arch with the Cyrinthian symbol. "How did you get these to work?"

"A magician we captured in Colombia showed us how to seal the circle and activate the corresponding symbols. We sent all our reinforcements to the arch in Queens Gate."

I'd never bothered using one since the omniarches were far more practical. "Let me tell you something about the dark place." I leaned in closer. "There's a creature inside that will completely destroy the world if it gets loose."

Jacob's eyes flashed wide. "Everything?"

I nodded grimly. "Everything. I recommend you leave those arches alone."

"Does this mean you won't kill me?"

"We're not murderers, Jacob." I straightened and folded my arms, a parent chastising an idiot child. "Supers have existed peacefully among noms for thousands of years. We've saved the world multiple times. Not all of us are perfect, but we don't want war."

Elyssa nodded. "We want peace with Razor, not war."

"It doesn't matter if you're peaceful," Jacob said in a low voice. "It matters that you exist. Either everyone has abilities, or no one does. The Overseer ordered the eradication or imprisonment of your kind. There are far more of us than there are of you and it's only a matter of time before you're all gone." He pointed to one of the other arches. "Any minute now our people will return from Queens Gate and they will put you back in the dungeon where you belong."

I didn't like the confidence creeping into his voice, but I let him run his mouth.

"Did your people make the underground prison?" Elyssa said.

"Yes. And there are more all across the world." Jacob's hate burned in his eyes. He bared his teeth. "Together we are stronger than you can ever be."

I wanted to punch the smug look off his face. *Devour the insignificant fool!* I flicked to demon vision. Hungry tendrils snaked around his halo and grasped it. It wasn't like feeding off emotions. I was a snake constricting my victim's soul and swallowing it, piece by piece.

Jacob gasped. His legs gave way and he dropped to the floor.

"Justin, what are you doing?" Elyssa grabbed my arm.

I ignored her and tightened my hold. *Devour!* "Your kind will perish beneath the might of Kalesh," I growled. Flames flickered in my vision. "I will reap your souls and leave a mountain of skulls as memorial."

"Justin!" Something hit me so hard the world went black for an instant. I stumbled to the side. The tendrils of my essence retreated, and my vision returned to normal. Kalesh's laughter faded inside my head.

I blinked and met Elyssa's concerned eyes. "I didn't mean to do that. That wasn't me!"

Jacob drooled and gibbered on the floor.

"You completely lost it." Elyssa gripped my hands. "Justin, we've got to find Emily Glass. You're getting worse."

I hadn't even realized Kalesh had taken control. I'd nearly devoured a man's soul and it hadn't seemed bad at the time. I knelt next to Jacob, but he was in shock and wouldn't be answering any questions for a while, if ever.

I tried to collect my scattered thoughts. "What do we do about this place?"

"We might be able to free more prisoners before the rest of the army comes back." Elyssa grabbed the back of Jacob's lab coat and dragged him behind her toward the soldiers. "We can use an omniarch to send them somewhere safe."

"We need to warn your father about Razor. We need to assemble the troops."

She nodded. "I tried to call him, but something's blocking my signal. He might not even be in Eden yet."

"No doubt one of Razor's anti-magic devices." I stopped in front of our ragtag crew. "Razor invaded Queens Gate. They could come back at any moment, or they might be a while. We can free more prisoners and take the chance that the enemy could return and trap us, or we can run."

"I'm not letting these bitches keep our people." Clarissa hauled up one of the conscious prisoners by her hair. "They want us dead for no reason!"

"Evil-assed people," another vampire said.

"I figure it ain't right to leave folks behind," Tommy said. "Let's get to it, shall we?"

A few of the vampires looked at each other nervously, but no one admitted to wanting to leave. I held up Pari's badge. "The comm badges we took should open the cells. Tommy and I already cleared a third of the cells. Start in the row near the elevator and work your way to the far side to make sure."

Clarissa glared at me. "You're too good to get your hands dirty?"

"You are the most ungrateful—" I sliced the air with a hand. "I'm going to open an omniarch portal to the prison below so we don't have to use the elevator, okay?"

She scoffed. "Sure, if you say so."

I didn't want the guards to know the omniarches worked, so I made a lassoing motion with my finger. "Round up the prisoners and dump them in the cells. Send me a picture of the elevator door so I can open a gateway."

"I'll do that." Elyssa dragged Jacob onto the elevator. The vampires took five guards onto the elevator after her, and they descended.

I turned to Stacey. "Can you look around their camp for the gadgets they use to track us? I want to take some for us to examine."

"Of course, lamb." She wound her long blonde locks into a bun and dashed away in human form.

"These are some right twisted folks, Justin." Tommy looked warily at the two conscious soldiers. "Is it just me or are there a lot more women than men in uniform?"

I was used to female warriors and leaders. The Mzodi fleets were captained almost exclusively by women and their soldiers were predominantly female as well. Males dominated most military forces in Eden. And yet, only three of the twenty plus Razor soldiers we'd captured were men.

"You're right, but I don't know why." I knelt in front of a conscious soldier. "Why are most of you female?"

She stared at me. "What does it matter? We are humans and we will stop you."

"Stop us from what?"

"Existing." Her hard gaze held mine. Oddly, I didn't see so much hatred as I did determination.

"Someone lied to you. Commander Edge or the Overseer might have told you that we're evil and out to rule the world." I shook my head. "We're not. We just want to coexist in peace."

"Your lies won't sway me, beast." She continued to glare at me. "Just know that you'll all die, either by my hand or another. Humans will win."

I thumped her gently on the temple and sent her to dreamland. Before her comrade could comment, I did the same to her. "They're complete fanatics."

"Aye, mate." Tommy grimaced. "They're worse than bloody vamplings. Won't stop coming until they're chopped to bits."

"I don't want to have to kill them, but we may have no choice if it comes down to war."

"There's always a choice, mate." Tommy sighed. "Thankfully I haven't had to make many life or death choices."

"I have, and it costs me something every time." I knocked out the other conscious soldiers. "At least I can imprison them in their own cells without feeling bad."

Tommy chuckled. "Bloody right."

The elevator doors opened a moment later and Elyssa emerged. She held out her phone, a picture on the display. "The signal blocker wouldn't let me send it to you."

I took it and frowned. "I'd like to know how they're blocking the signal since these phones use aether leylines."

"Me too." She walked with me to the omniarch as the vampires gathered more soldiers. "I just don't get how Razor could exist all this time and the Templars didn't even know about it. Things like anti-paranormal military forces don't just go unnoticed, Justin."

"Pari told me the paranormal units from several countries formed Razor. I don't think it was around before we left for Seraphina."

She scowled. "The Templars we left behind seriously slacked off."

"Considering everything that's happened since we left, it's a miracle they kept the Overworld together as long as they did." I walked past several omniarches slashed with red paint and stopped in front of one marked green. I knelt and pressed a finger to the silver circle around the ten by ten structure and willed the circle to close.

Aether crackled as the circuit closed and trapped it inside. I gave it a moment to charge then stared at the picture Elyssa had taken. *Open portal.* The omniarch hummed. A silver line split the air vertically and slashed open into a window straight to the prison below.

Vampires already waited with newly freed prisoners. The vampires with the captive soldiers took them through to the cells below. Clarissa pushed through a group of bedraggled Arcanes in dirty robes. "Spectacular. Does that mean you can help us now?"

I rolled my eyes. "Yes, I'm free to help now."

I just hoped we had enough time before Razor returned.

CHAPTER 28

I took a while by supernatural standards, but our ragtag group of vampires, Arcanes, and the lone Flark freed all the prisoners from Razor's clutches. Before I had a chance to feel good about the big rescue, Adam hit me with bad news.

"This prison is only one of dozens." He pulled up a global map pimpled with red dots. "They've got Thunder Rock, El Dorado, and even the Grand Nexus under their control. Each one houses an underground prison. They also control fifty percent of the primary waystations."

"Did they build prisons under them?" I asked.

"A couple, but most of their facilities are located in cities nearby." Adam shook his head. "I don't see how it's possible they accomplished so much in less than a decade. Governments aren't known for getting things done fast."

"They did it. That's all that matters." Elyssa zoomed in on the map. "What are the blue dots?"

"Potential targets." Adam scrolled down to reveal a map legend. "Atlanta is blue because they suspect a waystation is there, but they haven't dedicated resources to find it."

I felt mildly relieved. "So the Grotto is safe for now?"

"Hopefully." Adam closed the laptop. "I want to dig deeper into Razor's network, but not here." He looked down the central aisle at the mass of disheveled prisoners. "We need to get somewhere safe."

"That's the problem." Elyssa frowned. "We don't know what's safe anymore."

A dangerous idea formed in the back of my head. It would either work wonderfully or fail spectacularly. "We should take everyone to Queens Gate."

Elyssa's forehead scrunched. "Are you serious? Razor's invading Queens Gate right now."

"Yeah, but they're attacking from the waystation. They have no idea what the pocket dimension is like." I spread my arms in a feeble attempt to convey size. "The valley is huge, and we have all the resources of Arcane University and Science Academy at our disposal. Since Razor can only send a few troops through the doors at one time, even a handful of us could defend it."

Adam held up a fist. "This is Sparta!"

Elyssa tilted her head. "You know, that's not a bad idea."

"Oy, what a stink." A doughy pancake squeezed through the mass of freed prisoners and popped back into the shape of Tommy. "What's the plan now, boss?"

I looked at Elyssa. She nodded back at me. I pointed to the crowd. "We need to move them back so I can open another omniarch portal to Queens Gate."

Tommy blinked. "Ain't that the bloody place Razor's attacking?"

"Yes, but we're taking everyone straight to Arcane University. The healers there can patch them up and get them ready to fight." I searched the crowd for our vampire helpers, but they were hard to find among the throng of freed prisoners.

A black panther blurred around the arches and dropped an overstuffed backpack at my feet. Bones crackled as it morphed into a naked Stacey.

Adam stared at her boobs for a moment before blinking out of his stupor. "Uh, any luck?"

"Unfortunately, no." Stacey opened a fanny pack and slipped into yoga pants and a sports bra. "The contraptions Razor uses burned up and melted whenever I touched them. It was bloody annoying." She shrugged. "So I simply wrapped them in towels. Problem solved."

"Fascinating." Adam pushed a finger up the bridge of his nose. "Self-destruction mechanisms!"

"How are you supposed to find out how these things work if they self-destruct?" Elyssa asked.

He shrugged. "I don't know yet, but it'll be fun experimenting."

Clarissa barged her way through the prisoners. "Mind telling us what's next, or should we sit around and wait for Razor to slaughter us?"

I cupped my hands around my mouth and shouted," Everyone move back. I need space around the arches."

After mumbling, bumbling, and stumbling in confusion, the crowd shuffled backwards. They did pretty good considering most of them looked as if they'd been drugged or tortured out of their minds for days or weeks.

I turned to Tommy. "Did anyone free the leecher?"

He nodded. "Yeah, but we drugged it to keep it from killing anyone."

Adam grimaced. "Aren't leechers really bad?"

"No worse than vampires," Elyssa said. "Provided they aren't so starved they can't control themselves."

"Healers will do the trick," Tommy said.

"I hope so." I went to the first operational omniarch and sealed the silver circle. I vividly remembered the Mansion, but I didn't want to send them there. They needed medical attention and Arcane University was the best place for that. I pictured the great domed library of the university and willed a portal into existence. A gateway sliced open. The university appeared on the other side.

I motioned Clarissa over. "Get them to the healing ward in the main castle. I'll open more omniarch portals to speed up the evacuation."

"Uh, Justin." Tommy tugged on my sleeve and pointed to a humming arch in the middle of the numbered arches. "I think we have a problem."

"Crap!" I blurred over to the arch just as a gateway opened. A group of bloodied Razor operatives blinked in surprise when they saw me. I channeled a thick shield of Murk over the portal and flipped them off.

"Alert! Alert!" One of them shouted at someone I couldn't see.

I tied off the shield weave and dashed back to the omniarches. I opened portals in the two others marked green and lit a fire under the prisoners' asses. "Razor is coming! Get through the portals fast!"

Elyssa had already assembled the vampires into a defensive force by the time I returned to the gateway.

Commander Edge regarded me coolly from the other side. "How did you escape?"

"Pari just let me go." I shrugged. "She said you're an idiot and she hates you. Oh, and she says you always have onion breath and never trim your nose hairs."

Elyssa snorted, but kept a straight face.

Edge motioned to someone off to the side. "I doubt that. She is completely loyal to the cause."

"The cause?" I scoffed. "You people are no better than a mob with high-tech torches and pitchforks. What gives you the right to attack people who have done nothing to wrong you?"

"Your very existence wrongs us." Edge's lips peeled back into a sneer. "Humanity will not be snuffed out by mutants and freaks."

"We're not trying to snuff you out!" Reasoning with her was impossible. I glanced over at the dwindling mass of freed prisoners and gauged how long I had to stall this maniacal nitwit. "Look, maybe we could sit down and talk this out. Imagine how much good magic could do for humanity."

Her lips peeled back even further. "Good? There is no good in magic. All it takes is one individual to annihilate cities and incinerate millions!"

"We have supernatural police who make sure that doesn't happen. Don't you think if we wanted to do that we would have done it a long time ago?"

Edge wasn't listening. "We will wipe your scourge from the planet." A woman with a wide-muzzled rifle stepped into view. Edge pointed at the barrier. "Destroy it."

I remembered my last encounter with that weapon. It had destroyed my shield in seconds. The woman aimed and fired. Gray rings of energy rippled out. The Murk barrier cracked. More and more soldiers gathered on the other side of the gateway. In a few seconds, we'd be hip-deep in bad guys and I had no idea how to stop them.

Destroying the arch wasn't an option. It took way too much power to knock down one of these puppies. We didn't have any furniture to shove in the way and channeling another shield wouldn't do the trick. There was one thing that might stall them, but it was so simple I wasn't even sure if it would work.

"You're doomed, boy." Edge cackled. "I'll oversee your death myself once Pari is finished experimenting on you." She rattled on like a street preacher outside a strip club.

I didn't say a word. Instead, I knelt, pressed my hand to the Cyrinthian symbol in front of the arch, and prayed this worked. *Close portal.*

Edge's annoying rant went silent.

"Are you kidding me?" Elyssa stared at the deactivated arch. "You just turned it off?"

I grinned. "Those idiots don't know how to keep portals open."

A gateway split open in the arch again. Edge's face burned crimson. "Destroy that shield!"

I stuck out my tongue at her and deactivated the arch again. I chuckled and turned to Elyssa. "They don't realize that you have to will the arch to stay open if you want to keep someone on the other side from shutting it."

The portal activated again. I turned it off before Edge could even utter a word.

Elyssa chuckled. "Oh, man. She's got to be pissed."

A moment later it flicked on again. Edge shouted, "Stop it!"

I cut her off again. This went on for several minutes, a breach appearing every few seconds and vanishing just as quickly when I willed it off. Edge's shouts grew shriller every time.

I laughed. "Oh man, she's so freaking tilted!"

Another portal flicked on. Edge's glowing red face glared at me. "You—" I shut it off.

I braced for the next portal, but the seconds ticked by and it didn't open.

Elyssa cast a worried glance at the evacuation then back at me. "Did you break the arch?"

I shook my head. "No. Maybe they gave up." I channeled more Murk into my shield and repaired the cracks just in case I needed it.

"Fat chance of that." She looked toward the world map at the front of the control room. "Any chance they could activate the Obsidian Arch in the main waystation?"

I shook my head. "Not without an acknowledgement from this station."

She paced away, looking up and down the rows of other arches. "Do any of these other ones connect to here?"

"I don't think so." I hadn't used the numbered arches simply because the omniarches made them obsolete. It was a good thing Edge hadn't gotten omniarches to work, or we'd be dead meat. I tapped the symbol in front of the arch. "Every control room has an arch with this symbol. To use it, you have to know the symbol for the particular waystation." I pointed to a symbol in the upper corner of the world map.

Elyssa nodded. "As long as I don't have to worry about them popping out of another arch."

Adam walked over to us. "About seventy percent of the prisoners are through. We just need another ten minutes."

"I think I can manage that." I stared at the arch, readying myself to close it the instant it opened. That instant came less than a minute later. The arch hummed to life and a gateway flashed open. Something was different this time. A woman in Arcane robes knelt in front of the symbol. The bruises on her face and the crusted blood on her arm told the story.

Razor was forcing a prisoner to hold open gateway. I tried close it, but the woman's will was a distant wall I couldn't breach.

Edge bared her teeth in a savage smile. "You're mine now, boy." She made a chopping motion with her arm and two soldiers leveled their anti-magic rifles at my shield. I summoned more Murk and encased the arch in it, hoping the thickness would slow them down. The first cracks formed and the aether began to dissolve.

I looked at Adam. "I think we're out of time. Grab the stolen tech and get out of here right now."

He hesitated. "Without you guys?"

"Yes, without us!" Elyssa pushed him toward the omniarches. "Now go!"

The Murk barrier crackled and shifted like a block of melting ice. We had seconds to go before it shattered. I tried to close the portal again, but with the Arcane holding it open, there was nothing I could do.

Or is there?

Maintaining your concentration while under pressure was a skill Arcanes learned early. I could probably throw a cup of cold water on that woman's face and she wouldn't falter. Anything short of a bullet to the head wouldn't break her focus. I could probably pierce her skull with a ray of Brilliance and end this right now. But the thought of sacrificing her made me sick.

"We're not getting out of here are we?" Elyssa said.

I turned my back on Edge and took Elyssa's hand. "I've got an idea, but it's risky as hell."

"Let's hear it." I wasn't sure if she looked more worried before or after I told her, but she nodded her head. "Let's do it."

I cupped my hands around my mouth. "Tommy, I need you!"

The Flark squeezed out of the mass of evacuees and sprinted over to us. "Aye, mate?"

I whispered the plan to him as the Murk barrier shifted and cracked again. "Can you do it?"

"I'll give it my best." He took a position to the side of the arch.

Commander Edge rubbed her hands together like a child about to get her grubby mitts on a bowl of ice cream covered in chocolate sprinkles. More soldiers gathered behind Edge, ready to storm through the portal the moment the Murk shield fell. I could practically see them counting down the seconds in their head.

That's why they weren't ready for what happened next.

I channeled into the Murk shield with one hand. "Now!" I dissolved the shield in an instant and hurled a blazing ball of Brilliance at the floor between us and them. It went off like a flash grenade, the light so bright, it hurt my eyes even though I looked away. Cries of surprise echoed behind me.

I spun back around. Tommy's arm stretched like a rubber band beneath the gray anti-magic rays. Soldiers fired blindly. Electro guns unleashed a volley of black spheres. I channeled a small shield just in time to deflect them. Tommy's elastic arm snatched the Arcane woman and yanked her through to our side.

Tommy whooped. "Bob's your uncle!"

Edge bumbled blindly, hands outstretched. "Kill them all!"

But her soldiers were just as blind as she was. Another burst of inspiration hit me. *We can capture that evil bitch!* Before I could ask Tommy to grab Edge, the Arcane we'd rescued shut off the gateway and the chance was gone.

"Y-you saved me!" The woman slumped against Tommy, tears trickling down her cheeks. "Oh, thank you."

"You're welcome, Miss." Tommy patted her head. "All safe now, love."

I wove another shield around the arch just in case Edge tried to open it again. Elyssa took my hand and squeezed it. "I can't believe that worked."

My nerves were so shot I couldn't keep my hands from trembling. "If even one of those electro bullets hit us, we'd have been toast."

The last of the evacuees raced through the portals, leaving us alone in the control room.

"Yeah, well they didn't." Elyssa tugged my hand. "Now let's get out of here!"

Tommy hefted the Arcane and ran through a portal. I deactivated the other omniarches and went to the last one with Elyssa. Edge's arch hummed to life again and I couldn't help but laugh at her determination.

Even though she couldn't see me, I extended the middle finger in her general direction and hopped through the portal with Elyssa. I was tempted to wait until Edge made it into the control room so I could goad her, but that would be a stupid move. We didn't want her to know the omniarches worked. I willed the portal to close and it winked away.

When I turned around, the weight of the world settled back down on my shoulders. Hundreds of freed people milled aimlessly outside the stone walls guarding Arcane University. The huge castle looked a lot worse than I remembered it. One of the towering spires ended in broken stone. Black pockmarks marred the white walls. Sections of the perimeter wall lay in crumbled ruins. Only the great clear dome of the library looked unscathed.

Elyssa's mouth dropped open. "My god, this place looks like a warzone."

"Do you think Razor did this?"

She shook her head. "I don't know."

Clarissa appeared through a breach in the wall and sauntered over to us. "The entire building looks abandoned. There's no one in the healing ward."

"Abandoned?" I couldn't believe it. "How could Arcane University be abandoned?"

"I wouldn't know. My kind was never welcomed here." Clarissa arched an eyebrow as if blaming me personally. "It appears your safe haven is no more."

My brilliant plan was an epic fail.

CHAPTER 29

Elyssa took charge before I started feeling sorry for myself. She vaulted easily to the top of an unbroken section of wall and shouted for everyone's attention. "Are there any healers in the crowd?"

Hands raised.

"Great." Elyssa pointed to her right. "All healers please gather here. Battle mages over there. Anyone who's injured, group next to the healers." She continued to organize until everyone who was well enough to help had been sorted from those in need of medical attention. Within twenty minutes, she had healers and helpers guiding the injured inside the building to the healing ward. A makeshift scout troop spread out to search the environs and report back to her.

I walked up to the wall and bowed. "All hail the commander."

She hopped off the ten-foot wall. "At ease, smartass. Does your phone have a signal here?"

I'd been so focused on leading a prisoner escape, I'd forgotten to check.

The arcphone screen showed full bars, but when I tried to call Shelton, it failed.

A robotic voice greeted me instead. "Your phone is not registered on the Overworld network. Please visit a government authorization center to see if you qualify for an exemption."

"You've got to be kidding me." I ended the call. "Since when do we need authorization to use the phone network?" I checked the aethernet, but every website was blocked with the same message.

Elyssa sighed. "I guess we'll have to do this the old-fashioned way."

"Which is?"

She pointed up. "We need a flying carpet or broom."

I strained my brain to remember the layout of the university. "I think there's a broom closet just inside the main entrance."

She flourished her hands. "Lead the way."

The giant wooden doors of the main entrance hung open, gouged deep and charred by battle. Elyssa paused to trace a finger down giant claw marks then proceeded inside. The healers she'd sent ahead of us stared in horror at a pile of bodies in the middle of the corridor. Some corpses oozed gelatinous goo, a sign of decaying demon bodies. A cloud of flies buzzed around the corpses of real flesh and blood.

Elyssa's fists clenched. "I feel as if we escaped a warzone in Seraphina only to fall straight into hell."

"Arcane University is dead. The Overworld is under attack." I shook my head. "How can we beat Baal if our entire foundation is destroyed?"

"I don't know." Elyssa walked toward the crowd. "All we can do is keep moving forward." She clapped her hands once to get everyone's attention. "Can I get volunteers to separate the real bodies from the fake ones and arrange for cremation or burial?"

"I'll help." The Arcane we'd saved from Edge stepped forward. "We need to record the names of the dead and find out how they died."

"Are you a healer?" Elyssa asked.

She shook her head. "No, but I worked in forensic magic for the Custodians before Xander took control."

"Excellent." Elyssa held out her hand. The other woman looked at it for a moment and returned the grip. "I'm Elyssa Borathen, daughter of Thomas Borathen, the commander of the Templar legions."

Gasps resounded from the crowd.

"Why didn't you mention this before?" a man said.

"Are the Templars coming back?" another asked.

Elyssa held up her hand to ward off a barrage of questions. "Yes, the Eden army is returning, but right now we need to get the university in full working order. If you're a healer, please report to the healing ward and help get the wounded back on their feet. If you want to help with the dead, please stay and report to—" She looked expectantly at the Arcane woman.

The woman blinked. "Oh, I'm Kara."

"Kara is in charge here." Elyssa straightened her shoulders and gave a commanding look at the group. "Let's get to it, folks."

Before long, the group had dispersed, leaving behind six people to deal with the bodies.

Elyssa tugged my arm. "Let's find flying brooms."

"One sec." Kara's mention of the Custodians reminded me of Emily, so I went over to her. "Kara, did you ever work with Emily Glass?"

The woman blinked. "I haven't heard that name in years." Her gaze went distant. "I never directly worked with her, but sometime after the Crystoid Incident, she never reported back from a mission."

Cold dread worked into my stomach. "Did she die?"

"I don't think so. Someone said her boyfriend went missing, and she left to hunt him down." Kara shook her head. "The Custodians are just a shadow of what they used to be. If you could find George Walker, he might know."

"Yeah, he worked with Emily, right?"

Kara nodded. "He was Emily's handler."

"Any idea where he might be?"

"Probably somewhere in North America." She shrugged. "I'm sorry, but I don't know much else about the situation over there."

"Thanks, Kara." I took another look at the pile of bodies, searching with dread for familiar faces. Thankfully, I saw none. I went with Elyssa down the hall to the broom closet.

The door was smashed open. The inside looked as if it had been razed by fire spells. There were plenty of broomsticks if you counted splinters and ash. I dug around but found nothing operable.

I huffed. "What do we need brooms for anyway?"

"To scout the city and Science Academy. I need to know the extent of the damage." Elyssa went back into the corridor. "Surely there's at least one functional broomstick in all of Arcane University."

I snapped my fingers. "I'll bet the dormitories have some."

"Let's go." Elyssa jogged down the corridor to the rear exit.

We emerged on a field of mud and blackened grass that made running treacherous. Elyssa hooked left down a wide pedestrium. Three towers at the end crowded around a giant fountain. I'd never been inside any of the dorms because all the rooms were assigned by the time I'd been admitted to the university. It hadn't mattered that much because I ended up living in the original Mansion down on Greek Row. Daelissa later destroyed the house so we'd built the underground house in the Burrows to replace it.

For some reason, the tower in the middle called to me, mainly because it looked wonky. It was a square building, squatting in front of huge cylindrical towers. Turrets of all different sizes and shapes protruded along the towers, as if the builder had just tacked them on at random, making it a curious mix of chaos and order.

The other buildings were plain in comparison. The red brick mansion to the right reminded me of an old-fashioned insane asylum. The other, a gray stone affair with black iron balconies and somber stone statues resembled a fancy apartment building.

Elyssa didn't question me when I made a beeline for the weird building. She knew me well enough by now to know I'd go for the odd duck. The door hung open, but it didn't look damaged. The air inside was slightly musty and a thin film of dust lay over everything. I knew this was the right place when I saw the engraving on a marble tablet in the wall.

Welcome to Moore Keep

Elyssa grunted. "What a coincidence."

Somehow, I knew it wasn't. "If the old man gave Conrad his powers, maybe his ghost can help me find a flying broom."

A strange museum filled with hyper-realistic paintings and statues occupied most of the first floor. We wandered up staircases and found our way to a common room in between the two towers. A broom closet there held dozens of functioning brooms, including several high-performance models.

"Yes!" I snagged one and zipped around the room to reacquaint myself with broom riding. It was like riding a bicycle—you just don't forget. I flew through the window and zoomed up to the top of a tower. From there, I could see the entire campus, or what was left of it. Green fields and gardens were nothing but muck. The white walls of the main castle were pockmarked with damage.

Elyssa hovered next to me. "The world went to hell while we were away."

"Yeah, it really did." Colossus Stadium had taken a beating during the war against Daelissa and it looked like no one had bothered to repair it in all the time we'd been gone. All that remained of the plush gardens and lands of the university were blood and mud. Only the Fairy Gardens looked healthy, but the estate of the Arcanus Primus still bore the scars of Shelton's fury. After Mr. Bigglesworth, the evil Flark, killed his stepfather, Shelton tried to annihilate him with flaming meteors and destroyed the house instead.

I patted the broom's leather saddle. "This thing isn't as fast as a boom-stick, but it's not bad." I pursed my lips. "I wonder if Rai is still around. Maybe he could fix us up with faster rides."

"I hope so," Elyssa said. "We need to reconnect with as many people as possible." She shuddered. "Even Underborn."

"Ew." I wrinkled my nose. "He's probably plenty happy with all the chaos. It's good for business."

"I doubt that." Elyssa frowned. "This much chaos is bad for everyone."

"We also need to check out the underground mansion. There's no reason it can't be our new base of operations around here." I barely recognized Greek Row. All the houses were gone save one, and it occupied the plot where the original Mansion once stood. It was much smaller than its predecessor.

"The underground mansion is on my checklist." Elyssa jabbed a finger toward the valley. "But first, we need to make contact with Science Academy and the Queens Gate government."

"Gotcha." I gripped the handle of the broom and accelerated. "Let's get it done."

I'd spent a lot of time on sky ships, but it felt amazing to finally be on a broom again. We zipped out over the valley and straight toward the silvery curves of Science Academy. The main building, a great dome, bore battle damage significant enough to see from this distance. Even the cliff displayed its share of blast marks.

As we neared the campus, I noticed a strange shimmer in the air. "Stop!"

Elyssa veered in a U-turn. I edged closer to the shimmer but before I reached it, little orange signs popped up in front of me.

Science Academy is on lockdown. Please come back later.

"Guess that settles it." Elyssa peered at the campus. "The sidewalks aren't active, and I don't see anyone down there."

"Maybe they locked it up and left." I shrugged. "As usual, Science Academy isn't getting involved in Overworld affairs."

"Probably for the best." Elyssa looked down at the valley. "Just seeing this place reminds me of Victus's robots and airships attacking us the day he stabbed us in the back."

My face grew warm and Kalesh stirred inside. *We will destroy our enemies.* The timer to find Emily was ticking down, but how could I locate someone who went missing years ago?

"Let's check out Queens Gate." Elyssa directed her broom down toward the city.

From here, the place looked a lot like downtown London. Tightly packed row houses lined the roads on the western side of town. Single family homes dotted the land to the east. The city itself didn't look as if it had suffered damage from fighting, but portions looked abandoned. Weeds sprouted through cracks in the streets and sidewalks. Cracked paint and crumbling brick gave a sad history of the city during my absence.

There wasn't a lot of foot traffic in the streets or in the skies, either. It wasn't until we neared the government buildings at the city center that our approach triggered a response. Four carpets bearing men in Arcane robes lifted off from nearby rooftops and moved to intercept us. We probably could have sped past them, but I slowed down.

"Hopefully these are Galfandor's people," Elyssa said. "We need to tell him about Razor."

I waved to the Arcane on the lead carpet. "Take us to your leader."

The man's forehead pinched into a V. He gave a confused look to a comrade on a neighboring carpet before turning back to me. "Who dares fly against ordinance and comes demanding an audience with Overlord Xander Tiberius?"

Someone could have jammed an icicle up my ass and it wouldn't have been as cold as the shock to my system. "Say what?"

Elyssa's voice echoed my sentiment. "Xander is in charge?"

"State your names," the man said.

"I'm Billy Joe and this is Terry Lee Joe Bob." I bowed. "We didn't know Xander was the leader now."

"Those names sound made up."

"Most redneck names I ever heard," said another Arcane. "You two brother and sister?"

The lead Arcane scowled. "Arrest them and confiscate their brooms. We've got enough problems to deal with already."

I held up a hand. "How about you keep your grubby hands to yourself and I won't send you screaming for your mommies?"

A female Arcane laughed. "Look out. We got a big man on our hands."

The leader snorted. "It's been a while since I taught someone manners." He cracked his knuckles and took out a wand. "This ought to be fun."

Elyssa's hand blurred. Her light bow unfolded to full length and a blazing arrow sizzled into existence, the fiery tip aimed for the leader. "I really don't feel like shooting anyone right now, but I will if I have to."

The fourth Arcane gasped. "What kind of weapon is that?"

"It was gifted to me by Adonis, the leader of Atlantis." Elyssa showed her teeth in a feral grin. "I've fought dragons and angels with it, so a few of Xander's minions shouldn't be too hard to deal with."

"These people are crazy," the female Arcane said.

The leader summoned a shield. "Your fire arrows can't get me now."

Elyssa's grin widened. "Wanna bet?"

I noticed a dozen more carpets rising from the city center and figured they'd called for backup. Much as I wanted to put these punks in their places, the last thing we needed to do was kill Arcanes when we faced a possible full-scale invasion from Razor Echelon. I held up a hand. "Let's calm down. No one needs to die right now."

"Who said anything about dying?" their leader said. "We're going to give you a beating you won't forget."

Something flashed. I dodged right, but the spell grazed my cheek, leaving an angry burn. My rage-o-meter went from irritated to furious in two shakes of a lamb's tail. Kalesh roared with approval. I summoned a blazing ball of Brilliance in my right palm and formed a shield of Murk in my other. "Then feel the fury of my wrath!"

I will kill them all!

CHAPTER 30

The man who'd fired the spell screamed and nearly dropped his wand.

"He's a Seraphim!" the woman shouted.

In an instant, all four fired their wands at me. My shield held easily. *They cannot defeat me!* I zipped my broom to the side and fired a torrent of Brilliance. The Arcanes scattered, but not before I ignited the leader's carpet. He tried to put it out with an ice spell, but the white fire spread.

I roared with laughter. "You will all die by my hand!"

"Justin!" Elyssa's voice pierced the haze of bloodlust. "Control Kalesh!"

Kalesh? I fired another beam of Brilliance. The female Arcane barely avoided being struck. "These puny mortals dare fight me? I will burn their bodies to ash and consume their souls!"

"Justin?" Realization formed in the eyes of one of the Arcanes. "Justin Slade?"

"Yes, he's Justin Slade," Elyssa said. "And he's pissed!"

"Retreat!" The leader managed to put out the flames, but his carpet still smoldered. "Retreat!" he shouted again. The four veered around and made like bats out of hell. The reinforcements saw the panicked faces and waving hands and got the message well before they got close. The Arcanes flew back to the government building and a dome shield rippled on.

Though my anger still demanded blood, I roared in victory. *Nothing will save them from my wrath.*

Strong hands gripped my shoulders and shook me. "Justin, snap out of it!"

The anger melted away. Self-awareness crept back into my mind and with it the realization that I'd been ready to murder every last Arcane if they hadn't run from me. "Oh, shit."

Elyssa's eyes filled with worry. "Justin, we don't have any time to waste. Baal's demon seed is a time bomb."

My hands shook with anxiety and relief that I hadn't rampaged. "Emily Glass is missing. How am I supposed to find her with the entire Over-world under attack?"

"I don't know." She put a hand to my cheek. "You've got to hold on a little longer. We need to find out what happened to Shelton, Max, and Thal. If the Queens Gate waystation came under attack before they got into the pocket dimension, they might still be stuck in London."

I turned my broom toward the double doors at the far end of the valley that led out of the pocket dimension and into the waystation. Even my super vision had trouble picking out the details, but it appeared as though a mob of people in white robes stood around the exit. *Xander's people, no doubt.* Thankfully, we had a secret weapon. "Let's get to the Mansion. We'll use the omniarch to scout the waystation."

Elyssa put a hand on my arm. "We've got to be extra careful if we get into a fight. That Arcane barely nicked you with a spell, but it drove you into a rage."

"I know, I know." I pinched the bridge of my nose. "But what else can I do? Medicate?"

"Maybe." She pursed her lips. "I'll talk with the healers. We need a way to bring you back if Kalesh takes over again."

"That's just it." I shook my head slowly. "It doesn't feel like he's in charge. It still feels like I'm the one driving, but I'm not aware of how awful I'm acting."

"It reminds me of the issues you used to have with Brilliance." Elyssa accelerated her broom toward the university. "It triggered your demon rage."

"I had a talk with my inner demon to fix that." I paced her on my broom. "I kept him locked up. This is different."

"We've got to figure out something before you go on a rampage." Elyssa compacted the light bow and holstered it. "Your demon side seems to think he's invincible, and we both know that's not the case."

Elyssa was right. When the bloodlust took hold, it completely blinded me to everything else except the fight. It was literally a mental impairment that could get me and my loved ones killed. This time, a simple talk with my inner demon wouldn't fix it.

We flew back up the cliff, Elyssa checking our six every few seconds as if Xander's minions might decide to follow us. When we reached Arcane University, we flew to the edge of the Dark Forest and landed next to a copse of shrubs. The branches were crooked and broken, but still concealed their secret.

What had once been a field of grass where Vallaena taught me how to manage my demon powers looked as if it had been overrun by an army of monsters and churned into mud and gravel.

Elyssa peered at the edge of the forest. She picked up a stone and tossed it. It should have bounced off a shield. Instead, it ricocheted off a tree. "Uh, this can't be good."

"The shield is down?" I tossed another rock to confirm. "Oh, crap."

"Those giant claw marks on the university door looked familiar." Elyssa turned in a circle as if something might jump her at any moment. "I think the tragon made them."

"No wonder the university is abandoned. If all the monsters in the Dark Forest got loose, they probably attacked anything they saw."

Elyssa hopped on her broom. "You go to the omniarch. I've got to warn everyone at the university before someone gets eaten." She sped away without waiting for a response.

I'd used the tragon as a weapon on a couple of occasions, but that didn't make us friends. He'd eat me in a heartbeat, given the chance. "Guess I'd better add monsters to our list of problems." I caught a whiff of BO from my armpits. *Damn, that's rank.* I added my stench to the mounting list of issues standing between me and saving the realms. Now I had every problem imaginable, from the destruction of the world all the way down to personal hygiene. I felt complete.

"Well, universe, what else are you gonna throw at me?" I squeezed through the thick shrubs and found an old stump. I pulled up on the correct root and it swung open to reveal stone stairs descending into darkness. I went down and closed the hatch behind me. A sphere of Brilliance floated from my hand and led the way.

I followed the winding tunnel down a steep grade until it leveled out. From there, it was a straight shot to more stairs and a door. I climbed the stairs and released the door latch. The door slid open to the marble-tiled floors of a bathroom and a surprised man sitting on the toilet across from me.

"Son of a bitch!" He jumped up, giving me a show that made me want to bleach my eyeballs.

"Christ Almighty, Shelton! I'm happy to see you too, but can you pull up your pants?"

A grin split his face even before he yanked up his pants and buckled them. "Hot damn, you're alive!" He gripped me in a hug and I didn't even care that he hadn't washed his hands.

"Man, I'm glad to see you!" I slapped him on the back and backed away. "How'd you get away from the ambush?"

"Thal worked some hocus pocus and got me and Max out." Shelton shook his head. "We didn't even know where to start looking for you."

"You wouldn't have found me without a lot of luck." I gave him a quick recount of our escape and what I knew about the attack on the Queens Gate waystation.

"Yeah, we fought them back, for now." Shelton grunted. "Even Xander's minions helped. I guess the Overworld can band together when it has to."

"Maybe." I shrugged. "Elyssa and I didn't even know Xander was in charge until a few minutes ago."

"Speaking of Elyssa, where is she? And where's Adam?"

"The university." I pointed up. "Adam's helping resettle the former prisoners. Elyssa went to warn them that the Dark Forest is unshielded and the monsters are probably on the loose."

"The shield is down?" Shelton grimaced. "No wonder everyone abandoned the university. Victus had an entire army of monsters in there."

"I've had some episodes with my demon too." I shook my head. "Since Emily Glass went missing a few years back, I don't know who else can help me."

Shelton's eyes brightened. "I don't have Emily Glass, but another kind of help is already on the way." He washed his hands at the sink and dried them. "Um, if anyone asks why we were in the bathroom together, just give them a weird look and don't answer."

I chuckled. "Aw c'mon. You know us guys always have to go to the bathroom together."

He snorted. "Yeah. Gotta have guy talk." He unlocked the door and went into the hallway.

I stepped outside and was shocked to see the number of people bustling through the hallway. A female Templar lifted an eyebrow, but brushed past us and into the bathroom without comment. I walked down the hallway, trying to make sense of everything. "Were all these people here already?"

"Hell, no." Shelton grinned. "We opened a portal with the omniarch and went back to Kratos. We're unloading a ship at a time and bringing everyone to us."

My hopes rose just a fraction. "We've got an army."

"Yes, sir we do."

I smacked a fist into my palm. "Time to kick some Razor ass."

"Hellz yeah!" Shelton clapped my back. "Now let's go talk to Thomas about the monster problem."

I followed him down the hallway. "Did Ivy and the others make it to the Glimmer?"

"Yeah. Conrad, Ambria, and Max are around here somewhere." He dodged around a golem servant. "Conrad mentioned something about finding giant spiders." He chuckled. "I never know what to expect from those kids."

"That's for sure. I like them, but Conrad can be a little spooky at times."

"Max seems pretty normal. A bit down on himself, probably from all the bullying he took from his siblings." Shelton's jaw tightened. "But he's a fast learner."

"Better be careful, Shelton." I grinned. "He might see you as a father figure or something."

Shelton worked his jaw back and forth. "Damn. I thought I'd hate the idea, but it kinda makes me feel like I have a purpose, ya know?"

I nearly tripped over my own feet. "Dude, you've got plenty of purpose."

"Yeah, but this is different." He shrugged it off. "Eh, I'm probably just getting old."

"Yeah, or more mature." I shuddered. "Perish the thought."

His lips peeled back in a grimace. "Oh man. Don't scare me like that."

I didn't really think about where we were walking, but I probably didn't need to since Thomas was in the first place instinct led me—the war room. The conference table inside looked beaten up and scarred like everything else in Queens Gate, but the room was clean and ready for use.

"Justin." Thomas didn't look the least bit surprised to see me. "You escaped from Razor."

"Yeah, but don't act too happy about it."

Thomas's icy blue eyes betrayed a hint of amusement as he walked over and gripped my hand. "You have a knack for overcoming long odds."

"Well, we're up against really long odds this time." I tapped a finger to my temple. "And Baal's demon seed is driving me insane."

"Maybe the Eden army can hold down the fort while Justin and I go on the hunt for Emily Glass," Shelton said.

Thomas pursed his lips. "I requested a meeting with the faction heads. We'll meet in half an hour to discuss options. I'll ask them to put out feelers to locate Emily Glass."

Shelton grunted. "Do they even have feelers left after all these years?"

"I suspect we'll find out." Thomas set an arctablet on the table. "Where's Elyssa?"

"She's fine." I pointed up. "Went to the university." I remembered the other important thing I needed to tell him. "The shield is down around the Dark Forest. The monsters are loose."

Thomas nodded as if it were the most routine thing imaginable. He tapped on his arctablet. I leaned over and saw he'd compiled a list of problems longer than mine. I nonchalantly sniffed near him, but his deodorant was holding up just fine.

He raised an eyebrow. "Anything else I should know about?"

I blinked a few times and realized he might want to know about all the prisoners we'd rescued. "Yeah, there's a lot you should know." I told him about the Three Sisters and all the devices we'd stolen from Razor. "Adam's working on cracking their laptops and finding out how their devices self-destruct when supers touch them. He's probably in a lab at the university right now."

"Interesting." Thomas studied the notes he'd taken.

I knew better than to interrupt when he was playing chess in his head, so I leaned on the table and waited.

Thomas projected a holographic map of the world from his arctablet. Pinpoints of light shone green across the globe, each one a marker for a waystation. He tapped those occupied by Razor, turning them red. He marked the occupied special waystations like the Grand Nexus, Three Sisters, and El Dorado orange.

"Adam's got a map he stole from Razor," I said. "He could probably add to what you've got."

Thomas nodded. "I'll take all the data I can get."

"Razor ain't playing around." Shelton grimaced. "Who'd have thought the noms would take over?"

"The noms have had various supernatural task forces for centuries." Thomas put a hand to the globe and spread his fingers to flatten the map. "From massacres to witch burnings, exposure of the supernatural has rarely led to anything positive. The Templars planted agents in nom governments to cover up evidence and hide the truth. It appears these protections are gone."

"What I don't get is how they got all that fancy equipment in such a short period of time." Shelton took off his hat and scratched his head. "Those electro guns are easy enough to make, I guess, but what about the rifles that break shields? The cubes that detect supers?" His eyes widened as if a terrible though just hit him. "Son of a butter-eating goat herder. The only place that could or would come up with that sort of stuff is Science Academy!"

"Whoa." I shook my head like a wet dog. "Why would Science Academy help the noms?"

"It wouldn't have to be the entire academy." Thomas crossed his arms. "Victus once had quite a presence there. I wonder if he enabled a failsafe procedure in case of his death or imprisonment."

"Dollars to doughnuts he did." Shelton scowled. "We need to go to the academy and clear this up right now."

"It's on total lockdown," I said. "The only way in is by omniarch, but I wouldn't be surprised if they have portal traps all over the place."

"Yeah, probably." Shelton chewed on the inside of his lip. "Why don't they use ray guns or regular nom bullets?"

"They apparently want to capture and study as many supers as possible," Thomas said. "But it's also possible these electro weapons can be used lethally."

"They're also guaranteed to take down most supers, whereas bullets might not." I shook my head. "Once they knock someone unconscious, they can have their way with them."

Shelton shuddered. "Let's hope Adam can reverse-engineer the samples you stole."

I nodded. "If anyone can do it, he can."

"What is the meaning of this?" Kassallandra strode through the doorway, crimson hair coiled like a crown atop her head. "My feet have barely savored Eden soil and already you call for a war council! I will not abide this, Commander Borathen. The Daemos will not fight."

CHAPTER 31

The war council hadn't even started and the Daemos were already bowing out.

Komad Rashad, leader of the vampires, entered a moment after Kassallandra. His gaze took in our tense looks. "I take it Paetras Kassallandra has already voiced reservations about a war council?"

When Komad used her formal title, it usually meant he was angling to come down on her side of an argument, or at least brown-nose her enough to gain her support.

"Indeed, I have, Komad." Kassallandra's full red lips compressed into a line. "We are home. It is time to reestablish that which we left behind during our long exile in Seraphina. We must rebuild and grow strong, not throw ourselves into war."

"Against whom do we war?" Komad raised his other eyebrow. "We left Baal a world away. Are there some loose ends left from Victus's reign that the mighty Templars cannot tie?"

Thomas watched the pair posture for a few moments before responding. "What I have to say affects all factions."

"Then say it!" Kassallandra drew herself up haughtily. "I would hear why you have delivered us to this place instead of a waystation where we might find passage home."

Thomas yielded about as much as a brick wall. "We'll discuss it when the others get here."

I leaned to Shelton's ear. "They don't know about Razor?"

"Of course not." He chuckled. "Old war dog didn't tell them a thing as usual."

"I will not wait." Kassallandra turned as if to leave. "It is time to return home."

Thomas looked back down at his arctablet, ignoring her declarations as she inched toward the exit.

Even if Kassallandra walked out of the door, she couldn't exactly get back home without the omniarch portal. I imagined hundreds were filing through from Kratos, so it wouldn't be available anytime soon. On the other hand, it was better to keep her marginally happy instead of ignoring her.

I walked over to her and offered a curt bow. "Paetras Kassallandra, the entire Overworld is threatened. I implore you to remain that we might hear your wise council."

A red eyebrow arched. "Your honeyed tongue has swayed me, Kohvaniss." She laced her arm in mine and walked me into the corridor.

Komad paced behind us. "I would also learn more, young Slade."

"You should wait with the others," Kassallandra told him. "I must be convinced to stay."

"As must I." Komad tutted. "This is no time for politics, Paetras."

My honeyed tongue was about to turn acid. "I'll let Commander Borathen do the talking. Please wait for the others and believe me when I say it will take all the factions to set the Overworld right."

Kassallandra's lips pursed into a rosebud. "My piqued curiosity is the only reason I shall remain."

"That, and there's nowhere to go while the omniarch is employed." *Unless they want to walk.* I held out my arms helplessly. "It will make the wait less boring."

"We shall see." Komad checked the time on a gold pocket watch. "I will return in time for the meeting." A group of subordinate vampires gathered around him as he walked away and just as quickly dispersed, no doubt tasked with finding out what I knew.

Kassallandra marched down the hallway, high heels clicking on the stone, and vanished around a corner.

Shelton chuckled behind me. "Smooth talker."

I didn't have a chance to turn around before a beefy man with mutton chops and curly red hair padded around the corner. Colin McCloud bared his canines in a toothy grin. "Greetings, lad. No time for war like the present, aye?"

"Well, it's not like we have a choice." I gripped his hand in a hearty shake. Despite all our ups and downs, I'd generally been able to count on McCloud and the lycans, even if there had been some bumps in the road during our time in Seraphina.

"It's damned good to be back on home soil." He took a deep breath even though we were in a cave underground. "I can nearly smell Scotland from here."

I looked past him down the hall. "Where's Saber?"

"He and the other felycans are coming on the last ship." McCloud shrugged. "They didn't want to be cooped up long, I suppose."

"Did you see my parents?"

He nodded. "Alysea and David were supposed to come on our ship, but David hadn't come back from Heval yet." McCloud made a face. "I don't

315

much care for those strange folk on Olympus. They look a bit too inbred for my tastes."

Shelton snorted. "I mean, they live on a rock."

I'd only been to Heval a couple of times and didn't much care for it either. "I guess my parents and Saber will miss the war council."

McCloud clapped me on the back. "Convince me, and I'm certain Saber will come along for the ride."

I didn't know if that was true. Felycans were notoriously independent and hard to organize. I didn't know much about Saber, but the giant man had literally herded cats and formed an army out of them. He and McCloud had established mutual respect, but I wouldn't go so far as to call it friendship.

Even so, I let it slide. Saber hadn't abandoned us yet, so it was likely he would join the fight against Razor. "Oh, I think we'll convince you."

"Aye. No rest for the weary." He looked around. "Does this place have scotch? I'd kill for a bloody drink."

"Sure does." Shelton pointed down the hallway. "Take the first door on the left up there to the kitchen. Victus and his goons left a fat stash in the pantry."

McCloud rubbed his hands together. "I can taste it already!"

I watched the lycan until he vanished into the kitchen. "Now if only I could call Elyssa and let her know what's going on."

"Oh, yeah." Shelton huffed. "I figured out the deal with that. The big update that our arcphones downloaded when we got back to Eden was pushed out from Magicsoft and Orange at the orders of our beloved Overlord Tiberius. I'm working on hacking the code, but it's gonna take a while."

I stated the obvious. "We're screwed without communications. Do com badges work?" I'd lost mine after being taken by Razor.

"Those should work." Shelton frowned. "Provided we even have enough to go around these days. We paid a visit to the Ranch, but a nom squatter nearly cleared out the armory."

My jaw dropped. "Say what?"

His jaw tightened. "Nasty business." Shelton shook his head. "I locked him in a room upstairs. The Templars can deal with him when they have time. Unfortunately, the Ranch is out of supplies. Max and the others helped me loot anything useful and we brought it all back here. I don't remember finding any com badges."

"Probably because we took them all to Seraphina with us." I blew out a breath. "We've got no supplies or supply chain. It's like we're starting over again."

"Yeah. So the next thing we need to do is knock Xander off his perch and get things back into production."

"I don't know if that's a good idea." I bit the inside of my lip. "You said Razor mounted a major attack on the Queens Gate waystation. Just because we stopped them once doesn't mean they won't be back in greater numbers. We'll need everyone on the same side instead of turning the city into another warzone."

"You might be right, but don't ask me how we'll get Xander on our side." Shelton huffed. "I'm gonna see if I can hack the arcphone lockouts. That'll at least be something off our plates."

"I'll take anything right now." I clapped him on the back. "It's damned good to be back here, isn't it?"

He grinned. "Back at the Mansion. Seems like old times." Shelton sighed. "Might be a little nicer if it wasn't so much like old times. Damned maniacs and their plans for world domination."

I added a sigh of my own. "I hear you."

Shelton went down the hall to his makeshift workroom and I moseyed to the kitchen for a snack. I hadn't made it far when a man cried out.

317

The bathroom door burst open and a vampire stumbled out, nearly tripping over his pants as he tried to yank them up.

Elyssa dashed out after him and stopped, a stunned look on her face. "What in the world is going on here? Why is there a vampire in the bathroom?"

I howled with laughter. "Oh man, the look on your face."

"I just walked in on a vampire taking a leak, dude!" Elyssa stormed down the hall toward me. "He was standing there, pants around his ankles, whistling."

I doubled over with laughter. "Oh man, I'm gonna pee myself."

"Why didn't you tell me there were people here?" She tried to keep a serious face but couldn't keep from laughing.

I planted a kiss on her luscious lips. "Well, the phones don't work, and I don't have a com badge anymore."

"Oh." Elyssa booped my nose. "So, why are there people here? I thought they all stayed at the university."

"Better if someone else explains it." I took her hand and led her to the war room.

Elyssa flinched. "Dad?"

Thomas Borathen looked up from his arctablet and smiled at his daughter. "It's good to see you, daughter."

She dashed over and gave him a hug. "Where are Mom and the others?"

"Helping with the evacuation. Shelton reached us just as we were leaving Atlantis and used the omniarch here to portal us to the Mansion." Thomas told her about the upcoming meeting and the topics. "I could use your advice on how to deal with what's left of the Overworld."

Elyssa beamed. "Definitely. It's time for the Templars to get Eden back in order."

"That's all well and good, but we've got some smaller issues to deal with too." I told them about the Ranch and our lack of essential supplies. "We've got no armor, no com badges, and a handful of ASEs."

"That does pose a problem." Thomas pursed his lips. "Somehow we need to get word out to our former suppliers, but it appears Xander Tiberius controls all arcphone communications."

"Shelton's working on that." I leaned on the table. "We need to get Adam down here so they can put their heads together."

"So the entire university was abandoned." Thomas frowned. "And there's a monster army on the loose."

"We might shed some light on that." Conrad stepped into the room with Ambria and Max at his heels. "It's good to see you in one piece, Justin." He tentatively put a hand on my shoulder, as if unsure what to do.

I grinned. "Thanks, Conrad."

"Thank god you're okay!" Max clapped his hands. "Shelton was worried to tears about you."

Elyssa snorted. "To tears?"

"He was devastated. Cried like a baby." Ambria grinned. "I'm glad to see his worries were unfounded."

"Nothing like a good torturing session, but it could've been worse." I sat on the edge of the table. "What do you know about the monsters?"

Conrad clasped his hands behind his back. "Victus assembled a monster army to take over the university. Evadora rallied the tragon, and our spider friend, Shushiel, gathered the ruby spiders to fight them." His eyes grew distant, as if visualizing the battle. "We won. Most of Victus's frogres and other monsters were killed. We left Galfandor in charge to

319

reset the shield in the Dark Forest and to clean up. Unfortunately, it seems Xander Tiberius fought him tooth and nail."

"My father wanted power more than anything in the world." Max scowled. "I'm certain he'll do anything to keep it, even if it means losing to Razor."

Thomas grunted. "So if the Templars raided the city, you think Xander would fight to the death?"

"Definitely." Max shook his head sadly.

"So that's why the university was abandoned," Ambria said. "All the monsters ran loose. The tragon scared everyone away from the university before Shushiel and the ruby spiders convinced him to return to the forest."

"Convinced him?" I snorted. "He's too dumb to understand."

"Oh, he's smarter than you think," Ambria said. "Evadora was quite taken with him."

I didn't believe her, but that wasn't important right now. "So the monsters are back in the forest?"

"Yes. The ruby spiders destroyed the mutants." The female voice came from overhead.

I looked up just as a monstrous spider blurred into view. A screamed ripped from my throat and I did a combination backward somersault and flip to vault off the table and hide behind Elyssa. "Jesus eight-legged Christ!"

Ambria burst into laughter. "Oh, Shushiel, that was beautifully done."

The spider dropped lightly onto the table in front of Thomas and bounced up and down.

The commander didn't even flinch. "Shushiel, I take it?"

The spider dipped its forelegs in a bow. "Yes, sir."

"We owe the ruby spiders a debt of gratitude for controlling the forest." He held out a hand.

Shushiel extended a furry foreleg and touched his hand. "We are here to help, especially in these times of dire trouble."

"That's very good to hear." Thomas check the time on his arctablet. "The war council meets in ten minutes. Would you join us as an ambassador for your people?"

"Happily!" The giant spider bounced up and down a few times then crawled off the table to stand next to Ambria.

Elyssa looked over her shoulder at me. "Justin, you can come out now."

With a sheepish grin, I stopped cowering behind my girlfriend and came out. "Uh, sorry. I wasn't expecting you to drop right in front of me. I'm totally fine with spiders. Not scared at all." I puffed out my chest and patted it to demonstrate my manliness.

"Ambria thought it would be funny." Shushiel's mandibles twitched. "I am sorry, but it was amusing."

"Amusing? It was hilarious!" I walked over and shook her foreleg. "Welcome to the team."

"Thank you, Justin." Shushiel's mandibles twitched again.

That was when my mother rushed into the war room, a worried look on her face. "Justin, your father is missing."

CHAPTER 32

I blinked. "Mom? I thought you were still in Atlantis."

"I was." She cast her worried gaze around the room. "David went to Heval at the request of Archon Hippias. That was more than two days ago. Hippias said he met with David for two hours, and that was the last he saw of him."

Thomas pursed his lips. "I'll send my best scouts back to Atlantis with you. They'll find him."

"Dad has gone off on his own before," I said. "Though why he'd do it now makes no sense."

"He always tells me when he does that." Mom pressed a hand to her forehead. "This doesn't feel right."

I hugged her tight. "I'll come with you. We'll find him." There were tons of secret passages in Mount Olympus. We'd explored a lot of them, and Dad had expressed interest in taking a few days to poke around in them. I couldn't imagine him doing it in the middle of an evacuation, though.

"No." Mom put a hand on my chest. "They need you here. I was briefed on the current situation of the Overworld, and we can't afford to divert too many people right now."

Thomas motioned to a Templar at the door. "Have Glover and Hatch help Alysea find David."

The Templar pressed a hand over their chest. "Yes, commander."

"Thank you, Thomas." Mom kissed me on the cheek. "I'll see you soon."

"Glover and Hatch are the best," Elyssa said. "They'll find him."

Mom managed a smile and left.

I probably should have been more concerned but, knowing my father and his love of flying by the seat of his pants, it was highly likely he was sipping ale and enjoying the view from the tip top of Olympus. Despite Mom's concerns, he'd gone on unannounced walkabouts plenty of times in Seraphina and worried her half to death.

"You don't look worried," Elyssa said.

I chuckled. "Yeah, it's my dad we're talking about. He's probably in Olympus playing cards with Shakespeare right now." I nodded at Thomas. "Thanks for sending help, though."

"Of course."

McCloud walked into the room, a glass of amber liquid in his hand, and leaned against the wall. "'Tis pure heaven to have scotch again."

"I prefer wine." Komad glided inside and took a spot across from Thomas. He turned to one of his assistants and sent him to fetch a glass.

The other faction leaders filed in right on time. Kassallandra arrived a minute late, no doubt on purpose. Thomas began his briefing and got right to the point with a map of Razor conquests.

"This cannot be." Kassallandra stared at the red dots. "How did the noms gain such power?"

"Aye, what a bloody mess." McCloud slapped a hand on the table. "The entire Overworld is nothing but a shambles."

"Oh my." Captain Takei, leader of the Blue Cloaks and Arcane forces, shook his head. "This is quite grim."

"The solution is simple." Komad raked a sour gaze across the table. "The Templars must restore order. Dethrone the usurper, Xander, and exterminate the rogue noms."

Kassallandra nodded. "Agreed."

"I'm afraid it's not that simple." Thomas displayed a screen with troop numbers by faction. "The Templar forces are down by nearly sixty percent since our exile to Seraphina. All of our combined forces are barely over two thousand."

"Deserters account for a great deal of the attrition rate," Komad said. "They left to make lives of their own, thinking we would never return to Eden."

"Be that as it may, the Templars simply don't have the manpower or resources to challenge Xander and face Razor." Thomas highlighted a number labeled *Refugees*. "This is the number of prisoners rescued from just one of Razor's detention facilities. We hope to recruit some help from them, but they're nowhere near battle ready."

"So you call on the Daemos to ally with you once more." Kassallandra's lips peeled into a sneer. "The Templars and Custodians left behind have done a poor job maintaining order. Now it is up to us to restore everything."

"We didn't expect to be gone for years," Elyssa said. "We left behind a skeleton force to maintain operations while we fought Cephus. They simply weren't enough to hold down the fort indefinitely."

"The Daemos will help." Kassallandra offered a shrewd smile. "But we require certain recompense for our aid."

Komad raised an eyebrow. "Such as what? More power in the conclave? A greater say in Overworld matters?"

"I will discuss it with the commander after this meeting," she replied.

"Lest you forget, we are still beholden to the Overworld Conclave. Just because the government is no more, does not make the treaty less valid."

"Oh, I think it does." Kassallandra returned a confident gaze. "The conclave is dead, the government defunct. Article Nine states that without a governing body, the Overworld Conclave is dissolved."

"Are you insane?" McCloud pounded a fist on the table. "The conclave was steady and functional for hundreds of years. And now you want to dissolve it and revert to supernatural anarchy?"

I knew for a fact that Kassallandra didn't want to dissolve the conclave. She had something different in mind. "It's a bold move, Cotton. Let's see if it pays off."

Elyssa gave me a confused look. "Huh?"

"Oh, just watching the spectacle." Between the vampires and the Daemos, these meetings were always entertaining.

"Article Nine requires unanimous approval." Thomas gave each of the faction members a momentary look. "Since Xander is the reigning Arcanus Primus, he would also be required to vote."

"He's also the self-proclaimed Overlord!" McCloud growled deep in his throat. "Let's get everyone together and show the wee bastard he's the ruler of nothing."

"That would be unproductive," Thomas said. "We need to engage him in talks and form a temporary truce if we hope to defeat Razor."

"As I said, the Daemos require recompense for our aid." Kassallandra crossed her arms. "Otherwise we will withdraw."

"And I would hear these demands." Komad mimicked her stance. "For the Red Syndicate will not allow the Daemos a greater share of power in the Overworld."

"Which no longer exists," Kassallandra shot back.

I rolled my eyes. "Actually, it does." I planted a finger on the table. "Right here, right now. This is the Overworld Conclave. We have the Daemos, the vampire, the lycan, and the Arcane leaders gathered right here. Just because Xander created an illegal government and made himself the grand poohbah doesn't mean the Overworld is gone."

"It is all but vanished from Eden." Kassallandra's eyes shaded from green to red. "It is gone."

I held up a hand. "Okay, sure. It's an Overworld apocalypse. Is that what you wanted to hear?" I didn't wait for an answer to my rhetorical question. "I would argue that the Overworld is far more than a form of government."

Komad's forehead pinched. "How so?"

I made a circle with my finger to indicate the assembly. "We've been together through hell and back. We've sacrificed friends and loved ones, bled for one another, and fought tyranny to preserve our way of life. I have come to respect everyone in this room because they have proven time and time again that there are things worth fighting for. Things that matter more than wealth and power." I pounded a fist on the table. "We fight for life and liberty. We fight for our friends and loved ones."

All eyes focused on me, so I pressed onward. "Throughout our countless battles I've seen lycans die for vampires. I've seen vampires drag wounded Daemos and lycans out of harm's way. I've seen Arcanes shield soldiers of every faction even while under threat of death themselves." I let my gaze linger on each of the faction leaders. "We are not merely allies anymore. No, we crossed that bloodstained line long ago." I held up a hand and clenched it into a fist. "Now we are brothers and sisters, united. We are family."

"Bloody right!" McCloud howled and burst into applause. "Brothers and sisters united!"

Elyssa wrapped her hand around my upraised fist. "Family united."

Kassallandra swallowed hard. "You are sickeningly optimistic, Kohvaniss."

"Agreed." Komad scoffed. "This boy tore us from our homes and our realm to drag us into foreign wars. I've not known a moment of peace since taking up arms to follow him." He sighed. "However, he is not wrong. I know each of you better than I want to. I suppose that makes us more family than not."

"In war, family is the man or woman standing next to you." Captain Takei reached across the table and put his hand on mine and Elyssa's. "I am proud to call you family."

Thomas joined his hand to ours. "Family united."

Conrad, Ambria, and Max walked over and joined their hands to ours. "Family united!"

"Family united." Shushiel extended a slender foreleg. "Regardless of shape or form, we are family."

McCloud hopped up on the table and slapped his hand to the pile. "Family united!"

Kassallandra and Komad heaved a collective sigh and walked solemnly around the table. They extended their hands in unison and touched them to ours. "Family united." They sounded like two kids forced to eat their vegetables.

Tears glistened in Ambria's eyes. "I think I see why Justin is a hero now."

Max grinned. "The greatest that ever was."

His grin was infectious, and my lips spread from ear to ear. "Family united!

We threw our hands into the air and cheered—well, most of us did. Kassallandra and Komad were somewhat muted in their appreciation of the moment.

"We will follow your plan." Kassallandra returned to her side of the table. "As per usual."

"Red Cell and the Red Syndicate stand ready, Commander Borathen." Komad returned to his place. "We must reestablish the old order."

"It goes without saying the Arcanes are here to serve." Takei pounded a fist to his chest.

"As are the Lycans." McCloud slid back across the table and slapped Komad on the back. "Just like old times, eh?"

Komad sighed.

"Elyssa will present the briefing." Thomas stepped back to let his daughter take over.

She tapped arctablet screen and took a moment, as if reviewing her notes. It was mainly for show, because Elyssa was a veteran when it came to presentations. A holographic image of Queens Gate flickered on above the table. "Xander is holed up in the city center and surrounded by hundreds of loyalists and innocent citizens." The view shifted toward the end of the valley where double doors in the cliff face led to the waystation. "Another hundred or more loyalists control the waystation. There are several hundred refugees being held there as well. According to our sources, Xander isn't letting any more people into the city without thorough vetting."

Takei leaned toward the image. "Are they Arcanes or mixed?"

"Mixed." Elyssa rotated the image back toward the city. "Our sources tell us that the refugees are trapped between Xander's people and Razor. We don't have much time before the situation boils over and the refugees fight Xander's people. That's provided Razor doesn't attack first. Early indications are that Razor is prepping for a much larger assault."

"So we rescue the refugees from the waystation and increase our own numbers," McCloud said.

"We could, but there are other considerations." Elyssa tugged on the fabric of her shirt. "We are severely short on the essentials. Com badges, armor, and even weapons. Xander controls the government buildings, one of which is a warehouse the Templars once used. We need access to that warehouse."

"Red Cell is also in dire need of armor and weapons." Komad tapped a long, black fingernail on the table. "We are unable to contact any suppliers due to the communications lockdown by Xander's government."

"I say we bum rush the bastard." McCloud stroked mutton chop. "We take the city and everything we want."

"We can't afford to lose more people on our side or Xander's," Elyssa said. "What I propose is a truce with him. We will offer him a continued role in the government for his aid in defeating Razor."

"Surely, you jest." Kassallandra scoffed. "The man proclaimed himself Overlord. I will not allow an Arcane power over the council."

"And what of Takei?" Komad nodded toward the captain. "Surely you don't mean to have two Arcanes on the council?"

"I will gladly step aside if it means preserving the Overworld." Takei nodded at Elyssa. "Diplomacy is certainly the best option, and possibly our only hope."

Komad frowned. "What, precisely, would be Xander's role?"

Elyssa folded her arms across her chest. "He would remain Arcanus Primus and keep his seat on the Overworld Council. At the end of his term, he would be subject to another election."

"I sincerely doubt he'll agree to such terms." Kassallandra pressed her lips together. "Even under the threat of civil war."

"We'll have to try." Elyssa turned off the holographic projection. "Justin and I will extend the olive branch immediately after this meeting."

"What if he captures you and uses you as hostages?" McCloud shook his head. "Better just one of you goes rather than both. We can't afford taking a chance that bloody big."

"I'll go," said a small voice from the other side of the room.

All eyes turned to a blond boy—Maxwell Tiberius.

Max cleared his throat. "I may be the son he doesn't like, but I might have a better chance persuading him."

"What about your brothers?" Ambria said incredulously. "They might torture you to death just for fun!"

"We're going too." Conrad put a hand on his friend's shoulder.

"Oh no you don't." Shelton stood in the doorway. "I'll take him."

"This isn't an argument," Ambria said. "We refuse to let our friend go without us."

"I'm old enough to make my own decisions, Ambria." Max scowled at her. "I won't risk you and Conrad. The Overworld needs you more than it needs me."

"No, it bloody doesn't!" Ambria's fists clenched. "You're not the brightest in the world, Max, but you're like a brother to me, and I'll be damned if I let that rotten family of yours take you away."

Max's eyes watered. "Ambria, you're embarrassing me, but I love you." He grinned. "You're the best sister a guy could have."

"Oh, Max, you little fool!" Ambria hugged him.

"I have really had enough of these familial antics," Komad said. "Can you please decide on your ambassadors?"

I raised a hand. "Shelton and Max, you're with me. The rest of you stay behind."

"If Justin and Shelton can't keep me safe, no one can." Max disentangled himself from Ambria. "Okay?"

She sighed but nodded. "I suppose you're right."

Conrad patted Max on the back. "Good luck."

Max took a deep breath. "I'll need it."

"Then it's settled." Elyssa didn't look entirely convinced of my decision, but she also didn't question it in front of everyone. "We can't plan against Razor until we know the outcome of diplomacy with Xander. I suggest you get underway immediately, because we're running out of time."

The refugees in the waystation might rebel against Xander's people, or Razor might attack at any moment. Either situation would be a blood-bath. There was no telling how much time we had.

"We're off." I kissed Elyssa on the cheek and whispered in her ear. "Love you, babe."

"I love you too," she murmured back.

Komad groaned.

Shelton and I grabbed the two brooms Elyssa and I had taken from Keep Moore. The broom closet down the hall held four more in working order. Max grabbed one and we went back down the hallway to the bathroom with the secret exit. Shelton tried the door, but it was locked. He banged on the door. "Hurry up in there, it's an emergency!"

"I've got an emergency of my own!" a man shouted back. "There's like five more bathrooms in this place!"

Shelton growled. "Yeah, but we need this one."

"We? What sort of nasty fetishes are you in to?"

"Son of a—" Shelton pointed his arcphone at the lock and picked it with a spell. The door cracked open to reveal a middle-aged man reading a romance novel on the toilet.

"You people are crazy!" He covered his crotch with the book.

"Ah, put a cork in it." Shelton opened the secret exit and we filed out. He flourished a bow to the man on the toilet and closed the hidden door.

"Whose bright idea was it to put a secret entrance in the bathroom?" Max said.

"Might've been mine." Shelton shrugged. "Seemed like a good idea at the time."

"He wanted to design it so the entire toilet slid aside to reveal the stairs into the tunnel." I snorted. "Thank god that option didn't make it off the drawing board."

Max laughed. "That could have been disastrous."

"Maybe funny as hell, too," Shelton said. "But the plumbing would've been a nightmare."

We exited through the hatch at the other end and mounted our flying brooms. It took us ten minutes to reach the shield perimeter guarding the city center and another five or so before a man in white robes flew up to speak with us.

It was time to make peace with a dictator.

CHAPTER 33

"**F**lying without a permit is punishable by law." The man's wrinkles and narrow eyes gave him a hardcore case of resting bitch face.

Off to a great start already!

"Good to know," I said. "We're here to talk peace with Xander. I'm Justin Slade. These are my companions, Harry Shelton and Maxwell Tiberius."

The man blinked and looked at Max. "Your father will see you, but the others must wait here."

"No can do," Shelton said. "We're all going in."

"I think not."

"Look, we have an army ready to sweep through here like Genghis Khan." I put on my intimidating face and hoped it didn't look like I had constipation. "But Razor is a bigger issue. It's best if we avoid a civil war and unify to defeat them. Is Xander really willing to sacrifice the entire Overworld?"

The man's jaw worked back and forth. "I will present your proposal to the primus and return."

"We don't have time to waste." I pointed toward the far end of the valley and the waystation. "We've got a situation that could turn into a bloodbath any moment. You need to let us in now."

"I don't have the authority." The man turned his flying carpet away. "You will have to wait."

I threw up my hands, but before I could argue his decision, he flew away. "Well, great. The clock's ticking away and we're stuck waiting."

"I don't have the juice to take down the entire shield, but I could make a hole," Shelton said.

"Better not." I stared at the government buildings a few blocks away. "We might provoke a bad response."

"Xander is a coward." Max shifted in his broom saddle. "As long as he has walls to hide behind, he'll do what he wants."

Shelton scoffed. "He won't feel so safe once Razor smashes down the walls."

Two more broom riders rose above the government buildings. Max stiffened. "Oh no."

"What is it?" Shelton asked.

"My brothers, Rhys on the left and Devon on the right." Max shuddered. "This can't be good."

Two young men in their late teens rode boomsticks with blue chrome accents and narrow racing saddles. Both wore their platinum blond hair long. Aside from their blond hair, neither bore much resemblance to Max. Their narrow jaws and high cheekbones gave them a somewhat sinister appearance. They only furthered that first impression with matching grins. Though they were identical twins, a freckle on Rhys' cheek mirrored the one on Devon's.

"Oh, little brother. You've found more playmates?" Rhys flashed white teeth.

Devon put on a hurt look. "Is this why you never play with us anymore?"

"Oh, shame." Rhys rubbed his eyes as if he were crying. "We miss you so."

Max looked at Shelton and straightened in his seat before responding. "Is there a reason you're here, other than to make asses out of yourselves?"

"What a sharp tongue, brother." Devon tutted. "That's no way to talk to your elders."

Rhys scoffed. "Yes, be polite, or we'll send you on your merry way."

"Well, I guess we'll just let Razor Echelon have their way with you." Max turned to me. "Let's leave them to their fate, Justin. Once Razor is done, we'll bring the Eden army down here and clean up what's left."

I wasn't sure if this was a ruse, or what, but I played along. "They'll probably take prisoners and experiment on them, so I doubt anyone will be left."

"I hear their laboratory prisons are real nightmares," Shelton added. "Probably be a nice place for two teen wizards to get anally probed by scientists."

Devon paled, but forced a smile. "You wouldn't leave family to die, Max. You're such a needy little thing."

Max chuckled. "Needy? I already have everything I could have wished for. Razor can take my family"—he made air quotes—"and do what they want with them. I'm just here to save the people who can't escape your mad little kingdom."

Rhys opened his mouth to say something, but for once, he seemed at a loss for words.

"Either take me to Xander so we can work out a deal, or get ass-probed by Razor, *brothers*." Max bared his teeth. "The clock is ticking."

Devon's hands clenched into fists, but he didn't retort. "I'm certain you feel rather smug with the mighty Justin Slade at your side. Just hope I don't catch you alone." He took out an arcphone and pointed it at the shield. A section shimmered, and a hole opened. "Come through before I change my mind."

Max didn't move. "I don't think you're sincere. Maybe if you say please, we'll come help you."

Rhys groaned so agonizingly I wondered if he just popped a blood vessel.

Devon's knuckles turned white where he gripped his broom handle. His arms trembled, and his face turned red. He abruptly relaxed. A fake grin slithered across his face. "Please, Max. Come with us."

"See, being polite isn't so hard." Max motioned Shelton and me ahead of him and waited until we were through before he came.

I watched the arcphone in Devon's hand, half afraid the asshole might close the shield before Max was through. Thankfully, he did not.

Rhys jetted ahead without so much as a by-your-leave and headed toward the tall domed building to the right of the plaza at the city center. A group of men in red Arcane robes approached when we landed at the bottom of the stairs.

"No magical instruments allowed in the presence of the Overlord." The leader wore a purple badge on his chest and a thick Chester-the-molester mustache on his upper lip. "Prepare to be searched."

"Are you serious?" Shelton wrapped his duster tight. "I ain't giving up my arcphone."

"Is this really necessary?" Max said to his brothers.

Rhys sneered. "Yes."

"Then let's go back." Max mounted his broom and rose into the air.

"Stop them," Devon commanded.

The guards reached for wands. I summoned a sword of Brilliance and a giant sledgehammer of Murk in my hands. "Let us go in peace, or Justin smash."

Shelton unpacked his staff and summoned a miniature sun at the tip. "You don't want to mess with us, boys."

The guards looked at each other, fear in their eyes.

Rhys made a strangled noise. "Can't we just kill them?"

An insane light flared in Devon's eyes. "We could, dear brother."

"Stop!" A tall man with a shaved head stood at the top of the stairs. "Escort our guests inside. There is no need to search them." He spun, the silver trim on his black robes flashing in the sunlight, and vanished inside the building.

"Someone just saved you from a royal ass-beating." Shelton extinguished his spell but kept his staff handy. "Lead the way, kiddos."

Rhys and Devon walked ahead of us, muttering threats I only heard because of my super hearing. "Jesus, these kids are dark." If they weren't serial killers already, they would be one day. They were real front-line material for the next battle. If they'd bullied Max as much as I thought, I couldn't imagine how he made it through childhood without becoming a psycho himself.

Max walked between us, a big grin on his face. "That was awesome, Shelton. I kinda hoped we could kick their asses."

Shelton clapped him on the back and chuckled. "Anytime, ace."

Max's grin grew wider.

The marble stairs stretched nearly as wide as the building and about fifty feet high. I had no idea why the architect thought more stairs were better, but they certainly made entering the building an incredible chore. Our escorts were breathing heavily by the time we reached the top. Two more Arcanes in red robes opened the massive wooden doors at the top and we walked inside like we owned the place.

Dozens of massive portraits lined the walls of a wide foyer. Thick burgundy carpet ran down the center of a white marble floor. Bronze busts sat on intricately carved wooden pedestals. Another set of tall wooden doors opened in front of us to reveal a cavernous room with little else but a tall marble pedestal in the middle. A golden throne sat atop the pedestal, but there were no stairs to reach it. I assumed it took a flying carpet to get up there.

"Why's this place so big?" I asked. "You could seat Congress in here and still have room left over. Queens Gate can't possibly need such a large government."

"It's one of the official hosting places for the Overworld Conclave." Shelton nodded toward the marble pedestal. "Podiums rise up out of the floor for the faction members to use, and the members of the pocket dimension governments sit on flying carpets around the room."

"Seems really inefficient."

"Yeah, it is. I don't even remember the last time the entire Overworld Conclave met." He shrugged. "Looks like it's gonna be a while before we have another real government anyway."

Xander wasn't perched on his throne, which was a surprise, but he rode a flying carpet a few feet off the floor so he could look down on us. His glossy platinum locks reached past his shoulders. Cold blue eyes peered out over a long narrow nose. Rhys and Devon favored him, but his slightly squarer jaw gave him a less effeminate look. Even so, his gold-trimmed black robes looked like something out of a Victoria's Secret catalog.

The bald man in similar black robes stood to his right. Intricate tattoos patterned his scarred face, and his left hand resembled slightly melted plastic.

"It is good to see you, son." Xander drifted toward us, about twenty of his red guards pacing him. "Have you come to take a place in my government?"

"Of course not, Father." Max motioned to his left. "This is Harry Shelton, the most powerful Arcane in the world, and this is Justin Slade, hero of Eden."

Shelton's chest puffed out.

Damn, he gave Shelton top billing. It was definitely different seeing someone give Shelton some hero worship.

"We're here to negotiate a truce," I said. "Razor Echelon—I'm sure you've heard of them—are mounting another attack on the Queens Gate waystation. We need to unite and fight them back."

"I'm quite safe behind my shield," Xander said. "Why should I throw my forces into battle?"

"Razor has weapons that destroy magical shields," Max said. "You're not even remotely safe here. Razor will take the city first, but we'll be safe at Arcane University."

Xander looked as if he wanted to argue. Instead, he motioned to the bald man. "I have demands that must be met before I'll accept a truce."

The bald man held up a parchment and read from it. "Xander Tiberius shall remain Overlord for the rest of his natural life. The title of Arcanus Primus shall also remain his for the same duration. The Over-world Conclave shall be restored, but the Overlord's word is final on all matters." Baldy rattled off demand after demand until my eyes glazed over.

I held up a hand to stop him. "Stop. Just stop." I shook my head. "Let me tell you what's acceptable to us." I enumerated with my fingers to make it more official. "One, you remain Arcanus Primus until the next election. Two, there is no Overworld overlord, so that goes away completely. Three, you get immunity from prosecution for aiding and abetting Victus Edison. Four, you get to survive the shit storm about to sweep through this place." I raised an eyebrow. "Fair?"

"We will survive no matter what." Xander seemed awfully sure of himself. "As I said, Razor cannot penetrate our shields."

"Are you kidding me?" Shelton projected an image from his phone. In it, a Razor operative fired a shield breaker rifle at a barrier and disintegrated it in seconds. "That's going to happen to your precious shield."

"I think not." Xander waved away the comment like a fly. "Our shield is not magical. You see, Victus left behind a major cache of weapons and technology from Science Academy. We have tested their shields in the field against Razor, and their weapons are useless against it."

That smug son of a bitch. "Then they'll siege you and starve you out. Either way, you lose."

"Once Razor began assaulting the pocket dimensions, we knew it was only a matter of time before they found Queens Gate." Xander smiled easily. "So they cannot merely starve us out. Queens Gate is the last safe bastion in the Overworld, you see. This is why we've refused to allow in more refugees and why we will refuse your truce unless my demands are met."

"You think it's better being trapped in this city for the rest of your life than to take a little blow to your ego and step down?" Max waved a hand out toward the city. "You will be overlord of ashes and rubble, Father. Razor will either leave you to rot here or find a way through the shield eventually. Either way, you lose. What if by joining forces with us you became something more—something not even Victus Edison could ever achieve. You could be a hero of the Overworld."

Xander blinked, whether from surprise or contemplation, I couldn't tell.

"Don't listen to him, Father!" Devon clapped his hands. "The runt is an idiot."

"And a liar," Rhys added.

"I believe he speaks wisdom, for once in his insignificant life." A tall, fair-skinned woman drifted down from the balcony far up in the dome, riding a golden carpet. Her hair was so white it appeared silver. The two young women standing on the flying carpet behind her could have been clones. "I will not abide being trapped in this dying city with the whole world out of my reach, Xander."

Xander's shoulders slumped as if her words physically struck his back. "My darling, Faria, we should not be so hasty—"

"Hasty?" Faria laughed haughtily. "I have been kept from Paris and Milan for weeks because of this foolishness. Karenia and Rushmia are beside themselves with boredom, and we are sick to death of the local cuisine."

"It's miserable, Father!" One of the girls stomped her foot on the flying carpet with every word. "We want to travel again!"

"But you shall, you shall!" Xander stiffened his spine, like a man bravely facing a grizzly bear just before it disemboweled him. "We will drive off Razor, and I will rule the Overworld!"

Faria dismounted the carpet and strode over to Max. She caressed his face, not in a tender way, but like someone sizing up a prize horse. "Your words carry weight with me, Maxwell. I had always thought you a worthless runt, but I can see that my genes run stronger in you than I hoped. We agree to the truce, so long as the entire Tiberius family is immune from prosecution or seizing of assets, even those that may have come into our ownership after Victus, bless his wonderful soul, took power."

I didn't even want to think about the war crimes this god-awful family committed during Victus's brief reign. It made me sick to think that this agreement would give them a free pass, even if we found out they'd eaten babies and killed puppies. I began to question whether any deal we made with them was worth the blow to my conscience.

Max looked at his mother's hand as if it were a slug smearing his face with mucus. He backed up a step to get away from her touch. "I think that can be arranged, provided your forces report straight to Commander Thomas Borathen for the duration of this war."

Faria snapped her fingers at the bald man. "Fitwit, draw up the papers at once. I will have this properly signed and agreed to by Justin Slade. I am certain the hero of Eden's signature will carry the weight of law with his people."

I gave her the fakest smile possible. "Oh, it will, Lady Faria."

She pursed her lips and looked me over. "You're a feral one, aren't you, boy?" Her proper British accent made it sound completely improper. "Too bad your genes are polluted."

Fitwit didn't even look twice at Xander before dropping to his knees and scrawling away on a piece of parchment. Xander stared helplessly at his wife as she took away his hopes and dreams, showing everyone who really wore the pants in this government.

"I want all the political prisoners released too," Max said. "That includes Galfandor."

Xander moaned as if physically ill.

"Yes, more grist for the mill," Faria said. "Add it to the document, Fitwit."

I took Max and Shelton to the side. "I'm starting to rethink this. Do you really think we should let war criminals off the hook?"

"Oh, they won't be," Max said. "Believe me, we'll get them one way or another once Razor is beaten back."

"I agree." Shelton covered his mouth with a hand to keep anyone from lip reading him. "Let's get this done."

I sighed. Nodded. "I don't like it, but I guess it's the best way forward."

I caught a smug grin from Devon and returned it. These war criminals were going to pay, provided we survived Razor, Baal, and Xanos.

CHAPTER 34

F itwit was remarkably fast with his magic quill and had a document ready in minutes. But Faria made him tear it up and start over three times before she was pleased with the final document. I read it over three times to make sure he hadn't sneaked in anything about making Xander ruler for life. It wasn't great for either side, which meant it was about as good as it got.

Xander would remain Arcanus Primus for two terms. The Tiberius family was absolved of any and all crimes of the past and kept all the property they'd acquired. I made sure the government buildings and treasury were exempt from that condition.

I let Max and Shelton examine it for safe measure. I wanted Thomas's and Elyssa's sage advice too, but even if Xander granted my phone access to the aethernet, Elyssa's phone still wouldn't work. Flying it up and back would simply take too long.

"I think it's solid," Shelton said. "I don't see any red flags."

"It's what we came for." Max looked sideways at his sisters. "Guaranteed they'll make a beeline out of here the moment they can."

I took the quill from Fitwit's burn-scarred hand and signed on the dotted line. Xander looked pained as he took the parchment from the man. "We could have had it all, darling. Why sign it away?"

Faria's eyes narrowed to slits. Xander hastily signed the document.

I prayed I hadn't given away the kingdom. "Can you duplicate the document, Fitwit?"

The cleric, or whatever he was, created a duplicate copy without signatures, and we signed it as well. I figured that was official enough.

"First things first," I said. "We need to evacuate the refugees from the waystation and get them to safety before Razor launches another attack. I also need the lockdown on arcphones deactivated, and as many com badges as you can spare."

"Demands, demands." Faria sighed. "Fitwit, you are our envoy. Be sure they have what they need, but don't give away the castle."

The bald man clicked his heels together and bowed like a good little minion, then motioned us to follow. Xander started whining to his wife before we were even out of earshot. I didn't feel the least bit sorry for him.

Fitwit led us out of the auditorium and the building. Lumbering behind him was maddening when I just wanted to hop on my broom and zip to the supplies. Thankfully, we didn't have to go far. The Romanesque Overworld Courthouse had been converted into a makeshift warehouse. It held a treasure trove of weapons that might have been copied straight from a classic sci-fi movie. Fitwit led us to a crate filled with silver com badges shaped like stars.

"These are the surplus you may take," he said in a quiet voice. He took us to another crate of shiny chrome pistols. "These as well."

"What about flying brooms or rocket sticks?" Shelton looked around. "Hell, even flying carpets would do."

"Only a few brooms and carpets." He showed us a stack of musty-smelling carpets. "You may take these."

"What about those boomsticks Rhys and Devon rode?" Max wore a calculating look. "We could use those."

"I will requisition them for you." He jotted down a note on his parchment. "Shall I have everything delivered to the university?"

"That would be great." I was a bit surprised by his helpfulness but didn't question it.

He must have detected my curiosity, because he held up his injured hand. "Razor did this to me when they raided the Seattle waystation. They took my family. I don't know if they're alive or dead."

"I'm very sorry to hear that." I tilted my head. "Why are you with Xander?"

"He speaks for the common Arcane. He would keep out the vampires and other undesirables who want power over us." Fitwit made more notes. "I want Razor burned to the ground. To that end, I will do what I can to help. But I still believe in Xander. I think he is the only one to restore order to the Overworld. My loyalty lies with him."

Despite his ignorant rhetoric, he sounded intelligent. I couldn't imagine what the Overworld had gone through without the Templars to maintain order. There were probably a lot of scared people who struck out in fear. If we could defeat Razor, maybe we could get rid of the fear—well, at least until Baal and Xanos destroyed everything.

"I understand. Please get everything delivered as soon as possible."

"It will be delivered within the hour." Fitwit led us back outside. "I will have Magicsoft and Orange transmit the codes to unlock arcphones so they can use the aethernet again."

"Now we're talking." Shelton sighed. "It was a pain in the ass breaking the cipher."

"We'll need as many soldiers as you can spare too," I said. "Can you get them assembled and ready to go?"

"I will have them on standby in the plaza." He motioned to the square between the buildings.

I couldn't think of anything else, so I hopped on my broom. "Thanks, Fitwit."

He offered a slight nod and walked back inside the courthouse.

"Man, this feels almost too easy." Shelton looked back as we flew away. "I hope we can trust those bastards."

"You can trust my mother's desire to see Milan again," Max said. "She looked miserable all cooped up in there."

"Yeah, you're probably right." Shelton grinned at him. "Damned fine work in there, by the way. You're smarter and better than that bunch by miles."

Max's face flushed, and a pleased grin stretched from ear to ear. "Thanks, Shelton."

I shuddered. "How did you survive your family?"

"I stayed with my Uncle Malcolm mostly." He pointed to small farmhouses further south. "He's not a great person, but he mostly kept to himself and let me be."

A guard still hovered on a carpet near the shield and opened a hole for us to exit. We gained altitude and flew up over the edge of the cliff. People bustled about around the university wall, lifting chunks of broken mortar and stone with spells while others patched the broken sections. Elyssa had used her mad organizing skills to put the able-bodied refugees to work.

My phone began vibrating as we neared the hidden entrance to the underground mansion. I took it out and saw code flashing on the screen. It rebooted, and a moment later, I had a signal.

Shelton whooped. "Back in business!"

I called Elyssa as we entered the tunnel.

She answered right away. "Babe?"

"Yep!"

"You got Xander." She didn't sound surprised.

"Thanks to Max." I gave her the lowdown as we walked. By the time we got to the secret door in the bathroom, she was up to date and off the phone.

No one waited in the bathroom and I soon found out why. Someone had posted a sign on the door. *Do not use. Secret entrance for pervs in the wall!*

Shelton guffawed. "Oh man, that's funny."

"Pervs!" Max giggled. "As if I want to see people poop!"

Templars dashed in and out of the war room, making it difficult to squeeze inside. Faction envoys watched Elyssa and Thomas chart a plan for evacuating the waystation and setting up defenses. Komad and Kassallandra were probably charting their own courses somewhere in private just in case everything went to hell.

"The entrance to the valley is a bottleneck." Elyssa marked a holographic image of the double doors. "If we hold them here, they can't get into the city."

"Fitwit should give the Arcanes in the waystation the all-clear to evacuate soon," I said. "We need some people to meet and organize them."

"Already done," Elyssa said. "We need to free up the omniarch so we can send troops down there immediately."

Thomas turned to a woman with an arctablet. "Evacuation status?"

"All Templars present and accounted for. Ninety percent of Daemos present, fifty-five percent of vampires, ten percent lycans, and no felycans. Total evacuation stands at fifty-nine percent."

"Maybe she could be more precise," Shelton muttered to me.

Max laughed.

I felt at loose ends while Elyssa and Thomas focused on planning, so I came up with some work of my own. "I'm going down to the waystation. I want to make sure the evacuation starts right away."

Elyssa nodded. "That's a good idea. Send them straight to the university. I've got people organizing newcomers into functional groups."

"Of course you do." I pecked a kiss on her cheeks. "Call me if you need anything."

Shelton and Max had plans of their own. "We're headed up to the university to help Adam with the Razor gadgets." Shelton grabbed his broom. "We also want to make sure Fitwit delivers the goods."

"I can hardly wait to get my brothers' boomsticks." Max rubbed his hands together. "Those things are sick!"

We took the secret tunnel back to the surface again and stumbled upon Conrad and Ambria meeting with Shushiel at the edge of the Dark Forest.

"You'll never believe what happened!" Max ran over to his friends, the story pouring from his mouth faster than his tongue could tell it.

"Oh, I wish I could've seen their faces." Ambria spat on the ground. "Devon and Rhys can burn in a fire!"

"That's amazing, Max!" Conrad squeezed his friend's shoulder. "What kind of boomsticks do they have?"

"Totally customized." Max described them down to the wood grain.

I mounted my broom. "I'm headed to the waystation. Wish me luck."

"Oh, what for?" Conrad asked.

"The evacuation."

"I'd like to come." Conrad had his own broom. "Ambria could you help Shushiel organize the monster army?"

Shelton's eyes flared. "You're making a monster army of our own?"

"We're trying, but the ruby spiders aren't keen on leaving the forest to fight." Ambria threw up her hands. "I tried telling them that Razor doesn't care if we're man or monster. They want us dead!"

"I am doing all I can to recruit my people, but it is not going well." Shushiel sagged a little. "The cobalt spiders are still a threat, and some of Victus's mutants still roam free."

Ambria kissed Conrad. "I'll do what I can. Just be careful. If Razor attacks, you need to get out of there immediately."

"I will." He kissed her cheek and hopped on his broom. "Ready when you are, Justin."

We zipped to the south, over the cliff and toward the double doors. I could tell trouble brewed before we even arrived, mainly because fifty Arcanes in white robes stood outside the doors, wands aimed threateningly toward the inside.

I hopped off my broom the moment I landed. "What's going on?"

The men did a double take. "Who are you?"

"Justin Slade." I raised an eyebrow.

"Oh, yes. Fitwit told us to expect you." He didn't sound happy about it.

I raised an eyebrow. "And you are?"

"Pog." He didn't hold out a hand. "I am the waystation manager."

I nodded. "So why are you standing here acting like you want to blast whoever comes out of the doors?"

"Because of the animals." He flicked a hand in that direction. "See for yourselves."

At first, I thought he meant the animals in the stable, but when Conrad and I walked into the waystation, I saw what he really meant. Dozens of white robes herded groups of people away from the doors while motioning for others to get in line for evacuation.

One man resisted and turned on the Arcanes. He blurred toward the closest and knocked the wand from the man's hands. Spells flew. Fangs flashed. The vampire was fast, but not fast enough and went down hard.

"I've had enough!" Someone shouted. "Kill the oppressors!"

A mob surged toward the Arcanes. Some grew fangs. Others morphed to giant wolves. The Arcanes formed a line and opened fire. The infighting I'd feared had already started, thanks to Xander's idiots and their discrimination against non-Arcanes.

Screams erupted and the entire place broke into panic and fighting. A sharp pain stabbed into my ribs. I looked down and saw blood and burnt skin.

"A spell hit you!" Conrad grabbed me and pulled me out of the way as another volley streaked past.

I felt the familiar surge of rage. Felt my consciousness fading as the other half of me reached for control. If I lost it in here, I'd rampage until they killed me.

Reason slipped through my fingertips. I grabbed Conrad. "Knock me out. I'm losing myself."

"You're what?"

"Can't control—" It was too late. "I will bathe the world in blood!" I roared in a deep guttural voice. "All will perish before the might of Kohvaniss, the supreme devourer of souls!" I leapt into the melee, claws outstretched. Before I even swung a fist, a familiar face caught my gaze. Someone who would perish at my hands. I roared and ran toward him.

A tremendous force crashed into my back and the floor rushed to meet me.

"Hush, little baby, don't say a word," whispered a voice in my ear. Darkness descended.

My bleary eyes blinked open. My head ached so much I could barely stand it. "Holy smoking shit balls." I groaned and pushed myself up, pain stabbing into my feet and hands. I was no longer in the waystation. Hell, I wasn't even in Queens Gate anymore. I stood on a narrow plateau of obsidian no more than a hundred feet in diameter. A forest of black trees spread out below. The sun hung low on the horizon, casting an orange glow. I turned in a full circle before looking down at my feet. A complex pattern encircled me. Crimson liquid filled the precise grooves.

It was a demon-summoning pattern. I inspected my aching hands and found crusted blood all over my palms. My feet looked the same. My super healing had taken over, but whatever happened to me must have been traumatic for the wounds still to ache.

My side was completely healed, which meant these wounds were more recent. I knelt and inspected the pattern. The crimson coloring wasn't from anything so innocent as crayons. It was blood—my blood. "What in the hell is going on here?" I tried to walk out of the circle, but an invisible barrier held me in.

How is a pattern trapping me? They usually didn't work, thanks to my Seraphim half.

Faces bobbed into view on my left, bodies rising aboard a large flying carpet. I recognized all three of them. The first, a short blonde with a notepad, was Serena. She was the human equivalent of a roach, surviving every potential apocalypse and moving on to aid the next attempt. The second one regarded me with inhumanly large eyes and hair that flowed as if underwater. Lying behind her was a large black coffin. I felt a sense of finality.

This is where my road ends.

CHAPTER 35

I tore my eyes off the coffin and looked at the last person.

He wore a face that only faintly resembled one I knew, but he was the last person I'd expected to see Melea with. He was also the one I'd seen in the Queens Gate waystation.

"Melea, what are you doing with him?" I stared at the man. "I thought you backed Xanos."

"Xanos refused my aid long ago." The Siren stepped off the carpet with the others and flowed toward the pattern. The portal necklace rested in the hollow of her neck. "My master wished for me to test you, so I asked you to join the Apocryphan."

"Yeah, and I refused." I glared at the man—at Baal's infernus shell. "And I refuse to help you too, Pop Pop."

Baal grinned. "I'm not here to ask you again." He shrugged. "You're a man of virtue, and I respect that, no matter how misplaced it is."

My eyes found the coffin again. Despair nearly drove me to my knees. *I don't want to die!* It was funny how I'd faced battle so many times without a thought about how a stray spell might headshot me, or a giant battlebot might crush me. To be a prisoner and faced with my own mortality like this felt unfair.

I swallowed the lump in my throat. "So you're here to kill me."

"I would never kill one of my greatest assets." Baal made a shooing motion. "No, I need you, grandson. You will play a pivotal role in events to come."

I was so relieved, I nearly cried, but held onto the tough guy act. "Not for you!"

"That is where you're wrong, boy." Serena consulted her notes. "Soon you'll be doing double the work for us whether you want to or not."

"Mind control?" I paced back and forth. "Do you plan to make infernus copies of me?"

"He's perceptive when he needs to be." Baal stepped up to the edge of the pattern. "Just as these shells can contain only a fraction of my being, so is an infernus is far too crude to capture your broad powers. That is why I devised something a bit better."

Serena raised an eyebrow. "Technically, I devised it."

Baal ignored her. "You are strong indeed to have resisted the demon seed I planted. But we've been watching you, and it seems as if the seed has finally borne fruit."

"Yes, we must harvest before it's too late." Serena rubbed her hands together. "This has been a long time coming, boy."

My eyes found the coffin again. "If you don't mean to kill me, what's the coffin for?"

Serena held out her wand and the coffin levitated to my right. That was when I noticed another pattern etched into the stone. A series of wavy lines connected it to mine. The coffin settled upright into the center. Metal clanged. A muffled cry of pain from the coffin sent me stumbling backwards in surprise.

Blood trickled from holes in the bottom of the coffin, the crimson liquid spreading into the channels of the pattern as if directed by an unholy force.

"Who's in there? What are you doing!" I rammed my shoulder against the invisible barrier, but it wouldn't yield. "Let me out of here!"

The coffin sprang open, a maw filled with tiny bloodstained spikes. Serena yanked the coffin out of the pattern with a flick of her wand, then quickly knelt and pressed a finger to the edge to seal it. A bloodied, naked man lay in the middle, his back to me. Blood dripped from dozens of tiny stab wounds.

They began to heal within seconds, meaning the man had supernatural healing. "Who is that?"

Serena giggled like a schoolgirl. "This is for what you did to my Gloom fortress. For murdering Daelissa. For all the harm you have caused me, boy. I will enjoy this moment and cherish it. I pray it stains your soul for the remainder of your miserable life."

The man groaned and rolled over on his back. And that was when I knew what she meant.

That man was my father. "Dad!"

David squeezed his eyes tight and blinked them open. He pushed up to his knees and looked around. "What?" His gaze found me. "Justin? Where are we?"

"Serena, I will tear you to shreds if you hurt him." I felt the demon rising. "I will drag you to the Abyssal plane and feast on your soul for eternity!"

Her eyes shone with fervor. "Oh, yes, boy. Get angry. Stoke the seed in your soul."

This is exactly what she wants.

"Baal." Dad grinned as if he hadn't a worry in the world. "So, Father, I guess you missed me so much you kidnapped me?"

"You've always been a major disappointment, son, but you are family." Baal walked towards him. "Vallaena was the one who understood what I wanted. Meanwhile, you ran away and bedded a Seraphim." He tutted. "Thankfully, your seed produced something unexpectedly powerful. Now it's your turn to make me proud." He held up a fist. "Be strong."

David held his arms open. "What, no hugs?"

"Not this time." Baal nodded at Serena.

Dad's chat with Baal had diverted my attention, cooling my rage and sending the demon half back into its cage. If Serena wanted me angry, that meant I had to keep my cool no matter what.

"How did they get you, Dad?" I needed answers. "Mom said you went to Heval and vanished."

"I met with Hippias, but something happened to me on the way out." He shrugged. "Now I'm here."

"We'll get out somehow." I took deep breaths to keep the demon at bay.

"Let's do this the hard way." Serena walked up to my pattern and put a finger across where the invisible barrier held me. "Isn't it infuriating, boy? I could walk across this line without worry, but you're helpless to escape."

I tried to grab her finger and missed. "By all means, step across the line." I refused to be goaded. "Maybe we can chat and play cards."

"What is the meaning of this, Daddy?" Dad casually leaned against the invisible barrier as if it were a wall. "And where are we? Is this still Eden?"

"Not quite. I needed somewhere special for this to work." Serena struck something from her notes with a slash of her pen. "And now it's time for this diversion to end." She flicked her wand and a bolt of energy struck me full in the chest. Skin blistered. Heat and agony raked their claws across my flesh.

My scream of pain turned to a guttural roar. Reason fled without so much as a backward glance, and all I felt was complete certainty that I was the absolute master of the universe. Even Baal was no match for me.

My body swelled. Spheres of Brilliance flared in my hands. "You will die for that insult, mortal!" I unleashed everything I had at the insignificant speck. But the barrier absorbed my strikes.

"This pattern is imbued with your blood, fool." Serena grinned. "When you fight it, you fight yourself."

"Speaking of which." Baal motioned toward David. "Let's get this over with."

"Gladly." Serena smiled at my father. "Goodbye, you little thorn."

"That's not what your mother said." David bared his teeth in a feral grin.

I slammed my fists against the air. I unleashed all my power on the stone at my feet. "I will destroy you all!" Blue fire flickered in my vision. "Your souls are mine!"

"He's a bit more vicious than I imagined," Baal said.

"He can be trained." Serena took a bloody cloth and dripped scarlet liquid into the channels between the patterns.

The pattern began to buckle. The ground beneath me began to quake. I roared and felt the powers of the universe boiling through me. Murk and Brilliance mixed with Stasis. I pushed with everything I had and felt the pattern begin to break.

"He's actually breaking the pattern!" Baal's eyes shined with glee. "So much power."

Serena tapped her wand to the bloodied channels. "And now it's ours."

David stiffened. Fire and ice climbed my spine. They gripped every muscle and nerve fiber in my body until I could no longer move. A giant hand seemed to grip my insides and slowly tear them out of my body.

Kalesh cried out in my mind. *What is happening?*

Through the blaze of blue around me, I saw a ghost separating from my body. It was red as the blood in my veins and looked exactly like me. Its face contorted with rage, but the spirit could no more escape this torment than I could. It slipped across the barriers and into David.

Dad? Reason returned to me. My conscience was back. I tried to shout for my father, but I still couldn't move.

The blue flames in Dad's eyes turned red. His body contorted. Whatever held us vanished and we tumbled to the ground. Dad thrashed about, screaming and shouting. His bones cracked, muscles popped. His back arched, and his mouth sprang open in a rictus of pain. Blue fog coursed out, swirling like a miniature tornado above the center of the pattern. A tiny rift tore open and sucked the smoke inside.

Dad rolled onto his side, away from me, his flesh distorted by shifting bones, blood seeping from his pores.

"Yes, it's working!" Serena danced in a circle. "My greatest creation!"

"Dad!" I pressed against the invisible barrier. "Dad!"

He sat up, still facing away. Pushed to his feet and looked around. Then he turned toward me. The man I faced was no longer my father.

It was me.

Red flames danced in his eyes. "Insignificant speck." His voice sounded just like mine, but a lot meaner. "I am glad to shed your weak flesh."

"What in god's name have you done to my dad?" I staggered back. "What did you do, you crazy bitch?"

"David is gone." Serena smiled. "Please meet the new and improved Justin Slade."

An animalistic scream tore from my throat. "Dad!"

Baal watched me like a scientist observing a lab rat. "Loss is an important part of life, son. I hoped to bring you around to reason, but you forced me to action." He shrugged. "It's better that I rule so I can defeat Xanos. As many resources as I have, she is a formidable threat."

Serena leered at me. "I will savor this precious moment, boy. I have returned the grief you inflicted on me. My only wish would be that I could triple it. May my sweet Daelissa smile down upon me."

Her words stabbed me like swords. Pummeled me like hurled stones. I dropped to my knees and looked up at their creation—my twin. I couldn't grasp how this was possible. Couldn't grasp that my father was gone. The pain was so great I could hardly bear it. Tears blinded me and sobs wracked my body.

"What have you done?" I moaned. "What have you done?"

"The demon seed suffused you, assimilated your being." Serena jotted more notes, a cold smile on her face. "Once it reached a critical point, we had to transfer it to a shell that could handle all that is you. An infernus is still merely a shadow of the being it copies. It contains only a shard of the original soul. What we have done is copy you precisely, boy."

"Now, you are on my side." Baal walked to the other Justin. "Are you ready to take your place by my side, grandson?"

The other Justin smiled coldly. "Yes, I am, Pop Pop."

Baal raised an eyebrow. "We'll have to work on that personality of yours." He spat on the ground and rubbed it over the outer line of the pattern holding my twin.

The other Justin stepped out. He closed his eyes and took a deep breath as if smelling freedom for the first time. "Man, it feels great being in my own body." He looked down at me. "All those conflicting emotions and garbage floating around in your head are exhausting."

Serena held out a hand. "Come, Justin."

He looked down his nose at me. "I don't like that name." He bared his teeth. "I'm not like this pathetic boy." He tapped a finger on his chin. "Call me Cain."

Baal chuckled. "Cain. I like the biblical aspect." He nodded toward the carpet. "Come, Cain. Let's go."

Melea had remained quiet and watchful the entire time, but as the others left, she approached me. "Do not despair, Justin. You still have great works to do."

I forced myself to my feet. "Are you just going to leave me here?"

Baal stopped and slowly turned around. "No, I think you've been through enough today."

A faint melody drifted into my ears. It numbed the pain and made my eyelids heavy as lead. Melea's lips parted and the strange, discordant tune relieved the terrible burden on my shoulders. My legs wobbled, and it was all I could do to stay on my feet.

Sleep, the song whispered in my mind. *Rest and recover.*

I knew what she was doing to me, but there was no point in resisting. So I lay down and let the song take me.

CHAPTER 36

I woke up in a bed. Birds chirped and a gentle breeze whispered through the leaves of a tree outside. I sat up and threw off the covers to find I was fully clothed. *Was it a dream?* I hoped against hope that everything had been a nightmare. I felt calm, refreshed.

Yellow wallpaper decorated the walls, and a floral design patterned the bedspread. A neatly carved chest of drawers stood in the corner, pictures of a man and woman smiling back at me. I got up and looked around, trying to identify where I was.

Shouts echoed in the distance. I tried to make out what they said, but they were too far away. I opened the door to the bedroom and stepped out into a dim hallway. It was a stark departure from the bedroom. Wooden lathe showed like old bones through broken plaster. Scarred wooden flooring creaked beneath my feet. A musty odor tickled my nose.

I ran down the hallway, dust puffing beneath my feet. A couch with rusting springs sat against the wall of a family room. A broken table leaned crookedly in a corner, and shattered glass lay all over the floor. I found the front door and yanked it open. Stepped onto a cracked cobblestone road beneath an orange sun.

A great cliff rose in the distance, another to the right and behind me. *This is Queens Gate.* But where?

Shouts echoed faintly from my left. Great explosions thundered, and the horizon flashed with lightning. Fog clouded my thoughts and it was all I could do to concentrate, to understand what it was I saw. My gut reaction was to run in that direction, so I did.

I raced through empty streets, past abandoned houses until I reached the city center. Xander's shield prevented me from passing through, so I ran around it. A flock of Arcanes in red robes lifted off on carpets and brooms and flew south. The explosions grew louder the further I went.

I couldn't think of anything except reaching the commotion. I cleared the crest at the edge of town and the fog in my mind cleared. Hundreds of carpets and brooms floated ahead. Spells flashed and thundered. Somewhere, lycans howled, answered by the thunderous roar of a great feline.

"Razor!" I pushed through the back ranks of vampires, working my way toward a great floating platform hovering in the middle of squadrons of Blue Cloaks. I couldn't see who was on the Templar command platform, but I knew Thomas and Elyssa would be there.

"Elyssa!" I shouted. People looked at me confused expressions on their face. "I need to get up there. Does anyone have a carpet or a broom?"

"Is that Justin Slade?" someone behind me said.

I grabbed a Templar. "I need a flying carpet."

His forehead pinched into a V. "Commander Slade?"

"Yes! How do I get to the command platform?"

"All the carpets and brooms are in the battle, sir. I don't know how to get up there."

I let him go and continued running. Then I stopped and patted my jeans pockets. I felt the hard bulge of my arcphone. "I'm an idiot!" I still wasn't thinking clearly. I took out the phone and dialed Elyssa.

"Justin!" Relief filled her voice.

"Elyssa, it's me. I'm here below you."

"Where have you been?" She drew in a shuddering breath. "Oh my god, I thought you were dead."

"How can I reach you?"

"Justin, we're fully engaged against Razor. I'll see if I can spare a broom." I heard her shouting, but explosions muffled her voice. Finally, she returned. "Conrad is coming with a spare, but he'll need help finding you."

"I'll throw up a flare." I looked at my right hand, almost worried that my powers wouldn't work. But Brilliance channeled into my palm without hesitation. I flung a starburst into the air. A moment later, a distant figure on a broom zipped toward me. "He's coming. I'll see you soon." I ended the call.

Templars cleared an opening and Conrad alighted a few feet away, eyes wide. "Justin, what happened to you? We—we all thought you'd died. You ran into the riot mob and vanished."

I choked back grief. "I'll explain later." I held out a hand and he gave me the blue-chrome boomstick Rhys rode the last time I'd seen them. "I need to see Elyssa."

He nodded. "We could really use your help. It's absolute madness."

As I rose into the air, I saw why. The double doors to the waystation lay in pieces a few hundred yards away. A long scar ran horizontally across the cliff face, a blackened slit giving Razor a beachhead into the pocket dimension. Two massive tanks sat where the doors had been, firing electro-shells into our ranks. Shields intercepted some of them, but others exploded overhead, showering troops with crippling electricity.

Entire platoons collapsed, to be quickly dragged away and replaced by fresh troops. I circled above the platform and landed on the ledge. Templars manned consoles and shouted orders. Thomas and Elyssa stood in the center, a holographic image of the battlefield in front of them.

"Justin!" Elyssa hugged me. "I thought you were dead."

Thomas met my eyes with an unsure gaze. I wanted to scream and cry, but now wasn't the time.

"I was taken by Baal." I waved off the questions I knew were coming. "I can't explain right now. We have to beat back Razor first."

Her shoulders stiffened.

I looked down at the mess. "Did they blow up the cliff wall?"

"C-four charges on the inside." She waved a hand at the standoff below. "Now they have the perfect vantage point to take down our troops. We can't get close enough to the tanks, and their armor is magic resistant."

"Shit." I put my hands on my head and walked in a circle. *Razor is too strong. We're going to lose.* And if we won, then what? Dad was gone, replaced by that monster Baal incubated inside me. I hadn't even had a chance to start looking for Emily Glass and now it was too late. "What am I going to do?"

Elyssa grabbed my arm and pulled me aside. "Justin, you need to tell me what happened right now." She jabbed a finger at the battle. "We're fighting for our lives here and you sound like you've totally lost it." Concern shone in her eyes. "Is the demon seed corrupting you again?"

Tears burned my eyes. "No, it's gone." My voice broke and it was all I could do to hold myself together. Even so, the curious gazes of nearby Templars found me.

"Gone?" Elyssa blinked. "What do you mean?"

"Baal kidnapped me, Elyssa. He had Dad too." I took a deep breath to keep the grief from tearing me apart. "He transferred whatever he put inside me to Dad and it turned him into me."

"That doesn't make any sense." Elyssa gripped my shoulders. "Your Dad became an infernus?"

"No. They ripped out my father's soul and put the demon seed in his body. Dad is dead, and now there's an evil version of me helping Baal."

Elyssa's mouth hung open. Explosions rippled through the air and the entire command platform shuddered.

"Elyssa, we need you." Thomas held onto a smoking console. "The left flank is failing."

Elyssa pressed a hand to my cheek. "Justin, I'm so sorry. I wish we had time, but we don't. We have to beat Razor or it's all over." She kissed me. "I love you." Then she turned and ran back to her father, shouting orders to other Templars.

I watched Elyssa return to duty. Thomas's eyes caught mine. *Did he overhear what I said?* He simply nodded and turned back to the battle.

I looked down, held hostage by warring emotions, unable to act as the Razor electro tanks pushed forward, flanked by hundreds of soldiers. There was no way we'd beat them, not with their magic resistant armor and weapons that could disable even the hardiest supers. Even if I fully manifested, I'd fall beneath a hail of electro rounds.

Our left flank melted away, replaced by a swarm of hellhounds and Daemos. The electro rounds slowed the demon spawn but didn't stop them. Hellhounds plowed into the ranks of Razor soldiers and a great cheer went up from our troops.

"They can't stop them!" an overexcited Templar said.

"Bring up the other Daemos," Elyssa ordered.

But the jubilation was short-lived. The sea of black uniforms parted and a unit of Razor operatives in gray filed through to meet the threat, bearing crimson rifles. They lined up and fired. Glowing blue spheres arced through the air and exploded, leaving behind a wall of translucent mist.

"What is that?" Elyssa zoomed in the view on her console.

The first wave of hellhounds reached the mist. Howls and yelps of pain died abruptly. The mist was thin enough to see why. Demon flesh bubbled and lost all cohesion, turning into goo within seconds. A massive scorp spawn raced toward the mist. Giant claws clicked madly, a human face screaming beneath the black skin where a head would be.

I'd fought those things before. Their magic-resistant carapace and incredible strength made them formidable. But the instant its claws touched the mist, the carapace melted like plastic in an oven.

"My god. The mist dissolves demon flesh." I wondered if it would have the same effect on infernus. "How do they counter every damned thing we do?"

Elyssa spoke into her com badge. "Daemos, hold your ground. Do not advance."

The hellhounds and other demonic terrors retreated, forming a line before their masters.

"We've got nothing, and they know it." I tried to think of something, anything that could beat back these assholes, but came up empty. "We could use some divine intervention right about now."

Someone behind me spoke. "When we fought Razor in the waystation, we used their own electro tank against them by sealing the barrel with Murk."

I flinched, having forgotten Conrad hovered on his broom just off the platform. "But how do we even get close?"

"I don't know. But if we can, we might be able to take over a tank and fire on their own people." Conrad shrugged. "They seem to be able to take everything we throw at them."

And that's when an idea hit me. "I need all the Arcanes we have casting shields in front of our troops. Then we blitz them with everything we've got."

"You want to rush them?" Elyssa gave me an incredulous look. "They'll tear us apart before we even get close!"

"Not if we hold our shields long enough." I looked at the mass of troops below. "If we throw everyone at them, they can't stop us all." I pointed at Razor's positioning. "Their tanks can't fire on us once we close the gap. The rest of Razor's troops are behind the cliff wall. All we need to do is reach the troops outside."

Elyssa shook her head. "And then what?"

I grinned. "Easy." I explained my reasoning.

Understanding lit her eyes. "That's stupidly easy."

"Brilliant!" Conrad snapped his fingers. "This might just work."

Thomas came up behind us. "Will it work on the tanks?"

I shrugged. "Maybe. We won't know until we try."

Elyssa shook her head. "We have a lot of ground to cover." She tapped her com badge and opened a link to the faction leaders. "All Arcanes report to the front line for shield duty. Daemos, feint your hellhounds to the enemy left flank to draw out the gray troops, then send them to the far right. Vampires and Templars, you will follow behind the Arcanes." She laid out the plan I'd given her.

"What insanity is this?" Kassallandra's cold voice emanated from the badge. "We must throw ourselves into the line of fire?"

Elyssa took a breath. "I need as many hellspawn as you can throw at them. If you do what I say, this will work."

Kassallandra didn't sound convinced. "Are you certain using hellspawn this way will work?"

Elyssa gave me a hopeful look. "It should. They are supernatural creatures, after all."

"Then we will do our duty," Kassallandra said. "Daemos, bring forth hell on earth!"

"We do not have hellspawn, but we are fleet of foot," Komad said. "We are faster than even the Templars. Give us a chance for vengeance against the noms."

"You will have it," Elyssa said.

"The lycan are no slowpokes either," McCloud added. "Give us a shield and we'll throw everything we have at them."

"But the tanks." Captain Takei sounded doubtful. "One of their electro shells will take out an entire wave of Arcanes, no matter how well shielded. The electro bullets might not be lethal, but the tank rounds fry every neuron in the brain at close range."

"We just have to get within a hundred feet of the tanks. At that range, they'll fry their own circuitry." Thomas stared at the mechanical beasts. "We'll have to do our best."

I envisioned our blitz, the waves collapsing in toward the enemy hundreds of yards away. By the time we reached them, we would lose hundreds to the tanks. "What if we dive-bombed the tanks?" I said.

"We already tried," Thomas said. "They have surface-to-air missiles that are faster than even the fastest brooms we have. Once you go above a hundred feet within a certain radius, they'll open fire."

"So I can keep low and be fine." I no longer felt aimless. My path was clear. "I'll draw the fire of one of the tanks. I can shield myself long enough to give one flank the space it needs."

"I can make space too." Conrad summoned a crackling gray sphere. "I can intercept the electro shells in the air."

"Yeah, but if they explode near you, your broom is toast," Elyssa said.

"You need to be at least a hundred or more feet away." She slapped a com badge on my chest.

"Then that's what I'll aim for." Conrad nodded at me. "Sound like a plan?"

I grinned. "Yes, it does. Let's make some space." I hopped on my broom. "I'll be back."

Elyssa's eyes tightened. "You'd better be."

"As you wish." I blew her a kiss and jetted away.

"All troops, signal ready!" Elyssa's voice came through my com badge.

"Blue Cloaks ready," Takei reported. "Arcanes on standby to shield the front lines."

"Lycans are a go," McCloud said.

Komad reported next. "Vampires ready."

"Daemos and hellspawn await your command." Kassallandra sounded cool and calm.

The others reported in, and I couldn't help but think of Dad. He usually gave me unconventional advice for situations like this or offered a quick quip. But now he was gone. *This is for you, Dad.* Not because Razor was responsible for Baal's actions, but because I had to get through these bastards so I could get my revenge.

There will be blood.

CHAPTER 37

"Justin, you okay?" Conrad reached over and touched my shoulder.

I nodded. "Yeah. Let's kick some ass."

We veered down, crossing over the heads of the troops.

A few cheers rose as we passed overhead, but the faces below were tense, uncertain. I wished I had time for a battle speech, but with the relentless pounding of the tanks, there was none to spare.

"Keep below a hundred feet to avoid the anti-air missiles." Conrad pointed out several gray pods behind the enemy troops. "They're so fast you'll barely have time to react."

I'd missed the entire start of the battle, so I hadn't seen them in action. "I'll take your word for it."

Conrad threaded his fingers and hands through a pattern, weaving a glowing blue shield in the shape of a V. I formed one from ultraviolet Murk, making it just large enough to act as a windscreen. Electro bullets crackled in the air, their range too short to reach us. A tank turret rotated our way, but the other continued firing at our right flank.

"Good luck." I gave Conrad a thumbs up.

"You too, Justin."

With that, we veered off in opposite directions. The tank on my left tracked me. I was past our troops now, out over what had once been pastures and tree groves. Now it was little but sizzling muck.

A giant round exploded from the tank muzzle. My senses heightened and time seemed to slow as my reflexes took over. I could easily dodge the tank round, but it would land on our troops. To keep the detonation from taking out me and my broom, I had to hit it at the perfect range of a hundred feet. The further my destructive magic travelled, the weaker it became.

I only had one chance not to screw this up. I swung the shield out of the way and fired a tightly focused beam of Brilliance straight ahead. It speared into the black sphere. The casing peeled away and crackling blue energy burst from within. The electrostatic discharge rippled through the air. The outer ring washed past me in a superheated wave. Turbulence rocked the broom so hard, I thought it might break.

Another explosion rocked the air. I turned my head in time to see a wave of electricity wash over Conrad. His broom bucked like a bronco and lost power. Trailing smoke, he plummeted toward the ground.

"Conrad!" I threw out my hand, but he was almost two hundred yards away.

Another boom drew my attention forward. Another electro round hurled toward me. I pierced the shell like the last one. The shockwave nearly threw me off my broom. A fine crack ran down the broom handle and my momentum slowed. One more hit, and I'd go down like Conrad.

I looked back over my shoulder. Arcanes on carpets and brooms led the advance of our troops, so far unimpeded by tank rounds. Another detonation thundered. I looked right and saw Conrad miraculously still flying, despite black smoke trailing from his broom.

I couldn't destroy another round, not unless I did it far outside a hundred feet. But I was already straining to reach that far. *Brute force is not always the answer.* Fjoeruss's words echoed in my mind. Jeremiah had told me something similar as well. But how was I supposed to destroy tank rounds without force?

There was one thing that might work. The next round fired, and I prayed my plan worked. I wove a sphere of Stasis and launched it at the electro shell. The shell passed through it and quickly lost momentum and altitude, angling beneath me and toward the ground. It slammed to earth and detonated, throwing my broom far up into the air.

"Shit!" I held on for dear life, but the broom handle gave up the ghost and snapped in half. The part with the throttle fell from my grasp, but the back part with the saddle shot straight up at full speed. I gripped the saddle with my thighs and clung to the stubby front, but without the controls, I couldn't steer.

I flew higher and higher, up into the clouds. And that was when I heard the roar of something else. I looked down and saw three missiles streaking toward me, white contrails drawing lines to my death.

The broom tail seemed determined to carry me into outer space. I was on a one-way ride to a freezing vacuum or a fiery explosion. The broom couldn't actually reach outer space, but I didn't need to get that high to die from lack of oxygen. So I did the only thing I could. I let go of the broom and plummeted toward the ground.

The missiles zipped past me in pursuit of the broom. A brilliant explosion told me one found its mark. I expected the other two to veer around and come after me, but they didn't. Instead, they climbed before slamming into an invisible barrier and exploding. I wondered if that was the outer limit of the pocket dimension.

I'd gained enough altitude to have a moment of contemplation before I went splat, so I took advantage of it. The Stasis hadn't worked. It arrested the electro shell's momentum, but the casing protected the charge inside from the neutralizing effects. At this point, it didn't matter. In a few minutes, more missiles would launch and turn me into fine red mist.

Yet, they didn't.

I've only got one chance at this.

I concentrated. Pain sliced through my shoulder blades. Energy wings unfurled and caught the air, allowing me to glide. Fire blossomed from far below and the roar of missiles sounded. They'd found me again.

"Go to hell, you bastards!" My trajectory took me out over the tank, hundreds of feet below. Unfortunately, I'd never reach it intact. I released the channel maintaining my wings and went into freefall. No shield I channeled would protect me from the missiles, but maybe, just maybe, I could dodge past them and take them into the tank with me.

The missiles climbed straight up and soared completely past me as if they'd suddenly lost their lock, exploding against the invisible barrier again. I didn't know what was going on but took advantage of it and channeled my wings again. More missiles launched, and the answer dawned on me.

They lock onto magical heat signatures.

The moment I used magic, they launched. I released my wings again, and they zipped past me. This time, I waited until they nearly reached the invisible ceiling before channeling my wings again. The missiles veered around and came straight for me. No new missiles launched, which meant they probably limited the launches to three per target.

I folded my wings to the sides and dove straight at my tank. Far below, I saw Conrad closing in on his target. Our troops swarmed across the ground like ants. The flank I'd protected faltered under fire from the tank. I had to reach the target no matter what happened to me. I looked back. The missiles were directly on my tail.

That was about to be literal in a moment. I released my angel wings.

The missiles held course as I hoped, but now I had another problem. In seconds, I'd impact the tank like a human missile.

Ironically, Baal's demon seed had taught me a new trick.

I called on my inner demon. *Kalesh, are you there?*

I am you. You are me. We are here.

He sounded a lot different than before. In fact, he almost sounded like a team player. I didn't have time to wonder. *I need to spawn wings. Help!*

Then spawn and force them to grow.

I manifested my demon form. Horns spiraled up from my forehead and black claws pushed out my fingernails. A tail sprouted from my backside, lashing in the wind. I could spawn on autopilot. But the wings were something else. I concentrated on my back, willing them to form.

Like this.

An image of bat-like wings flashed into my mind, muscle threading across bones, flesh webbing between them. It felt as if someone took a hammer and smashed my shoulder blades. I hurled to earth, a meat missile screaming like a lunatic, limbs and tail thrashing helplessly.

Then I felt something new, something different. Something my evil twin had taught me without meaning to.

I spread newly formed demon wings. Terminal velocity threatened to tear them from my back. I gritted my teeth and endured the pain, holding them as level as possible. Just feet away from plowing into the tank, I caught air and soared over the heads of the enemy troops.

They must have watched the aerial chase, because instead of firing on me, they ran for their lives away from the tank. Three explosions rocked ground. The shockwave flung me forward into a grove of trees. I smacked into limbs and nearly lost consciousness.

"Not this time." I roared in fury and leapt to the ground. "I will not sleep through this battle!"

I ripped through the trees and emerged back on the battlefield. The burnt-out shell of the tank smoked. Dead and wounded Razor soldiers lay around it. Those who reached a safe distance formed ranks and opened fire on the tide of furious supers coming for blood.

A dazed soldier not far from me grabbed her weapon and tried to aim it. I blurred over and snatched the rifle. In that moment, I knew my master plan would work. Why? Because the rifle popped and smoked, self-destructing at the touch of a super.

Lycans and vampires blurred past me, touching weapons left and right. Most didn't bother to even strike the enemy soldiers before moving on to the next targets. Enemy weapons popped and exploded, becoming useless hunks of metal, all thanks to the mechanism designed to keep supers from using them against Razor.

Oops. Guess you didn't think that one through.

Lycans howled in victory. I reared back my head and roared, unleashing all the pain and rage boiling inside me. Tears met the demonic flames in my eyes, hissing and spitting.

The Overworld was all but destroyed. My father was dead. Baal was one step closer to ruling.

We would win this day. Eden would claim her victory, but it was a small, hollow thing. I was a tiny, insignificant being in the grand scheme laid out by Baal and Xanos. How could I hope to stop even one of them?

Our forces drove Razor from the waystation. Most of their troops escaped through portals in the control room, but they left behind over two hundred operatives. As with the other troops, the ratio of women to men was nearly three to one, every last one fanatical in their devotion. The captives refused to give up even a hint of information.

Elyssa found me an hour after the battle ended. I'd reverted to human form, content to help round up any stray enemies and deliver them to Templars.

"Are you okay, Justin?" She put an arm on my shoulder. "You look as if we just lost."

"We won a battle against the noms." I scoffed. "This is child's play compare to what Xanos and Baal have in store for us."

"We need to talk about your father." A tear trickled down her cheek. "I know you're in incredible pain right now, but—"

I shook my head and gave a scornful laugh. "I'm so far past pain right now, I'm numb. I feel even more powerless than when I faced the tsunami in Thailand. Please, tell me how we could beat even one of these godlike beings?"

"I don't know." Elyssa's gaze hardened. "But this isn't the Justin I know. This isn't the man who found hope even in the face of Daelissa's unstoppable army. This isn't the man who destroyed goliaths by sheer will alone." She grabbed my arm so hard it hurt. "Everything and everyone has a weakness, Justin. Even Baal and Xanos."

"Name one."

"I don't have the answers." Elyssa got in my face. "But if anyone can find them, we can. If the Sirens trapped the Apocryphan in the Abyss, we can damned well do it to Xanos again."

"But how? Why do you think we can find it?"

"Because I believe in you, Justin." She pointed to herself. "I believe in me, and I believe in us." Elyssa's eyes glowed violet. "Why do you think Baal hasn't tried to kill you, Justin, hmm? Haven't you wondered why he didn't finish you when he had the chance?"

"He said I had work to do. I still don't know what he meant."

"Baal is devious. He doesn't do things in a straightforward manner like you." Elyssa put a hand on my chest. "What's more useful to him than killing you?"

I thought about it a moment. "Using me against my enemies?"

She nodded. "Yeah. And we're his enemies. But what's even deadlier to an enemy than weapons?"

I shrugged. "Cholesterol?"

"Don't be a smartass." Elyssa pushed harder on my chest. "It's what's in here."

"My heart?"

"Hopelessness. Grief. Fear. Anger. Hate." Elyssa put a hand to her chest. "Faith. Love. Hope." She put a hand on my cheek. "Don't you see? Everything Baal has done, it's been to demoralize you, to take away what makes you so great. It was your hope that carried us through the war with Daelissa. It was your faith that made us believe we could defeat Cephus. If Baal steals that from you, if he turns you into a pit of despair, you'll drag all of us down with you, because you're a symbol, Justin. You're the person everyone looks to when things look hopeless."

I stumbled as if someone threw back a curtain and revealed a monster. Elyssa saw the dark, ugly truth of Baal's plan. People might look to me for hope, but she was my pillar of strength. Whether she admitted it or not, everyone looked to her as well. She was brains and brawn, all in one beautiful package.

"That bastard." My voice shook with anger and grief. "Killing my father just to play mind games with me."

"Yes. And we'll have to work to restore your spirit, Justin." Elyssa took my hand. "But we can do it."

I felt strength just from touching her, just from looking into those fierce eyes. "If anyone can heal me, you can." I swallowed a lump and changed the subject before I got too emotional. "Is Conrad okay?"

She nodded. "He lost his broom, but he melted the other tank to slag when he got close enough. Ambria flew in and rescued him before the Razor troops got to him."

"Sounds like we both have strong women protecting us."

Elyssa grinned. "We protect each other, Justin. We're a team."

"Yes, we are." My soul was in pain, but even if we lost the war, I refused to let Baal destroy my hope.

CHAPTER 38

Thomas made the decision to demolish the aboveground entrance to Queens Gate, sealing the tunnels for miles to cut off access. We set up portal-blocking statues in the waystation so Razor couldn't reach us that way. The only thing we couldn't protect against were the omniarch portals outside the waystation, but Razor still hadn't demonstrated a knack for using them.

We put our omniarches to good use, securing supplies from the outside world and building up our defenses. Once again, we were cornered, just as we had been in Atlantis. At least now we were home.

Mom was among the last refugees from Atlantis to come through. I met her at the portal and instantly choked up when I saw her worried face. Tears pooled in her eyes when she saw the look on my face. Mothers just know bad news is coming.

"What is it, Justin?" The tears spilled down her cheeks. "What did you find out about David?"

I took her down the corridor and into the empty gauntlet room before I told her. She took the news about as well as expected and that was all it took to break me again.

"No." Mom's chin quivered. "No!"

I hugged her and cried and cried some more as Mom sobbed against my chest.

The grief I felt was as bad as it had been with Nightliss, but different. This was the man who'd raised me. Who'd declared Fridays as movie and pizza nights. Who'd supported me whenever I failed and tried to teach me how to be a normal kid.

It had been a façade, of course. There was nothing normal about my family, but at least Dad and Mom tried. For the first eighteen years of my life, they'd let me know what it was to be human. That was something neither Baal nor Xanos could ever understand.

Dad meant the world to Mom, but she was too strong to grieve for long. She took a deep breath and dried her eyes. "I'm going back to Atlantis."

"What? Why?"

"I'm going to find out how they took David, and I'm going to make sure the Atlanteans are ready for war." She bared her teeth. Brilliance glowed in her eyes. "I will scour Seraphina clean with my bare hands if I have to."

"Mom, just don't do anything crazy, please." I gripped her shoulders. "I can't lose you too."

"Does Ivy know?"

I shook my head. "She's in the Glimmer. Maybe you should go see her first. Maybe you can help Cora revive her people. We need all the fighters we can get."

Mom nodded. "You're right. I'll go there first." She straightened her shoulders. "Baal just signed his death warrant."

I couldn't believe this was my mother talking like this. Then again, I'd known her just a fraction of her life, and she was thousands of years old. "I'll go with you."

"I'd like that." Mom sniffled. "Ivy deserves to have us both there."

We went to the Mansion first, so I could let Elyssa know where we were going. I found her in the war room with Thomas and Nightliss. Shelton and Adam were there as well, excitedly discussing something.

The diminutive Darkling smiled with delight when she saw us. "Oh, Justin. It's so good to be back here, isn't it?"

"Yeah." I hugged her and tried to muster a smile.

Her eyes narrowed. "Something's wrong."

Adam interrupted before I could reply.

"Justin!" Adam pointed to a nom laptop on the conference table. "I think we found something huge."

Thomas's eyes pinched when he saw Mom. Only he, Elyssa, and Conrad knew what happened to my father. I planned to tell Adam and Shelton next. "How are you, Alysea?"

"Not well, I'm afraid." Mom swallowed hard. "We're going to the Glimmer to see Ivy."

"I understand."

"Dude, take a look." Shelton guided me to the laptop and pointed to a video. "This is a recording of a communication to Commander Edge from their grand leader."

Curiosity made me take a look. "The Overseer?"

"Yeah." Shelton started the video. "They used standard nom video conferencing software for this."

Edge's image appeared in a box in the lower left corner of the screen. "How does this work again?"

"Just press this call button." A man next to her moved into view and did something. "It's dialing now."

"I don't care for technology." Edge's lips curled up. "Now leave me."

The man nodded and left through a door behind her.

A middle-aged woman's face filled the screen. Her graying hair and fine wrinkles lent her something of a matronly look. "Hello, Dolores."

Edge scowled. "Do not call me by my first name."

"Young lady, don't you talk back to me." Steel filled the older woman's voice.

Shelton snickered. "Who is this woman?"

Edge swallowed hard. "Yes, Overseer."

The others must have already seen it because Mom and I were the only two to flinch back when we heard the name.

"She's the Overseer?" My mouth dropped open. "But she looks like a grandma."

Shelton put a finger to his lips. "Just hush and listen."

Edge was already speaking. "Queens Gate has been found. Our troops prepare for an assault even now."

"Very good, Dolores." The Overseer leaned back in her chair. She looked about sixty and thin, but with muscle tone to her arms. "The supernatural problem must be taken care of soon. We have even bigger threats to deal with."

"The demon lord." It wasn't a question.

"Yes, he prepares for an assault. We must secure this world before he comes."

"Queens Gate is the last bastion of the supernaturals," Edge said. "Refugees from all over the world fled there, making an easy target for us. After we defeat them, we'll have only stragglers to deal with."

"The list of new prisoners you sent me mentioned a Justin Slade." The Overseer's eyebrow arched. "I want him brought to me."

"He's very dangerous," Edge said. "Are you certain?"

The Overseer's eyes narrowed. "What did you say, Dolores?"

Edge flinched. "Apologies, Overseer. I will have him transported right away. May I ask why?"

The kindly smile returned to the old woman's face. "He freed me from my prison. I owe him a chance at joining our cause."

The commander looked almost ill. "But he's a super, Madam Overseer. A vile, disgusting demon hybrid."

"And a powerful tool to use against his own kind." The Overseer leaned forward, her dark eyes swirling with infinity. "Bring him." She leaned back, all smiles again. "God speed in your battle at Queens Gate. I will talk to you after your victory." The Overseer's video ended, leaving the recording of a confused Command Edge trying to turn off the program.

Adam stopped the video. I reached for the mouse pad, but he slapped away my hand. "Dude, don't touch the laptop or it'll self-destruct."

"How are you touching it?"

He tugged on a finger, revealing transparent, skintight gloves. "As long as my skin doesn't touch it, we're good."

"Man, I got so many questions, I don't know where to start." Shelton rewound the video to the part where the Overseer leaned forward. "That grandma frightens me half to death."

I stared at her long and hard. "I've never seen her in my life. How could I have freed her from prison?"

"We wondered that too," Elyssa said. "In fact, we couldn't figure out how this woman united all the nom supernatural agencies together into Razor. On the surface, she looks harmless."

"Complete disconnect." Adam put the tips of his fingers together and moved them apart. "We thought she might be someone you freed from Kobol Prison during the war with Daelissa, but there weren't any prisoners, per se, kept there."

"Yeah, just cherubs in null cubes," Shelton said. "Not any old ladies."

I couldn't stop looking at the old woman's creepy eyes. "She's definitely not someone I freed from Kobol Prison, because I'd remember an older woman among ageless immortals."

"I dug through all the recordings, but this is the only one from the Overseer," Adam said. "So I ran it through an analyzer to see if we could identify the woman from her voice patterns and appearance. If she's a nom, it's likely they'd have a record of her."

"But the analyzer picked up something weird." Shelton pulled up an audio file and played it.

"Bring him," the Overseer said.

"Did you hear that?" Shelton said.

I blinked. "Yeah?" I dragged out the word to make sure he understood I missed his point. "What am I listening for?"

"Again." Shelton played it three more times. On the last time, I heard what he meant.

"Do you have better speakers? This laptop is garbage."

"No. We can't transmit it to an arcphone, because the laptop is locked down to prevent file transfers." Adam turned up the volume and played it again.

The Overseer spoke. "Bring him." It sounded as if several voices spoke at once, some higher, others lower than the grandmotherly one. The tinny laptop speakers made them difficult to hear at first.

That was when two dots connected.

Elyssa spoke before I could. "I want to know if you reached the same conclusion we did."

"Please let me be wrong." I took a deep breath, remembering the voice with many voices that belonged to someone I'd freed from a prison. "Is it Xanos?"

Adam and Shelton nodded in unison.

Elyssa added her own. "Xanos controls Razor."

Mom scoffed. "As a grandmother?"

I could hardly believe it, but the more I thought about it, the more sense it made. "How else would this woman know Baal is aiming for Eden? Why else would she want to get rid of the supers here?" I slapped a hand on the table. "That harmless looking old woman is using noms to get rid of us so we can't interfere with her plans."

"Holy smoking cannoli." Shelton whistled. "We fought Xanos and didn't even know it."

I scoffed. "We didn't fight Xanos. We fought an army of her minions. If the Apocryphan are so strong, why didn't she face us herself?"

"We think she's still too weak from millennia in the Abyss," Thomas said. "That means if we defeat Razor fast enough, we can send Xanos back to her prison."

"Why disguise herself as an old woman?" Shelton shook his head. "Why not a badass rocker chick in leather tights?"

"And how did she raise such a fanatical army?" Elyssa bit her lower lip. "I hope she doesn't have mind control powers."

I grimaced. "Oh man, not that again."

"She would need incredible strength to control so many minds," Nightliss said. "I believe her followers are true believers."

Thomas nodded. "Meaning they're even more dangerous."

"But if Xanos is weak right now, we need to push back hard." Elyssa pounded a fist into her palm. "We need to take the war to her."

"Yeah." I couldn't stop thinking about Baal.

Nightliss studied my face. "What's wrong, Justin?"

I figured I might as well get the terrible news out of the way. "Baal killed my dad."

Nightliss gasped. "No, this can't be true!"

"What in the hell?" Shelton slammed a fist on the table. "I'm gonna murder that bastard!"

"Oh man, I'm sorry." Adam shook his head. "How did it happen?"

I swallowed the lump in my throat and told the story.

Tears trickled down Nightliss's cheeks. "Did Baal absorb your father's spirit when it left his body?"

"I don't think so. It looked like it went through a breach, probably banished to Haedaemos."

"Are you certain?" Nightliss gripped my forearm. "Is that exactly what you saw?"

"Yeah." I envisioned it again, the blue smoke pouring into the rift. I'd seen it before when Daelissa's minions tried to banish his demon to the spirit realm.

"Then David is not dead—at least not yet." Nightliss took a shuddering breath. "His spirit lives, and so does his body."

"But his body changed." I shook my head. "It's not him anymore."

"If we could remove the demon seed and replace it with his spirit, your father might return." Nightliss wiped her tears. "I just don't know how to do it."

I knew of one person, but I had no idea how to reach her. "We need to find Emily Glass." I smacked the palm of my hand. "If I'd just found her the moment we arrived, this never would have happened."

"She's missing, Justin." Elyssa put a hand on my shoulder. "We've had nothing but obstacles since we got here."

"Then that's our next step." Mom wiped fresh tears, but she looked more relieved than sad. "We'll do whatever possible to find Emily."

"Do you still want to tell Ivy?" I asked.

She nodded. "It wouldn't be fair to keep this from her."

"I will do whatever I can to restore your father," Nightliss said. "Please let me know how I can help."

"You've already helped more than you know." I cupped her chin. "You've given us hope."

Shelton clapped my back. "I'm with you all the way, fam."

Adam chimed in. "Me too."

Elyssa gripped my hand and squeezed three times. "I love you, and I'm with you to the end."

Tears burned my eyes.

The Overworld had collapsed beneath two dictators, and now Xanos wanted to end it for good. But she was weak, and our people had a strength hers could never match. Baal had done his best to steal that strength, but in the end, we'd held on. We'd rediscovered the one thing that neither he nor Xanos could defeat.

Hope.

And hope would win us this war.

BOOKS BY JOHN CORWIN

THE OVERWORLD CHRONICLES

Sweet Blood of Mine

Dark Light of Mine

Fallen Angel of Mine

Dread Nemesis of Mine

Twisted Sister of Mine

Dearest Mother of Mine

Infernal Father of Mine

Sinister Seraphim of Mine

Wicked War of Mine

Dire Destiny of Ours

Aetherial Annihilation

Baleful Betrayal

Ominous Odyssey

Insidious Insurrection

Utopia Undone

Overworld Apocalypse

Assignment Zero (An Elyssa Short Story)

OVERWORLD UNDERGROUND

Possessed By You

Demonicus

Coming Soon: Infernal Blade

OVERWORLD ARCANUM

Conrad Edison and the Living Curse

Conrad Edison and the Anchored World

Conrad Edison and the Broken Relic

Conrad Edison and the Infernal Design

Conrad Edison and the First Power

STAND ALONE NOVELS

Mars Rising

No Darker Fate

The Next Thing I Knew

Outsourced

For the latest on new releases, free ebooks, and more, join John Corwin's Newsletter at www.johncorwin.net!

ABOUT THE AUTHOR

John Corwin is the bestselling author of the Overworld Chronicles. He enjoys long walks on the beach and is a firm believer in puppies and kittens.

After years of getting into trouble thanks to his overactive imagination, John abandoned his male modeling career to write books.

He resides in Atlanta.

Connect with John Corwin online:
Facebook: http://www.facebook.com/johnhcorwinauthor
Website: http://www.johncorwin.net
Twitter: http://twitter.com/#!/John_Corwin

Made in the USA
Coppell, TX
19 November 2023

24475994R00236